She dialed. The phone number was still in her memory.

Where he lived, it was already a couple of hours later. Kai wasn't surprised that he answered the phone.

"It's Kai," she said evenly when she heard his voice. "I've been arrested." She paused for a breath. "I'd like you to defend me." In the silence that followed, her heart seemed to stop—and to resume beating only after he spoke.

"Are you sure?" he asked.

She took another moment to repeat the question in her mind. Could she trust him to defend her?

"Yes," she said.

"I'll be there in the morning," he replied. "Just get someone else to arrange your release tonight."

Neither felt there was anything more to say. Kai lowered the receiver into the cradle.

Yes, she told herself once more, she was sure. If he could be the one to rescue her, there could be no more perfect justice.

SENSATIONS

Save **25%** and more at
Hilton International Hotels
with the **Great Escapes Summer**
from ⑦ Signet and ⓔ Onyx!

* * * * * * *Look for these titles this summer!* * * * * * *

June
REVERSIBLE ERROR
Robert K. Tanenbaum
RELATIVE SINS
Cynthia Victor

July
GRACE POINT
Anne D. LeClaire
FOREVER
Judith Gould

August
**MARILYN:
THE LAST TAKE**
Peter Harry Brown &
Patte B. Barham
JUST KILLING TIME
Derek Van Arman

September
DANGEROUS PRACTICES
Francis Roe
SILENT WITNESS:
The Karla Brown Murder Case
Don W. Weber &
Charles Bosworth, Jr.

SAVE the coupons in the back of these books.
REDEEM them at Hilton International Hotel and receive a 25% discount off regular rates and much, much more...because, *the more GREAT ESCAPES coupons you collect, the more you get!*

2 coupons: Save 25% off regular rates at Hilton International Hotels
4 coupons: Save 25% off regular rates <u>plus</u> upgrade to Executive Floor
6 coupons: Save 25% off regular rates <u>plus</u> complimentary Fruit Basket to welcome you
8 coupons: Save 25% off regular rates <u>plus</u> Fruit Basket and Bottle of Wine to welcome you

----

B O N U S

And to get you started, here's a BONUS COUPON!
GREAT ESCAPES

• This bonus coupon is valid only when sent in with three or more coupons found in our GREAT ESCAPES titles (see above)

Employees and the family members of Penguin USA, Hilton International, and their advertising and promotional agencies are not eligible to participate in THE GREAT ESCAPES SUMMER. Offer subject to change or withdrawal without notice. Coupons valid until 3/31/94.

B O N U S

SENSATIONS

by

Jessica March

AN ONYX BOOK

ONYX
Published by the Penguin Group
Penguin Books USA Inc., 375 Hudson Street,
New York, New York 10014, U.S.A.
Penguin Books Ltd, 27 Wrights Lane,
London W8 5TZ, England
Penguin Books Australia Ltd, Ringwood,
Victoria, Australia
Penguin Books Canada Ltd, 10 Alcorn Avenue,
Toronto, Ontario, Canada M4V 3B2
Penguin Books (N.Z.) Ltd, 182-190 Wairau Road,
Auckland 10, New Zealand

Penguin Books Ltd, Registered Offices:
Harmondsworth, Middlesex, England

First published by Onyx,
an imprint of New American Library,
a division of Penguin Books USA Inc.

First Printing, March, 1993
10 9 8 7 6 5 4 3 2 1

Copyright © Jessica March, 1993
All rights reserved

 REGISTERED TRADEMARK—MARCA REGISTRADA

Printed in the United States of America

PUBLISHER'S NOTE
This is a work of fiction. Names, characters, places, and incidents either are the
product of the author's imagination or are used fictitiously, and any resemblance
to actual persons, living or dead, events, or locales is entirely coincidental.

With love to those
sensational people,
C, D, and M

SENSATIONS

Prologue

"Sometimes, when he's touching me . . . I'm not sure if he really *feels* me or if . . . ."

As she had so many times during the past forty minutes of struggling to explain her deepest feelings, the lovely young woman paused to gaze away pensively at the ocean view beyond the window, the eternal surf breaking at the near end of a shimmering golden path laid down by the setting sun.

After a silence, the young man sharing a sofa with the woman leaned toward her, evidently to coax out her unfinished thought.

Seated in a chair facing the couple, Kai Wyler quickly raised a finger, signaling a reminder to the man not to speak. As part of the instructions she gave every couple at the start of their initial session, she always told them to listen to each other—listen not just to the words, but to the silences.

As the pause lasted, Kai Wyler's bright turquoise eyes switched between the two people across from her. She couldn't help appreciating how attractive they were. Well, not merely attractive—beautiful, ideal physical specimens of man and woman. Of course, that wasn't uncommon in their profession. Among Kai Wyler's clients were many movie and television stars. She was used to dealing with beautiful people, and she understood how their beauty was often part of their problem.

Yet even in a milieu filled with exquisite women and ideal men, the couple with Kai now were a cut above the norm. Jenna Lyle, a month shy of her twenty-fourth birthday, was currently appearing on eighteen hundred screens nationwide in a romantic comedy about a young policewoman who goes undercover and falls in love with the son of a mafia don who wants to be a veterinarian. The movie had already made a hundred and forty million dollars, and it was Jenna's second straight box-office blockbuster. For the moment, at least, this young woman with the wide-set gray eyes, retroussé nose, full mouth, and short auburn hair was Hollywood's top female star. She could earn four million dollars whenever she worked.

Her husband's success was even greater. A decade ago, Ron Carpenter's sole claim to fame had been winning a bronze medal for Canada in an Olympic weightlifting event. His rippling muscles and blond boyish good looks had brought offers to appear in low-budget action movies, and he had spent five years working in that vein. Then one film about a super-being sent back from the future had broken through to make hundreds of millions around the world. Each subsequent film had been bigger than the last, and he began making other kinds of films—at a salary of fifteen million dollars each. When the two stars had met at a celebrity tennis tournament two years ago, the romance that blossomed had become a perennial front-page staple of the tabloids. Their wedding, the birth of a child, had only intensified the attention.

At last Jenna Lyle resumed. "I guess I don't know if it's really me he's touching, or some idea of me that comes from . . . my publicity." The actress turned back to Kai. "Can you understand? It's as if somehow I'm not real anymore. Not to him. What I am . . . is more what people see on a screen, than *this*." She touched herself, laying her hands flat against her chest.

As the sun sank lower, the light in the room had grown dim, but Kai didn't turn on a lamp. The people who came to her often talked more easily when they couldn't be clearly seen. "And when you touch Ron," Kai asked sympathetically, "how do you feel?"

"Oh god," the actress sighed, "he's so perfect . . . his body is so wonderful, I can't help wondering what he wants with me. Well, look at him. Be honest, Ms. Wyler, don't you want to fuck him?"

Kai was used to dealing with such jabs from clients, anxious to deflect the microscope from their own problems. "I thought we were here to talk about love," she said, "not just lust."

"You're famous as a sex therapist," the actress countered. "Well, sex is fucking, right? So don't try to dodge my question."

Kai's voice remained level. "What difference does it make, Jenna, how I feel about Ron—or how *they* feel, the millions of women who see his movies, then go home and have fantasies about him? The only thing that should matter is how you feel—and how he feels about you."

"Sounds easy when you say it," Jenna said quietly, her assault defused. "But you should see when we go to one of his openings—the crowd of women fighting to get near enough to grab his crotch. Some are pretty damn good-looking, and he could have his pick. So when he's with me . . . well, its just so hard to believe I'm the one—"

"How many times do I have to tell you, Jen?" Carpenter broke in. "I don't want anyone else. I love you!"

Jenna nodded, but didn't look at her husband. Ron turned to Kai. "Well, there it is. How do we get past this? I can't stop women from lining up to see me—or sending me their underpants in the mail. Hell, I don't want to stop them. It's what put me where I am. But the way it affects Jen . . . well, it's screwing up our lives. We can't last much longer this way. Every time we've been in bed lately, she acts like there's two hundred other women right there on the sheets with us. She freezes up, or else she just rushes through it. At the beginning we had such great sex, but . . . ." He trailed off, shaking his head.

Kai stole a glance at the small Tiffany clock discreetly set among books in a shelf across the room. The session was almost over. Preparing to sum up, she thought over all she knew about the couple from her research and what they had told her. Jenna Lyle was the product of a broken home, sexually abused by a stepfather while she was in her early teens. Ron Carpenter was one of three brothers born on a farm in Ontario to a couple who were still married after thirty-eight years. A volatile mix in the best circumstances, but these two people were working against other problems, too.

"Listen, both of you," Kai said softly, "the most important thing is that you love each other. You wouldn't be

here if you didn't. You'd be right where last week's *Enquirer*
said you were.''

''Splitsville,'' Carpenter echoed the headline. ''The bastards.''

Kai went on. ''Forget that. You can stay together and
prove them wrong. But that doesn't mean you won't have to
get through a rocky period. Both of you spend your working
lives acting out fantasies that send audiences home thinking
their own lives are pale by comparison. But what happens
when you get home? You wonder, too, why reality can't
match the make-believe. You're stars, aren't you? That's
the word you hear again and again to describe yourselves.
Stars . . .'' Kai paused, and the couple gazed back at her
attentively. ''And what's a star?'' she went on. ''A heavenly
body, aflame with heat and light. It follows that a star is
supposed to have heavenly love, heavenly flaming sex forever . . . with none of the problems that bother mere mor-
tals.''

The actor and actress glanced at each other with smiles
of recognition.

''But whatever the publicity says,'' Kai continued,
''you're just a man and a woman in love. As for sex, even
if it started with a big bang—as the astronomers say—when
two stars collided, that doesn't guarantee the fireworks continue automatically for all eternity. Get caught up in all your
own Hollywood bullshit that sex isn't worth anything unless
it's instant magic every single time, and you'll give up on
each other too quickly because the magic isn't always
there.'' Kai looked at Jenna. ''You're afraid Ron must want
someone else more than you—or want the fake you more
than the real you. The fear keeps you from giving yourself,
so you're trapped in a vicious cycle. Unable to enjoy him
because you're so afraid of losing him.''

''That's right,'' the actress whispered. Even in the dim
light, the glistening of tears could be seen as they spilled
from her eyes.

''Well, you can get the magic back,'' Kai said. ''But not
without taking time to look for it. Love is fuel for the fire,
but we may have to strike some fresh sparks. If you'll work
at it, though, I can help you.''

''How?'' Jenna asked plainly.

''A combination of things. Curing your doubts. Getting

you to talk to each other, let each other know exactly what your needs are in bed. And, if your pride can stand it, maybe even a few lessons in basic technique.''

''Sure we'll do it,'' Carpenter said. ''I want this marriage to last forever.'' He reached out for his wife's hand. She hesitated only a moment before placing her hand in his.

''Okay, let's set up a schedule.'' Kai switched on a table lamp and took up an appointment book.

Despite the actors' complicated schedules—films to be shot in different parts of the world—a number of sessions were finally set, and Kai walked them to the door of her office. As her usual parting advice after an introductory meeting, she told them to enjoy simply being together, not worrying so much about when the fireworks would begin again. ''You'll get the magic back,'' she told them. ''I'm sure of it.'' They went off holding hands.

Alone, Kai sat down at her desk and, as she always did, jotted down observations on a yellow legal pad about the session just completed. In the midst of making notes, she set down the pencil and swung around to look at the Pacific. Long shadows from the last rays of the sinking sun accented the fine bone structure of her exotic face, gilded her naturally tawny skin, and lit up the sparkling golden flecks in her remarkable turquoise eyes. Her long, lustrous copper hair came alive with reddish highlights. She was as startlingly beautiful as any of the film stars, rich Hollywood wives, or models who sought her help. Against the half-darkness outside, Kai could see a faint reflection of herself in the window. She regarded herself without vanity, however, thinking only of how much she resembled her mother. The fading orange sun caught her in a way that was so reminiscent of the firelight flickering on Lokei's face that night Lokei had taught her how to dance. . . .

Kai lifted her eyes to search the far horizon of the ocean. Across those waters her life had begun almost forty years ago. Lately she found herself thinking more and more about the journey she had taken from there to here. Her successful private practice had brought her the chance, two years ago, to bring her advice on sexual fulfillment to a wider audience on her own cable television show, *Heatwaves*. She was celebrated and successful for the work she did to mend the fraying fabric of other people's lives. Yet for all the wise things she said to the world about the importance of love in achieving true fulfillment, she hadn't found it any easier to anchor love in her own life.

Kai forced her attention back to the notes she had started to make, a reminder to work with Jenna Lyle on coming to terms with the effects of the sexual abuse suffered as a teenager on her current insecurities. A vision came into Kai's mind of a young woman, her wrists bound with silken curtain ropes and tied to bedposts . . . and it was a moment before she realized it was not suggested by anything the client had told her, but a fragment floating up out of memory. Eager to blot out the ugly picture, Kai pressed her pencil to the pad and went on with her notes.

The ringing phone interrupted her.

Even before she could speak, a man's voice came through the receiver. "Thank god you're there, Kai . . . jesus, you've got to help me. . . ."

It came out somewhere between a moan and a whisper, but Kai recognized the voice nevertheless. "For godssake, Mitch, what's wrong?"

"You've got to believe me, Kai, I swear I never meant—" He broke off, and she could hear his sobs coming through the phone.

"Damn it, Mitch," she said sharply to cut through his hysteria, "tell me where you are and what's happened."

"I'm with Annie," he stammered in reply. "She came to the hotel and, oh god, I—I don't know why, but I—" The sobs overtook him again.

"What, Mitch?" Kai demanded. "What did you do to her?"

"She's not breathing, Kai. I think she—"

Kai cut in; there wasn't time to worry about getting the picture crystal clear. "Call an ambulance, Mitch—the second I hang up. All right? I'm on my way."

She replaced the phone, in a hurry to get moving. As she ran from the office, the sound of his sobs echoed in her mind. In the twenty years she'd known Mitch Karel, she'd never heard him cry—never imagined he was capable of breaking down.

The beautifully landscaped driveway in front of the Beverly Palace Hotel, the new flagship of the hotel chain owned by Mitch Karel, was clogged with police cars and TV news trucks. Kai left her car at the end of the drive and went on foot, skirting the sidelines of the activity away from the news teams' bright lights, hoping not to be recognized.

But as she was crossing the crowded lobby, a stocky gray-haired man in a well-cut dark suit hooked one hand around her arm. Relieved to see he wasn't holding a microphone, Kai didn't resist as he pulled her into an alcove. "Ms. Wyler," he said urgently. "I'm Richard Lofton, the night manager. I thought we should talk before—"

"Where's Mr. Karel?" Kai cut in. "I came because he called."

"He slipped out of the hotel before the police came."

That was Mitch, all right, Kai thought ruefully. Dragged her smack into the middle of things, then didn't have the decency to stay around. "What about the woman?" she asked quickly.

"I can't tell you much. The ambulance people showed up, said they'd had a call from the penthouse suite, and I let them in. The girl was badly beaten. They rushed her straight out of here."

"So she was alive," Kai said, a twinge of relief coming amid the horror. "Where did they take her, which hospital?" At least she could keep a vigil for Annie Raines. Poor Annie. Whatever had happened to her, Kai couldn't deny a share of responsibility.

"I don't know the hospital, Ms. Wyler. But before you go anywhere I wanted to warn you . . ."

"About what?"

"When I went up with the ambulance crew, I found an envelope addressed to you—a note from Mr. Karel." He paused.

Kai waited, expecting the manager to hand the note over.

"I gave it to the police as soon as they arrived, turned it over the way I found it—with the envelope sealed." Lofton shrugged his large shoulders apologetically. "Since I know you and Mr. Karel are friends, I thought the least I could do was prepare you. I mean, tell you about the note . . . and one other thing. The hotel also keeps an automatic record of all phone numbers dialed from each room, and the time of the call. The detectives on the case have already take a copy of the record."

Even without knowing what Mitch had written in his note, Kai realized she could be in deep trouble herself. Though the manager didn't say he was aware she'd been called after the beating took place, his mention of the phone record betrayed his knowledge.

"The way things are," the manager said, "well, I thought you might want to contact a lawyer before you talk to the police. You can use my office to call."

At this stage, Kai thought, seeking the shield of a lawyer carried with it an intimation of guilt. And she was far more anxious to learn exactly what had happened than to spend time protecting herself. "I'll talk to the police," she said.

Kai headed for the bank of elevators. A couple of uniformed policemen with walkie-talkies were checking everyone who went up to make sure they were guests, or involved in the investigation.

"I'd like to talk to the detectives," Kai told the officer who stopped her. "My name is—"

"I know who you are, Miss Wyler. I've seen you on TV." Into the walkie-talkie the policeman said, "Tell Captain Vargas that Kai Wyler is on her way up."

When she stepped off at the penthouse, a man was standing so close to the elevator that Kai had to dodge sideways to avoid bumping into him. She had already started away when he spoke:

"No need to go anywhere, Miss Wyler," he said in the gravelly voice of a heavy smoker. "I'm the man you want to see."

Though not quite as tall as she, he was powerfully built, with broad shoulders, a bull neck, and a large head capped with glossy black hair worn in a marine-style brush cut. Gold-rimmed spectacles masked eyes as black as his hair, and a thick mustache arched down around a mouth set in a cynical frown. He looked, thought Kai, like a cross between a bookish professor and a Mexican bandit.

"Captain Hector Vargas, LAPD," he introduced himself. He pulled an envelope from a jacket pocket. "While the girl was lying there bleeding, Mr. Karel took the time to write this. Maybe you should read it before we talk."

It was clear from his tone that he was not in a mood to be friendly, or even diplomatic. Kai accepted the opened envelope from him without a word.

"K. Wyler" was scrawled across the front. She unfolded the letter from inside and read the few hastily scribbled lines.

> I was so out of my mind, I didn't even think of the ambulance. Thanks. Forgive me, Kai. Remember, everything would have turned out better if only you'd given me what I wanted.

He had signed it "Love always," but without his name.

Kai lowered the sheet of hotel stationery to find Vargas's intense black eyes targeted on her. He plucked the paper out of her hand and restored it to the envelope.

"What's he mean at the end?" he demanded. "About giving him what he wanted."

Kai felt bullied by the detective. "Can I sit down somewhere, Captain Vargas? All this may be routine to you, but for me it's quite a shock."

"Sure," Vargas said, "let's sit down." He waved her toward an open door across from the elevators.

They entered the luxurious penthouse suite reserved for Mitch, as owner of the hotel. A few men were milling in the large living room, and through a doorway leading to the bedroom, Kai glimpsed a man dusting a night table for fingerprints, and a photographer taking flash pictures of bloody sheets. The surge of adrenaline that had propelled Kai since Mitch's phone call seemed to wane, and she was left with a sick, hollow feeling at her core.

Vargas pointed to a seating area in a corner of the living room. While she took a chair, he went and murmured something to the men clustered in conversation. They moved out into the hallway.

The detective came back and stood in front of Kai, arms folded. "Now that we're all cozy and quiet, want to start explaining?"

"Explaining what?"

"That letter, for a start—where he says maybe things went wrong because you didn't give him what he wanted. Just what did he want from you?"

"He wanted," Kai replied flatly, "for me to love him."

The detective eyed her coolly. "And was Karel such a hard guy to love? He owns this hotel, twenty more like it and god knows what else. How much money has he got—two billion dollars, three?''

Kai didn't respond. Was it necessary to say that money, no matter how great the amount, couldn't buy love?

The detective went on. ''You must've been really good friends, though. You're the one he called as soon as there was trouble; you're the one who came running. Or was that purely a matter of friendship?'' A harsh edge came into his voice. ''Wasn't business involved, too? This girl who was here with Karel . . .'' Vargas paused to snatch a notepad from his jacket pocket. He glanced at it. ''This Annie Raines, wasn't she one of several girls who work for you?''

Kai knew now where the questioning was headed. ''No, Annie didn't work for me,'' she snapped. ''Annie worked for herself.''

''Okay, have it your way. But she was here because you thought it was a good idea, wasn't she? And she was in this room for the purpose of having sex, selling her—''

''Wait a second,'' Kai tried to interrupt.

But the detective overrode her. ''Maybe you didn't have any interest in loving Mitch Karel—maybe you even knew he had the kind of brute violence inside him that made it sensible to keep your distance. But that didn't keep you from making arrangements for some hooker to come in here and—''

Kai bolted up from her chair. ''That's enough, Vargas! Annie Raines isn't a prostitute any more than I'm a pimp. She's a third-year graduate student in psychology at UCLA, earning some desperately needed money for her education by working as a sex surrogate. And what *I* am, Captain Vargas, in case you don't know, is a sex therapist. I help people with their problems, and sometimes women like Annie are involved in the process. The use of surrogates, women trained to deal sympathetically with people who suffer from various kinds of sexual dysfunction, is a known—and pretty well accepted—part of therapy.'' Kai's fury wound down; there was nothing new about having to defend herself or her methods. She regretted letting Vargas bait her into spouting off so defensively.

Vargas bobbed his head tiredly, as if he'd expected the speech. ''Therapy,'' he echoed. ''Sure sounds like a good thing the way you put it, Miss Wyler. But in the situation we've got here, I can't write it off as anything so fine and noble as simply helping a nice man with his little problems. Mitch Karel is an animal; he beat this woman senseless— then ran out of here through the back door like any two-bit hoodlum escaping from a mob hit.''

Kai sank back into her chair. Even if she could find the words to defend herself, there was little to be said for Mitch. In fact, it seemed harder with each moment to forgive herself for having played a role in what had happened.

Vargas looked down at her. ''You know, Miss Wyler,'' he said at last, ''you didn't have to tell me what your business is. It happens my wife is a big fan of that TV program of yours. Sometimes I come home from a night shift, and I can tell she's been watching 'cause she'll be so goddamn full of ideas about what's wrong with the way we make love.''

Kai gazed at the detective. Was this the real reason for his hostility toward her? That she'd interfered in his love life?

''Used to be okay just to get it on,'' he continued, ''but now all the time she's telling me I should do this or that, telling me it's no good unless—'' Abruptly he caught himself spilling out his personal grievances and shifted gears. ''So maybe you think you're helping people, but sometimes it just leads to a lot of bad shit. Like tonight. Whatever you thought you were doing when you let that girl come in here to service that son-of-a-bitch billionaire, the fact is he killed her and you've got to face the consequences.''

Kai's head jolted up, and she stared incredulously at the detective. ''Killed her? But she was taken to the hospital, I thought. She—''

''Dead on arrival,'' Vargas said bluntly.

Shock and grief swept over Kai, immobilizing her. An image of Annie Raines rose in her mind, a lovely young woman of thirty-one. As with all the surrogates, Kai had given her a rigorous screening before allowing her to participate, making certain she had the personal history and intelligence required to fill such a unique role without being thrown off balance. A college graduate who had endured two short, failed marriages by the time she was twenty-four, Annie had engaged in several years of extreme promiscuous behavior before she had decided to return to school to educate herself about psychology. Though no longer promiscuous, she had retained an uninhibited attitude about sex, and frankly recognized that there were few opportunities to earn the substantial tuition she needed, yet still leave herself time to attend school and study. "But I don't want to do a lot of this," she had stipulated to Kai. "One patient . . . just one client during any one period of months, no more than that." And the stipulation had been met. During her three years of being associated with Kai, Mitch was only the fourth man Annie had served as a surrogate.

The voice of the detective sliced into Kai's reflections. "C'mon, Miss Wyler, I've gotta take you downtown." When Kai remained another moment in her chair, stunned, Vargas reached down, grasped her wrist, and pulled her to her feet. "Please. Make it easy, and I won't have to use the cuffs."

It sank in. She was being arrested. "What are the charges?"

"I can't say exactly what language the D.A. will use. But it boils down to pinning you with a good share of the blame for the woman's death."

Her will to resist neutralized by shock and guilt, Kai let Vargas prod her toward the corridor. But then her pride asserted itself. There would always be plenty of people— like Vargas—who were too bound by old customs and old ways of thinking to regard the work Kai did in a sympathetic light. But she knew its value, she knew her own motives. And she understood that tonight had thrust her into a battle to justify them.

Kai turned to the detective. "Before we leave, Captain, would you allow me to call a lawyer?"

"You're certainly gonna need one," he said, and obligingly pointed out a phone on the table.

Kai went and picked up the receiver. A lawyer. To defend her. Only one name came to mind. She had never forgotten seeing him in action, winning an acquittal. The best in his field, she thought. But on the brink of making the call she reminded herself there had been a time when she would have met this man in a courtroom only to be a witness against him. Reminded herself that this was the only man she had ever really hated—hated enough, she had felt once, to commit murder herself.

She dialed. The phone number was still in her memory.

Where he lived, it was already a couple of hours later. Kai wasn't surprised that he answered the phone.

"It's Kai," she said evenly when she heard his voice. "I've been arrested." She paused for a breath. "I'd like you to defend me." In the silence that followed, her heart seemed to stop—and to resume beating only after he spoke.

"Are you sure?" he asked.

She took another moment to repeat the question in her mind. Could she trust him to defend her?

"Yes," she said.

"I'll be there in the morning," he replied. "Just get someone else to arrange your release tonight."

Neither felt there was anything more to say. Kai lowered the receiver into the cradle.

Yes, she told herself once more, she was sure. If he was the one to rescue her, there could be no more perfect justice.

BOOK
ONE

Chapter One

Oahu, Hawaii—June 1959

Precisely at midnight, the first rocket streaked up into the night sky and exploded in an immense shower of red, white, and blue sparks. At this moment Hawaii was beginning a new era. The lawmakers had put through the legislation, President Dwight D. Eisenhower had signed the necessary documents, and now this group of islands had officially become the fiftieth state of the United States of America. The fireworks began in earnest, rockets shooting up in groups and detonating with a cannonade of booming explosions into mushrooms of multicolored light.

On the open lanai of a small cottage beside a long white beach, an exotically beautiful young woman stood gazing up at the wondrous rain of colored sparks. Exciting as the fireworks were, Lokei Teiatu saw that none lasted more than a few seconds before fading and being swallowed up in the night. It seemed to Lokei that the event they celebrated would be no different: a moment of light—the bright, burning hope that statehood would bring her life a change for the better—would quickly fade back into darkness. Becoming a full-fledged American citizen was supposed to symbolize gaining complete freedom and equality, but Lokei couldn't imagine never being truly free or equal. Whatever the Americans wrote in their history books, whatever homage they paid to their great Abraham Lincoln and his famous Emancipation Proclamation, Lokei could not escape the realization that she was a virtual slave with no prospects for release.

From across the nearby fields came the sound of throbbing drums and the languorous whine of steel guitars. The plantation workers had begun celebrating hours ago. Lokei could see the glow of their bonfires above the coconut palms, could smell the tantalizing aroma of roasting meat carried on the soft breeze. If she were free, wouldn't she be there, too? There was nothing she'd like better than to be at a luau dancing the hula or the *olapa* with the others. . . . Yet she dared not leave the cottage.

Hearing a noise behind her, Lokei turned to see her seven-year-old daughter in a doorway. Wakened by the exploding rockets, the child moved onto the lanai clutching a blanket.

"Why are the stars falling down, Mama?" she asked fearfully.

Lokei knelt and gathered her daughter into her arms. "It's nothing bad, Kaiulani. Those are fireworks. Didn't I tell you there was going to be a big party tonight?"

"For a birthday, you said."

"A kind of birthday. Hawaii is being born into a new life."

The child nodded. As the haze of drowsiness lifted, she recalled more of the things she'd heard from her mother, and at the one-room plantation school she had started to attend. "We're going to have our own star on a flag," she said.

A fresh burst of fireworks flared high above them, and the little girl looked up, lost in gaping wonderment at the spectacle.

Lokei, meanwhile, gazed with similar amazement at the face of her daughter. How miraculously lovely she was. *Kaiulani*—"heavenly beauty" was the translation of the Hawaiian word Lokei had bestowed on her baby in the first flush of maternal pride. With the passing of each year she became more aware of how fateful the choice had been. The child was truly magnificent. Slender and perfectly proportioned, with long legs, blue-green sloe eyes that seemed to glow with an inner light, a trailing mane of silken hair in a unique shade of coppery red-gold, and flawless skin that appeared tanned to the color of pale honey even when the rainy season kept her out of the sun for weeks.

Yet in the wake of admiring this "heavenly beauty," Lokei felt a rush of fear for her child's future. Hawaiians generally harbored a superstitious belief that great danger attached to beauty, and evil spirits reserved a special cruelty for any child who became too proud or vain. It was *kapu*—

taboo—to be proud of one's own appearance, or even to praise it in others. Children were taught to avoid mirrors. To discourage vanity they were never too openly admired, but routinely addressed by such endearments as *keko* or *mo'o*—monkey, lizard. Lokei's fear for her daughter went beyond such unreasoned tradition, however. No matter how pleasing Kaiulani was physically, Lokei knew there would always be those who looked at the child and saw nothing but corruption and impurity because of the strains of mixed blood that ran in her veins. From her own experience Lokei knew how a life could be marked and limited by such bigotry. Many doors had been closed to her because she was herself a *hapa*—literally, a "half"—conceived as the result of a union between her full-blooded Hawaiian mother and a white mainlander who had been stationed at the U.S. Army's Schofield Barracks in Honolulu twenty-five years ago. To be a *hapa* was by definition to be less than whole, and therefore somehow less of a person, less deserving, less decent. It wasn't only the mainland whites who looked down on those of mixed blood, but also many of the native Hawaiians, who were proud of their heritage and angry at those who were weakening the strain—another kind of surrender to the mainlanders. Lokei brooded often on the very different life she might have had if she were not a *hapa*. Someday perhaps, as more native Hawaiians mixed with mainlanders, such cruel distinctions might fade. But for the present it terrified Lokei to think Kaiulani might be similarly branded.

"Mama, listen." The child's attention had wandered from the fireworks to the music drifting from the fields. She twisted loose from Lokei's embrace and went to the edge of the lanai. "Is that the birthday party, too?"

"Yes. It will go on until the sun rises."

Kaiulani sniffed the air. "It smells so good. Let's go to the party, Mama!"

"It's too late to be going anywhere." Lokei lowered her voice and looked out at the darkness. "At this hour, too many evil spirits are hiding in the tall pili grass and the *'ohe 'ohe*."

"No one else is afraid of spirits tonight. Please, Mama." Kaiulani darted across the thatched porch and grabbed her mother's hand. "It's the birthday for Hawaii!"

Lokei looked down at her daughter's lovely, eager face.

What excuse would satisfy her? Would it be enough to say simply that Mr. Trane might be coming soon? As little as Kaiulani grasped about the truth of their circumstances, Lokei had already explained that their home did not really belong to them—that they were allowed its use by Mr. Trane because he was "a good friend." Often in the daytime, when Kaiulani wanted to play on the beach or take a walk with her mother, Lokei was forced to say that Mr. Trane might be coming, and send her daughter off to be tended by one of the old women who lived in the workers' shanties along the cane fields.

But it was much harder for Lokei to disappoint her daughter tonight. For one night couldn't she dare to forget that she was Trane's *manuwahi*? Couldn't she take the chance he wouldn't come to her tonight? In the big plantation house on the hill, there was also a grand celebration going on. It would surely last long into the morning.

Even so, her obligation to Trane was clearly spelled out; she must be here for him whenever he wanted, whenever he came. He need never inform her in advance; he was her *haku*, her absolute master. This was the contract she had made in order to provide for Kaiulani, to shelter her in the comfort of this cottage while she tried somehow to find a way to steer her daughter into a better future than her own.

But for just tonight—just an hour—couldn't she risk turning her back on this bargain with the devil and pretend to celebrate freedom?

"Quickly, Kaiulani. Go and put on your prettiest sarong."

They rushed inside, to their separate bedrooms at either side of the cottage. Just before the child disappeared to dress, she stopped and called to Lokei. "I want to dance tonight, Mama. I want you to teach me."

Lokei smiled. She knew that the various old women who often looked after Kaiulani had told the little girl that her mother was much admired for her graceful hula and *olapa*.

"Yes, my darling," Lokei said, "tonight we'll both dance."

On the huge terrace behind the large white plantation house, a floor of polished teak boards had been laid over the flagstones, and a crowd of men in sleek tuxedos and women in their best gowns and jewels were dancing to Broadway show tunes played by the orchestra that had flown over from Los Angeles for the occasion.

Standing alone by the balustrade at the edge of the terrace, Harley Trane sipped the last champagne from his glass and looked across the floor at his wife, a slender brunette with very pale skin, swaying to the music in the arms of her partner. She danced, thought Harley, the way she fucked—hardly moving, the sculpted features of her beautiful face set in an expressionless mask. Was her current partner in the dance someone she'd already allowed to make love to her, Harley wondered idly, or one of her new prospects? There had been quite a few others, he knew, men tempted—as once he had been—to test their talent as lovers against the task of arousing this cool ice princess. Harley smiled at the thought of the disappointment that lay in store for all of them.

Turning his back on the fancy crowd, he gazed down the long hill to the fields far below. At this distance the bonfires made by the plantation workers looked hardly bigger than flames burning at the tip of a match, and all he could see of the revelers were masses of tiny shadows. But he could easily imagine the excitement that was crackling around the fires down there. The *kamaaina* knew how to have themselves a really good time. None of this dainty two-stepping around by tight-assed frigid women laced into their thousand-dollar designer creations, their faces so carefully painted on. None of the jocular clubhouse patter of these men in monkey suits—the island power brokers laying their plans so that no matter what status Hawaii acquired, they would lose nothing by it. Down in the fields, the *kamaaina* would be going wild. Getting drunk on that two hundred-proof stuff they brewed up, and never worrying about who saw them. The women would turn themselves free, dancing to the drums, their shiny panther-black hair swirling around their sensuous golden bodies. That was his kind of party. . . .

He was a big man with blond hair allowed to grow shaggy, a handsome face that had once been finely chiseled but now bore the effects of years of dissipation, and a certain way of holding himself that indicated there was a hard frame under the softness accumulated in recent years. In his teens, before the war with Japan, Harley Trane had spent time on the beaches watching the young native men practice the island sport they called *he'e nalu*, "wave-riding," standing on long homemade wooden boards specially shaped and smoothed, and propelled along by the curling ocean breakers. Harley had made himself a champion at the sport. If his father had not pressured him onto a different path, he would have been happy to go off around the world with his surfboard, searching for bigger and bigger waves to ride.

A hand clapped down onto his shoulder. He turned to see his younger brother, Ken.

"You haven't danced all night, Harl'. Don't you like the band?"

"They're okay, I'd just rather be drinking. Which reminds me—" He raised his empty champagne glass and started to sidle away.

Ken grabbed his arm. "Is it too much to ask that just one goddamn time you won't embarrass the rest of us? Can't you stay sober and mix in a little bit? And how about dancing a little with Vicky? You have to make such a show of pushing your own wife off onto other men?"

"If I embarrass you, little brother, maybe you shouldn't invite me to this big, beautiful house of yours."

The snarling emphasis Harley put on his final word summed up all the bad feeling that had grown up between the brothers—reaching its peak fourteen months ago when their father had died. Daniel Trane's will had left instructions that it was the younger Kenneth who was to take over running the plantation and other real estate interests, the canning works, the sugar refinery, the bus line and car dealerships—all the enterprises that made the Tranes among the wealthiest of the *aliilani*, the small, closed aristocracy of white planters who had ruled the islands for almost two centuries. Thus established as head of the clan, it was Kenneth who also became the owner and occupier of the traditional seat of Trane power—Windward House. Harley had received only a minority share in some of the businesses, and a comfortable but considerably less imposing house originally built for a plantation foreman. He was not really surprised that he had been passed over. He knew that the love of surfing he'd once displayed had made his father doubt his abilities in business. "No serious, sensible man," Daniel Trane had told him, "would want to spend all his days romping in the ocean like one of the native boys." Since then he had found himself always left one step behind Ken, always treated as less capable, less important. Even their two sisters were treated more generously, given enormous tracts of land outright for their dowry when they married. Long before Daniel Trane died, Harley had already felt the sting of his rejection and had sought to dull the pain with the anesthetic effect of alcohol, or overwhelm it with other sensations.

Kenneth Trane stared back at Harley with a mixture of sympathy and contempt. Shorter, darker, well manicured and tailored, he made a stark contrast to his rumpled older brother. Quietly he said, "I never wanted to lock you out of anything, Harl. If you'd only pull yourself together, I could use your help."

They were interrupted by a uniformed maid who passed holding a chilled bottle of champagne to refill guests' glasses. Ken shook his head, but Harley grabbed the bottle, then waved the maid away.

"So you want my *help*," Harley said, cutting off any protest from Ken. "For what, little brother? To fan the flies away from your head, bring you a cool drink?" He pushed his face closer to Ken's. "I'm not your fucking servant."

Determined not to let their disagreement escalate into a scene, Ken held back a reproof. "You want to handle something of your own," he said, "you could have that, too. You just have to straighten out—show me you're ready to work hard."

"I don't have to show you shit. I've already got something of my own to handle. Now that you mention it, I think it's time for me to go off and handle it right now." Harley showed his brother a smug smile.

Ken had no trouble understanding his brother's inference. The two men had argued increasingly about the *hapa* mistress Harley kept in one of the guest cottages spread along the miles of beachfront owned by the Tranes. For generations it had been common enough within the society of rich planters to possess such a native *manuwahi* that even Daniel Trane had never held this against his elder son as much as his sheer idleness. But now that Ken was the head of the clan, he wasn't willing to tolerate the arrangement much longer. This kind of old-fashioned sexual feudalism might provide a flashpoint in the new society that was going to evolve with the coming of statehood. If plantation workers understood nothing else about gaining full citizenship, they realized that they could never again be treated as property, and would rebel against anyone who violated that right.

"I've told you, Harley," Ken reminded him now. "It can't last much longer. Not the way it is. If you've got to keep a love nest, put it somewhere else, not right on the plantation. And treat the woman a little better. I don't want trouble."

"Then don't make any. Things are fine just as they are. Vicky doesn't give a damn, so why should you?" It was true that Harley's wife knew about the mistress and tolerated the arrangement, content with her own affairs.

"Because the world, our world, changed more than you realize when those rockets went up tonight. In little ways, it's going to affect us all."

"Statehood," Harley sneered. "If you and your friends were really worried about it, you wouldn't be celebrating. Statehood may mean we have some new kinds of politicians, sitting in new offices in new places. But the *aliilani* will go right on owning them."

"Let's hope so," Kenneth said. "But we won't able to boast about it. That's what democracy is, Harley: it lets you be as rich and powerful as a king—as long as you're careful not to make all the people at your feet jealous and angry, as long as you don't step all over the illusion that they're just as good as you are. That's the problem with your *manuwahi*, big brother. The way you treat her may make some people wonder whether their own dreams are getting stepped on." A cold, hard edge came into Kenneth's voice. "I don't want her on our land anymore, not a woman whose only work is to be your whore."

"I've told you she's got a child," Harley said. "Kick her out and you'll make the little girl homeless, too." He was not by any means humanitarian, but he would use any argument that served his own ends.

Ken understood his brother's cynicism. "You also told me you're not the father. So what difference does it make to you?"

"None. But if what worries you is getting the rest of your other workers pissed off, then you'd be stupid to throw this pretty little girl out in the cold. I could get some strong resentment fired up over that kind of treatment."

Ken stared back coldly. His older brother might be lazy, but he had the same cruel, cunning gift for surviving on his own terms as any jungle animal. "Okay, your *hapa* whore can stay for the time being. But for godssakes keep her out of sight, and keep her from making trouble. Keep her satisfied."

"Oh, I can do that, little brother," Harley gloated.

Ken stalked away onto the dance floor, and cut in on the man dancing with Vicky Trane.

Harley watched his wife dancing with his brother for a few moments, long enough to ask himself the usual questions. Then he turned to look again at the fires burning far down the hill.

A moment later, he threw his champagne glass down on the floor with a loud smash that momentarily caused the dancers nearby to pause and glare in his direction. Then, carrying only the bottle, he climbed onto the stone balustrade, jumped to the ground below, and began to march in a lurching, unsteady step toward the distant pinpoints of flame.

Holding tightly to her mother's hand as they walked through the thick stands of pili grass and giant ferns bordering the path to the fields, Kaiulani peered into the darkness on either side. As brave as she'd sounded earlier when pleading to be taken to the party, she couldn't forget the evil spirits that might be lurking. Or, if she was lucky, she might see one of the tiny *menehune,* the elf-like people who were said to have lived here since the islands had been thrust up out of the ocean by the volcanoes. If you saw one, you could ask for a wish to be granted. Among the *kamaiina* it was a custom to leave food outside their shacks to tempt these magical little spirits into the open. Often, after her mother had gone through several days of seeming particularly sad and quiet, Kaiulani would see that a bowl had been set out behind their cottage filled with the yams and *'opihi* that were supposed to be special favorites of the *menehune.* None of the little people had ever come, though.

The path broke suddenly out of the high foliage and into a gigantic field, flat and open since the cane had been cut. Dotted around it many glowing coal fires were being used to roast whole pigs, yams, and taro, and at the center of the broad open space was a bonfire, a mountain of flame climbing up to the dome of a blue-black sky frosted with stars. Everywhere men, women, children, all with flower leis draped around their necks, were laughing, singing, and drinking from hollow coconuts. The sound of drums and steel guitars filled the air.

As they went toward the arena of light cast by the bonfire, Kaiulani recognized many faces—children from the plantation school, workers she saw on days when her mother sent her to the fields while Mr. Trane was in the house. Some returned a nod or a smile, but she also noticed the queer way everyone looked at Lokei—surprised or even a little afraid to see her among them.

"Aloha ku'u keko!" a voice sang out. A wiry little man wearing frayed *palaka* shorts and a shirt decorated with a vivid multicolored print of orchids emerged from the crowd. He crouched to nuzzle Kaiulani's cheek, and she giggled. She was so glad to see Prince Makelahi. When he greeted her as "my monkey," it always struck Kaiulani as particularly funny. With his bowed, skinny legs and thin arms, the fuzz of graying black hair on his round head, the glittering black eyes, and the small, flat nose in the middle of his wizened nut brown face, no one looked more like a monkey than the prince himself.

The little man rose from his crouch. *"Aloha,* Lokei," he said.

"Aloha, Mak."

"It's nice that you could join us tonight."

"The child wanted so much to dance."

"Ahah! Then you shall, little *keko,"* the man said, smiling down at Kaiulani. "This is certainly a night to dance— a night to invent new dances!" Most Hawaiian dances, Kaiulani knew, consisted of movements with certain meanings that added up to stories of old legends and great moments in island history.

"But before we will allow you to dance," said Mak, "you must join the feast. Come!"

Kaiulani happily scampered after the little man. Unlike

many of the other *kamaiina,* Mak and his wife, Lili, were always nice to her and Lokei. Mak did all kinds of mechanical repairs and carpentry jobs around the plantation, as well as helping the other workers to keep the ancient shanties where they lived from collapsing. Insisting that he was a descendant of the early tribal kings who had come to Hawaii from islands far across the sea, he called himself Prince Makelahi, but Kaiulani wondered why a prince would work as a handyman instead of living in a castle as big as the Tranes' mansion. She had asked her mother about it.

"Our kings and princes have always been good men who didn't like to fight," Lokei said. "They were no match for other men who came with many weapons and took all they wanted."

Kaiulani still couldn't understand why a real prince would be so poor. Yet she also believed Prince Makelahi was kind and trustworthy. On days when she was sent out of the cottage because Mr. Trane was coming, her favorite places to go were Mak's little repair shed or the shack he shared with his wife, Lili. Lili's full name was actually Lilikoi—which meant passion fruit—and she was bigger than her husband, round as a drum, and had the brightest smile anywhere on the island. Not long ago she had told Kaiulani it would be all right to call her *tutu*—as if she were actually Kaiulani's grandmother.

They came to an area where a line of makeshift tables stood spread with pineapples and papayas, and trays of meaty roasted pork bones. There was also several large wooden barrels from which people were ladling liquid into their coconut shells.

"I want something to drink," Kaiulani called out to Mak. "Some of that!" She pointed to the barrels.

The people around her began to laugh. Kaiulani flushed with embarrassment. Then she saw Lokei laughing, too. Her mother was always so beautiful—and especially tonight, with a huge white poinsetta tucked behind one ear and her prettiest silk sarong draped around her perfect figure. But when she laughed, she was even more magically lovely—and it happened so rarely. "I must have some of that!" Kaiulani repeated. She would ask over and over if it kept Lokei laughing.

Mak led the child over to one of the barrels. "If you drink

a cup of this, *keko*, you won't dance tonight. It's a liquor made from *ti* plants called *okole hao*. Can you guess why?''

Kaiulani knew the meaning of the words—''iron bottom''—but couldn't see how they applied to a drink in a wooden barrel.

''Because,'' Mak explained, his black eyes twinkling, ''if you drink a cup of this, you won't be left standing straight up unless you've got an iron bottom.'' He slapped his posterior, and the crowd laughed once more.

He brought her to a table and gave her a coconut shell filled with pineapple juice. But as Kaiulani drank, she kept a worried eye on her mother, who was drinking some of the Iron Bottom.

Mak held out a pork rib. ''Now, if you want to dance, you must first eat this.''

Kaiulani wasn't sure what one thing had to do with the other, but she took the bone and began chewing the delicious meat. Suddenly she saw a circle had formed, a crowd watching. She stopped and stared back curiously.

''Aren't you hungry?'' Mak said. ''Go on.''

She hurried to finish so that they would all stop watching. Soon Mak stepped forward and took the bone from her hand. He raised it in the air and called out. ''Do you see what the little *mo'o* has done?'' There were murmurs of approval all around.

Kaiulani felt puzzled and worried. But then her mother was beside her. ''It's an ancient belief of ours,'' she said, ''that when a very young girl eats all the meat from a bone, as you have done, it's a sure sign she will be a most wonderful dancer.''

Kaiulani beamed with delight. Many of the ancient beliefs she heard from her elders struck her as odd—how could the way she ate determine her ability to dance?—but there was nothing she wanted more than to be as graceful as her mother.

At a cool distance from the blazing bonfire, a number of workers with musical instruments were performing together, seated on hollow logs as they strummed ukuleles and pounded drums, or standing to run their hands across the strings of the bench-like steel guitars that gave Hawaiian tunes their distinctive twang. Women in several separate groups were doing the hula, their hips rocking gently, arms moving from side to side as they undulated in a liquid rhythm. With Mak and Lokei, Kaiulani moved closer to watch the dancers. Some of the older ones seemed very unsteady, as though they had been drinking *okole hao* but didn't have the necessary iron bottoms. But the younger women looked incredibly graceful. A few danced in the most ancient native tradition, wearing only skirts made from sheaves of grass, and thick leis of plumeria that hung from their necks to cover their nakedness. As the flickering light from the bonfire played over their swaying bodies, the best of the dancers seemed to have found some mystical synchrony with all the elements, moving in time not only to the music but to the rhythm of the flames and the fluttering shadows. Kaiulani began to imitate what she saw, lifting her arms and reaching out to one side, then the other, and trying to sway her hips with the same fluid ease.

Mak smiled and nudged Lokei.

But as she watched her daughter's fledgling efforts, she felt something besides pride and pleasure. The hula, and its more ancient version, the *olapa*, were sensuous, seductive dances. It was because she did them so well herself, Lokei recalled, that she had first attracted the attention of the man who was now her *haku*. Often just before they made love, he would command her to dance naked for him.

Did she really want her little girl to become so skilled in the moves of this powerfully seductive dance?

Or was it wrong to let her own unhappy history poison her view of something that could also be joyous and beautiful and innocent?

Lokei watched her daughter for another moment, then moved up beside her. "Lift your arms a little higher, Kaiulani," she said gently, "like this." Lokei fell into the rhythm, demonstrating as she danced. "Don't just make yourself move. Feel the movement coming from inside you . . . like a warm breeze that blows softly along your limbs . . . from the shoulder, along your arms, trickling off the fingers as if they were the tips of little leaves. . . ."

Kaiulani listened, and watched the way her mother did it. Her own movements quickly became smoother and more sinuous.

"Remember, too, that you can be telling a story with your hands, your eyes, every part of you." The dance they had just joined, Lokei explained, told the story of a woman who sails across the waves to find a lover who went looking for a huge fish to feed his starving tribe and did not come back. The waves were represented by undulations of the arms and hips; pressing the hands together and swooping them in looping arcs depicted the fisherman diving after his quarry.

With each step Kaiulani matched more closely her mother's graceful movements. The women around them soon gave up dancing to watch. They didn't approve of Lokei Teiatu; the status she had accepted demeaned all native women. Still, she had always been the best of dancers, and there was nothing more enchanting than to see the beautiful young child perfectly mirroring the grace of her beautiful mother.

Kaiulani smiled back at the circle of spectators that formed, thrilled by their approval. Her blue-green eyes flashed with delight when she saw that Mak's wife had joined the circle. *Tutu* Lili was pridefully beaming her enormous smile. As Kaiulani felt her own mastery of the dance quickly developing, she became even more bold. She initiated some steps of her own, beginning to circle around Lokei. The spectators clapped and murmured approval. Again, Kaiulani saw her mother laugh. She had never been so happy.

All at once there was a change in the mood—vague at first, a sense of something different in the air, like the faint prickle of electricity on the skin that precedes a lightning storm. Then Kaiulani became aware of voices rising from the crowd around her.

"*Aloha,* Mr. Trane." "Good evening, sir . . ."

Kaiulani glanced at Lokei and saw that her happy expression was gone, her mouth was tight, her glance skittering anxiously over the circle of people around them.

A moment later, a gap opened in the circle of spectators, and Harley Trane stepped through it.

Lokei froze instantly, but Kaiulani continued to dance—unwilling to stop, to let such a magic moment end. Her mother grabbed her gently waving arms and pulled them down. "No more," she said, barely louder than a whisper.

"Don't stop now!" Harley Trane shouted out. "You know how I love your dancing, Lokei!" Taking a step deeper into the circle, he waved the champagne bottle he was holding almost as though it were a conductor's baton.

Lokei hesitated. From his weaving stance and slurred speech, it was obvious Trane was drunk, and Lokei knew well that if she disobeyed him when he was in this condition, he could explode at any second into vicious behavior.

"C'mon," he cajoled. "Lemme see. The kid, too. Even better to watch you with the kid." As Trane advanced on Lokei, Kaiulani huddled closer to her mother. He glanced down at her. "Good to start 'em young, right? Teach her to follow right along in your footsteps—teach her to do it like you do, everything . . ."

"Kaiulani is tired now," Lokei said, desperate to save her child from humiliation. "Come to the cottage, Harley. I will dance for you there." She gestured to the musicians to stop playing. The music trailed off.

Harley took a swig from the champagne bottle, still keeping his eyes trained blearily on Lokei. "Not ready to go yet," he said. "Tonight's a special night, isn't it? So let me make a gift to everyone. You dance alone for me all the time. I want everyone to see—"

"They've seen me, Harley. Let's go—"

"No!" he roared ferociously. "I want you to do it now!"

The circle of spectators did nothing to interfere. Whether or not Harley was directly in charge of the plantation, he was a Trane; he was one of the *aliilani;* he was connected to power and could deprive them of their jobs or worse.

Even Mak was slow to respond, hoping Trane might be controlled by Lokei. But now he moved forward to stand in front of Kaiulani. "We're pleased to have you join our party, Mr. Trane. But you'll enjoy it more if you come with me and have some *okole hao.*" As he spoke, Mak lightly prodded Kaiulani toward Lili. "Come, Mr. Trane, let me give you—"

"I don't want anything from you, goddamn little toad." Harley thrust out one of his large hands and shoved Mak so hard that the little man staggered backward and fell. Lili and Kaiulani cried out, but Mak quickly gestured to them that he was all right and hopped to his feet. "Seems I could use more of an iron bottom myself," he said lightly, moving toward Trane again.

Knowing Mak would be hurt more seriously if he challenged Harley again, Lokei headed him off. "It's all right, Mak. He just wants me to dance . . . so I'll do it."

Lokei threw a look of reassurance at her daughter, whom Lili had pulled into a protective embrace, her huge arms forming a fortress around the child. Then Lokei called to the musicians to play again. As they did, she began slowly to sway. Mak backed away to stand beside Lili.

Lokei closed her eyes and forced herself into the rhythm, and soon she was performing almost as well as before.

For a minute Harley watched. Then he staggered closer to Lokei. "You can do better than that, sweetheart. Need to loosen up, though . . . do it the real traditional way."

Lokei realized what Harley wanted from her now, and felt sick at the prospect of being debased in front of Kaiulani. But even before she could protect herself or call to Lili and Mak to take the child away, Harley grabbed the part of her sarong draped across her shoulder and tore it away.

A chorus of gasps rose from the onlookers. The music faltered again. Lokei stopped moving and crossed her arms over her bare breasts. Kaiulani started to run to her mother, but Lili held her back, afraid of Trane's unharnessed brutality.

"Something wrong?" he shouted at the crowd. "Isn't that the way it's supposed to be done?" He whirled on Lokei again. "C'mon, lover, keep dancing."

Mak edged forward. "Go home, Mr. Trane. Leave Lokei alone tonight. You're *ona nui*." Very drunk.

Other workers chimed in. "That's right." "Let her be." "Go home."

Trane focused a burning glare on the crowd. "You're telling *me* what to do? Think you can give *me* orders?" A rough growl of a laugh rose from his throat. "You really think anything has changed because some man thousands of miles away signed a few little papers? Every inch of the land you're standing on, living on, is still owned by me and my family! And no one's going to take that away. You want to eat tomorrow? You want a job? Then back off, and don't you dare forget your place!"

It was a brazen boast since Harley knew that his brother would never go along with firing any workers because they defied him in this situation. But Harley also perceived that the ingrained reflex of the workers was to fear any member of the *aliilani*. It would be a long time before they dared to rebel. He turned to Lokei again, put his hand out, and touched her breast.

"Bastard!" Mak cried out. He would have taken a run at Harley, but Lili grabbed his sleeve and held him back.

"Stay out of it, Prince," Harley called over his shoulder, "or you'll lose your balls the way you lost your throne."

Still, Mak might have torn loose from his wife to go on the attack, but Lokei cried out: "Go home, Mak. Take Kaiulani and go. I'll be all right." Mak hesitated and glanced to his wife.

"Don't let him make you do it, Mama!" Kaiulani screamed. "We have a star on the flag. You don't have to do anything you don't want."

Harley tossed his head back and laughed, and Lokei cried louder to be heard above him. "Go, Mak! Take her, Lili!"

Lili bent to Kaiulani and said softly in her ear, "Come, *keko*, we must go."

Kaiulani put up no resistance as the two started to lead her away. Her mother's submission to Mr. Trane had left her shocked and confused. Without completely comprehending the reasons, Kaiulani realized that Lokei had no choice—had never had a choice—but to do what Mr. Trane wanted.

As she was led away, Kaiulani heard the music resume. Glancing over her shoulder, she could see her mother standing in front of Trane, half nude, a distant golden figure across the dark field. Slowly, Lokei's hips began to sway, then she lifted her arms and extended them at her sides and they began to move gracefully, so gracefully, as if a warm, gentle breeze was blowing from within, rippling down along her arms and off the tips of her fingers.

Tears filled Kaiulani's eyes, and she could watch no more. She didn't think she would ever want to dance again.

Chapter Two

Her waist-length copper hair streaming behind her, Kai raced along the winding path through the workers' settlement, took the rickety steps up to the narrow veranda of Mak's shack in a single leap, and lunged through the mosquito net across the open door.

"Have you heard?" she called loudly as she dropped her schoolbooks and ran across the empty front room. The shack was small, consisting of a room used for sleeping and sitting, and a small kitchen tacked on at the rear. There was no bathroom, only a privy and an outside shower in a coconut grove, shared with several nearby workers' shacks. Kai knelt in front of the old television set Mak had rescued from a junk pile and switched it on. "Come and see, *Tutu*!"

Lili emerged from the kitchen holding the meat of a coconut she'd been shredding. To supplement her husband's earnings as a handyman, she baked cakes for a Honolulu hotel that sent someone across the island twice a week to pick them up.

"Why are you home early from school?" Lili asked.

"The science teacher let us out of a lab. He said we should all go home and try to see the television pictures."

"What pictures? What's happened, *mo'o*?" Both Lili and Mak still used the same endearments they had applied to Lokei's daughter when they first began caring for her. These days not another soul would ever have thought to refer to Kaiulani Teiatu as "monkey" or "lizard," not even for the sake of observing the superstitious *kapu* against acknowledging beauty. At fifteen, Kai—as she had been known since starting high school—was tall and leggy, with a figure that had advanced well across the frontier from girl to woman. The dewy loveliness possessed as a child had evolved into a stunning physical presence that was even more spectacular. Beyond the visual effect of her face and form, the flashing turquoise eyes and golden skin and lithe coltishness, she projected some intangible magnetic aura, a vibrant inner energy and appetite for life, that heightened her attractiveness.

Kai watched the screen, waiting for an image to form. "A spacecraft landed on the moon today. You know what that means? Space travel is real. In a few years we'll be able to send men to the moon!"

Lili shook her head in annoyance. "This is not good. Men should stay where they were put in the beginning."

"*Tutu*, if everyone stayed where they were put in the beginning, you and I wouldn't be Americans. Our ancestors across the Pacific would never have climbed on their rafts and sailed to Hawaii."

"Sailing the ocean is not the same as shooting big bullets at our beautiful yellow *mahina*. If the spirits of the moon get angry, who knows what they will shoot back at us?"

The black-and-white picture faded in—an episode of a mainland soap opera. Kai flipped the dial. There was nothing about the moon shot on any channel. She switched off the television in disgust. "Don't they think this is news?" she complained to Lili. "The Russians have landed a spacecraft on the moon. It's going to send back pictures! We're going to see what it looks like up there. Isn't that amazing, *Tutu*?" After so many years of addressing Lili as if she were her grandmother, Kai had practically forgotten that no actual blood relationship existed.

"You say the Russians did it? Then why should we be glad? We're Americans, *mo'o*. The moon spirits might be annoyed with us, but they know we're nicer people than the Russians. Oh, they are sure to be very angry now. They may switch off the light of the moon for weeks and weeks." Lili stalked back to the kitchen.

Laughing, Kai followed her. "*Tutu*, the moon has no light of its own, it only reflects the sun. Spirits or no spirits, it can't be turned off like a lamp."

Lili resumed shredding coconut into a bowl. "It is a great thing to be educated, Kaiulani," she said haughtily. "But no matter how much you learn, you must always leave room in your heart and mind for magic.''

Kai picked up a piece of coconut meat, found a knife, and set to work alongside Lili. She understood how deeply rooted were some of the spiritual customs and beliefs of the Hawaiians' ancient Kahuna religion. Lokei, too, harbored a genuine fear and respect of the Kahuna spirits that were believed to control the sun, the moon, the sea, the plants and rocks—all of nature—and some of this had been instilled in Kai as a child. Science had become one of her favorite subjects in school precisely because it liberated her from these childish fears. Now she struggled with the dilemma of sharing this love of learning, yet continuing to respect the sacred beliefs of her elders.

''I want to believe in magic,'' she said. ''Often when I walk from here back to the beach, I still hope to see a *menehune*. I have so many wishes I'd make. But there are other ways to make wishes come true besides magic. The *aliilani* don't believe in spirits; they're powerful and rich because of what they *know*. That's why I want to learn.''

''You want to be powerful?'' Lili asked.

''More than Mr. Trane, anyway,'' Kai said grimly.

Lili glanced sympathetically at Kai. She knew the pain and frustration that plagued this beautiful girl because her mother continued to endure being Harley Trane's *manuwahi*. In recent years Trane had divorced one wife, married another, and had more children. Yet he hadn't stopped his frequent visits to Lokei Teiatu's beachside cottage. Throughout Kai's younger years, there had been many times Lili would hold her for hours while she wept, never able to accept her mother's humiliation. More recently there were no tears; Kai's sorrow had curdled into bitterness.

Groping for words to ease the inner wounds of this child she loved so much, Lili said, ''There are some things you may never be able to change, Kaiulani. Don't blame yourself if you cannot always save the people you care about. Sometimes it's because they won't let you help.''

Kai brooded silently. It was true she had tried dozens of times to encourage her mother to cut the ties to Trane, and Lokei had always resisted her arguments, insisting that things would be no better elsewhere, and probably worse. When Kai had been younger, she hadn't believed this could be true; away from Trane, things would have to be better. But over the years, having gained a greater understanding of the hard realities of life in the islands, Kai was no longer so naive. Being a *hapa* woman with little education or developed skills, did Lokei have so many chances to earn a good living, dwell in a comfortable house on the beach, feed and clothe her child? Yet, being that child, Kai could not escape the feeling that she was also accountable for the profane bondage in which her mother was trapped.

"She stays for me," Kai said at last, "to give me a home. She's always done it for me. So who else can save her?"

Before Lili could reply, Mak entered the shack and shouted, *"Aloha!"* from the front room. She and Kai called out greetings in return.

"Come and see," Mak summoned them. "There are going to be pictures sent from the moon on television."

Lili muttered to herself and went on shredding coconut, but Kai ran to the front room. Mak had found a news bulletin, and the black-and-white television screen was filled with a fuzzy image of patches of light and dark.

The picture was certainly not as magical as seeing the glowing yellow ball that hung in the night sky, Kai had to admit.

"This means that before long men will also go," Mak said.

"I know." But suddenly Kai felt less thrilled by the prospect. She was oddly troubled by the idea Lili had planted, that the price of knowledge was a loss of something mysterious and romantic. The crude pictures being transmitted from a Russian spacecraft did reduce the moon to nothing more than a huge, uneven field of gray dust. "Do you think you'd like to walk on the moon, Mak?" Kai asked.

The little man smiled. "I don't have to. I know already exactly what it's like."

"You do?"

"I have walked on the slopes of volcanoes after they have erupted and cooled. It's the same there, the ground covered with fine white dust, nothing living for miles around."

"I thought the volcanoes have all been dead for a long time."

"Here on Oahu, yes. But this was on the big island. I picked sugarcane there when I was a young man. Two volcanoes there are still alive. Perhaps I can take you some time.''

''Oh, please, yes.''

The short broadcast of pictures from the moon ended. Kai's feeling of disappointment lingered. ''Maybe Lili is right,'' she said. ''Maybe it's foolish to shoot big bullets at the moon.''

Mak looked at her in surprise. ''I suppose,'' he guessed, ''that she has been saying we'll make the spirits angry.''

Kai smiled. ''That's not what worries me. I just wonder . . . if there's really any point. Will life here change for the better because we've sent men to the moon? These things we get so excited about, sometimes it seems that they could be . . . like tricks that are played on all of us.''

Mak remained silent. He sensed that Kai was leading up to something else.

''Remember how happy everyone was when Hawaii became a state?'' Kai gazed through the screened doorway window toward the fields. ''How full of hope we were. But nothing really changed. Nothing's better than it was, not for us. And now we're so excited because someday we'll send men to the moon.'' She turned her luminous eyes on Mak. ''But how will that really make anything better?''

Like his wife, Mak was sensitive to the problem that troubled Kai above all others. When she expressed a longing for change, he knew that she was thinking only about her mother.

He placed his wrinkled brown hands on the shoulders of the kneeling girl. ''You talk as if you believe all changes should happen easily, by themselves, the way the seasons change, or the oceans rise and fall. But the things you want to change, *keko*, will happen only if people make them happen. That is what we learn by seeing the surface of the moon, by knowing a man or a woman will walk there someday. It teaches us that we can go very great distances—even fly up into the heavens. But only when we stop dreaming about it, and work to make it happen.''

Kai nodded slowly. True, she had yearned for changes and expected them to occur without her making any effort. Of course, it was the habit of a child to think that way, to expect things to be done for her. But it was time to break the habit, to dare to make things happen.

"I must take Lokei away," she said with sudden urgency.

"Where would you go?"

"Anywhere. Just so long as she's safe from Mr. Trane. I can't stand anymore to think of—of what she must do for him." Kai's fists clenched at her sides. "I've been hoping Mama would have the strength to break with him, lift herself up. But if she won't, then I have to be the one to make it happen."

"You know I'll help any way I can."

Kai looked at him imploringly. "Would you go, too, you and Lili? You're also my family."

Mak rocked back on his stool, thrown off balance by the thought of revising his own life overnight.

"You're so good at fixing things," Kai continued. "I don't know how I could go to school and still earn money. And without money, I'm afraid that Lokei . . . well, she only knows one way. But, Mak, you could earn your living anywhere doing the same thing you've done here. Fixing cars, and tools, and building things . . ."

Mak leaked a slow smile. Within the space of a few moments he found the idea taking hold. Why not accept the challenge of making a fresh start? Both he and Lili would be miserable separated from Kai. They had often acknowledged to each other that the love they felt for the girl could have been no greater if she were their own.

"Lili!" Mak shouted suddenly, springing to his feet.

Mak's wife scuttled in from the kitchen holding a mixing bowl.

"Kaiulani is planning to go away," he announced.

The Hawaiian woman's broad face instantly collapsed with dismay, and the bowl dropped from her hands.

"No, wait!" Mak said over the sound of crockery shattering. "She wants us to go with her. To help rescue Lokei from Mr. Trane."

Lili needed only a second, too, to digest the idea, and then her mouth split into a smile of pure joy. "But where are we going?" she asked.

Kai shrugged. "I haven't thought about that yet. I only know it can't be far. We have no money to travel."

"Then I know exactly the right place," Mak said.

Both the women turned to him questioningly.

"We'll go," he said, with a wink at Kai, "where I can take you for a walk on the moon."

Will I miss it? Kai asked herself as the path emerged from the grove of palms and she walked along the white sand beach toward the cottage. It was a pretty place, certainly, a white frame wooden house with lanais on all sides—open porches that could be closed to the heavy rains or sea winds with large shutters—set back from the powdery sand in a grove of white poinsettia and ohia trees with their scarlet blossoms. She'd always had her own large room, on the opposite side of the house from her mother's, its windows facing the east so she often woke to the sight of the sun rising over the ocean. It would have been a perfect place to live—if only its charm was not blotted out by the ugliness of knowing it represented the largest part of the payment Lokei received for her services to Harley Trane.

No, Kai assured herself, she would never regret leaving here.

She had spent another half hour with Mak, making plans. Mak knew a fisherman who owned a boat large enough to transport four people. He had repaired the boat's engine several times, often without being paid for months, since the fisherman usually had little money after being unable to use his boat. Now the favor could be returned. The boat could take them directly from the plantation beach, and by the next day they could sail from Oahu to the island of Hawaii. The Big Island was less settled than all the others, more of a frontier, representing more opportunity. Being bigger, it would also be an easier place to "get lost in"—as Mak put it—just in case Harley Trane tried to chase after Lokei.

"I can arrange it whenever you're ready," Mak said.

It all sounded so easy that Kai wished she had spoken to him about leaving years ago.

Yet she didn't expect Lokei's agreement to come automatically. Just as the steady drip of raindrops wears through a rock, her mother's will seemed to have been worn down by the constant indignities she had suffered. Despite the pain and shame Trane had inflicted on Lokei over the years, Kai had also heard her speak of feeling some gratitude because he had provided a better life for her than what her own mother had endured.

Only within the last couple of years had Kai begun piecing together some of the history of her family. Once, when she had been very young, Kai had plied her mother with questions about her background, and Lokei had replied sharply that her parents were people who had "insulted the spirits"—a crime for which they had been punished by Pele, the god of the volcano, who made them both disappear in a cloud of smoke. Kai was sufficiently frightened that she didn't ask any more about Lokei's origins for years afterward. When she grew older and resumed asking the kind of determined, logical questions that could not be silenced with scary tales, Lokei had been more evasive.

"It's better you don't know too much," she told Kai. "My mother was a native, my father a mainlander who was here with the army, then went away again. The same thing happened to me. Your father was a mainlander who left. There's nothing more to know, nothing that matters."

Kai did not give up so easily. She went on trying to pry loose a few details about her father—his name, what he looked like. "I've forgotten him, and so should you," Lokei would insist. Finally, when she lost all patience with Kai's questions, Lokei exploded furiously. "He's dead, he's not part of our lives and never can be. So don't ask me anymore." The command was given with such intense, anguished conviction that Kai had not since dared to disobey it.

But she asked Mak and Lili what they knew about her father, about her mother's background, about how Lokei had met Harley Trane. They were evasive, too, at first. But as Kai reached her teens, they began to sketch in the outlines, always in a context of encouraging her to be sympathetic to the hardships her mother had survived.

"You must understand what the islands were like thirty years ago," Lili said one night. "There was nothing here but the plantations, and the big American bases for their ships and their army. Nothing for the women to do but work in the fields—or work at entertaining the sailors and soldiers." However delicately Lili attempted to deliver the facts, in the end Kai realized that Lokei's mother had been one of the hundreds of prostitutes who worked in the brothels situated near the Schofield Barracks in central Oahu. Even thirty years ago, long before the wars against the Japanese or the Koreans, Schofield had been one of the biggest installations of the American army—and, like all such places, it provided a magnet for vice. Lokei's mother had become pregnant by one of her customers and had given birth to a daughter. As for Lokei's father, under the circumstances it was impossible to determine who he was.

Knowing this much had made Kai reluctant to pursue more of the story. It was bad enough that Lokei had given herself to Trane. How much worse if she had followed in the same path as her mother, become a common whore.

Could this explain why she would never tell Kai anything about her father?

But Lili calmed the worst of her fears. "Your mother was luckier," she told Kai. "She was saved by Laka—the goddess of the dance, who gave her a gift that she could sell instead of her body." Left on her own after her mother died—not of an illness, after all, but of alcohol poisoning—Lokei had earned her living as a hula dancer in tourist shows at the Honolulu hotels, and it was there that Harley Trane had seen her.

"But my father," Kai persisted, "who is he? Why won't Lokei talk about him?"

"We can't tell you," Mak said. "Because, truly, we don't know."

Only Lokei could provide the answers, if ever she would. But sometimes Kai thought that—just as her mother had insisted so often—it might be better not to know.

Approaching the entrance to the cottage, Kai rehearsed the pleas she would make if Lokei had any resistance to leaving. *You stayed here for me, Mama, I know that, but I'm not a child anymore, and I can't let you do this to yourself for me. . . . I know it's better than what your mother had to do, but it's still not good enough. . . . You'll be happier away from here, away from* him. . . .

How could Lokei not agree? Charged with hope, Kai hurried into the cottage.

Unlike the small front room of Mak's ramshackle hut, this one was spacious and comfortably furnished with rattan chairs, lamp tables, a sofa arranged on a soft carpet, and a fairly new television set. All provided by Harley Trane.

Kai usually found Lokei curled on the sofa, watching television or reading one of the fashion magazines Trane often brought, secondhand from his wife. Because there was no way to predict when Trane would claim her evenings, Lokei always made an effort to spend time with her daughter when she arrived home after school. Usually she was waiting right there, eager to sit and talk.

Then Kai realized she was back an hour earlier than usual because the science teacher had dismissed everyone from lab. "Mama," she call, "I'm home."

Silence. The house seemed empty. Kai guessed that her mother had gone for a walk, or to the plantation store, where she had a regular allowance for food and other supplies.

She put down her bag of books and went to the kitchen. Unlike kitchens in the workers' shacks, this one was neat and up-to-date, with a glossy linoleum floor and modern electric appliances. Kai took milk from the refrigerator and poured herself a glass. As she stood drinking it, her eyes swept over the clean, shining space around her. This, all of this, was what Lokei had bought with her obedience to Trane. There might be nothing as nice where they were going . . . but, no, she wouldn't miss it. Kai finished the milk, rinsed the glass in the white porcelain sink, and headed for her bedroom.

As she crossed the living room, she heard a faint bumping sound from the opposite side of the house. Her mother's room. Kai stopped and looked across toward the closed door. She hadn't even thought to check the room before, assuming Lokei would have answered her call.

At the door Kai knocked softly, then called. "Mama . . . ?"

There was a noise, like a muffled cry. Kai went rigid; her eyes locked on the solid wood panel in front of her, as though trying to burn through it with the heat of her gaze, to see without being forced to make the choice of opening the door.

Her hesitation lasted a second, then her hand went to the knob. Another indistinct whining sound came from inside the room as Kai slowly pushed the door back on its hinges.

Her blood froze in her veins. In one shocked instant, every ugly detail of the scene was etched into Kai's mind with the same rough power of a lethal acid searing grooves into metal. Her mother and Harley Trane on the bed, his

naked body stretched over hers, pinning her. His hands
pressed over her mouth to keep her from crying out. Lokei's
beseeching eyes aimed at the door. A nearly empty bottle
of liquor . . . and a syringe lying on a night table.

And the ropes—braided silken ropes; Kai had seen such
ropes dangling from curtains in the windows of the Trane
mansion when she'd done gardening there last summer to
earn extra money. Four short lengths were knotted around
her mother's wrists and ankles, each tied to a corner post
of the bed, holding her mother's naked body splayed out on
the sheet like a specimen butterfly.

Kai's brain rebelled against the reality.

Then a pathetic squeal came from Lokei as she tried to
say something, and her body started to writhe, attempting
to break free.

Kai sprang forward, her arms extended, fingers clawed as
she leapt at her mother's torturer.

Trane stayed on the bed, as though unconcerned about
defending himself. But he threw back his head and let out
a hideous laugh—and at the same moment he pulled his
hand away from Lokei's mouth.

Instantly her desperate shriek filled the room. "*Aole*, Kai!
Don't!"

Kai froze, her feet rooted to the floor. *No . . . don't?* Kai
stared straight into Lokei's glazed eyes. Didn't she *want* to
be saved?

Lokei answered the question before it was spoken. "Leave
us alone. *Holo* . . ."

This had to be a nightmare. Her mother couldn't be telling her to go, to run.

Trane laughed again. "That's it, sweetheart, don't go.
Have to learn sometime. Stay right here and watch me fuck
your mother." He reared back, showing his erection to Kai
as he took hold of the throbbing red shaft and guided it into
the nest of shining black hair between Lokei's thighs.

For another moment Kai remained paralyzed. Why was
Lokei silent now, unprotesting? Then the spell of horror
broke. Kai sprang across the room and grabbed for the nearest of the silken ropes, her shaking fingers fumbling at the
knot around Lokei's ankle. She was only vaguely aware
of Trane still laughing. But the angry scream that tore
through the air froze Kai again.

"Hele oe!"

Go away? And that tone in her mother's voice—more fury than shame. Kai shook her head, still refusing to believe.

Lokei averted her eyes, but the words tumbled once more from her lips in a regretful moan. "Please . . . go away."

Kai's sense of purpose collapsed. She moved slowly away from the bed as thought retreating from a nest of snakes that mustn't be disturbed. Her feet carried her backward, out through the door, across the floor, the sound of Trane's laughter and the vision of him with her mother still filling her brain, blocking everything else from sight, that last whisper echoing loud as thunder inside her head.

She turned finally and broke into a blind, stumbling run from the cottage. She nearly collided with the trunk of a cocoa palm, and staggered past it onto the wide belt of white beach. A wave of nausea dragged her down to her knees, and she retched onto the sand, but in a minute she was on her feet again, running alongside the surf, running until her lungs burned and her heart was pounding so hard it seemed that it would explode.

Finally she dropped again, gasping, unable to move. The cold edge of the ocean surged around her. She gazed out at the sea and sky. Imprinted on the azure horizon was that terrible image of her mother trussed to the bed; the soft whisper of the surf was drowned by the wretched scream inside her head: *Hele oe.* Go away.

All her life, Kai had believed that Lokei had been pressed by circumstances into being the slave of a man she hated. Now she knew a different truth. Her mother hadn't wanted to be saved. Lokei neither hated Trane nor the way he treated her. If she said she did, then it was part of a ritual she had performed for her daughter's benefit.

But what could make her—could make any woman—willing to endure such humiliation? The question rolled through Kai's mind as relentlessly as the surf washing up onto the shore.

The sun sank below the horizon, the night turned cold. But Kai stayed on the beach, only moving far enough to avoid the advancing tide. She couldn't go to Mak or Lili to unburden herself, not this time. How could she admit to them that her mother was no less corrupt than Harley Trane?

As the hours passed, and drowsiness mercifully made the

ugly image fade, and the voices inside her head grow calmer, Kai found herself finally staring at the moon, bright silver tonight and almost full.

Perhaps, she thought, Lili was right about making the spirits angry. How different this day would have been if men had not been shooting at the moon.

"Mama . . . ?"

In the half light of dawn, Kai crept toward the figure reclining on the bed, sheets wrapped around it like a shroud. Kai had fallen asleep on the beach, but as soon as she opened her eyes the image had been there—and the storm of emotions that came with it. She had raced back to the cottage. Now, along with pity and disgust and sorrow and anger, Kai felt an icy fear that Trane's warped desire might know no limits.

Lokei lay on her side, facing toward the window, her back to Kai. Her body deathly still.

"Mama!" Kai cried, suddenly certain her intuition had been correct. She ran around the end of the bed.

Lokei's eyes were open, staring at the dawn sky. Even in the dim light Kai could see they were rimmed by dark circles.

Tentatively, still afraid, Kai knelt beside the bed and reached out. "Mama," she whispered.

Lokei rolled over, hiding her face again.

Kai took a deep breath. A very long silence passed. The light in the room grew brighter.

"Why, Mama?" Kai said at last. "Why do you let him do that to you?"

Lokei refused to speak or to look at her daughter.

"Has it always been like that?" Kai persisted. "Does it have to be? Talk to me, Mama. Please . . ."

Lokei said nothing.

The answers were not important, Kai decided. All that mattered was stopping it.

"We can't stay here, Mama. We're going away. I've arranged it with Mak. We'll go to the Big Island, he knows a man who will—"

"No." Quietly as Lokei spoke, the word struck Kai like a hammer striking an anvil.

"But you can't want this, Mama."

"It's all we have," Lokei murmured.

"But it's *wrong,*" Kai said, her voice rising. "I don't care about staying in this damn house. What's the good of a beautiful view outside the window, when inside I see things that are so . . . so . . ." The word *dirty* was all that came to mind, though she couldn't bring herself to say it. Lokei had suffered enough humiliation already.

Kai rose from her knees to perch on the bed. She leaned over her mother's prostrate form. "Mama, there are men who would love you, treat you with respect—I know there must be. Don't you want that instead of a man who hurts you?"

Slowly, Lokei rolled over to look up at Kai. "My mother was a whore, too," she said in a small, trembling voice.

Kai lay down alongside her mother and put her arms around her. Beneath the sheets she felt Lokei's body shivering like a child needing to be comforted after a bad dream. Kai recalled the times when she was very small and she would wake to the fierce thunder and lightning of a tropical storm, and Lokei had held her like this to reassure her.

"Don't be frightened, Mama," Kai said, echoing the words her mother would speak to her. "I'll take care of you."

They lay together until Kai heard her mother's deep, even breathing and realized she had fallen asleep. Then Kai rose quietly and began to go through the house, gathering the few possessions they would take with them into a new life.

Chapter Three

In the Hawaiian archipelago of eight islands, the eastern-most was the one that actually bore the name Hawaii. More than three times larger than any of the others, it was hardly ever called anything by the natives but the Big Island.

Only on the Big Island were the volcanoes still alive. Across one entire quadrant the earth was continuously opening in rifts and craters to disgorge streams of molten lava that flowed down the volcanic slopes for miles. Where they cooled, huge fields of hard black lava were left behind—as desolate as the moonscape Kai had glimpsed on television.

Kai had been excited about the prospect of seeing the volcanoes from the moment Mak mentioned it. Her knowledge that these soaring cones that spewed steam and molten rock into the air were a vision of how the earth had been born, inspired her curiosity. As soon as they arrived at the docks in Hilo, the island's largest town, Kai started asking Mak when they would see a volcano.

"Patience, *keko*," he said. "We have more important things to do first."

The group set about the task of finding a place to live and ways to earn money. As Mak had hoped, they were given temporary shelter in a dormitory run by one of the Christian missions that had been active ever since the first white settlers had arrived on whaling ships at the beginning of the nineteenth century. The missionaries were still happy to shelter anyone who would spend a few minutes in the chapel attached to the dormitory.

Every day Mak and Lili went separately through the town to find work, and Kai went along with Lokei. Hilo was not filled with opportunities spurred by the kind of booming tourist trade that existed in Honolulu. The small port served mainly to ship the sugar and pineapples that came from the island's plantations. Mak visited the few old hotels that stood along Hilo Bay, proudly presenting himself as a man who could fix anything. In one he was offered a job shoveling coal into an outmoded boiler. In another a position was open for a baggage carrier, work too strenuous for a man of his years.

Lili's search turned up openings at the local canneries, jobs that involved sitting over a conveyor ten hours a day, gutting and cleaning fish for less wages than plantation workers received. The prospect was depressing compared with the relaxed independence Lili had left behind.

Kai intended to continue public high school as soon as the others had jobs and a home was established. But she went along as Lokei made the rounds of places offering the sort of work that might be managed without too much experience. A florist shop. A couple of clothing stores. Hotel reception clerk. Arriving together, the strikingly beautiful mother and daughter were always quickly received. Dressed in nothing more than flowered *muumuus* with blossoms tucked behind their ears, both outshone most other women in gown and jewels. But where job openings turned up, Lokei's extreme passivity during interviews dissuaded prospective employers from believing she could handle any responsibility. More than once Kai was offered a tryout, but she would not accept work while her mother was being rejected.

By the end of the fourth day, no decent job had turned up. That night in the mission dormitory, Kai took Mak aside. "Forgive me," she said tearfully, "it's my fault you're here. I'm the one who made you and Lili change everything, and I've ruined your lives. I even wonder if Mama's going to be better off."

Mak cheered her. "You were smart and brave to make her break with Trane, *mo'o*. Never doubt that. And Lilikoi and I are here because we love you, and we knew it was right to help." He hugged Kai as he added, "It's much too soon to talk of mistakes. Tomorrow we will visit someone who will surely help us with our search."

"Who?"

"A friend of Lili's—someone with much influence."

"Lili has a friend here?" Kai asked in astonishment. Why hadn't they spoken to this person as soon as they arrived?

"Your mother knows her, too," Mak said.

"Who?" Kai repeated eagerly. "Tell me who it is."

Mak gave her a slow smile. "Pele," he said.

Ruler of fire, maker of mountains, eater of forests, melter
of rocks, the goddess Pele was hallowed in Hawaiian legend
as the most beautiful, powerful, and temperamental of their
deities. The daughter of Haumea, the Earth Mother, and
Wakea, the Sky Father, she also had a murderously cruel
sister named Na Maka, who was goddess of the sea. According to legend, these volcanic islands had been created
when Pele tried to escape from the wrath of her sister. The
beautiful goddess of fire ran from one island to another,
digging deeper each time, getting nearer to the core of the
earth. But Na Maka found each refuge and destroyed it until
at last Pele came to the Big Island. Here she dug so deep
that Na Maka was never able to find her.

"And so," Lili concluded the legend she'd been recounting to Kai, "Pele remains to this day deep, deep in her
impenetrable fortress home—the great firepit of Mount Kilauea."

They were riding on one of the buses that regularly made
the thirty-minute run from Hilo to the area where the island's two active volcanoes, Mauna Loa and Kilauea, were
located. Kai shared a seat with Lili, though she had barely
more than the edge, since the rest of the space was consumed by Lili's girth and a hempen bag filled with food the
mission had donated for a picnic. Ahead of them sat Mak
and Lokei, turned around as they listened to Lili's tale. A
number of tourists were also on the bus. Kai noticed them
eavesdropping, not bothering to conceal smirks provoked
by the quaint native legends. Kai was annoyed by their smug
amusement, but no less disturbed by the look of intense
devotion on Lokei's face—as though she took the myth for
literal truth. Kai didn't think that Mak's intention in making
today's journey was seriously to ask the help of a goddess,
but more to raise their morale with a day of sightseeing. Yet
lately Lokei had seemed so lost in her own thoughts, Kai
felt uneasy about encouraging her belief in any fantasy as a
way out of their problems.

But as they arrived at the volcano area, Kai's worry eased.
This was not, after all, a wild, spooky terrain dominated

by the kind of fire-spitting mountain natives that could be seen worshiping in foolish old Hollywood jungle epics Kai had watched on television. On either side of the road were slopes of cooled black lava. At intervals, plumes of steam rose from the ground, gathering at some places into clouds that obscured the sun. But there were also houses and stores—indeed, an entire mountain village called Volcano was the terminal point for the bus. The value of the volcanoes as a natural resource and tourist attraction had been officially recognized by the government when it designated the area Hawaii Volcanoes National Park in 1916. There were snack bars and a visitors center where the geological phenomena that formed the volcanoes were explained. Gleefully, Mak showed Kai a printed notice saying that astronauts now training for the first moon landing in two years would be spending time in the park, walking the lava fields to prepare themselves for dealing with the lunar surface.

As for the titanic and unpredictable power of the mountain's resident spirit, Kai felt her awe greatly reduced when she hiked behind Mak up to the Halemaumau—the half-mile-wide crater at the summit of Kilauea—and saw that a large, busy hotel called the Crater Inn had been built right at its edge. Mak told her the inn had been there for forty years.

Still, for all the surrounding encroachments of a modern world, when Kai approached the crater and looked down into the yawning cavern of flame and burning rock, she was mesmerized by this dark vision of the earth's tempestuous inner forces. The air was filled with the kind of sulfurous fumes that might rise from the fires of hell. Even with her scientific knowledge, Kai couldn't help but feel a stirring of some unreasoned trust in myth and magic. Moving closer to the rim, she leaned over and tried to see even deeper into the hellish recesses of the crater. Beyond the smoke, there were glowing orange spots—like eyes staring up at her. . . .

Two hands at her waist suddenly pulled her back. "Not too close, *keko*!" Mak warned. "It's easy to get dizzy from the gases." He pointed to one of the signs posted along the rim explaining that the fumes of sulfur, hydrogen, and carbon dioxide could produce dizziness if breathed for too long.

Kai glanced at her mother, who was standing at another point on the rim with Lili. Her dark eyes were half closed, her face slack. Perhaps the gas had affected her, too. Kai walked over. "Move back, Mama." She grasped Lokei's arm to pull her away.

Lokei resisted. "Not yet. We must leave our offering with the others." She gestured to the ground.

A mound of leaves had been heaped up nearby at the edge of the crater. Then Kai noticed another little pile of leaves a few feet farther on—and as her gaze traveled farther, she realized there were hundreds of identical mounds spaced at intervals along the entire sweeping rim of the vast crater.

"The leaves of the *ti* plant," Lili said, bending over the hempen bag she had brought along. She took out a package wrapped in newspaper and opened it to reveal several handfuls of green *ti* leaves. Kai guessed they had been brought all the way from the plantation, that Lili had always planned to make this offering.

While Kai and Mak watched, Lili and Lokei knelt on the ground and arranged the leaves in a circular mound. Lili chanted some Hawaiian words softly, and then Lokei joined in.

"In the old days," Mak whispered to Kai, "the people left animals . . . and long before there was a time when children and young maidens were thrown into the firepit as sacrifices to Pele."

Looking at her mother, Kai saw her face set in an expression of fierce concentration, her eyes aimed toward the crater as though truly praying to the spirit of the volcano for deliverance from her doubt and suffering. Kai was glad when the little ceremony was finished and they all sat down on a bench in an observation area to have their picnic.

Afterward, Mak spent a couple of hours hiking with Kai over parts of the vast lava fields. Lili hadn't the energy to climb around the slopes, and Lokei showed no interest, but Kai wanted to visit some of the more unusual formations created over the years by volcanic action—craters and tubes at the site of small past eruptions. Even if the main crater of Mount Kilauea had not recently exploded, the crust of the earth was constantly cracking open in so-called "rift zones" to vent the steam and molten rock bubbling up from underneath.

Mak and Kai hurried back to the village of Volcano in the middle of the afternoon to catch the bus back to Hilo.

The bus was waiting at a stop across from the old inn, Lili and Lokei standing in a crowd of passengers waiting to board.

"You may as well relax," Lili said. "The driver just told us the bus has broken down." She pointed to the front of the bus, where the driver was looking under the raised hood of the engine compartment. Kai drifted along as Mak went to the front and poked his head in next to the driver's.

"What's wrong?" Mak asked.

The driver pulled his head out from under the hood and frowned at the little man, clearly annoyed by his interference. "Won't start," he growled. "Have to be towed. Go wait somewhere for an hour or two, and we'll have another—"

"Perhaps I can fix it," Mak said. "I know all about mechanical things."

"So do I," the driver snapped. "Can't be done. Needs a new part."

"May I try?" Mak leaned toward the engine compartment.

The driver looked as though he might grab Mak, but then he threw his hands up. "You better know what you're doing, bud, 'cause if you damage anything you'll pay."

Mak reached into a pocket of his *palaka* shorts, took out a camping knife, flipped open the screwdriver, and began tampering with the engine. Removing various pieces one by one, he examined them, then reattached them. At one point he held something up to his mouth and blew into it.

At last he turned to the driver. "See if it starts now."

The driver made a face, but he climbed into the bus and switched on the ignition. The engine instantly purred to life.

The crowd of waiting passengers broke into applause. A couple of Hawaiians called out, *"Shaka!"*—well done! Mak playfully bowed and doffed his crumpled straw planter's hat. It was a small achievement, yet it made Kai feel proud to know him. To be the best at anything in life, she thought—even if it was just to be the best mechanic—made a person special.

They were lining up to board the bus when a tall gray-haired man in a tan suit crossed the road and tapped Mak on the shoulder. "Excuse me, I heard you say before that you're good with all kinds of mechanical things."

Mak nodded.

"The way you fixed this bus," the man said, "well, I imagine you must be in a hurry to go, but I'd be very grateful if you could put off leaving to try repairing something for me."

Mak switched his gaze to Lili, who gave a nod of encouragement. When Mak agreed, the man gestured along the road to the Crater Inn. "It's in there," he said.

As they walked, the man introduced himself and explained his problem. His name was Francis Swenson, and he was the present owner of the inn. Since the day it was built, the heat and hot water in the forty-room hotel had been provided by harnessing the energy of the volcano, but it took a system of pumps, and the main pump and a backup had both given up a few hours ago. Normally it wouldn't have been a problem—he kept a handyman on the staff of the hotel. But over the weekend the man who did the job had quit to help his son run a restaurant in Honolulu, and Swenson had yet to find a replacement.

"I can't get a repairman out here from Hilo until tomorrow," he said, ushering Mak through the lobby. "I'd rather not leave my guests without heat."

"Of course," Mak said. "We must give them all the comforts."

Swenson guided them to a stairway leading down to the basement, where the systems were located. He stopped and turned to Lili, Lokei, and Kai. "I think you ladies would be much happier sitting in our snack bar. You're welcome to drinks and dessert. As my guests, of course."

"You're very kind, Mr. Swenson," Mak said. "But before I look at the pumps, may I tell you my price?"

"By all means."

"If I succeed in making the repair, I want the job as your maintenance man."

Swenson blinked in surprise. "You want a job? But . . . I thought you were all here as tourists."

"No," Mak said. "My wife would like work, too. She's a wonderful cook. And perhaps Lokei could—"

"Hold on," Swenson said, though he was laughing amiably. "I'm not sure I can promise you all jobs, though I'll do my best. But first you have to fix that pump."

"Oh, it's as good as done, sir." Mak smiled and continued jauntily down the stairs, with Swenson following.

For all his skill, Kai thought Mak was being awfully cocky. How many heating pumps had he fixed in his life—especially the kind connected to volcanic energy? But then she noticed Lili smiling and patting her hempen bag as she watched Mak disappear.

Lili caught her staring. "You see, *mo'o*," she said. "You must always leave room in your mind for magic." She took Lokei's arm and they started across the lobby toward the snack bar.

Kai gave a puzzled shake of her head. Of course, it was only the luckiest of coincidences that the bus had broken down and the owner of the inn had seen Mak fix the engine when he was in need of a repairman.

But it was also a few hours ago that Lili had made her little offering to Pele. And hadn't Mr. Swenson said it was just about then that both his pumps had stopped working?

Chapter Four

Kai finished filing the registration cards for the group of geology teachers from Seattle who'd just checked in, and turned back to her general checklist. Fresh orchids ordered for the dining room. Done. Call the telephone company to report that the lines had briefly gone dead again this morning and request an inspection. Done. Write up bills for tomorrow's check-outs. . . . She took out a blank billing form and began adding up charges for the ebullient young couple who had come from Iowa to spend the last night of their Hawaiian honeymoon at the Crater Inn. "Couldn't think of a more appropriate place to start a marriage," the groom said, "than right on the edge of a volcano."

Being situated practically on the rim of the steaming mouth of Mount Kilauea, the Crater Inn tended to attract a clientele that was generally more adventurous than run-of-the-mill tourists. Kai enjoyed making contact with diverse personalities from working on the reception desk, and she had proven adept at keeping guests satisfied by smoothly handling the problems that arose.

Francis Swenson hurried into the warm, wood-paneled lobby from the corridor that led to his office suite. "Seen Mak around?"

"I sent him up to Room Seventeen," Kai said. "The guest says the closet has a squeaky hinge; it scares her."

"Scared by a squeak?" He gave a little tug to his polka-dot bowtie that Kai had come to recognize as a kind of nervous twitch.

"She thought it was a mouse," Kai explained. "Be sympathetic, Mr. Swenson, some people—"

"Of course, I understand. I'm glad you took care of it. I'm going over to pick up the mail, Kai. As soon as Mak's free, ask him to have a look at the typewriter in my office."

"What's wrong with it?"

"Nothing's wrong. It just needs a new ribbon." He left.

Kai smiled to herself. Francis Swenson was a lovely man. Gentle, considerate, and generous. But he was hopelessly baffled by anything mechanical—not the most fortunate shortcoming for a man who owned a hotel.

But Mr. Swenson had done far more than keep Mak busy. As soon as he became aware of the circumstances that had brought Mak and the three women to his doorstep three months ago, he had found jobs for all of them. Lili was assigned to the kitchen as a pastry cook. Kai, while continuing her studies at the public high school in Hilo, served a few hours each evening in the dining room and filled in as a chambermaid on weekends. And Lokei was started out on the reception desk, rotating with Swenson's wife, Georgette, and a middle-aged, unmarried Hawaiian woman named Celia who had been hired by the previous owners of the Crater Inn—twenty-five years ago, just a week before the Japanese attack on Pearl Harbor.

But Francis Swenson's generosity didn't stop at providing four paychecks. When he had learned his new employees also needed a place to live, he suggested to Mak that the small basement workroom customarily provided for the maintenance man could be combined with a couple of adjoining storerooms to make an apartment for all of them. The ground-level windows were small but adequate; the washroom was down the hall and did have to be shared with other employees. But there was enough space to allow for two narrow bedrooms and a sitting room. Light cooking could be done on a hot plate, anything else in the hotel kitchen.

Mak made an inspection and gratefully accepted the offer. The three women were disheartened by the sight of the dingy storerooms cluttered with old hotel furniture, broken lamps, and moth-eaten rugs, but Lili and Kai trusted Mak's promise that his carpentry would soon turn it into a comfortable home.

Only Lokei kept sulking. "I must be near the beach," she said. "I need to see the waves. They always made me feel clean."

"The beach is miles away," Mak pointed out. "What could be better than living right here where we work?"

Kai understood how much her mother missed the charm of the cottage, the restful view of sunsets over the ocean. But why wasn't the prospect of a future free from Harley Trane's abuse more important than the view from a window?

"Mama," Kai consoled her, "if we don't have to spend what we're earning on rent and transportation, we could save enough money between the four of us to put a down payment on a house."

"And we'll make sure it has a good view of the beach," Lili said.

Lokei stopped protesting.

Mak made good on his promise. With one partition hinged to another, he even managed to make one end of the sitting room easily convertible to a third bedroom, so that Lokei could have a separate sleeping space from Kai's. He knew where to put closets and how to construct shelves and cabinets so that the small rooms seemed cozy rather than cramped. Lili made curtains and pillows, and Kai hung scenic posters the Hawaiian Tourist Board had distributed to the hotel.

Yet Lokei remained discontent and spent her time in the apartment brooding, sitting for long stretches, gazing at the blank wall below one of the small, high windows as though she was actually looking out on the ocean.

Unfortunately, Lokei ended up being the least busy of the four. Only two weeks after she started working at the reception desk, Mr. Swenson had taken Mak aside to say Lokei was being replaced. "I feel awful if it means losing you, too," Swenson told Mak. "But after what's happened I don't see how I can use Lokei at all."

Reluctantly, because he felt an explanation was due, Swenson said that he had received a report from a male guest that Lokei had whispered an offer to come to his room late that night. "I doubt it would have been mentioned to me except this man happened to be a minister and he was concerned about saving the young woman's soul. I don't like to be hasty in a situation like this, Mak. I know Lokei could have said something completely innocent that was misunderstood. But I worry that there have been other instances . . ."
The deciding factor was that Swenson had heard from a female guest who complained that Lokei had been inap-

propriately flirtatious with her husband when the couple was checking in. "I know there are two sides to every story. A woman as beautiful as Lokei, it wouldn't take much to make a nervous wife jealous. But you understand, Mak, I can't take any chances with this kind of—"

"No need to say more, sir. You're absolutely right. Can we have a day or two to look for another place?"

"That's not necessary," Swenson said. "I don't want Lokei involved with the guests anymore. But if things can be kept under control, I want you to stay. I'm more than happy with your work, Lili's desserts are a great addition to our menu, and Kai is terrific at whatever she does. In fact, I'm putting Kai on the desk evenings and weekends to fill the gap. You'll just have to be sure Lokei stays out of trouble."

Mak gave his assurances.

When Kai was told about the changes in jobs, Mr. Swenson said it was because there had been some lost reservations. Lokei herself refused to answer any of Kai's questions about problems on the desk. But because the apartment was so small, and only a thin partition separated Kai's bed from the room where Mak and Lili slept, Kai overheard them discussing the true reasons late one night.

Alone in the dark, Kai cried softly. "Oh, Mama, what's wrong with you? Why can't you be happy now?"

Kai never revealed to Mak that she knew why Lokei had lost her job, but in the weeks that followed she joined in keeping a watch on Lokei, tracking her whereabouts as much as possible and making sure she stayed out of trouble. It would have been difficult if Lokei was active and independent, but she rarely left the apartment. On a few occasions when Kai noticed her going out of the hotel at a moment when it was possible to step away from the desk and follow discreetly, she had seen Lokei do nothing more than walk across the smooth black lava slopes to the rim of the volcano and make an offering of *ti* leaves.

As Lokei increasingly confined herself to the basement rooms, Kai constantly sought some way to cheer her mother and lift her spirits. Having proven her own capability, Kai was left to oversee certain aspects of the hotel operations, such as keeping the many floral decorations fresh. She asked her mother to make flower arrangments and replace those in the lobby and dining rooms as soon as the flowers began to wilt. For a few weeks Lokei did the job well. But then Kai noticed that most of the vases were simply crammed with unsorted blooms, and soon all through the hotel flowers were being allowed to wilt and drop their petals. Unable to confront her mother, Kai had simply resumed doing the job herself.

Now, with the end of the school term approaching, Kai was expecting she'd soon be asked to work full-time during the summer.

When Francis Swenson reappeared after making a trip to the post office in the village of Volcano, he asked Kai to come into his office. There he made it official. He wanted her to do a full day shift through the summer, Sundays off, for which he would pay $115 a week. "And I'm giving you a title to go with your responsibilities—Daytime Hospitality Manager."

Kai thanked Swenson. The money was almost three times what she'd been earning for her part-time hours. But as she was about to leave the office, she paused. "About my mother . . . isn't there something she could do?"

Swenson looked down at his desk for a long moment. At last he faced her again. "I'm sorry, Kai, not here. I'll ask in the village, though."

Kai knew seeking work outside the hotel would be futile. Volcano was basically an artists' colony. Except for a few shops individually run by their owners, the village was occupied mainly by studios for artists, ceramicists, and a couple of photographers. Kai had struck up acquaintances with some of them—one of the photographers was always asking her to pose for him—but she knew they were independent people who didn't need assistants.

In mid-afternoon, as her shift was ending, Kai was joined at the desk by Georgette Swenson. A shapely, vivacious blonde from Texas, she had met her husband when they both had management jobs at a chain hotel in Honolulu, before purchasing the inn.

"Congratulations on your promotion, honey," she said to Kai in her folksy Texas drawl.

"Thanks, Georgette. I'm sure you were in on the decision."

"Sweetie, you know I wouldn't mind if you took this whole place over someday."

Weeks ago it had become apparent to Georgette that Lokei's apathy left Kai without a mother's guidance. Georgette took it on herself to provide advice to Kai about everything—cosmetics, hygiene, vitamins, schoolwork, and career possibilities. Impressed by Kai's conscientious work at the hotel, Georgette had suggested she think about making a future in hotel management.

Kai was about to leave the desk when Georgette added, "Francis also told me you were worrying about your mom. I've thought of something that might help."

Kai brightened. "That's wonderful. If she just has another chance—"

"It's not a job, Kai. I was thinking it might do Lokei good if she went to a doctor."

Kai was puzzled. "She hasn't said anything about not feeling well."

Georgette put an arm around her. "Honey, the kind of doctor I'm talking about is a psychiatrist."

"Mama's not crazy!"

"Plenty of people can use help getting their thoughts straightened out even when they're not really in bad shape."

Kai had learned there was a strong vein of common sense in most of what Georgette Swenson had to say, though she didn't automatically take her advice. She listened as Georgette went on:

"A psychiatrist wouldn't do anything but talk to your mother, listen to what's bothering her, ask her to explain why she's unhappy, and tell the things she dreams about, or wishes for."

"I've tried plenty of times to get Mama to talk about those things. But she just says to leave her alone, she's okay. Then she goes on staring at the wall."

"That's why you need a doctor to do it," Georgette said sympathetically. "Just the way a surgeon spends years learning to operate, a good psychiatrist is trained to get people to open up. Once he finds out what's bothering 'em, then he's able to do something about it."

"I'd give anything to see Mama happy. In my whole life I don't think I've heard her laugh more than once or twice." For a second Kai was transported to that night when she'd asked Mak for a drink of *okole hao*—and heard the rare sound of her mother's laughter. "I'd like the name of one of those doctors, Georgette," she said at last.

Returning to the apartment after work, Kai found her mother sitting as usual in one of the old leather lobby chairs Mak had repaired, her dark eyes aimed at a blank spot on the wall. They were alone; Lili and Mak usually worked until after the guests had finished dinner. Kai wished she could share the good news about her job; the bigger pay-check would mean more savings for the down payment on their house. But seeing Lokei took away any impulse to announce her achievement.

"Mama," Kai asked, "what do you think about when you sit there all day?"

"Nothing."

Kai had asked the question before, and failed to get any real answer. But tonight she wasn't going to give up so quickly. "It can't be nothing," Kai insisted. "You can't just keep your mind a blank. Not if you're awake—"

"Leave me alone," Lokei said, curling into the chair.

"You've been here alone all day. You have to stop locking yourself in silence. Tell me what's wrong. Tell me . . . what you'd wish for right now if a *menehune* came through the window."

Slowly, Lokei shifted her gaze from the wall and smiled at Kai. "I'd wish to go back and do it again," she said.

The answer stunned Kai; it hinted at what she dreaded most—that some unredeemable strain of corruption made her mother want to be with Trane no matter how badly he had treated her. Kai didn't want to hear any more. She went to her room and tried to study for her end-of-term examinations.

But her mother's words—the wish "to go back and do it again"—kept pushing into her thoughts.

Perhaps Lokei hadn't been referring to her time with Trane, Kai mused, but to the larger span of her life. Wishing for a second chance.

The next day, Kai received a slip of paper from Georgette on which a name—Dr. Lewis Parkes—and a phone number had been noted. "He's the only psychiatrist on the island," Georgette said, "but he's supposed to be good. He works at the hospital in Hilo."

When her shift on the front desk ended, Kai went to the hotel kitchen, where Lili was making desserts for the evening meal. Just as the hotel's hot-water system harnessed the natural geothermal energy of the nearby volcano, there were special baking ovens in the kitchen heated by ducts that tapped into hot air rising from the crater. Lili often said her cooking was done these days "with Pele's help."

Kai took Lili to a corner of the kitchen, showed her the slip of paper with the psychiatrist's name, and explained why Georgette had given it to her. "I was hoping you'd talk to Mama about this," Kai said. "She wouldn't listen to me, Lili. But if you told her seeing this doctor could do some good, maybe she'd try it."

"A doctor for her mind?" Lili said, frowning suspiciously. "I've heard of such things. But . . ." She shook her head.

"Mama's got to talk to someone," Kai pleaded. "Sometimes it seems to me she's—she's almost like a volcano herself. There's so much going on deep down inside her. I'm afraid if something isn't done to help her, it could break her apart."

Lili nodded slowly. "I have been hoping the evil spirits inside her might grow tired of haunting her and go away. But I think you may be right, *mo'o*. We must do something soon."

"Then you'll talk to mama, tell her to try this?"

"*Ae*, Kaiulani," Lili agreed.

The next Saturday, when Kai was working a morning shift on the desk, she noticed Lokei leaving the hotel with Lili, dressed in a long *holomuu* rather than the less formal *muumuu*. Kai kept a watch through the open entranceway, and when the bus for Hilo arrived she saw the two women file aboard.

In the middle of the afternoon, when Kai was in her room doing schoolwork, she heard someone enter the apartment. She left her desk and looked around the partition. It was Lokei, carrying the small sack made of red-dyed *tapa*—a cloth made from beaten tree bark—that Lili used as a handbag.

"Did your trip to Hilo go well, Mama?" Kai asked.

"Very well," Lokei said. "I'm going to get better, Kaiulani."

Kai smiled at her mother. To acknowledge that something was wrong was already a step forward. Yet a strangeness in Lokei's manner, an air of coy bemusement, seemed to hint that she was concealing something.

"Where's Lili—didn't she return with you?"

"Of course. She went straight to the kitchen to do her work."

Kai's sense that Lokei was holding back persisted. But before she could pursue it, Lokei said that she was exhausted from her journey and went to lie down.

Kai returned to her desk, still wondering about her mother's behavior. There was definitely something different about it, something she couldn't put her finger on. Or was it only that Lokei seemed a little better, more like her old self? She had not, after all, come slouching dejectedly into the apartment, and slumped down to stare at the wall.

Perhaps it was natural, too, that Lokei wanted to avoid talking about the doctor. If it had gone well, then she must have opened up to him. But she might still want to keep her private thoughts from everyone else.

Fine, Kai thought. As long as someone was listening to Mama, then whatever was boiling within would be released. The volcano wouldn't explode.

Chapter Five

Through the first half of the summer, from her place at the reception desk Kai watched her mother, accompanied by Lili, leave the hotel every Saturday morning to board the bus for Hilo. Kai was increasingly curious about Lokei's visits to the doctor. Exactly what did Dr. Parkes do to help her? Kai thought at times of switching shifts with Georgette or Celia so that she could make the trip, but decided it would be unwise to intrude. Once or twice when Kai had touched on the subject, Lokei had made it plain that she preferred not to discuss her treatment.

"How many more times do you think you'll have to go?" Kai asked on one occasion.

"I will go until I am told not to go," Lokei replied. "Now stop asking questions I can't answer."

One thing Kai had managed to learn was that Dr. Parkes was expensive. Mr. Swenson had suggested that the money she and Mak and Lili earned should be put in a bank, where it would earn interest. Unaccustomed to dealing with bank accounts, Kai and the others had agreed to endorse their checks back to Mr. Swenson to open a savings account at the hotel's bank in their name. He made any deposits or withdrawals they wanted, and kept a ledger of the account, which he showed them anytime they asked. Examining the ledger, Kai had seen that Lili was withdrawing fifty dollars each week, the only regular expense since meals and lodging were covered. If it went on too long, Kai realized, it could put back the plan to buy their own home by at least a year or two.

Yet she didn't doubt the value of the treatment. Lokei was obviously being helped. She was less moody, more active. She no longer spent days alone in the dim apartment.

"Where do you go all day, Mama?" Kai asked one evening.

"I go sightseeing," Lokei said. The Big Island was full of fascinating places to visit, she reported. "You've seen the beaches of black sand made by the volcanos. But did you know there's one with green sand? And there are many *heiaus.*"

These were elaborate stone platforms, usually situated in large open fields, that had served as the temples and sacrificial altars in ancient kahuna rituals. "The oldest *heiau* in all the islands is not far from here," Lokei said. "Often I stay there all day. I imagine what it was like for our ancestors to be there. I feel their spirits around me. I'll take you, Kaiulani. You must feel the spirits, too."

A renewed pride in her Hawaiian heritage—damaged in the past by slights she had suffered for being a *hapa*—seemed to be another element of Lokei's recovery. She enjoyed telling Kai about legends and traditions she had learned from reading books in the local library on Hawaiian history and religion. She talked about Algaloa, the sky god who shaped the clouds as a means of speaking to men about their future, and Milu, the god of the underworld, and Ukupanipo, the shark god who was known to adopt human children, giving them the ability to change into sharks at will. And of course she talked about Pele, goddess of the volcanoes, more powerful than all others. "It is said she likes to show herself in our midst as a beautiful girl who dances divinely."

When Lokei spoke about the feats of the gods, her eyes blazed so brightly with pious fervor that Kai wondered if her involvement was perhaps unhealthy. Yet these doubts meant little when weighed against Lokei's emergence from her former despair. She seemed well enough even to resume working in the hotel.

One morning before she left the apartment for work, Kai went to her mother's bedside. Lokei was sleeping, her lush black hair fanned out on the pillow. Kai stood admiring her beauty, hesitant to wake her. But then Lokei drowsily opened her eyes.

"I'm going to work now, Mama," Kai said. "I thought I'd ask Mr. Swenson if you could also have a job here again."

Lokei sat up abruptly and clutched Kai's sleeve. "No! You mustn't ask him," she whispered fiercely.

"Mama, you must start over, forget the past . . . and you can. If you just try—"

"I know I can," Lokei cut in sharply. "It isn't because I doubt myself that I won't work for Mr. Swenson."

"Why, then?"

"Because he's *haole*," Lokei hissed, her eyes burning with fury.

Kai was too stunned to respond. Because he was a white man?

"The *haole* are devils," Lokei seethed. "They ruined me, ruined my mother. I want nothing to do with them ever again."

"Mama, Mr. Swenson has been good to us. He supports us, lets us live here—"

"Here!" Lokei spat out the word disdainfully. "Under the ground, in the realm of Milu. I don't trust Mr. Swenson, Kaiulani. The damn *haole* ruin everything."

Kai's belief that Lokei was being helped by her treatments crumbled. Was it any improvement if her quiet despair had only been replaced by this hate and bitterness?

Or was the treatment responsible so much as her zealous embrace of native ideas? Perhaps everything that had seemed normal—even the daily "sightseeing walks"—had a hidden negative side.

"Mama, you mentioned taking me to see a *heiau*. I'd like to go. I'd like to see what you do there."

"Whenever you wish."

"Today. After work."

Lokei nodded and lay back on her pillow. She looked very pleased, Kai thought as she left, very happy.

The trek to the *heiau* took them first over one of the vast lava fields. Walking over an area of jagged lava that was hard on their feet, its sharp edges stabbing the soles of their sandals, Lokei explained that this was called *a'a*—thrown up by Pele to slow down men and gods alike who tried to sneak up on her kingdom. Lower down the slope, a smoother lava surface where molten rock had congealed into ropy swirls was called *pahoehoe*. Within the thick rope-like formations, Lokei pointed out, there were also many thinner filaments. These, she said, were strands of "Pele's hair." Closer to the ocean, where they saw three small extinct craters, Lokei identified them as "Pele's footsteps," formed when the goddess had first risen out of the ocean onto the island and climbed up these mountains to dive down a hole to her hiding place in the center of the earth.

Where the lava fields ended, a wall of greenery sprang up, the remainder of the forest that had been there before the floes of molten rock had cut through it decades ago as it coursed down to the ocean. Lokei led the way along a narrow path through dense, fragrant growths of heliconia, hibiscus, wild orchid, and torch ginger. Around them everywhere the tropical forest was alive with the sound of raucous bird calls. Sparks of color lit the air as sunlight flashed down through the leaves and feathered wings in brilliant hues flitted from branch to branch.

"It's paradise," Kai said when she and Lokei paused to rest on the petrified stump of a fallen tree.

"It should have been," Lokei said as she rose and moved on.

Just inland from a beach, they came finally to a clearing the size of two football fields. At either end stood imposing structures of large stones, stacked to form gigantic tables with hollow spaces beneath. Each of these, Lokei said, was a *heiau,* built many hundreds of years ago. Because the ancient temples had been built so close together, and because the bones of some chiefs were believed to be buried under one of them, the clearing was a place of rare power, where it was easy to commune with the spirits.

While Lokei settled on her knees at the center of the clearing, Kai circled both of the *heiau* on her own. Lokei had brought along Lili's red *tapa* bag, and when Kai looked over, she saw her removing a few things, setting them on the ground. When Kai came closer, she saw a number of rocks, bits of wood marked with paint, and a couple of dried gourds spread in a semicircle around Lokei. Kai sat down beside her mother.

"You asked to see what I do when I come here," Lokei said. "I do this, Kaiulani. I pray." She gestured to the odd assortment of objects around her. "My gods are here with me, in all these things—my *hamakau.*" Lokei explained that these were personal gods more powerful than all others except for Pele.

Kai glanced at the bits of stone and rock. It might have seemed pathetic to believe in their divinity—though why should a stone idol, or a cross of gold, be deemed any more worthy of worship? Why were sacred deities any more likely to inhabit a cathedral than a *heiau*?

The sun sank low in the sky. The jagged shadows of tall trees edging the clearing crept toward them, an image of titanic teeth slowly closing down on them. Lokei lifted her eyes and scanned the clearing. "This is a sacred *puuhonua*," she said, "a place of refuge. In the old days, there were many *kapu* that ruled the life of a woman. If her shadow ever fell across the path of a chief, if she ate when the men were eating, if she danced at certain times of the month—for many such crimes she could be put to death. She might be sacrificed to Pele, hurled into the volcano. Her one hope of salvation was to escape from her accusers and remain here until it was decided whether the gods forgave her." Lokei's gaze came back to her daughter. "I come to the place of refuge for the same reason: to ask my gods to forgive me for violating the *kapu*."

Until this moment Kai had not fully comprehended the grip that the ancient kahuna religion had on her mother. She had seen Lokei reading the pamphlets, had heard her talk with pious respect about all the ancient traditions. But suddenly Kai knew beyond doubt that these beliefs had become more than a crutch, more like an obsession.

"There are things I will tell you now," Lokei said, "because we are here, and because I have prayed now many times and believe I am forgiven. My failing, the *kapu* I violated—as my mother did—was to give myself to the *haole*. . . ."

Having lived with her mother in a brothel near the Schofield army barracks, Lokei explained, she had lost her virginity at fourteen in a rape by a drunken soldier that went unreported and unpunished. She had done her best to avoid the soldiers thereafter, had dreamed of becoming a dancer. But she was just sixteen when her mother died, poisoned by alcohol and weakened by the infections that came with being constantly used by many strange men. Left alone, with little education, without the support of a father, she had tried nevertheless to avoid falling into prostitution. She had gone to Honolulu to find work as a hula dancer in one of the tourist shows, but all the best jobs were already taken, and she had landed instead in a bar near the naval base at Pearl Harbor, where, along with dancing, she served drinks. Sometimes, too, she slept with the sailors who frequented the bar—though only if she liked them. She had stayed there for two years.

And then she had had some luck. "Or what seemed like luck at the time," Lokei said. A naval officer had come to the bar, a nice-looking, soft-spoken man who impressed her because sailors were usually so loud and messy. He had told her she was the most beautiful *wahine* he had ever seen, taken her to bed, and afterward sent her the first bottle of expensive perfume she'd ever received. Then he'd asked if she would like to work for him. It would bring her much more money than she earned at the bar—and there would be more perfume and other wonderful gifts.

That was how she had become part of a group of girls organized by this officer exclusively to service other officers at the naval base. "For me this was a great success," Lokei said. "I thought that I had gone far beyond my mother. I lived in a nice room with my own kitchen, and was paid two hundred dollars each week! The men who came to me wore neat uniforms decorated with gold stripes. I was, you see, the *kaimana* in the ring of girls—the diamond—to be used only by the men of very highest rank. There was even an admiral. . . ."

With each mention of a man, Kai listened for anything that might hint of her father. But Lokei gave no clue.

For a year Lokei's routine had remained unchanged. The men she served were always officers, and there were always new ones rotating through because the war in Korea made Pearl Harbor busy again as ships sailed in and out of active duty.

Then a scandal threatened to expose everyone involved in the call-girl ring.

"One of the girls was murdered in her apartment," Lokei said, her eyes blank, as if looking inward at the past. "This *wahine,* a *hapa* like myself, was found naked, stabbed many times—the act of a madman. The rest of the girls knew the killer could only be one of the dead girl's customers, an officer." Lokei's tone, flat and unemotional until now, turned slightly darker. "So nothing was done at first. As in all wars, it was important to keep morale strong, to keep civilians proud of all their soldiers and sailors. Rather than punish a murderer, the navy covered up the killing; they broke up the ring of girls and put us in jail so that we could not tell anyone about our customers."

"You went to jail, Mama?" Kai blurted. How many more grim revelations would there be?

"For a few months," Lokei answered.

She would have stayed much longer but for an honest local policeman, a Hawaiian, who refused to let the death of the woman be ignored. Despite obstruction from the navy, he continued to investigate, and at last he charged the corrupt officer who ran the call-girl ring with the murder. Since the accused was in uniform, the navy claimed the right to administer justice by court-martial. Both prosecutor and defending attorney were appointed from the navy's Adjutant Corps.

"In return for a promise to help the prosecution with their testimony," Lokei explained, "all the girls were released from jail. But the defense lawyer, another officer, also wanted to talk with us to prepare his case. Many times he made me return to go over and over everything I could tell him about the man who organized our ring. When I asked the defending officer why he was working so hard to help this murderer, he told me he was certain the man was innocent—that the navy had provided evidence against him and wanted to punish him for the crime because there was someone much higher in rank they had to protect. I was surprised the lawyer would tell me this since he was also in the navy, but it convinced me he was an honest man, determined to do the right thing."

The court-martial lasted weeks, and in the end, against all odds, the defending lawyer won acquittal for his client. The corrupt officer was immediately sent back to the mainland, no further investigation was done into the murder, no officer of higher rank was ever charged. The scandal was buried. But her own life, Lokei said, had been changed forever by the case.

"Through all the time I spent with this fine lawyer, I found myself wanting to stay near him—not only because he was handsome, but because he seemed decent and brave. When the court-martial ended, he came to me and said he wanted me, too. So I went to live with him, Kaiulani. We spoke vows of love. I was happier than I had ever been.''

So there it was, Kai thought. *This* was her father. She breathed a sigh of relief. She had not been born to one of Lokei's brothel customers, not an anonymous personality formed of unknown, ignoble traits. Her father was courageous and principled, a defender of the innocent.

But her relief evaporated as she remembered the bitter oath against the *haole* that had spurred her mother's confession.

The rest of the story came with a matter-of-fact swiftness that bespoke the years and years Lokei had spent coming to terms, even trying to forget. In an attempt to scatter all trace of the ugly incident that threatened the navy's prestige, the defending adjutant was given a quick promotion and transferred back to Washington. He promised to send for Lokei after he was settled. She never doubted they would be reunited. Their vows of love had been affirmed. A navy chaplain had performed a wedding on the base.

''He was gone from me only a few weeks before I learned that I was pregnant,'' Lokei concluded the story. ''I never heard from him again.''

Kai felt the cold shock of betrayal. She could imagine the devastation her mother must have suffered. So why did Lokei's account end there? ''You were married, Mama,'' Kai declared. ''That gave you legal rights. Didn't you ever think of trying to trace this man, your *husband*, forcing him to accept responsibility?''

Lokei stared down at the *hamakau* around her, the sacred manifestations of her gods, as though drawing upon them for the strength to bear her memories. ''I went to the navy and asked for help. But the men in charge thought only of protecting themselves—they were officers who could not afford to admit they knew me.''

She had been refused any information about the transferred officer, and told that no record of a marriage performed on the base had been found in the files.

Lokei fell silent again.

Kai could supply for herself the part of the story that linked Lokei's devastating abandonment to her liaison with

Harley Trane. Deserted, with a child to feed, she had done whatever was necessary to survive.

Many things Kai had never understood before were suddenly clear. She understood why Lokei had kept the past in darkness, understood how hard she had fought to retain even a minimum of dignity, understood why laughter was so rare for her.

The sun was below the tops of the trees now, and a chill gloom was settling over the field. "We should go soon," Kai said. "But there's just one more thing I'd like to know, Mama. My father—his name. I want to try again."

Lokei gave her daughter a wary look. "Try what?"

"To find him."

"No," Lokei said with quiet resolve. "We want nothing to do with him, Kaiulani. He is *haole*."

"Mama! No matter how much you hate him for what he did, you have to deal with this. You never did anything about the marriage, did you? And you're still young. Suppose someday you want to marry again. . . ."

"My heart is a stone," Lokei said. "I will never marry again. But it would not matter anyway. There is no marriage, Kaiulani, they told me it didn't exist."

"Because the navy was afraid, you've explained that. But it was seventeen years ago. It must be different now. Those men who had to protect themselves, they're probably retired. If we—"

"No!" Lokei cried out, a desperate wail that echoed off the ancient stones around them. "My soul cannot rest unless I have nothing to do with the *haole* ever again, nothing!"

Abruptly, Lokei got to her knees and began placing the *hamakua* gently into the *tapa* bag.

It couldn't be left like this, Kai thought. Her mother's recovery could progress no further while she was committed to this irrational rejection. "Mama," Kai appealed, "you can't hate them all because of what one man did. We depend on Mr. Swenson. And I know he'd give you another chance if only you'd take it."

Lokei shook her head and got to her feet. "I must obey the rules," she said, fixing her eyes on Kai. "The next time I violate the *kapu,* I cannot be forgiven. I have been told by the *kahuna*.'' She turned and started across the field toward the path up the mountain.

The *kahuna*. The priest. Kai stared after her mother a moment, struck by a realization. It wasn't the religion itself Lokei meant, but a priest. Somehow she had found her way to one of the native men who taught the old ways. The *kahuna* had told her she would die, had turned her against all *haole*. Kai rushed to catch up.

"Listen, Mama, it's crazy to believe in those ideas. Haven't you talked to Dr. Parkes about this?''

Lokei gave her a puzzled glance. "I talk to no doctor,'' she said. "Only to the *kahuna*. He knows what is right for me.''

"But your trips to Hilo—'' Kai started, and then the words died on her lips as comprehension came over her with the crushing force of one of the huge waves that curled down onto the shore. Lili had never taken Lokei to see the doctor!

Reliving now that moment when she had given Lili the doctor's name, Kai recalled that Lili had merely agreed that it was time to arrange help for Lokei. But the old woman had relied instead on her belief in magic. Lili had found a local *kahuna*—all her weekly payments had been tribute given for his pronouncements. A total of nine hundred dollars paid to date so that Lokei could be told she was guilty of a sacred crime for loving a white man, and would die if she attempted to resolve the dangling threads of her past.

They climbed back up the mountain in silence. Rather than being prepared to live fully again, Kai realized now, Lokei had only sunk deeper into illusion. But she didn't know what to say or do that would break the hold of primitive superstition on her mother's fragile mind.

As much as Kai tried to maintain respect for native beliefs, and knew that Lili had sincerely meant to help by taking Lokei to the *kahuna,* she couldn't forgive the waste of money, and, worst of all, the setback to her mother's well-being. Yet Kai avoided speaking to Lili for two days after Lokei's revelation, so furious she was afraid she might say something that would damage beyond repair her relationship with the woman she regarded as a grandmother.

On the third day, at mid-morning when the lobby was

quiet, Lili came to the desk from the kitchen. "You cannot stay angry with me forever, *mo'o*," she said.

"Damn it, *Tutu*," Kai replied, instantly pulling the plug on restraint, "I know you meant well. But Mama needs someone who can help her believe in *herself* again. The last thing that'll help is being told that she really has no power over her own life—that her fate is in the hands of a bunch of make-believe bogeymen who turn people into sharks and live in volcanos."

Lili's eyes flared with panic. "Kaiulani, you mustn't mock the power of the gods! Remember we are here because we made an offering to Pele."

"No! We're here because of a couple of lucky breaks. Lokei mustn't ever go back to that *kahuna*. She should see the doctor—should have been seeing one all along."

Lili reached to grasp Kai's arms in her big soft hands. "Not yet, *mo'o*. Your mother believes in this, this is what she wants. And there are more special ceremonies to be done."

Kai shook free of Lili's grasp. "What ceremonies?"

"To purify her. To protect her from evil spirits."

"Oh god," Kai moaned with exasperation. "It's got to stop. For all it's costing if for no other reason. Wait here!" Before Lili could protest, Kai darted from behind the front desk and ran to the hotel office. Mr. Swenson wasn't there, but she knew where he kept the ledger. She grabbed it off a shelf and ran back to Lili. "Taking money week after week . . . you don't realize how much this has cost us." Kai found the page with the account of their savings and spread it out on the desk. Even without looking at the figures, she started to recite them. "It adds up to a quarter of everything we—"

Kai stopped. No, not a quarter, she realized, staring at the latest balance, but almost half the savings were gone. Scanning the debit column, she saw that a full one thousand dollars had been subtracted only five days ago, at the end of the past week. Kai raised her eyes from the ledger.

Lili stared back at her. She had known without being shown. "It was my money," she said. "All that I've earned."

Kai was beyond anger now. "What was it for?" she asked.

"A special ceremony. To bless the *hamakua* and release their power."

Kai thought of the odd collection of nature's knickknacks that Lokei had shown her. "*Tutu,*" she said with sad finality, "it has to end. I'm not telling you or Mama to stop believing in your gods. But make your own offerings. These ceremonies—they can't go on. Not another day."

"You are making a mistake, *mo'o,*" Lili said quietly. But she turned and left without further argument.

Later, when Kai saw Mr. Swenson, she asked him not to allow any money to be withdrawn from the savings account unless she gave permission. When she explained the reason, Swenson agreed.

Kai didn't doubt she'd taken the right decision, even when Mak spoke to her and offered to use his own money to pay a *kahuna.*

"How can you be in favor of that, Mak?" Kai said. "You taught me to believe in science—not in gods who turn the moon on and off."

"It's your mother's belief that matters, *keko.* I have heard of experiments where sick people were given pills made of sugar and told they were strong medicine. Sometimes it cured them."

"And sometimes it didn't! It's safer to get the real medicine."

The visits to the *kahuna* were discontinued without any apparent ill effect. Lokei remained even-tempered, reasonably cheerful, still content to spend the balmy summer days hiking or relaxing on the beach. Kai never doubted that Lokei must be making trips to the *heaius,* continuing to commune with the spirits. But having separated her from the influence of a native priest and his backward ideas, she felt there was a possibility Lokei would mend on her own.

The volcano changed her mind.

In the last week of August, a new rift developed overnight on the side of Mount Kilauea, a tiny fissure that tore open in the skin of the mountain as quickly and explosively as a seam bursting in a fat man's pants. Molten lava bubbled up through the crack in the earth and ran down the mountainside in a thin, glowing stream, yellow as it emerged into the air, cooling to red, then turning to a steaming black ooze that flowed like thick syrup down the mountain and stopped where the slope leveled off. The rift was no wider across than the average doorway, so the release of lava was minor and the narrow stream did no damage as it rolled down to the point where it hardened.

When a park ranger came to the inn to inform Mr. Swenson about the overnight development, he emphasized that there was no immediate danger: tourists would not be kept away from the rift—which had already been dubbed ''Pele's Doorway.'' Mr. Swenson posted a notice about the new lava flow, which sent guests running for their cameras so they could photograph each other with ''Pele's Doorway'' in the background.

''It's quite a sight,'' Mr. Swenson told Kai when he returned from his own excursion to the new phenomenon. ''Go have a look. I'll get Georgette to take over the desk for a couple of hours.''

Before setting out, Kai went downstairs, thinking she'd fetch Lokei and take her along. But the basement apartment was empty.

At the site of the rift, on the opposite side of the volcano from the hotel, a crowd of several hundred tourists were gathered, scattered across the slopes at a respectful distance. There was still plenty of room to maneuver for a good view. Kai could see fiery molten rock spitting up through the vent in the earth, then cutting a golden line through the old lava field as it ran downhill. Wending her way among other observers, she moved up closer until she could hear the hissing of the viscous superheated liquid escaping into the air. Even across a gap of fifty yards, Kai could feel the radiant heat warming her skin.

Nearing the front ranks of the crowd, she noticed one person who had moved to a place halfway between all the others and the rift. Against the glow of the fountaining lava, the figure was only a silhouette, the low black pyramid of someone in a kneeling position. The foolhardy daring of this spectator was as much of a show for the crowd as the volcanic activity.

''The heat that close must be a real bitch,'' Kai overheard one man to her left say to a companion. ''Don't know how she can take it.''

 . . . *she* . . .

Sudden recognition sparked in Kai's brain. At once she

bolted across the open ground toward the kneeling figure. With every few yards she advanced, the heat rose a few degrees until she could feel the air drying her throat with every breath and her skin seeming almost painfully tight from the heat, as though it was shrinking around her bones.

Panting from the run, she dropped down beside Lokei to catch her breath. This close to the lava flow, the heat was nearly unbearable. Lokei was drenched with sweat. It dripped down her face, and dropped from the ends of her hair as thickly as a tropical rain sluicing off sheaves of grass. Laid out around her in a semicircle were her *hamakau*. "Mama, get up!" Kai pleaded. "You can't stay here."

"Pele has opened a door," Lokei murmured.

Kai perceived at once that her mother had endowed the appearance of the rift—along with the clever name someone had tacked on—with a supernatural significance. It was pointless to try talking her into leaving, Kai decided. She scooped the *hamakau* into the *tapa* bag lying on the ground, then gripped Lokei's arm and pulled her to her feet. To Kai's relief, her mother put up no struggle, but allowed herself to be led away from the intolerable heat.

As Kai escorted her mother through the tourists who had remained at a safe distance, she was aware of them eyeing Lokei with pity, could hear their whispers: ". . . sick, I guess." "Crazy."

Crazy. Not until she heard the word come from the lips of a stranger did Kai begin to accept the gravity of her mother's condition.

"Why did you come here, Mama?" she asked after they were away from the crowd, slowly walking back to the hotel. "Why were you praying?"

"Pele opened the door," Lokei repeated. Even though she had left the glowing rift behind, her eyes remained wide, as though she remained hypnotized by its bright fire. "She opened the door so she could speak to me."

Kai felt the sting of tears forming in her eyes. All this time she had believed her mother was on an even keel, she had evidently been deteriorating. "What did Pele tell you, Mama?" Kai asked.

Lokei stopped and half turned in the direction of the rift as though listening again for a faint voice. "I will not be forgiven,'' she replied. ''Not until I leave the *haole*. It is *kapu*, Kaiulani. I cannot do it anymore.''

Kai's gloom deepened. Lokei was convinced that accepting Swenson's hospitality was a violation of a sacred taboo punishable by death.

Lokei walked placidly the rest of the way back to the hotel. But she didn't look well, Kai thought, her tawny skin marked by a reddish caste, as though exposure to the extreme heat had left her with a burn. In the apartment, when Kai offered to make her some soup or tea on the hot plate, Lokei refused and went to lie down on the daybed. After arranging a blanket over her, Kai collapsed in a chair in the sitting room.

Looking grimly across the room at a stretch of blank wall below the high, small window, Kai wished now that she could see the ocean as it had looked from their cottage by the beach. Wished that Lokei could be at least as content as when they were there.

And yet, she reflected, that contentment had only existed along with depravity, and a pathetic resignation to being utterly worthless except to serve one man's perverted pleasures. Had there been any choice but to take Lokei away from there?

But where could she take her mother now to save her from running off again to speak to the gods through Pele's doorway?

Chapter Six

"From everything you've told me, Miss Teiatu, your mother is exhibiting severe delusional behavior." Dr. Lewis Parkes stubbed out his cigarette in the hollow half of a coconut shell that sat on a desk cluttered with papers and stacked books. "Dealing with the problem could require more intensive treatment than out-patient psychotherapy. Of course, I can't make a reliable diagnosis without talking to the patient."

Kai stared bleakly at the doctor. She had already reported that Lokei refused to come along to Hilo, ranting that the gods would punish her for "not trusting them." Lokei stayed in the apartment, while Mak, Lili, and the Swensons took turns sitting with her, making sure she didn't wander off and disappear.

"But if you can't help her, Dr. Parkes, who will? You're the only psychiatrist on the island."

"There are dozens in Honolulu, Miss Teiatu. Many have affiliations with the kind of psychiatric facility where your mother should be sent."

He was a wiry, soft-spoken man with curly black hair and warm brown eyes usually masked by spectacles with heavy tortoiseshell frames. Based on her limited experience with doctors—visiting the small clinic on the Trane plantation for routine vaccinations—Kai had expected Parkes to be considerably older and more formal, garbed in a stiff white coat. Lewis Parkes appeared to be in his mid-thirties, and he was dressed casually in khaki chinos and a yellow and red Hawaiian floral-print shirt. His small office in a wing of Hilo's eighty-bed hospital was equally offbeat, the walls adorned with bullfight posters and a corkboard to which cartoons and postcards from traveling patients were tacked. For all his easygoing informality, Kai sensed that Parkes was a caring professional, providing sound advice.

Which didn't make the advice easier to take. Kai swallowed hard and said, "By psychiatric facility, I suppose you mean . . . an insane asylum?"

He gave her a reassuring smile. "That's not what I meant at all. I didn't say your mother was *pupule*." He used the Hawaiian word for *crazy* as though hoping it might strengthen a bond of trust. "I do recommend confinement in a place where she can receive regular attention. But it would be a modern hospital. And, depending on how she responds, her stay there could be relatively short—perhaps no more than two months."

If Mama responded well. Kai sighed. "If only I'd brought her here myself, before she got all mixed up by a—a witch doctor."

"It wouldn't have mattered. From what you've said about your mother's early life, I'd guess what's happening now is only a manifestation of problems that developed over many years. If I'd seen her a year ago, I would've probably recommended the same treatment as now."

Kai slumped deeper in her chair. The best hospital would be in Honolulu. Of course, her mother should have the best, but it would take all that was left of their savings, even put them in debt. "She's not . . . making trouble right now," Kai said. "Can't something be done while she stays with me?"

"There are medicines that might be tried, tranquilizers. But with this kind of problem, Kai, your mother's moods and actions will remain unpredictable. Without treatment, I doubt she can resume a normal life."

There really was no choice, Kai realized. "But I have to figure out how to pay for it."

"Didn't you say your mother had married a navy man, and was never divorced?"

"Yes . . ."

"Then she can be treated free at a navy hospital. They have to accept responsibility for dependents of an officer. And the medical facilities at Pearl Harbor are superb. With so many Vietnam trauma cases pouring in, they're experienced at dealing with psychiatric problems. I could call Pearl right now, Kai, and ask about having your mother admitted.''

"All right," she said, barely above a whisper. It was hard to start the process that would send Lokei away.

Parkes reached for a rotary file of phone numbers and picked out a card. "What's your father's name?" he started to dial.

"I don't know. My mother never told me his name."

The psychiatrist replaced the receiver in its cradle. "Without it, there's no way she can get the benefits of navy coverage. There has to be some proof of her entitlement."

Kai bowed her head defeatedly.

"Hey, I didn't say we should give up." Parkes rose from his chair and came around the desk. "Go home, Kai. Get that name from your mother, then we'll start the ball rolling."

As she rose, Kai was thinking that even with the name, there was little chance. Lokei had said the proof of marriage had been eradicated. At the door, Kai remembered that she hadn't paid for the appointment. She plunged a hand into the pocket of her blue sundress and felt for the envelope of money she had brought from the hotel.

The doctor didn't even wait for her to ask the amount. "No charge this time—I insist."

"I don't know how to thank you," she said. "You've been so kind."

"Never mind. With a smile like that on a face like yours, I'm already feeling overpaid."

All Kai's attempts to explain the importance of knowing her father's identity did nothing to soften Lokei's resolve. The man was a *haole,* Lokei said over and over. His name must never pass her lips again.

Lili's opposition also undermined Kai's efforts. "Leave your mother alone," she pleaded. "It only upsets her more to argue with you."

Even Mak urged her to back off. "We'll take care of her here, Kai. Isn't it better for Lokei to be surrounded by people who love her than to be locked up among strangers? It would be different if she were violent or dangerous, but she's not."

Their pleas persuaded her not to keep pressing. Lokei's

condition also seemed less critical than it had when Kai visited Dr. Parkes. Lokei carried her bag of *hamakua* everywhere, and spent hours seated before them in the apartment, silently conversing with the voices she heard in her head. Yet she remained essentially manageable. She never challenged Kai's strict order that she mustn't wander out on her own, but only when someone was available to go with her. As for her objection to living under Mr. Swenson's roof, it went no further than muttering about it from time to time.

The summer season ended, and Kai went back to high school in Hilo. Two or three afternoons each month, at the end of a school day, she walked over to the hospital to see Dr. Parkes. Through their conversations about Lokei, a friendship had formed, and he encouraged Kai to drop in and discuss anything that was worrying her, free of charge. Being raised as she had, he said—with one dysfunctional parent, and a family tree whose male branches had been lopped off the last couple of generations—she was amazingly well adjusted. But he warned that she was vulnerable to drifting into what he called "neurotic patterns" if she nursed fears and misconceptions formed during her abnormal upbringing. One likely result might be a difficulty in trusting men in general. Kai had to admit that she was keeping her guard up, staying clear of the many boys in school who expressed an interest in dating her, cutting them off with the same cold hostility she used to control guests at the hotel who made rude passes.

"That's just what I'm talking about, Kai," he said. "You have to make a distinction between men who behave badly and the ones with whom you should have a normal relationship."

"Is there a distinction? They all want the same thing from me."

"No, they don't, Kai. There may be some who want nothing but sex. But you'll find others who want to love you—and sex can be one of the most powerful elements of healthy love."

As Kai learned to trust Lewis Parkes more, she spoke more freely. She began to delve below the surface of feelings, to comprehend the depths of an inner terror she had never confronted before. What she knew of her mother's and grandmother's lives had planted a notion that she might be powerless to escape a similar destiny. She would fall into prostitution, give birth to a child by a father she couldn't name. Once she confessed these fears, Dr. Parkes began helping her to deal with them. She visited him more often, and stayed longer if he had no other patients.

On a rainy afternoon in February, she stayed nearly until evening, and he suggested she come home with him for supper; afterward he would drive her out to the hotel. Kai called the hotel and talked to Georgette to explain her late return.

Lew lived a short distance from the hospital in a small ranch house, a specimen of the stamped-out, nondescript housing that had been quickly erected after most of Hilo was decimated by a freak tidal wave—a thirty-five-foot wall of water that had swept in from the ocean in 1960.

The clutter she had seen on his desk was magnified tenfold inside the house. As soon as they were through the door, he began apologizing for the mess as he darted around, gathering up the used dishes and glasses that been left out.

"Maybe it wasn't such a good idea to bring you here," he said. "At least not on short notice. I should've cleaned up first."

Kai told him not to worry even after she followed him into the old-fashioned kitchen and saw the sink piled full of dirty dishes and pots still sitting on the stove. "I can see you need someone to take care of you," she said.

"You're right. I really do."

Kai heard such poignancy in the reply that she turned to look at him. When their eyes met, she saw the same message nakedly revealed in his gaze. He didn't just need someone. . . .

For a moment they stared at each other. Kai sensed that he was just as surprised by his honesty as she was. She turned back to the sink, turned on the water, and started washing dishes. But she was intensely conscious of him as he went to the stove, collected the dirty pots, and brought them over to a counter beside the sink. As she swirled the dishes under the tap, she tried to deal with the confused thoughts swirling through her mind. He had told her—taught her—not to be afraid of love, of sex. Was it to make her ready for him?

The awkward silence lasted. Kai went on washing one dish after another, trusting that the slow repetition of the ordinary would bridge the awkward moment, make it disappear.

And then he touched her, his fingers sliding lightly along her bare arm. "I can't help it," he said huskily.

It was almost as though she'd been burned, the touch was so unexpectedly shocking. She let the plate clatter back into the sink as she retreated from him, speechless, shaking her head.

He moved toward her. "I've tried, Kai—god, I've tried not to want you. But it's not something I can control. You're so lovely. I just can't help it."

She backpedaled, putting more distance between them. "Please, don't say any more—don't come nearer."

But he kept coming, reaching out. "You know you don't have to be afraid of me. I love you, Kai. Just let me hold you, that's all I want. You've never let any man hold you."

She wondered if the balance between them could be made right again, if it wasn't as simple as granting that small request. It was true—she'd never been in the arms of any man. An occasional quick fatherly hug from Mak, that was all. Perhaps, as Lew had often told her, she did have to let herself be loved. Perhaps she owed him something for all his kindness.

He read her silence as permission. He moved closer and slowly put his arms around her. She felt him trembling as his embrace tightened, and then suddenly his mouth went to hers, his tongue forcing between her lips. She was afraid to stop him, afraid to anger him. Afraid to lose the support he gave her battered spirit.

His hands began to clutch her, move down her back. She tried to control the panic building within her; he was her friend, her guide, and she did need to be loved.

She felt him gathering up the loose fabric of her *muumuu,* his hands moving along her bare skin. His touch was electric as his fingers slid between her thighs. His breathing grew faster, his touch rougher. He whispered hotly into her neck, her throat. "I want you, I can't help it. Let me see you, all of you. . . . " He sank to his knees, pushed up her skirt. She felt his lips on her knee, then the tender skin above it. One hand was pulling her panties down.

She couldn't let it go on. "No," she murmured.

But he ignored her, his mouth moved higher along her leg. She cried louder, then pushed his head away and started to rearrange her clothes.

He looked up at her, his face damp with sweat, "But you know you need this," he said earnestly. "You need to be loved."

Staring down at him, she suddenly perceived with absolute clarity that even before he had touched her, he had violated her. "How could you do this?" she cried contemptuously. "I needed your help. I gave you my trust, and you used it against me." She turned from him and ran.

"Wait, Kai, please," he called after her. "I love you."

She pulled open the front door and escaped into the night.

He stood in the doorway, shouting, "I'm sorry. I love you. I couldn't help it."

Shivering all the way, Kai rode the bus back to Volcano. The echo of Lew's final declarations mingled in her memory with all the advice he had dispensed, all the encouragement to rise above the shame of her heritage. Was she right to feel the trust was shattered? His crime was no greater than wanting to love her. And it was beyond his control, he'd said—because she was so beautiful.

Perhaps, then, it was her fault, not his.

In the midst of her confusion, Kai felt strangely envious of her mother's delusions. In that inner world Lokei had made for herself, decisions were so much simpler, all dictated by her priests and gods.

During the months since the rift had first appeared, Pele's Doorway had gradually widened, the release of lava growing from a thin ribbon to a small river. The changes were monitored by volcanologists, who judged that the lava flow remained within safe limits and that tourists could still be allowed within viewing distance. Still, the developments were significant enough to bring television news crews and documentary filmmakers from the mainland to photograph Kilauea.

Since the time Lokei had endangered herself at the rift, it was understood that Pele's Doorway was off-limits to her;

whenever she left the hotel she was always supervised, if only by a bellboy or chambermaid pressed into extra duty.

But one evening when she and Kai were alone in the apartment, finishing their dinner, Lokei said, "You must take me to the doorway."

Kai stared back, her mind racing. How should she deal with this? "You mustn't go back there, Mama," she said.

"But it's opening wider, I've heard. I know it's because of me." There was no trace of hysteria in Lokei's voice. Rather, it was eerily calm and self-possessed.

"Mama, it's nothing to do with—"

"I have to go. Pele wants to talk to me." Lokei's hand came across the table to seize Kai's arm in a tight, painful grip that belied her tranquil tone.

If only she could call Lew Parkes for advice! Did she dare to indulge her mother's fantasy that the goddess of the volcano was summoning her? Would Lokei's agitation at being refused be even more damaging?

Neither choice was a good one. In fact, Kai realized now, she had avoided for too long the only course that offered any hope. Lokei needed to be hospitalized. "Tell me my father's name, Mama," Kai pleaded. "Please. I need it to help you."

Lokei started to shake her head.

"I'll take you to the doorway," Kai said with fresh urgency, "if you'll just tell me his name."

"Tomorrow," Lokei said after a moment.

The faint light of dawn was creeping through the high, narrow basement window as Kai lifted her head from the pillow, her senses alive, an odd tingling on her skin even before her mind was fully awake. What was it that had penetrated her sleep? A loud sound, a voice calling out? She peeled back the covers and swung her feet to the floor. She must go and check on Lokei.

The soles of her feet were no sooner planted on the flat basement floor than she felt the vibrations traveling through the concrete. They came in waves of shifting intensity: faint, then slightly stronger. A noiseless rumbling that seemed to be coming from deep within the earth.

The volcano! But surely not an eruption from the main crater. That would have already blown the inn away.

Kai leapt up and ran to the bed where her mother slept. Lokei was gone. The sheets and blankets had been stripped and left neatly folded.

Mak stumbled out of the room he shared with Lili. "You felt it, too," he said, rubbing his hands over his bleary eyes.

"And so did she," Kai said, nodding toward Lokei's bed.

Mak glanced over and went running back into his cell to change out of his pajamas.

Somehow Kai knew there wasn't time to change. She raced out of the apartment, still in her nightgown, her feet bare.

The lava fields stretched out before her to the horizon of a pink-striped dawn sky. Keeping to the smooth *pahoehoe*, Kai was able to run at full tilt without hurting her feet. On the treeless slopes she had a clear field of vision across the massive side of Kilauea, and in the crystalline morning air she could see all the way to the point where the circumference rounded to the other side of the mountain. She was alone on the bleak, black moonscape, no one visible ahead.

She stopped for a second to refill her lungs, then bellowed as loud as she could: "Mama!"

No answer came back, not even an echo. But as she stood there she felt the vibration once more. Stronger.

She started running again. As she rounded the mountain, she saw far ahead the rising spout of smoke and steam that marked the location of Pele's Doorway. It was shooting up much higher than the last time she'd been here, bringing with it a spray of molten rocks that fell back to the ground like a rain of gold. From this distance Kai couldn't yet see the rift itself, but the fiery river of new lava pouring out of it was sharply defined against the bare black slopes as it coiled down the mountain like a glowing red-yellow serpent. Her eyes swept across the broad vista, straining to pick out a human figure. Where was Lokei?

As her breath started to give out, Kai slowed down slightly. And at that moment she finally spotted a silhouette flickering against the serpent's glow, too far away to look like much more than a speck of ash.

"Mama!" Kai screamed as she resumed running as fast as she could. "Stop . . . please!"

Lokei kept walking in a straight line toward the place

where the snaking river of lava rushed out of the ground. Kai forced herself on faster.

Then suddenly she was running over a thousand knives—the smooth *pahoehoe* lava had ended and she was in a field of jagged, cutting *a'a*. The pain was too much to endure. Kai was forced to stop. She stood dumbly, watching Lokei retreating from her, moving closer and closer to Pele's Doorway. Then something in the foreground caught her eye, a patch of white, like snow lying on the black rock. Gingerly she picked her way over to it, trying to spare her feet, already raw and bleeding.

Lokei's nightgown lay on the ground. Kai raised her eyes. The dawn sky had lightened and she could see her mother's retreating figure more distinctly—the black mane of hair, arms and back and legs bare of clothes. Realizing Lokei was naked reminded Kai of the story her mother had told about the pagan punishment of women who had violated a *kapu*—how they were sacrificed to Pele. . . .

Kai snatched up the nightgown and ripped it in half, quickly wrapping each foot in a clumsy bandage. She charged forward across the *a'a*. Bolts of searing agony still shot up through her legs, but she kept running, closing the gap between her and Lokei. She called out a couple of times, then gave up. The effort only robbed her of breath, and Lokei probably didn't even hear, her mind occupied by other voices.

They were still a hundred yards apart when, mercifully, the ground reverted to the hard, smooth *pahoehoe*, and Kai was able to increase her speed. Lokei was near the rift now. Its radiant waves were visible in the air, undulating around Lokei as she walked through them. Her body took on the aspect of a shimmering wraith, a form without solidity. Now she changed direction slightly, walking parallel to the lava flow and heading straight for the gaping wound in the side of the mountain.

There was no hope of stopping Lokei, Kai realized, not even if she pushed herself on faster. But her burning lungs were no longer capable of holding the air. Staggering to a halt, she forced herself to take in one more hungry gulp of wind and screamed:

"Mama! *Aole!*" No.

The very effort of her cry seemed to drain all that was

left of her strength and breath. Kai sank to her knees, weep-
ing with frustration as she tried again to shout but found no
more than a soft cry emerging from her throat. *"Aole, Mama
. . . aole."*

Then, through her tears, through the rippling heat waves
that made all solid things seem to melt in front of her eyes,
Kai saw her mother stop and turn around.

The plea had broken through her trance! Rising painfully
to her feet again, Kai forced herself forward another few
steps. She saw Lokei raise her arm as a signal of recognition, and Kai raised hers, too, beckoning her mother to
return to safety. "Quickly, Mama!" she yelled. "Get away
from there."

Lokei didn't move for a moment. She kept her arm raised
high as in some kind of salute.

Even when the figure turned away and disappeared into
the bright yellow glow beyond, Kai didn't at first trust her
eyes. Through the wavering veil of heat nothing seemed
quite real. The air would change, her mother reappear. . . .

But she didn't. Kai cried out once, a howl of abject horror
and despair. Then a surge of adrenaline propelled her into
a stumbling, lurching run. She stopped only when she was
so close to the volcanic rift that the heat became as impenetrable as a wall, and she could bear to keep her eyes open
only by shielding them with her hand.

She could see, though, that Lokei was not there. Where
she had been a minute ago, there was nothing but the molten glow. She had walked through Pele's Doorway, had gone
willingly out of her private darkness into the domain of her
goddess. Now she was part of the light.

Chapter Seven

The gray jeep of the Navy Shore Patrol raced along the avenues of asphalt between the low buildings housing the administrative departments of the Pearl Harbor Naval Base. Through spaces separating the buildings, the harbor itself could be seen, glittering under the bright afternoon sun. Dozens of ships from the mammoth U.S. Pacific Fleet were lying at anchor, on their way to duty in Vietnam, or returning to be refitted or give their crews R&R.

Dressed in jeans and a fraying sweatshirt, Kai rode in one of the jeep's high, hard-bottomed rear seats. Her long copper hair whipping behind her like a flag caught the eye of many sailors, and a steady chorus of wolf whistles played in her wake. Brushing the hair from her eyes, Kai took in her surroundings. As she marveled at the immensity of the installation, she had to wonder if all she had gone through to get here would be for nothing. The arguments with Mak and Lili preceding a tearful leavetaking, their fearful cries that they might never see her again. The earnings she'd spent. The change of plan—to give up her schooling and pursue any information she might find, wherever it would lead. What chance did she have to crack through to a truth buried almost eighteen years if this massive military organization was determined to defend itself as it might repel any invader?

Well, she mused, Pearl Harbor had let down its guard once before, and all its mighty power had failed to defend it. There was always a chance she'd succeed with her own surprise attack.

She had arrived in Honolulu on a ferry from the Big Island just an hour ago, and had taken a taxi straight to the base. The two sentries guarding the main gate had explained the base was strictly off limits to civilians.

"But there's information I need," she argued, "and this is the only place to get it."

"I'm real sorry, ma'am," said one sentry, "but regulations say you can't enter the base without a pass."

Kai stood her ground, demanding to see someone in charge, until one of the sailors grabbed her arm and started dragging her away from the gate. When she fought to free herself, the second sentry joined in roughly trying to subdue her, and she gave him a kick in the most effective place. Next thing she knew, she was being clapped in handcuffs.

A battle won as far as she was concerned. She was sorry she'd hurt the young sailor, but it had gotten her onto the base, and that was all that really mattered. If there was a shred of evidence left on this earth about the identity of her father, then nothing was going to stop Kai from finding it. It was too late to save Lokei, but not to find the man responsible. There had to be a reckoning.

The jeep pulled up in front of a long, low building. On a small lawn in front were two flagpoles flying the American and navy flags, and a large sign, white letters on a blue field reading BASE COMMAND, U.S.N. PEARL HARBOR.

Inside, she was guided along a corridor and told to sit on a bench opposite the open door of an office suite. From her seat Kai could see a secretary typing at a desk that guarded a closed inner office. The M.P.s walked through to the inner office and returned a minute later.

"You can go in now, ma'am," one said, removing the handcuffs. "Just don't make any more trouble, or we'll have to come back for you."

The inner door had been left open when the M.P.s came out. As she went forward, she saw a large, carpeted room with a big window looking onto the harbor. At a desk in front of the window sat a scowling, hollow-cheeked man with broad shoulders, hair the color of a battleship and eyes like the sky over a stormy sea. His dark blue uniform jacket was encrusted across the chest with colored ribbons and shiny medals, and gold braid decorated the sleeves. Intimidated by his forbidding look, Kai stopped automatically at the threshold.

"Proceed," he snapped, waving her to one of two hard-backed chairs in front of his desk. "But leave that door open. Judging from what I hear about the ruckus you made, young lady, I may want a rescue squad to be able to reach me quickly." His voice was hoarse, and the words came fast, as though he couldn't break the habit of barking orders in emergencies. As she sat down, she read the brass name plate at the front edge of the desk: REAR ADMIRAL STEWART L. MCKEENE.

"Let me tell you something you may not know, miss," he continued. "A military sentry is charged with using any and all necessary means to keep unauthorized personnel from passing a guard post. In time of war, the regulations are strictly enforced—and we do have quite a nasty little war going on over in Vietnam. Technically, my sentries would be within their rights to shoot anyone who refuses to stop on command. Now, you sure don't look like some damn saboteur who means to blow up a munitions dump, so what makes you so damn eager to kick one of my men in the balls and take a chance on getting your ass shot off?" McKeene's eyes widened to a blazing glare.

Kai refused to let him frighten her. "I need the truth about something, sir. And this is the only place to get it."

"Truth about what?"

"Who my father is, and where to find him."

McKeene's eyes narrowed. A network of lines radiated out to both sides of his weathered face. "Why look here?"

Kai remembered Lokei saying that, as the *kamaaina* of the call-girl ring, one of her high-ranking customers had been an admiral. Could McKeene be the very one? No, too much time had gone by, she decided. Yet she spoke carefully, aware that she was in an uphill battle against a corps of men who would close ranks to protect one another.

"My mother brought me up alone, sir. I don't know my father's name. But I believe he was in the navy, and that he married my mother here at Pearl Harbor. She also told me that the navy covered it up, denied the marriage took place."

Rear Admiral McKeene's face took on a reddish tinge. "Then why isn't your mother here making these charges?" he demanded. "Why leave it to you?"

"My mother killed herself two months ago, sir."

McKeene studied Kai across his desk as if he was staring out from a ship's bridge looking for torpedoes below the surface. "All of it," he said. "Don't just give me guess-work. Tell me whatever you know."

Kai held nothing back, whether it stained the memory of her mother or insulted the honor of the navy. She had to pay with the truth to buy the truth. At the end she said, "My mother imagined a lot of things when she was sick, Admiral. I know it's possible she might've also made up a love story for herself. This officer she says was my father, maybe he was just a man she had a fantasy about. Maybe there wasn't any one man who loved her enough to marry her. You may doubt what I'm telling you, and I've probably got a lot of the same doubts. But I'm hoping that won't keep you from helping me sort out the lies from the facts."

For a long time after she finished, McKeene sat drumming his fingers on the desk. "What's your name, young lady?" he asked at last.

"Kaiulani Teiatu."

"How old are you?"

"Just turned seventeen."

"So all this happened almost eighteen years ago. Could make it hard—if not impossible—to trace any records. They may not even exist. A cover-up would mean records were destroyed."

"I know. But I have to try."

"What worries me is that you'll think we're still covering up if we can't find you an answer."

"Then let me find it, sir, and you won't have to worry."

McKeene's thin lips twitched with a brief, grudging smile. Abruptly his arm shot out to grab up one of three phones perched at his elbow. He dialed a few numbers, then spoke sharply into the receiver. "Commander Bolton? This is Admiral McKeene. Get over to my office. I've got an assignment for you."

Dressed in his tropical whites—short-sleeve shirt, no jacket—Commander James Bolton took the five-minute walk to base h.q. from the building that housed the Press Liaison section. With each angry stride Jim Bolton's determination to get the hell out of Pearl and back behind the helm of his patrol boat rose another notch. True, floating down the Mekong River at night, keeping a watch for enemy movements, was not a very comfortable place to be. One moonlit night this past March, his boat had come under fire from a detachment of Vietcong and Jim Bolton had been stitched across his arms and chest by four bullets from a machine gun, one drilling through bone and tissue just three inches from his heart.

Yet there were things about being on the boat that had his present duty beat hollow. For one, he enjoyed the camaraderie with his crew. More important, on patrol duty he was never bored and useless. Boredom, Jim Bolton thought, ran death a close second for a condition to be avoided.

For the past two weeks he'd been bugging every one of his superiors to give him a transfer back to active duty from this stupid desk job as "Public Relations Officer." He was sick of the steady schedule of running guided tours for reporters from the *New York Times* or the *Washington Post*, and visiting senators and their wives, showing them the U.S. Navy's power and preparedness, and, not so incidentally, convincing them that the war in Vietnam was absolutely necessary.

Bolton knew why the job had been shoved onto him. Not as a reward for suffering endured in battle, certainly not because any prewar experience prepared him to do P.R. for the navy. It was simply because he looked good in the uniform, looked like he belonged on a recruiting poster. Tall, with thick, straight hair the color of polished oak, pale blue eyes, and a strong chin ridged by the faintest hint of a cleft, Jim had always found his rugged handsomeness to be a combination of blessing and curse. Without the money he'd earned as a catalogue model he would never have managed to pay his way through college, then two years of Harvard Business School before he'd been pulled into the war out of a reserve officers unit. He had no complaint, either, about the edge his looks had given him with girls in high school, the coeds in college—though he supposed the reason he'd never built one steady relationship was because there was always too much choice. But when the escalating Vietnam conflict had caused his ROTC unit to be activated, and he'd found himself put up in front of a group of enlisted men as their leader, he'd been faced with their mockery and doubt about whether he was brave enough or smart enough to get them all home alive. "Pretty boy," they called him, and said—to his face—that they didn't believe he had the guts to lead. The ugly sons of bitches didn't mind taking risks, maybe didn't even mind dying so much. A pretty boy wouldn't want to take a chance on spoiling that face, or missing all the fun that must come with it.

Bolton had taught them otherwise. By the time of the attack they weren't surprised he was one of the three men wounded; he was always the first to put himself in harm's way, and he'd readily exposed himself to enemy fire in the course of dragging two other wounded men to cover.

Now, because of his looks, he was being made into a kind of store-window mannequin for the navy. That only made him hate the job more.

As he turned up the path to base h.q., Bolton's impatience to get back to meaningful duty was at an all-time high. What had McKeene said about this new assignment? Something about taking the daughter of an ex-officer from the Korean days over to Records to search for an old marriage certificate? Great. She was probably putting together a scrapbook for her parent's twentieth anniversary.

Marching into h.q., Jim decided to go straight in to McKeene and say he'd had it—dramatize the fact by refusing to take on one more fool's errand.

Then he saw the girl sitting on the bench outside the admiral's office. The sight of her stopped him in his tracks. She seemed to be daydreaming, her luminous blue-green eyes cast vacantly to one side, her head slightly tilted so that the long copper hair fell away from her face. He had never seen such breathtaking beauty.

Presenting himself, he took off his cap and put it under his arm. "Commander Bolton, miss. I'm here at the request of Admiral McKeene."

When her eyes found his, they kept their distant glaze for a moment, as though she was still captive to the daydream. Then she gave him a winning smile and introduced herself.

He saw now how young she was. Though he felt no less ready to help her, the feeling sparked by his first sight of her underwent a sudden, subtle change.

The personnel records were kept in a separate building. As they walked there, Bolton asked questions, clarifying for himself the reason for Kai's search. After hearing about the past cover-up intended to protect men of high rank from scandal, he wondered about McKeene's motive in handing the matter over to Public Relations. It could be taken two ways, Bolton thought. Was he supposed to keep the navy completely in the clear—even if it meant continuing to fudge the truth? Or had he been brought in for damage control in case the past scandal came to light? No surprise that the admiral hadn't specifically declared his wish; he was too shrewd to let himself get nailed with responsibility for anything that compromised navy integrity. The assignment he'd been given, Bolton knew, was to juggle this hot potato all by himself. Not quite as perilous as running the patrol boat— but not boring, either.

In the Records building were two floors, each with a vast open area where hundreds of gray file cabinets were lined up side by side in long aisles. One of several sailors who worked as file clerks was detailed to provide assistance in steering Bolton through the maze of files.

The problem with finding proof of a marriage performed on the base, the clerk said, was that it existed only in the form of copies of marriage certificates included in the service dossier of each man—which would be filed by name. There was no separate registry of all marriages. Without a name there was no way to find a certificate short of going through hundreds of thousands of files from A to Z.

"Back in Washington," said the clerk, "they're starting to use some kind of computer that's supposed to be able to search through millions of facts in minutes. But so far only current personnel are being filed that way."

Hearing this, Kai gave a despondent sigh. Bolton laid his hand lightly on her shoulder, a reflex touch of encouragement. Kai usually shied from such contact, but she understood instinctively that there was nothing more than kindness behind the gesture, and she gave the naval officer an appreciative smile.

Moved by that smile, he resolved that nothing would stop him from helping this girl.

Another approach to narrowing the search occurred to Bolton. What was known about the anonymous officer was that he had served in the legal division, the Adjutant Corps, and he had provided the defense at a court-martial held several months before the presumed marriage. "What about the court-martial?" he said to the clerk. "You keep any records of legal proceedings?"

Actual transcripts would be stored in an archive attached to the Adjutant Division, the clerk said. However, the files here did include a general record of courts-martial, and they could be tracked chronologically.

Kai held out little hope as they went to the next section of records. She recalled Lokei telling her everything had been done to conceal the scandal.

But twenty minutes later, the clerk was able to provide details on nine courts-martial that had taken place on the base during the two years preceding the time Lokei would have been pregnant. In seven cases the defendants were enlisted men. Of the two officers charged with offenses, one had been accused and found guilty of manslaughter after killing an enlisted man in a bar fight; the second had been acquitted.

"What's the charge in the second case?" Bolton asked.

"Funny thing, sir," the clerk answered, "it doesn't say. Just a blank where the information usually appears."

Kai and Bolton exchanged a look before he took the dossier out of the clerk's hands and told him he could return to his regular duty.

"This has to be it," Bolton said to Kai when they were alone. "It would leave too big a hole to pretend the court-martial never happened; too many people knew about it—witnesses, judges, lawyers on both sides. All that was really needed to paste over the scandal was to blot out the nature of the crime. I suppose the transcript might have disappeared, too. But with the defendant acquitted, the case was closed; nobody was apt to snoop too deeply into it." He smiled at Kai. "Of course, they didn't reckon on you showing up eighteen years later."

"The man my mother told me about," said Kai, "was the lawyer for the defense. Does it give his name there?"

Bolton glanced back at the dossier. "Here it is," he said. He put his finger down on the paper and turned it around toward Kai.

She read the name: Randall Wyler.

Now that there was a name, it was easy to go back to the main file. No copy of a marriage certificate was included, the officer's status was given as single at the time of his honorable discharge. But just as important to Kai, a home address was given—in Chicago, Illinois.

"Quite a coincidence," Bolton observed.

"What?" she asked.

"I was brought up in Chicago myself. Haven't lived there in many years, though. For that matter, this man Wyler might have moved on. This address dates back to the time of service. A man's apt to wander a long way in eighteen years; a young lawyer could easily have taken work in another city after being discharged from the navy."

"I know," Kai said gloomily. "But it's all I've got to go on."

Bolton brought Kai back to his office, where he immediately placed a call to the information operator in Chicago. When he supplied the name Randall Wyler, the operator gave telephone numbers for home and business. The navy officer asked for addresses, too, and jotted down all the information on a notepad.

"Well, that's one lucky break for you," Bolton said as he hung up. "Looks like he's still right there in Chicago." He pushed the paper across the desk to Kai. "That's everything you need to get in touch with him. What are you going to do now?"

"Go and find him."

"You're just going to show up on this guy Wyler's doorstep?"

Kai shrugged. She couldn't really think that far ahead—couldn't actually see herself standing in front of the faceless man who had deserted her. But she knew she was going to Chicago.

Bolton regarded the lovely girl with concern. "Kai, I know you've got a score to settle," he said. "It's none of my business, but I'd suggest you put out some feelers to be absolutely positive you're headed in the right direction. It's too soon to be a hundred percent certain Wyler's the right man."

"I know what my mother told me. She said he'd been the defending lawyer in the trial, that he'd won an acquittal."

Looking at Kai, Bolton felt an odd regret now for having helped solve the mystery. The way she had broken through the barriers to get here was evidence of her grit and determination. Yet he sensed a surviving softness, too, a vulnerability. It stirred a desire to protect her, save her from any more hurts.

"You'll be out on a limb when you get there," Bolton said. "If he denies everything, turns you away, will you have enough money to get back here? Because I could give you some—"

"I have enough," Kai said flatly. She'd left eight hundred dollars along with her clothes in a valise checked at the ferry terminal. The money was just a third of what had been left after Lokei's burial costs were paid.

The flat certainty of her answer silenced Bolton for a moment. There was no arguing with it, yet he couldn't let her go without offering something.

Then he thought of it. A gift as good as money, and easier for her to accept. With a call to McKeene, then to the military transport command, he was able to arrange a free seat for her aboard a navy plane that made stops in a number of mainland cities, including Chicago. "It's really a cargo plane," he said. "The seats in the passenger section aren't as soft as the commercial jets," he said, "but you can't beat the price."

The next flight left in an hour. He drove Kai into Honolulu to get her valise, and made it back to Wheeler Field in time to bring her out to the runway just as the giant C-130 Hercules started its jet engines.

"Thanks, Commander Bolton," she said as they stopped at the loading stairs, "I won't forget what you did for me."

Bolton had never felt awkward with women. But with this girl, all his usual instincts went haywire. Her beauty by itself was almost overwhelming, but he also admired her courage—and she possessed an undeniable sexual allure. It was simply part of her, Bolton thought, as innocently and instinctively present as the song of a bird.

As they said goodbye, in spite of all the rules of common sense, he wanted to reach out and tell her not to go. Wanted to gather her into his arms and beg for a chance to be the one to teach her about love.

But the big jet was revving its engine, and she was seventeen, and he was an officer and a gentleman. So he replied simply, "I'm glad I could help you, Kai. Take care of yourself."

He waited at the edge of the airfield and watched the plane take off. He watched until it soared up and banked away over the ocean, shrinking to a dark pinpoint in the clear blue Hawaiian sky.

Bolton stood watching even after it was gone, like a lover left behind.

BOOK
TWO

Chapter Eight

Chicago, August 1968

Having made several stops en route—San Francisco, Denver, Phoenix, Tulsa, St. Louis—the big navy cargo jet landed in Chicago at eight o'clock Tuesday morning, seventeen hours after departing Honolulu. The frequent landings, and the noise of six dozen sailors in the passenger section celebrating leaves and discharges, had made it hard for Kai to sleep, though much of the time she pretended to doze, saving herself from the leers and passes of the rowdier sailors. At each stopover she had looked out the window by her seat, and had seen coffins being unloaded. Stacks of them. The sight horrified her. She had known there was a war on—but not the size, not the toll. She had been too preoccupied with problems closer to home.

Walking through the terminal to the airport bus, she saw a large group of young men and women holding up hand-lettered signs tacked to long sticks and chanting slogans. "PEACE NOW"—"GET OUT OF 'NAM"—"MAKE LOVE NOT WAR." The navy men shouted angry remarks at the demonstrators, and there might have been a more serious clash if the sailors hadn't been so concerned with meeting their families.

Outside were more demonstrators. Kai got on the bus and took a seat at the front across from the driver. "Are they here all the time?" she asked the driver, nodding at the crowd visible through the windshield.

"Just this week." The driver explained that the Democratic party's convention to nominate a candidate for president in the November elections had opened in Chicago last night. The city was already packed with journalists and politicians, but more were still arriving, and a corps of demonstrators had stayed at the airport to get the anti-war message across.

The driver seemed friendly enough, so Kai showed him the slip of paper on which Jim Bolton had written down the addresses for her. "Does the bus go anywhere near these places?" she asked.

"Not too far. One's downtown, in the business district. The other's up on the North Side, residential," the driver said. "That's money country, kid. Whoever you're goin' to see must be big-time."

Looking at the sights passing on all sides as she rode toward the city, Kai felt a combination of awe, curiosity, and despair. Her father had fled so long ago, and had apparently become a man of wealth—which went with power and influence. Could she force him to acknowledge her if he chose not to? How could she have left behind people who cared about her and the lush beauty of Hawaii for *this*? There was so little open space in this city, so little greenery. Everything was gray and dingy—smoke pouring from tall factory chimneys of blackened brick, neighborhoods of wood-frame houses with peeling paint stretching on mile after mile. Instead of the perfume of tropical blossoms in the air, there was a hideous stench that grew stronger as they got farther from the airport. It became so overpowering that Kai pinched her nostrils.

The bus driver laughed when he noticed Kai holding her nose. "If you're planning to stay around here, kid, better get used to that smell."

"What is it?"

"The stockyards. Didn't you ever hear what they call this town—'Hog Butcher to the World'? Look over there." He pointed to one side. Beyond acres of railroad sidings lining the expressway, Kai could see a vast field of wooden pens filled with animals—not only pigs but cows and sheep.

"Does the whole city smell this bad?" she said.

"Depends on which way the wind is blowing. There's places you hardly get a whiff. That's what the rich folks pay for up on the North Side."

A taxi took Kai from the bus terminal to a neighborhood of imposing brick and stone mansions, some visible from the street, others hidden behind high walls and iron gates. Where the cab let her off, Kai found herself standing in front of a closed iron gate. Beyond the bars a mansion was partially visible at the end of a long tree-lined drive. Kai had thought it made more sense to come here rather than her father's office, but now she wasn't so sure. She saw an intercom set into the brick pillar at one side of the gate. She pushed the button.

A man's voice emerged from the speaker. "Wyler residence."

What words should she use to announce that she was walking back into her father's life? "I—I'd like to see Mr. Wyler."

"What is your business with him?" the voice asked.

To tell him I'm his daughter. "I have to talk to him, that's all. It's very important."

"He's gone to his office. You can contact him there." There was a click as the intercom was switched off.

Kai dug the paper out of her jeans and looked at the other address Jim Bolton had jotted down. Her thoughts stayed on the handsome officer for a second. He'd been so kind. There were good men in the navy. Did she dare to hope Randall Wyler might be a man like that, after all? No, if he had been that sort of man, she wouldn't be here alone, forced to hunt him down.

The law offices of Dawes, Lybrandt and Wyler occupied two full floors high in a fifty-story building on Adams Street in the city's downtown district, known as the Loop. Unable to find an empty taxi, unfamiliar with the bus stops, Kai had walked all the way from the North Side toting her valise. After the long walk, and the sleepless hours on the plane, she was exhausted. She thought twice about entering the building: perhaps she should wait until she was clean and rested before trying to see her father.

But she couldn't wait.

When she asked to see Randall Wyler, the sleek receptionist seated behind a marble-topped desk gave Kai's jeans, T-shirt, and unbrushed hair a scornful once-over. "Look, if you're one of those kids who wants to sue the city 'cause the cops beat 'em up for demonstrating against the war, Mr. Wyler can't take the case. He's no war lover himself, but—"

"It's not about any case," Kai said. "It's personal."

The receptionist looked her up and down. A crooked smile tilted the corners of her mouth. "Personal, eh? Well, Mr. Wyler isn't here, and won't be the rest of the day."

"Where is he?" Having come all this way, Kai couldn't wait another day to see him.

"Honey, don't you read the papers?" the receptionist said. "He's at the courthouse. They're summing up today in the Loomis trial."

In the cavernous lobby of the courthouse building, Kai passed a cubicle where newspapers, coffee, and snacks were being sold. The hunger that had been kept at bay by her focus on the search suddenly gripped her stomach. She bought three donuts and a coffee, and while gobbling down the food, she noticed a tabloid newspaper headlined LOOMIS MURDERS TO JURY TODAY. She bought the paper and scanned the story. Steven Loomis was charged with shooting to death his father and brother at the family estate in a suburb of Chicago. Since his mother had died of an illness years earlier, the deaths left Loomis the sole heir to a family fortune of eighty million dollars. "Final summations in the trial are expected today," the story concluded. "Speaking to reporters last night, defense attorney Randall Wyler predicted that the twenty-five-year-old heir to the Loomis Vacuum Cleaner fortune would be found not guilty. 'I've won every murder case I've ever fought,' Wyler said, 'and I've never felt as sure about a verdict as I do about this one.' " Brief as the quote was, it gave Kai a sense of Wyler's personality—his brashness, his vanity—and fueled her anger against the father she had never met. A photograph of a man accompanied the article, but the caption identified him as the accused.

Before going to the courtroom, Kai stopped in a public washroom and cleaned up. This was how he would see her for the first time, she thought, as she gave herself a final inspection in the mirror, satisfied that she looked clean and tidy enough.

Outside the third-floor courtroom, the corridor was filled with curiosity seekers who had been denied access to the spectacle, and an assortment of reporters and photographers taking advantage of a twenty-minute recess to shoot the breeze or smoke a cigarette. A stocky bailiff was guarding the doors to the courtroom. As Kai tried to take a quick look through one of the small round windows in the double doors, the bailiff tapped her.

"Sorry, the public galleries are full," he said.

After the separation of a lifetime, Kai was separated from her father now by only a door. "I have to see Mr. Wyler," she said.

"He'll be starting his summation any minute. See him at the next recess."

"Look, I've come a long way," Kai pleaded. "I have to get in. I'm his . . ." She couldn't bring herself to say it outright. "I'm a relative."

"Relative, huh?" The bailiff looked her over skeptically, but he was taking no chances. "Well, write a note and I'll bring it inside. If he gives the okay—"

"He wouldn't know who I am," she blurted.

The bailiff laughed. "A relative, but he doesn't know you. Long-lost cousin, something like that? Sorry, miss . . ."

She could simply wait to catch him outside later, but it might be hours and she couldn't stand to be so near for so long. She *had* to get in that courtroom.

She dropped the valise, crouched to remove more money, then stood and held out the bills. "I'll pay for a seat," she said.

The bailiff scowled. "Listen, you, you're talking to an officer of the court. If I took this for a bribe attempt, you'd be in real hot water."

"I'm sorry, I didn't mean to—"

"Go on! Just get the hell out of the building—or I'll run you in!" The bailiff fixed a hot glare on Kai until she had grabbed her valise and retreated down the corridor. Turning a corner to a bank of elevators, she leaned against a marble wall, her forehead against the cool stone, overcome by exhaustion—and an unreasoned fear that Randall Wyler might remain forever out of reach. Servants, secretaries, bailiffs— the guardians around him seemed harder to get past than armed sentries at Pearl Harbor.

Among the reporters outside the courtroom, several noted the beautiful girl with the tawny skin and long copper hair trying to scam her way inside by claiming she was a relative of Randall Wyler's. But only Jerry Vaughan broke from the group to drift after her. Vaughan's journalistic radar detected a hint of something extraordinary about the girl's hunger to get past that door. Maybe Wyler did know the girl; the successful lawyer was married to a rich, attractive socialite, but there had been scuttlebutt around the newsrooms that both husband and wife indulged in occasional affairs. Nothing solid enough to kill off the idea that Wyler should make a run for senator one of these days. But the sexy young girl presented all kinds of possibilities, the reporter thought. Who could say that she wasn't panting to watch Wyler in action because she was carrying a torch?

Rounding the corner to the elevators, Vaughan almost bumped smack into Kai, who was still leaning against the wall.

"S'cuse me, miss. I couldn't help overhearing the little problem you had back there," Vaughan said. "Just wondered if I could help."

The first thing Kai noticed about the man was the tag pinned to his lapel with PRESS stamped across the top in bold red letters. He was slight, a little shorter than her own five-nine, with lank dirty blonde hair in need of a cut, a small nose, and shrewd brown eyes. A notepad and several pens poked up from the pocket of his rumpled seersucker jacket, and an odor of stale cigarette smoke hovered around him.

"Jerry Vaughan," he introduced himself. "I'm covering the trial for the *Tribune*. Heard you butting heads with that goon on the door—you said something about being related to Randy Wyler?"

Kai suddenly realized that her story might have value to a newsman; Wyler was a public figure. But it wasn't going to help a delicate situation if, before he'd ever met the person claiming to be his daughter, the prominent attorney read about it in his morning paper. She answered carefully, "I'm not sure there's a family connection. I'm hoping to talk to him so I can find out."

"So you've never met . . . ?"

"No," Kai admitted.

Cross off the mistress angle, Vaughan thought. Looking into the girl's clear eyes and guileless expression, he'd have bet a Pulitzer prize that she wasn't lying, wasn't even capable of it.

''What makes you think you're related?'' he asked.

''Mr. Vaughan, I don't want to give you a story, frankly, because I'm not even sure I have one. I won't really know until I talk to Mr. Wyler. But if you help me get into the courtroom, and later I find out something worth telling a newspaper reporter, I'll give it to you first. Okay?''

Vaughan smiled at the girl. She struck him as an odd combination of naive and savvy, a bit of a hick but with sharp instincts. ''Where you from, kid?''

''Hawaii.''

''How does Wyler come by a branch of the family way out there?''

Supplying details, Kai realized, would open the way for the reporter to research the story himself. ''Do you think the recess is over yet?'' she asked, glancing toward the courtroom.

Yeah, cute and sharp, Vaughan mused. ''Okay, the story comes later. Right now let's see if I have any influence around here.''

The bailiff started to redden when he saw Kai returning, but the reporter hurried over first and huddled with him. A moment later, Vaughan gave Kai a come-ahead wave, and they were passed inside. Kai sat down beside Jerry Vaughan in one of the two rows of benches reserved for the press.

''Which one is Wyler?'' she asked.

''Not here yet,'' Vaughan said. ''Must've taken his client for a private conference during the recess.''

He had only just finished speaking when a side door opened and a stocky, balding man in a rumpled suit entered and took a chair at a table near the front facing the judge's bench.

''The D.A.,'' Vaughan murmured.

A minute later, two more men came through the side door, one wearing a tweed sports jacket and dark slacks, the other a charcoal suit. Even if Kai hadn't seen the picture of the accused in the paper, she would have known at once that the man in the suit was Wyler. She recognized him from her own image in the mirror—from that part of herself that came from him. He was tall and built powerfully, broad across the shoulders and chest. His hair, full and fine and perfectly cut, had not quite completed the change to a premature silvery gray, leaving several distinct irregular bars of black in a pattern suggestive of a tiger's markings. He was a man who commanded attention, and no sooner had he entered than the babble of spectators quieted, and their eyes followed Wyler as he walked across the front of the room and sat down with his client at the defense table.

A clerk called the court to order. "*Oyez, oyez!* All rise." A black-robed judge entered from behind the bench and sat down. He rapped his gavel, though the crowd was already quiet. It seemed to Kai that they had really been brought to order not by the judge, but by the entrance of Randall Wyler. Her father.

An urge to denounce him raged within her. If any one person could be held to account for her mother's slide toward self-destruction, it was this man. Murderer! she cried out in her mind.

"Mr. Wyler," the judge said, "we are ready to hear summation for the defense."

The courtroom itself was a reminder of the principle that all men were innocent until proven guilty. Kai sat back and waited to hear how Randall Wyler would defend a man against a charge of murder, as a clue to how he might excuse his own crime.

Randall Wyler stepped in front of the jury box and scanned the men and women staring back at him. Twelve good citizens, solid and dependable. He knew from their faces and names that they represented a fair microcosm of the diverse population that made up this remarkable city, the boiling center of America's melting pot—Irish, Italians, Lithuanians, Poles from the stockyards, blacks from the South Side. Wyler understood them. He had been born to such people himself, his father a track-maintenance worker on the web of steel rails that had fed into Chicago in the days when passengers and freight had been carried mainly by railroads. Randall Wyler's natural charm, linked with dogged application in school and ambition that burned hotter than a blast furnace, had raised him to the pinnacle of his specialized legal field, the practice of criminal law.

Yet as far as he rose above the rank and file, he never wanted to rise so far that he could no longer make genuine contact with these people who would always be the majority of any jury box. Knowing their fears and hopes was the foundation of the phenomenal success he enjoyed.

Of course, he reminded himself often, he had built wisely on that foundation by choosing exactly the right wife.

He began his appeal.

From her brief reading of the case in the newspaper, Kai couldn't imagine how the young man accused of shooting to death his father and brother could be found innocent. The fact that he had deliberately aimed and fired the murder weapon was not even being denied. The plea of temporary insanity seemed completely undercut by the motive to inherit an immense fortune.

But not long after Wyler started to speak, Kai felt the force of a passion to convey his own vision of justice casting a spell over the courtroom. Drawing together the evidence offered over several weeks, the case made by Wyler hinged on the fact that Steven Loomis had served as an infantry lieutenant in Vietnam. Discharged a year ago, he had returned with medals pinned to his chest, physically unscathed.

"But there was another kind of damage done to this valiant young man," Wyler said, his voice throbbing with conviction. "A year of combat against a shadowy enemy that came in endless waves left Mr. Loomis suffering from night terrors long after he had returned from the steamy jungles. The deadly guerilla army that once lurked everywhere around him had finally infiltrated his last defenses to prowl in the darkest jungle of all—the deepest recesses of his mind."

Wyler reminded the jury of the psychological experts he had produced to testify about the effects of war—what had been termed shell shock in the past and was now being called battle-induced psychosis. He repeated testimony given by a maid in the Loomis house that Steven slept with a rifle near his bed, and weeks before the fatal shootings had fired the weapon when he awoke in the middle of the night, convinced his foxhole was being overrun by Vietcong.

"The district attorney would like you to believe my client was being clever when he shot at phantoms that night—that he was laying the groundwork for a subsequent defense. But of course the district attorney was lucky enough not to serve in this terrible war, not to know the terrors that may lodge in a man's brain as surely and destructively as shrapnel from a grenade.''

Wyler rounded out his thesis. On the night of the shootings, Steve Loomis had awakened in a panic, gripped by an illusion that his position was being overrun. He had shouted for help, as any soldier might alert others in his unit, and grabbed up his rifle. Responding to his cries, his father and brother had come running through the darkness, and Loomis had fired a salvo of bullets to repel the enemy.

By this point in Wyler's speech, the courtroom was as still and silent as an abandoned battlefield. He moved to his conclusion: ''Our system of justice requires a man to be found innocent if a reasonable doubt of his guilt exists. But I would ask you to exercise, too, a reasonable *trust* in the goodness of this man who put his life on the line for his country—yours and mine. Would he defend us with his gun, only to use it against those who were even nearer and more precious? The two men who died were not murder victims. Like Steven Loomis himself, like tens of thousands of others, they were nothing less than . . . casualties of war.''

As Randall Wyler sat down again there was a clamoring exodus of reporters from the press section, Jerry Vaughan included. A good share of the newsmen were already betting Wyler had won, and were phoning quotes from his dramatic speech to their newspapers.

Kai was left simmering with doubt—though not about a verdict. She perceived how deftly Randall Wyler had appealed to the emotions of the jury. Yet she wasn't sure if he had designed a clever thesis solely for the sake of winning or if his compassion was genuine. What had he said about maintaining a reasonable trust in the goodness of men? She was hopeful now that he wouldn't turn her away.

The judge sent the case to the jury, and the jurors were taken to be sequestered.

As Wyler left the courtroom, a crowd of reporters mobbed him. Kai followed, wanting neither to let Wyler out of her sight, nor to speak to him until it could be private. Outside, on the courthouse steps, the movable press conference stopped. The questions shifted from the trial to politics. What were Wyler's views on the convention? As a political insider, did he think Ted Kennedy would be drafted to run for vice-president on the ticket with Hubert Humphrey?

What about Wyler's own ambitions—any truth to the rumor he would leave his lucrative legal practice to run for senator?

As he fenced with the reporters, Wyler's glance happened to land on Kai. Suddenly he broke off, distracted. She held her breath in anticipation. In a moment he would push through the crowd, ask her name, embrace her. . . .

But then his gaze traveled past her and he resumed his answer. "I've got to get over to the convention," he excused himself finally from the reporters, and ran down the steps to a waiting limousine.

As Kai watched the limousine disappear around a corner, Jerry Vaughan moved up beside her. "Ready to tell your story?"

"I still haven't talked to him," she said.

"You just let a good chance go by."

"You saw it was impossible."

Vaughan examined Kai curiously. He had observed her trailing Wyler, while keeping her distance. Both Bobby Kennedy and Martin Luther King had been shot in recent months by malcontents with murderous fixations. This beautiful girl seemed sane enough, but she might be worth keeping an eye on.

"He'll be at the convention," Vaughan said. "I can give you a lift if you want to follow him."

The main activity of the convention was at night, but by the end of the afternoon the amphitheater was a magnet for delegates and power brokers who had grown tired of wheeling and dealing in smoke-filled rooms at their hotels.

Security arrangements at the Chicago Amphitheater were intended to bar anyone from entering without proper credentials, but heavy traffic through many entrances and exits made it easy for Vaughan to take Kai past the guards by flashing his own press pass.

"Thanks again, Jerry," she said when they were inside. "Looks like I couldn't get through any door in this town if I was alone."

"These are nervous times, kid, and you've got the age and uniform that makes you the enemy. Tell you the truth, you scared me a little until we had a chance to talk in the car."

"What do you mean I scared you?" she asked as they made their way onto the vast convention floor.

"America's a violent place, Kai. People come out of nowhere to hurt other people for no reason. I'm still trying to figure out why you're so hot to get close to Wyler."

"Not to hurt him," she said.

In addition to the open floor where the different state delegations met, the amphitheater provided broadcast booths for television networks, rooms for caucuses and press conferences, dining areas, and miles of corridors on several levels that formed natural hives for hatching political intrigues. With all these separate meeting grounds, it was no easy task to locate any one person. Vaughan took Kai to the main floor and they checked the Illinois delegation, then looked into a few side rooms without finding Wyler.

When they went to the buffet-style dining areas, Vaughan couldn't help noticing that Kai hungrily eyed the food laid out on the long serving counters. "Have something to eat," he said, pressing a five-dollar bill into her hand. "Meantime, I'll go up to the press section and ask if anybody knows where Wyler hangs out."

Kai picked out a roast beef sandwich and a glass of milk, and ravenously finished them in a minute. To kill time waiting for Jerry to return, she went to the entrance of the dining area and watched the action in the corridor outside. Delegates wandered past wearing colorful sashes or straw hats emblazoned with names of their favorite candidates.

Suddenly Wyler came into view, accompanied by four men, all in animated conversation. She stepped into the center of the wide passageway to intercept him, not wanting to let another chance be lost.

Seeing her, he halted and whispered an aside to one of the men with him, who quickly hurried off. Then a second man left. He must be dispatching them so he could talk with her alone, Kai thought. But then he wheeled around and walked quickly in the opposite direction, flanked by the two men remaining with him.

"Mr. Wyler!" she called out, trotting after him. *Mister.* Her father!

He turned with his companions into a passage leading to the open arena. Out there, amid delegates and journalists crowding in for the convention's evening session, he'd be hard to find again. Kai broke into a run.

As she rounded a corner into the passage Wyler had taken, she smacked into a pair of security guards. They grabbed her by the arms. "Stop fighting us, bitch," said one as Kai struggled to break free, "or I'll break your fucking arm."

Kai could tell it was no idle threat. She was the enemy, as Vaughan had said. She submitted to being led away.

They took her to a floor below the arena, a large, windowless room with cinder-block walls set aside as headquarters for the security squad. Kai was searched, pushed into a chair, and questioned by the man in charge, a white-haired retired FBI agent. Why was she stalking Randall Wyler? Was she part of a group?

It was Wyler who had sent for the security guards, Kai realized. Without knowing who she was, he might have become alarmed by seeing her on the courthouse steps, then here at the convention.

Telling the truth to these guards, Kai thought, might only make her seem unstable, more of a threat. Would they believe the man she was following was the father who had never seen her?

"Listen," she said to the chief of security, "I'm not here to make trouble. I want to give Mr. Wyler a message from an old friend. If you're worried, keep me here. But let me write a note you can take to him."

The security chief gave Kai paper and pen. She thought for only a second before writing: "Your *kaimana* sends her love."

The security man glanced at it suspiciously, but took it away without asking any more questions.

She waited in detention. Two hours, three. From the floor above, the roar of thousands of delegates were heard as platforms were announced, speeches made, old heroes of the party brought back for a last hurrah. The security men debated turning her over to the police. If her note meant anything, they said, Wyler would have come by now.

Jerry Vaughan appeared, carrying the valise she had left in his car. He had tried and failed to obtain her release, he said. He promised to keep working on it, but he left with apologies that there were other stories he had to cover.

Another hour went by. The evening session of the convention had opened at eight o'clock; it was now almost midnight. The roars from the arena above had grown thinner, fainter.

"Everybody's leaving, kid," said the guard detailed to stay with her. "We're handing you over to the cops."

At that moment Wyler arrived. As soon as he walked through the door, Kai sprang from the chair where she had been sitting for hours. "Can you release her to me?" he said to the guard after identifying himself.

"If you're sure you want to take her, Mr. Wyler."

He walked over to Kai and looked her in the eye. "*Kaimana,*" he said after a pause. "Means diamond, right?"

Kai nodded.

"Took me a while to remember."

"Did you forget the diamond had a name, too?" she asked.

He shook his head. "What about you—what's your name?"

"Kaiulani."

"What's that mean?"

"Heavenly beauty."

He studied her silently again. "Suits you."

He said nothing else before arranging her release and leading her out of the convention hall.

In the streets outside, patches of fighting had broken out between policemen and anti-war factions, who kept a constant vigil. Kai found herself feeling sympathetic to the demonstrators. The treatment she'd received from the security guards, and her memory of all the coffins being removed from the military plane, combined to form opinions on issues that had never mattered to her before. As the policemen scattered demonstrators, Kai edged toward the street.

As though anticipating her impulse to join in, Wyler grabbed Kai's arm and steered her in the other direction. They walked down several back streets until they entered a small coffee shop with a counter and half a dozen booths. A few counter stools were occupied by men who appeared to be night laborers coming off their shifts. Kai supposed Wyler had chosen the place because he didn't want to meet anyone he knew while he was with her.

They took a booth and a counterman came for their order. Wyler asked for coffee, but Kai seized the opportunity to satisfy her lingering hunger. "I'll have a cheese omelet, bacon, fried potatoes, salad, and juice," she told the counterman.

"Still a growing girl," Wyler remarked wryly when they were alone.

"I haven't eaten much for two days," Kai said. "I've been too busy chasing you."

"Why?" he asked flatly.

She took a breath and riveted her eyes on him. "Because I'm your daughter."

He stared back implacably. He didn't look shocked, didn't rush to deny it, didn't laugh it off.

Once he'd admitted he remembered Lokei, Kai suspected that those hours he had left her in detention after receiving the note had been used to adjust himself, think through the possibilities. He was trained by his trial work to do that—prepare himself to hear testimony, ask no questions for which he didn't already have the answers, draw emotion from others and show little himself. Now he would use all his skills in his own defense.

"Tell me what happened to Lokei," he said. "I've always wondered."

So quiet, so reasonable. Was it sincere interest—or a clever tactic to disarm her? "This past spring," Kai said, wanting to rattle him, "she killed herself."

A flicker of pain pinched his expression, the first sign of any emotion. "I'm really sorry to hear that."

"Sorry?" Kai said, mocking him. "And would you be sorry to hear that she spent most of the years after you left as the sex slave of a goddamn sadist because it was the only way to give me a home? Are you sorry if it finally drove her out of her mind?"

"I'm sorry about all of it," Wyler said quietly.

Kai stared at him, at a loss for how to continue. This man seated across the table was her father; he hadn't attempted to deny it. Yet the way he was reacting to her made the fact seem barely relevant. It was as thought he had been mixed up with nothing more than a traffic accident eighteen years earlier.

"So it was because of her suicide," he said, "that you set out to find me. You hold me responsible."

"Is that so unfair? Her whole life would have been dif-

ferent if you hadn't lied to her, hadn't told her you'd send
for her and then . . . thrown her away.''

"Are you so sure she would have been better off coming
here? You've seen this city now. If I'd brought her, do you
think she would have been happy here?''

Yes, he was putting her on the stand, Kai realized, using
his courtroom techniques to argue the case—asking questions that put her on the defensive.

The counterman brought their order to the table and left.

"For godssake," Kai demanded, "if you knew it was
hopeless, why did you let it go so far? Marrying, starting a
family—"

"I didn't know it was hopeless," Wyler cut in hotly. "I
never even thought about where it would lead." The cool
pose was finally gone. He took a sip of his coffee, then
asked Kai abruptly, "Ever hear of Captain Cook?''

She knew the name, of course. The English explorer
James Cook, who had sailed to Tahiti in the late eighteenth
century, also figured in the history of Hawaii. On one voyage, when he had stopped at the Big Island to provision his
boat, he had been welcomed, given many gifts, and his
sailors had paired off freely with the native women; later,
when Cook landed again, an argument had blown up with
the Hawaiians, Cook had been killed, and his bones stripped
of their flesh for their *mana*—the spiritual power. Kai answered Wyler with a puzzled nod. Why bring the long-dead
explorer into the conversation?

He went on, "Imagine what it was like a couple of hundred years ago to sail away from civilization and arrive for
the first time in a place like Tahiti, or Hawaii. Like finding
Eden itself, I'd guess. They say Cook's men never wanted
to leave.'' He leaned across the table, as if to share a confidence. "It was like that for me. I'd never done anything,
been anywhere away from here until I joined the navy and
they sent me to the islands. The weather, the beaches, flowers everywhere, it was paradise. And then I met her. . . .''
He paused, looking down into his coffee cup, and Kai could
tell he was seeing her mother, remembering the first time.
At last he raised his eyes again. "I suppose you know why
they called her the *kaimana*.''

"I looked at files on the court-martial to find your name,''
Kai said.

His gaze remained distant. "From the first moment I saw her, I wanted her. A lot of men did—that's what got her in trouble. But with me it was more than just a casual thing. It's strange, but I can't say for sure that I loved her. What I do remember is that I desired her more than any other woman before or since—and I couldn't imagine there'd ever be a time when I didn't. Like a sailor who'd landed in paradise in a simpler time, I forgot the world I'd come from." He shrugged, then smiled self-consciously, as if suddenly aware these were odd admissions to make to a seventeen-year-old he barely knew, daughter or not. "If I could've stayed there, maybe we'd have been okay. But if you know about the court-martial, you'll understand why I was ordered back to the States right after it ended. The navy brass wanted everything and everyone connected to the case buried, forgotten. I didn't argue about being rotated back to the mainland—wouldn't have made a difference if I did. But I meant it when I said I'd send for her."

"You changed your mind as soon as you got back here." Kai was fighting to cling to her anger. She wanted to hate him, but it was more difficult than she'd expected.

"When I left, I didn't know she was expecting a child."

"If you hadn't cut yourself off from all contact, you might have found out! Even if you knew it was over, why didn't you have the decency to let her know instead of leaving her to guess—"

"Because I wanted to forget!" He raised his voice to match hers. "Because it was a mistake I had to erase the easiest way possible!" A couple of men at the counter rotated on their stools and looked at them. Wyler brought his voice down as he went on, his eyes fixed on Kai in a burning glare. "You want the truth? That's it. Way out in the middle of the ocean, I'd been in a dream where I thought I could marry a beautiful whore and it wouldn't matter. As soon as I was away from her, I woke up."

Kai had no trouble now finding her fury. "Well, wake up to this, Mr. Wyler: you're my father, and I'm not going to let you throw me away, too."

He looked into her eyes, as he had looked at the jurors, gauging their strengths and weaknesses. "Can you be sure you're my daughter? A woman like your mother always had many men."

"Not when she was with you. She loved you. She was faithful."

"There's no proof."

"I *am* the proof. Look at me."

He drained his cup of coffee before observing coolly, "That's not the kind of proof that stands up in a court of law."

All her sympathy was dead. He was talking about fighting her, after all, using the battleground he knew best. For a moment she was overwhelmed by the utter hopelessness that Lokei must have felt when he'd abandoned her. It was no less a turning point now, Kai thought. If she allowed him to deny her, she might never recover from the defeat. In desperation she reached down into a well of cunning she had never tapped before.

Almost as though listening to someone else, she heard herself calmly outline the threat. She had made the acquaintance of a newspaper reporter who had been tremendously curious about her reasons for pursuing Wyler. She had said nothing to him so far, but if and when she did, her story would certainly be printed. Which of course would lead to some backtracking into the history of his service in Hawaii, the cover-up of a military scandal. It wasn't the kind of story that he should want published—if it was true that he planned to run for high political office.

Wyler studied her grimly when she finished. "You got a lot more than her looks, didn't you? You're a fighter, ready to do whatever it takes to win." A smile of grudging admiration crept into his expression. "That's what you got from me."

He told her to finish her eggs, then try some of the apple pie, and he ordered another cup of coffee for himself. There was, he said, a lot more talking they needed to do.

Chapter Nine

Kai woke from a long, deep sleep. She got out of bed and threw open the curtains, letting the sun pour in. Last night, when Wyler had brought her to the hotel, she had been too tired to care what the room looked like. Now she saw it was drab but comfortable. King-sized bed, television, a separate sitting area.

The conversation in the coffee shop had ended with him agreeing to accept her into his life—though the agreement had been reached in an atmosphere of dry negotiation, more like two lawyers hammering out a contract than father and daughter embracing the demands of the heart. She could come and live with him, he said, but he needed a few days before any concrete steps were taken. He had a family—his wife, three children. It wouldn't be the easiest task to throw open this window on his past. He worried about the effect on his wife; women had walked out on husbands for less.

Glancing at a clock set into a night table, Kai saw she had slept through most of the day—it was almost four o'clock. She showered and pulled some clean clothes from her valise, an aqua tank top and a pair of white hip-huggers—island clothes. Wyler had left three hundred dollars in cash on the dresser. She stuck the money in a pocket and left the room.

The hotel was obviously not one of the hubs of convention activity. The lobby was small and shabby, but there was a coffee shop where Kai ate a hamburger before ambling outside. The sun shone in a clear sky, and a breeze was blowing along the street from the lake a few blocks away, a relief from the oppressive summer heat. She came to an intersection with a broad avenue. She could see the sky-scrapers of the Loop in the distance, nearer some low buildings with shining glass fronts that looked like stores. She set out with the idea of shopping, buying some clothes to help her fit into a new life—life in that mansion, behind the gates.

She had gone only a block from the hotel when she heard music coming from a large park across the avenue. She crossed over. Several empty squad cars were pulled up on a grass verge, groups of police standing nearby. Farther into the park, a rock group was performing on an outdoor stage, watched by a large crowd of young people. They sang along with the music, some clapping rhythmically. Here and there, couples were dancing.

As Kai walked among them, she felt enveloped in an amazing atmosphere of camaraderie. It wasn't like walking into a crowd of strangers so much as entering a party where she knew everyone. Her eyes met glances from other girls and young men, and they smiled in greeting. Friendly voices came at her. "Hey babe . . . welcome, sister . . . c'mon over here and stay a while." She smiled back and kept moving through spaces in the crowd until she was near the stage.

The rock group finished performing and were sent off with tumultuous cheers. A blues singer took the stage and did the current Ray Charles hit, "Crying Time," introducing it with the remark: "It'll be crying time in America as long as we're in Vietnam."

Kai forgot about shopping. Between singers there were speeches, some of them impassioned diatribes against the war, some funny and irreverent. The crowd roared with laughter when a young man named Abbie with straggly hair announced that the piglet he was holding in his arms would run as the presidential candidate of his "Youth International Party"—otherwise known as the Yippies.

The sun sank lower and floodlights were turned on. The crowd swelled, blankets were spread. Along with the shared political views and enjoyment uniting the crowd, there was something else in the air, a defiant pride in the right to express opinions.

But as night fell, another element entered the atmosphere, an intangible electric tingle. Looking around, Kai saw many more police cars pulled up onto the grass at the rear of the crowd. Their headlights were on, forming a fence of light. Kai's pulse quickened.

"You can leave, you know," said a girl standing behind

her. "No law says you have to stay and let the cops kick your butt."

Kai turned around. "You talking to me?"

"Yeah, you. Looked to me like you were starting to get uptight," the girl said. "And you don't seem cut out for getting your head cracked."

For a moment Kai was lost in staring at the girl, unquestionably the most amazing creature she had ever seen. To start with, her eyes were so wide and intensely blue that they were almost like the eyes of a cartoon figure. Their size was emphasized by thick mascara on the lashes and eyebrows that had been plucked down to pencil lines. The startling eyes were set off all the more by pale skin and yellow-blond hair hacked short in a waifish style that had surely been done by her own hand. Her mouth was small, the lips thin, but made to stand out with shocking pink lipstick. She was five or six inches shorter than Kai, but had a voluptuous, perfectly proportioned body evident under a tie-dyed polo shirt and striped Oshkosh overalls with broad straps. Pin-on metal buttons of every size and description covered the straps—some from old election campaigns for Truman and Hoover, some that were tourist souvenirs from Niagara Falls and the Eiffel Tower. The trousers of the overalls had been scissored off to the tops of her thighs, revealing legs surprisingly long and shapely given her height. On her feet were army surplus field boots that had been whitewashed, then painted over with rainbow stripes. The picture was completed by a blood red ribbon tied into a bow around an upright hank of hair standing atop her head like a sheaf of wheat.

Kai found her voice. "I didn't think *anyone* was particularly suited to getting hit on the head," she said.

"Well, some of us have been through the wars. We know how to put ourselves on the line without getting totally screwed."

"Maybe you should tell me," Kai said. She felt challenged by the girl's braggadocio to show her own courage rather than slink away.

The girl moved in front of Kai and brazenly eyed her up down. "I dunno," she said. "I've had my eye on you a while, and I get the feeling you'd be a lot better off going home."

Kai smiled ironically as she reflected that she had no home. "I'm as much in favor of ending the war as anyone else," she said. "I'm not going to be scared into running if staying could make a difference."

The girl gravely studied Kai another second, then a smile broke across her face. "Hey, you're all right," she said. "My name's Sylvie. What's yours?"

"Kai."

"Pegged you right, didn't I? This is the first time you've been to a demo."

"And you're right that I'm scared," Kai confessed. "Do you think the police might really break this up?"

"Yeah, they'll come at us now that it's getting dark. Tonight could be worse than last night."

"But all we're doing is singing and having a good time."

"That's what they hate about us most," Sylvie said. "They keep coming at us, and we're still here, still having fun. Makes 'em feel weak and ridiculous. Not all the cops are bad—hell, they're only human—we just bring out the worst in the ones that are, because we're young and they're fat, miserable, and horny." She slapped Kai on the arm. "Stick with me, though, and you'll be okay. Like any war, you can survive if you know the tricks."

The exchange with Sylvie simultaneously boosted Kai's fear and her resolve to take a stand. She felt slightly less anxious after Sylvie ran through a few detailed strategies for protecting herself from the worst elements of a police assault. The police would almost certainly use tear gas to clear the park, Sylvie warned. "If they do, remember, breathe through your mouth, and don't panic. The worst thing you can do is run, 'cause that makes you breathe harder and you'll get more gas. Your eyes will start to water, but for chrissakes, don't rub them, that'll make it ten times as bad." Sylvie produced a jar of Vaseline from the pouch pocket of her overalls. "I've got some of this in case the cops start spraying Mace. That burns your skin, but if you rub a little grease on your face and arms, it protects you."

There were still performers getting up on stage, songs being sung, speeches being given. While Kai and Sylvie stood together listening, they began trading stories about what had brought them to Chicago.

From the details Sylvie supplied about her life, Kai per-

ceived that the anti-war movement had filled a vacuum left
by the failure of more routine elements in her existence—
family, school, romantic attachments. Her full name was
Sylvie Tremblay—French in origin because her father had
been a French Canadian logger. Her mother, who came from
northern Vermont, had taken work as a cook in a Canadian
logging camp across the border, and had become pregnant
by one of the lumberjacks. The couple had stayed together
until Sylvie's father died in a logging accident twelve years
ago. From the age of nine, she had been raised solely by
her mother, who eked out a living with jobs in local short-
order restaurants when not incapacitated by alcohol. Six
years ago, Sylvie had dropped out of school to go to New
York City with an older boyfriend who dreamed of becoming an actor. The boyfriend had received a draft notice, and
Sylvie had started drifting.

"Some girls follow the rock groups around," she said.
"Me, I became a peace groupie. The life's pretty much the
same. You meet a lot of cool guys, go new places, and all
for a good cause."

"So this is all you do?" Kai asked. "Travel around to
demonstrations?"

"It's been a pretty busy spring and summer. I hitched to
California when Bobby Kennedy was running in the primary. That was a real high—till he got shot. Then I went
to the demos in Miami at the Republican Convention. In
between, I hang out wherever I am. I can always get work
waiting tables. Often as not, I'll hook up with a guy. Met
a cute one last night, stayed in his tent down on the beach.
Jesus, he was one of the best fucks I had this summer . . .
but he's gone, the scene scared him. Goes to show, huh? A
guy can have a big dick and still be a chickenshit weasel."

Kai didn't know whether to admire Sylvie or feel sorry
for her. She seemed brave and resourceful and good-hearted,
but also lost. In Sylvie, Kai saw the kind of rootless life
that would threaten her, too, if she wasn't given a home
with Wyler.

"What about you and guys?" Sylvie asked. "With your
looks, they must be crawling all over you."

Kai was slow to reply. She wasn't embarrassed to admit
her lack of experience, but she just didn't want to get into
the subject of sex. Before she could even say something

noncommittal, however, a loud scream came from somewhere in the darkness, then angry shouts rose from all corners of the park:

"They're coming!" "Rotten pigs!" "It's gas!"

Now Kai heard the rumble of engines from the cars and jeeps moving across the grass, their headlight beams catching the startled looks of faces in the crowd. Tear-gas canisters began to rain down among the demonstrators.

Sylvie dug the jar of Vaseline out of her pocket, scooped out a dollop with her fingers, and thrust the jar at Kai. "Get some of that on fast," she said as she started slathering her face and arms.

Nearby a young man cried out in pain as the one of the tear-gas projectiles glanced off his shoulder and rolled across the ground. Kai started toward him to offer help, but in the next second a plume of acrid smoke billowed up around her. She was immobilized by a powerful burning sensation in her eyes and nose and lungs. *Don't panic,* she told herself, remembering Sylvie's instructions. Through tearing eyes she peered into the thickening cloud of smoke.

"Sylvie?" Her call was lost among a hundred others, people crying names, directions, warnings. "Sylvie?" Kai screamed louder.

"Over here!"

Coughing and choking, Kai stumbled toward the voice. She thought of the boy who'd been injured by the tear-gas canister, and looked back in that direction, but she could see nothing except shadowy figures running through smoke.

She collided with someone.

"Kai, that you?"

"Yes."

"Grab my hand, I'll get us out of here."

Hands clasped, they moved in a direction where the smoke seemed less dense. The cries of those still in the thick of it fell farther behind, and the air became easier to breathe.

Then suddenly, as if they had merely circled blindly around, new shouts of panic and agony rose up ahead of them. A phalanx of policemen wearing riot gear charged into the crowd in a terrifying wave, swinging their truncheons like ringmasters at a circus cracking their whips at wild animals.

"Jesus," Sylvie said fearfully, "it's never been this bad."

Ahead, Kai saw the looming figures with their helmets and windmilling batons moving through the crowd. She tried to steer away from them, but they were everywhere, ghostly figures silhouetted against the haze of gas that seemed to glow from the headlights shining at the edge of the park. Kai threw up her arms to protect her head and caught a blow on her forearm. She expected other blows to follow. When none came, she glanced up and saw that the wave of police had rolled past like an unstoppable tornado.

Then she realized Sylvie wasn't standing next to her. Kai peered through the smoke, unable to keep herself from rubbing her stinging eyes, making the torment worse. Now she saw Sylvie crumpled on the ground a few feet away. Dropping to her knees beside her, Kai gasped in horror as she saw blood oozing through the blond hair and running down the front of Sylvie's face. Her eyes were open, but she was obviously dazed.

". . . fucking bastards . . ." Sylvie whimpered.

"C'mon, I'll get you out of here," Kai said. She was strong enough to lift the smaller girl to her feet and support her as they continued out of the park. Everyone was scattering now, pausing only to aid the injured.

"Look at that," Sylvie said, "look how much they made us bleed." And then she laughed. "They blew it, Kai! Fucking cops made us bleed too much. It'll take a while to sink in, but I think we're the winners!" She laughed again, then shoved away Kai's supporting arm. "It's okay, I can walk."

Kai let go reluctantly. "Your head looks bad. I'll take you to an emergency room."

"No!"

"But you probably need stitches and X rays and—"

"No hospitals!" Sylvie screamed. Then in a pathetic little-girl whine, she added, "Please . . ."

"Okay," Kai placated her. "My hotel's nearby."

Under ordinary circumstances, the hotel management would have stopped any guest seen bringing a bloody companion to a room. But there was nothing ordinary about tonight. Though the hotel was small and away from the avenue, by the time Kai and Sylvie entered the lobby, a number of other injured demonstrators were already there using the washrooms and telephones.

In her room, Kai made Sylvie comfortable on the bed, then soaked a couple of towels in cold water and washed the wound. Once the blood was blotted away, Kai could see a two-inch split in the scalp.

"You need stitches," Kai said firmly.

"Last time I'll say it, Kai. I'm not going to any fucking hospital. I'd rather die, I mean it." There was no mistaking the intensity of Sylvie's conviction.

"Okay," Kai said. "But I'd better go and buy antiseptics and bandages so I can take care of this properly."

On the way out of the hotel to look for a pharmacy, she checked the message desk. Even if Wyler had said it would be several days before he could resolve the problem of absorbing her into his life, she expected him to keep in contact. But there was no message.

Kai wrestled with the thought that Wyler might have moved out of reach again. A few hundred dollars, a room for a couple of nights, perhaps it was only a payoff. Right now he might be positioning himself to deny anything she could say to a newspaper reporter.

When Kai returned to the room, Sylvie was no longer stretched out atop the bedspread. She had shucked all her clothes into a mound on the floor, and gotten under the covers on one side of the king-size bed. Her eyes were closed, and she was breathing deeply, though slightly unevenly, as if being chased in a dream. Kai shook her gently, testing for a response.

Sylvie's eyes fluttered open; she looked at Kai and smiled. "Hope you don't mind," she murmured. "Such a big bed."

Kai shook her head and let Sylvie drift off again.

As she finished bandaging Sylvie's wound, Kai thought through the incredible events of the past twenty-four hours. She hadn't just located her father, she had found other pieces of herself that she hadn't known existed until now. She had taken a stand as a matter of principle. She had reached out to help this stranger, who had moved right into her bed.

It should have reassured her that she could handle anything that might happen in the days ahead. But she wondered how she would manage if Wyler didn't call.

And if he did—if she had to claim a place for herself within his family—would that be any easier to endure?

* * *

Sylvie was apparently suffering from a minor concussion. As soon as she rose in the morning, she felt dizzy and collapsed to her knees. Kai helped her to the bathroom, then back into bed.

When Kai suggested once more that Sylvie should really be in a hospital, Sylvie begged tearfully to stay. Then she told Kai the story that explained her terror of hospitalization. At the age of fourteen she had become pregnant by a boy in high school and had sought help from a rural doctor who was known to give back-room abortions. The treatment had led to a life-threatening infection, so Sylvie's mother had put her in a hospital.

"When the doctors figured out what caused my problem," Sylvie said, "the jerks told my mother. Thought she had a right to know. Well, as soon as the damn doctors told her, she went berserk. Came to my ward and started beating the shit out of me. Right there—in front of nurses, patients. A couple of interns pulled her off pretty fast. But that wasn't the end of it. She got the idea I should be—whattaya call it?—sterilized. Not just so I couldn't have kids, but so I wouldn't want sex, wouldn't feel it. She was taking all the doctors and interns aside, asking if they'd do the operation—offering them money. I found out from one of the interns. After I'd been in the hospital a few days, I was fucking him. He'd take me out of the ward to give me examinations, supposedly, but we'd go at it, then he'd tuck me back in bed. Anyway, I got scared shitless when I heard about my mother wanting to take care of me like I was nothing more than a cat. I thought maybe she had the power to get it done on her say-so. I ran away right after they let me go home, but I still can't get over this crazy fear that she might catch up to me someday—that maybe some kind of order has gone out to all the hospitals in the world to cut everything out of me if I ever give them a chance."

Kai willingly nursed Sylvie through the rest of the day. They spent time talking over meals ordered from room service, or while watching television. In the middle of the day the TV news programs began reporting that the Loomis trial had ended with a verdict of not guilty, and there were short interviews with Wyler and his client.

"So that's the sonofabitch," Sylvie said when Wyler appeared on the screen. Kai had told her about the search for her father. "Well, he's gorgeous, I'll give him that."

"He's off-limits!" Kai scolded, only half joking. The hospital story and other episodes Sylvie told from her life made it obvious that she had no inhibitions about sex, and no man was off-limits. Sylvie could hardly talk about anything—her travels, the jobs she'd held, the hometown she'd left—without referring to all the men she'd slept with in every place she'd passed through. Football players in high school, teachers, men who'd been her mother's boyfriends, waiters at restaurants where she'd worked, peace activists she'd met on the marches—married or unmarried. The list was endless.

But now Sylvie reassured Kai. "Hey, you're a friend. You'll never have to worry about me around anyone who belongs to you."

In any case, Kai wondered if Sylvie would ever meet Randall Wyler. More than a full day had passed since she had last seen him, and there had been no call.

Late in the afternoon, Kai traveled to the Greyhound bus terminal and fetched a large backpack with Sylvie's belongings from a locker. After a day of talking, Sylvie was no longer merely an acquaintance in need, but a friend. Sylvie was twenty-two years old, but the difference in ages wasn't a barrier between them. Yet because of her own fear of the power of sex, Kai was both fascinated and repelled by Sylvie's tales of constant sexual encounters. And when, over a room-service supper, Kai admitted she was a virgin, she inspired no less amazement in Sylvie.

"Holy shit!" Sylvie said, dropping her club sandwich back onto the plate. "Jesus, Kai, you could have any guy you want, any time. What's wrong with you? You're seventeen already, for chrissakes. I started years before that."

Kai gave a sheepish shrug.

"Look, being a virgin isn't the worst thing in the world," Sylvie went on apologetically. 'It's how we all start out. But, hey, isn't the suspense killing you? Aren't you dying to know how it feels?'

Kai smiled. "I can wait."

"Waiting for Prince Charming, huh? Well, I believed in it, too, back when I was reading fairy tales. But I gave that up a long time ago. I'd go batty if I couldn't get laid regular as clockwork.''

Her reluctance had nothing to do with Prince Charming, Kai confessed, as she opened up to Sylvie about the many factors that had turned her off sex.

Sylvie listened, wanting to be sympathetic, but her perspective was so different it was hard for her to understand Kai's problem. ''Hell,'' she said, ''there's nothing so terrible about what you saw that guy doing to your mom. I've let guys tie me up, Kai. It's a kick. You should try it sometime—well, I mean, once you get started.'' And when Kai told about being attacked by Lew Parkes, Sylvie said, ''Look, maybe he was really trying to help loosen you up. You know, Kai, you've gotta get over the idea that a guy must be a rat if you turn him on. You, especially, 'cause you're gonna walk through this world turning 'em on like a string of Christmas lights. Maybe you don't know it, but you're sexy as hell—probably the sexiest woman I ever saw.''

Kai blushed.

Sylvie went on, ''It's—it's like some people have a good singing voice, or they know how to paint. You've got this thing, Kai, this appeal. It's one of the reasons I started talking to you in the park. Hell, I'm not a guy, but even I can feel it.''

''But I don't want it,'' Kai said, agitated. ''It's *not* like having a talent. It's nothing to be proud of, nothing I'd ever want to use.''

Sylvie shook her head sympathetically. ''Poor kid. All this time everybody's worried about war and peace, and you've been fighting a war inside yourself. You can't change what you are, Kai. If you're sexy, you might as well make peace with it.''

''Like you do?'' Kai said, lashing out defensively. ''By getting into bed with every man you meet?''

Sylvie smiled ruefully. ''For me, that is making peace with myself. I don't fight what I am, and I don't hate myself for it. There are plenty worse things than being a nymphomaniac.''

''A what?'' Kai had never heard the word before.

''Nymphomaniac. Somebody's who's lucky enough to want sex all the time.''

"That's not my idea of lucky," Kai remarked.

"I suppose it wouldn't be mine, either, if I couldn't get laid when I want to. But I've got no complaints."

It was a difference between them they both recognized as unbridgable. Yet they realized, too, that there were similarities that bonded them—their fractured childhoods, growing up without fathers, being raised by mothers who'd been overwhelmed by their own problems. By the end of the day, after Sylvie had dozed off and Kai got into the big bed, she felt she wasn't merely lying down with a friend—they were really too different to be friends. Somehow Sylvie seemed more like a sister.

When Kai woke the next morning, Sylvie was already out of bed. Kai found her in the bathroom, in front of the mirror finishing off a haircut she was giving herself with a nail scissors.

"How do you like the new look?" she asked.

Kai stared. The central feature of the haircut was an island of white scalp that had been neatly clipped in a circle around Sylvie's head wound. Several other islands of scalp were scattered in the sea of blond hair—a triangle, a square, and a couple of five-pointed stars. Covering her injury was a fresh gauze bandage on which she had drawn a peace symbol with her pink lipstick.

"It suits you," Kai said, not merely being kind. There was something about this blond gamin with the wide blue eyes that allowed her to carry off even the most bizarre get-up, so she looked only more adorable and vulnerable. Though Kai said nothing about it, she noticed that a *muu-muu* pulled from her valise was part of Sylvie's new look.

They spent the day together again, but not in the room this time. "I've got my battle wounds," Sylvie said. "I'm entitled to some rest and recreation." In any case, the demonstrations were winding down. Hubert Humphrey had been nominated at the convention the night before; busloads of demoralized peace activists were already leaving town.

After breakfast they went shopping along the Magnificent Mile, Chicago's downtown collection of fine stores. "I'm only doing this for you, Kai," Sylvie said with a mock sacrificial air. "I can't afford to buy anything. But you've still got daddy's cash—and you need clothes!"

"I have things to wear."

"Not the right things," Sylvie declared.

Based on the wild outfits she had seen in Sylvie's wardrobe, she imagined that what she had meant could include anything from tie-dyed prison stripes to a circus trapeze-artist's costume. To the contrary, Sylvie said that what Kai needed were some demure, "serious" clothes to help her fit more easily into her father's home.

"You've got to make a good impression," Sylvie said. "And your new family's in the upper crust, from what you say. You can't walk around looking like a beachcomber anymore."

"Right now I'm not sure I should spend a nickle to look right for them. My father hasn't called, Syl, and maybe that's for the best. I wanted to find him because I thought it would mean something that I came from him. But it doesn't, really. Not if he wants to cut me off. It has no more meaning that he's my father than . . . than if one of the men you slept with in the last couple of months made you pregnant."

"Bite your tongue!"

"I'm just saying it's nothing but an accident. I understand why my mother didn't want to tell me his name. She knew what I'd do once I had it—and she wanted to save me the trouble."

"You talk as if you're ready to forgive this man," Sylvie observed, "let bygones by bygones, give up the fight. Kai, there's nothing you want from him that he doesn't owe you."

"And I started out thinking I'd do anything to collect. I even blackmailed him, sort of, threatening to tell my story to the papers. But it's not worth it. Even if he takes me home, that's only half the battle. I'll still have to win over his family."

They arrived in front of the splendid rococo exterior of Carson Pirie Scott, the grand old department store that had stood at the center of Chicago's shopping district since the turn of the century.

"Get the clothes," Sylvie insisted. "Because I'd bet my favorite pair of boots that daddy's gonna take you home."

"What makes you so sure?"

"The political thing. A story about turning his back on

his child for almost twenty years would look pretty bad if you were still out on the street.''

"He might just shut me out, deny everything.''

Sylvie shook her head. ''You're not thinking like a politician, kiddo. His best bet is to take you in, say you were kept away from him by your mother, and now that you need him, he's thrilled to have you. Make it a real sob story and get a lot of good publicity. What's more, you'll look great standing up behind him on the campaign trail. Oh yeah, baby,'' she concluded. ''He'll take you home any day.''

At the end of the afternoon, after wending their way through Scott, Marshall Field, and several boutiques along the Magnificent Mile, they returned to the hotel in a taxi. Two hundred and eighty dollars—spent from the cash given her by Wyler—wasn't an immense sum, but Sylvie was a shrewd shopper who'd shown Kai how to stretch the money to the limit. The haul included three dresses, a suit, a couple of good silk blouses, nylons, Kai's first pair of heels, and a pair of saddle shoes—Sylvie's idea of what polite society girls wore in the daytime. In spite of her own outrageous taste, Sylvie had sound instincts about which clothes offered the most understated elegance at the best price. Kai had rewarded Sylvie's help by treating her to something from Marshall Field—a fluffy pink angora sweater. They were in high spirits as they entered the hotel with their armloads of boxes.

When Kai stopped to pick up her room key at the front desk, the clerk also handed her a message slip. Only a phone number was noted on the slip.

"What'd I tell you!'' Sylvie said. ''This is it.''

From the room, Kai phoned the number. She was answered by the switchboard at Dawes, Lybrandt and Wyler. After giving her name, Kai was put through to another line.

"Miss Tattoo,'' said a woman, mauling the Hawaiian music in Kai's name, ''I'm speaking for Randall Wyler. A car will pick you up at the hotel at six o'clock.''

Receiving her instructions secondhand, Kai felt she might as well have been a client receiving a communication about a contract. It canceled any joy she would have expected to feel at going to join her father.

She collected her belongings and changed into one of the afternoon's purchases, an apple green shirtwaist with a scoop neck. There was still eighteen dollars left from the money Wyler had given her, and she insisted Sylvie take it. The room was also paid up for another night; Sylvie could stay. Kai wrote out Wyler's home phone number and made Sylvie promise to stay in touch. Then they went down to the lobby together to wait.

"What about you?" Kai asked. "Where are you going next?"

"I'll stay around here if I can find a job."

"Maybe I could get you something at the law firm."

"Forget it. I don't own a thing I could wear to an office and I don't want to. By the way, can I keep this moo-thing as a souvenir of our time together?"

"*Muu-muu,*" Kai said. "Sure. But don't talk as if we're never going to see each other again."

"I wouldn't fit in too well with the North Side crowd."

"Then neither will I."

Sylvie gave her a long look. "No, Kai, you'll do fine. Just hang in."

A bellhop interrupted to inform Kai that a car was waiting for her outside. He picked up Kai's valise and packages, and preceded her out to the sidewalk.

Sylvie followed along. They both stopped to stare when they saw a chauffeur in maroon livery taking the packages from the bellhop to load them into the rear of a silver-gray Rolls-Royce. "Wow," Sylvie said, "you struck gold."

They embraced, and the chauffeur opened the rear door for Kai. "Take care of your head," she said to Sylvie.

"And watch out for your heart," Sylvie answered.

Kai looked out the rear window at Sylvie until the car turned a corner. She was sorry their time together had been cut short.

Kai turned to survey the plush interior of the car. Yes, it seemed she had struck gold. Yet she didn't feel lucky. She longed for a home, a father. But Randall Wyler wasn't taking her in because he cared to provide either.

Chapter Ten

Election-night parties at the Wyler house were a tradition, famous for the best food and champagne, and for being the place to make the best connections. Memories of past parties were especially good since the movers and shakers who came were all Democrats—no sense being anything else in Mayor Daley's Chicago—and their party had won the last two presidential elections.

Tonight the champagne and food were as good as ever, but the memories were going to be something else. From each of the eight television sets rented for the evening and placed around the downstairs rooms of the Wyler mansion, news anchormen were heard reporting early computer predictions that Richard Milhous Nixon was going to be the thirty-seventh president of the United States.

A collective groan rose from the large group of guests around the television in the living room. Alexandra Wyler stepped to the console and turned down the volume. "Enough of this depressing bullshit!" she declared. "This can still be a hell of a party if we just pretend it's New Year's Eve—anything but election night."

"But my god, Alex," cried one elegantly gowned woman. "Four years of Tricky Dicky. It's not so much his politics that bother me, it's those suits he wears. Can we trust this man to run the country if he can't even find a good tailor?"

The crowd laughed.

"Listen, all of you," Alex Wyler called out. "I've still got plenty of the best champagne in town—"

"I'll bet!" a man shouted. "Left over from one of those truckloads your father got from Capone."

More laughs.

"Hell, no! That's so good I'm saving it for Randy's victory party in two years. Meanwhile, there's plenty of the good French stuff for drowning your sorrows.''

Alex moved away from the TV watchers. She beckoned over one of the waiters circulating with trays of champagne, exchanged her empty glass for a full one, and pointed him toward other guests running low on liquid cheer. Giving a good party was one of the talents on which Alex prided herself—along with her good taste, her knack for bringing interesting people together, and an ability in general to spend her considerable wealth generously on herself. Until recently, too, she had felt a justifiable pride in knowing that she was almost always the most striking woman in any gathering. Though she kept herself very thin, it suited the planes of her face, high cheekbones, straight narrow nose, and a sculpted chin. Her eyes, the golden amber of a wheat field, were complimented by her ivory skin and chestnut hair with its reddish highlights. Tonight her coloring was set off by a Givenchy straight classic gown of silk chiffon in carnation red, and a matching ruby and diamond necklace and bracelet. She had dressed with the conviction that this was a night to shine—though not because it would conclude the presidential campaign, but because it would launch her husband's career in politics. If everything stayed on track, in two years he would be a U.S. Senator—and that would be only the beginning. When Alex Wyler looked ahead, she could see all the way to the inauguration ball at the White House and years of state dinners where she would reign as First Lady.

It was to serve this dream that, when Randy had unveiled the vile news about this *daughter* of his who'd dropped out of nowhere, Alex had spent no more than two days fuming and mulling over a divorce action before giving her husband a green light to take the girl under his wing. She quickly recognized that slamming the door on Kaiulani Teiatu—Kai "Wyler," as she would henceforth be known—would leave everyone out in the cold, herself included, while there were benefits to be reaped from appearing generous and benevolent.

None of which changed the fact that Alex already bitterly resented Kai. How else was she supposed to feel? Alex had never been told until the girl turned up in Chicago that, at the time Randall Wyler was courting her and *marrying* her after his return from service in Hawaii, he was already the husband of an Hawaiian woman left behind on the orders of his superiors.

Seventeen years ago, when she had met Randall Wyler on a mild autumn night at a gala charity ball, it had been the start of a whirlwind courtship. By June that dance had led to the biggest society wedding of the season. Alexandra's father, Lionel Dawes, was acknowledged to be Chicago's foremost lawyer, counsel to the giant meat packers, to Marshall Field, and dozens of other major corporations. During Prohibition, Dawes had been one of several young lawyers who earned their daily bread keeping Al Capone and his men out of jail, but he had catapulted himself to respectability by marrying the daughter of a surgeon with society credentials, and extricating himself from shady work. It was only natural, when his own daughter chose a lawyer for her husband, that Dawes should invite Randall Wyler to become an associate at Dawes & Lybrandt. Wyler had soon proven himself a valuable addition, quickly earning his partnership. When Lionel Dawes had died nine years ago, he had left fourteen million dollars to his daughter, Alexandra, and had left leadership of his firm in the hands of his son-in-law. Without question, it was Randall Wyler's marriage that had launched his meteoric rise in the legal profession and brought him a life of consummate comfort.

At first Alexandra had never doubted that Randall's love for her was sincere. But several years into the marriage, as passion had cooled and friends started hinting to Alex that her husband was sleeping with other women, she looked back to their beginnings and saw how neatly she had fitted into his plan to snare a wife who would guarantee his future. It was a wound to her pride, but not a fatal one. After all, she was satisfied with her own end of the deal. She had her children. She had an enviably attractive husband whose achievements gave her a special status in the community. She had the satisfaction of knowing that her wealth would permit her to reclaim her independence anytime she wanted. And if Randall was going to have himself a fine time fucking whomever he pleased, then there was no reason why she couldn't do the same.

But her adjustment to the situation had been given a jolt last summer when Kai had arrived. Although Alex understood that Randy had seized on her as "a good catch," she hadn't dismissed the notion that he had also been attracted to her, loved her—at least in the beginning. Now, knowing he had lied from the start—had kept the secret of another wife, and a love child—gave a much darker shading to his opportunism.

But again Alexandra adjusted. She longed for nothing so much as a chance to move beyond the narrow sphere of influence of the Chicago elite to the wider arena of national and international power. These ambitions, tied as they were to her husband's, could not be served by rejecting Kai. As she had said to Randy, "When election time comes around, you'll be far better off with a half-breed in the family than a skeleton in the closet."

So she had accepted Kai into her household. But not without conditions. "Just keep her away from me," Alex raged at her husband the night before Kai arrived. "I'll let her live here; I know why it makes sense. But I don't want a damn thing to do with her. She's yours, Randy, all yours. You take care of her, and keep her out of my way."

Alex made the household arrangements so that she would have as little to do with the girl as possible. The bedroom given to Kai was not in the existing family wing, but in another corner of the vast house, where the servants slept. And Alex made every effort to keep her own three children separated from Kai as much as possible. It wasn't difficult to arrange. The teenage boy and girl had their own friends, and could be kept busy with their lessons and other activities. The three-year-old girl, Vanessa, had a nanny who was instructed to keep the child away from "Mr. Wyler's girl." However, as far as anyone outside the family knew, Kai was welcomed and loved.

Surveying the election-night crowd around her, returning the smiles and greetings of her guests, Alex felt content with the choice she had made. These wealthy Chicagoans would be Randy's backers when the time came. It did no harm if they saw him as a sentimental family man with a marriage strong enough to withstand an unexpected shock.

Alex spotted Tony Banks as he moved away from one of the TV sets and touched a match to one of the enormous Havana cigars that was always protruding from the corner of his mouth. A heavyset man with the look of a professional wrestler, Banks was a powerful political wheeler-dealer who had been involved in many of the decisions that had given the state of Illinois to John Kennedy in 1960, and to Johnson in 1964. He had sat this one out, though, convinced that Humphrey was bound to lose. Alex hurried over as Banks shook out the match. Knowing that he was the sort of man who might let a match fall to the rug rather than look for an ashtray, she held out her palm.

Banks dropped the match into it and laughed. "Always in the right place at the right time, aren't you, Allie?"

"For the little things, Tony, maybe not the big ones. The right place tonight may not be here but Nixon headquarters."

"Nah, I'll bet the champagne over there is the cheap California stuff. I like it better here."

Alex lifted her glass as if toasting his good taste, and took a sip. "Have you made up your mind yet?" She and Randy had approached Banks six months ago about running the Wyler for Senator campaign, starting with the primaries.

Banks eyed her shrewdly. "Don't let any grass grow, do ya?"

"There's a Republican moving back into the White House, Tony. Making it all the more important to keep the other side strong on Capitol Hill. The sooner we go to work the better."

Banks was still studying her. "Who wants this more, I wonder—you or Randy?"

"No question about it," Alex said tartly. "I do."

He laughed, his large stomach shaking behind his tight plaid cummerbund. "Well, I've got good news for you, sweetheart. I'm taking the job. You know what made up my mind? Coming here tonight . . . and getting a good look at that." He glanced toward a portal opening to the entrance foyer. Kai was clearly visible seated on a step halfway up the broad central staircase.

When Alexandra turned in Kai's direction, she had to fight against an angry urge to bolt rudely away from Banks. For she could see that her six-year-old, Vanessa, was curled up asleep in Kai's lap.

"In political terms she's solid gold," Banks explained. "Leaving aside that she's a knockout, there's this Hawaiian connection. Exotic blood in the family would've been a no-

no with a lot of voters ten years back. But now Hawaii's a state—brothers under the flag and all that crap. On top of which, the girl doesn't really look foreign. Any way we play it, we'll get some good mileage out of her.'' The big man took a puff on his cigar. ''You want to break the good news to Randy or should I?''

''You do it,'' Alex said. ''And tell him your ideas about the . . . about his daughter. He'll be interested.''

Banks started away, then stopped. ''Oh, Allie, you haven't forgotten our deal. . . .''

After making the first approach to Banks with Randy, Alex had gone back to see him on her own. To tempt him away from running any rival campaigns in 1970, she had promised him a $200,000 bonus if Randy was elected senator. ''I haven't forgotten, Tony.''

He blew a smoke ring and went off to look for his new client.

Alex pushed through the milling crowd and climbed the stairs to where Kai sat, cradling the sleeping girl in a nightgown. ''Vanessa should be in bed,'' Alex said, glaring at Kai.

''She heard all the noise and came down. I was just going to bring her back upstairs.''

''I'll do it, thank you.'' Alex reminded herself not to sound too severe. There were too many people within earshot. ''You stay here and enjoy yourself.''

Alexandra's arms remained extended until Kai stood and handed the sleeping child into them. ''Good,'' Alexandra said curtly. ''Now go and say *aloha* to my guests. Show everyone how sweet and pretty you are.'' Alexandra moved up the stairs carrying her little daughter.

Kai went downstairs to mingle. She didn't enjoy playing the part that was expected of her. ''Yes, you do have to be there,'' her father had insisted earlier when she had asked about being absent from the election-night party. ''These people expect to see my family around me—to know we stand together. That's an asset in a campaign.''

An asset. Kai couldn't count the times she had heard herself referred to that way since coming to live with Mr. and Mrs. Randall Wyler. Sylvie's predictions had been smack on target. Wyler had done nothing to cover up the story of a daughter materializing out of nowhere. He had just tin-

kered a bit with the facts to make himself out to be a hero
instead of a heel. In the version given to newspapers by
Wyler's public-relations advisers, Kai was described as his
child by a brief, unhappy marriage consummated in Hawaii
during his military service at the time of the Korean War.
The child's mother had received custody and prevented
communication between father and daughter ever since, but
she was an unstable woman who had committed suicide. As
soon as Wyler learned of the tragedy, he had brought his
daughter to Chicago. The story of their heartwarming reunion had been featured in all the Chicago papers and in
segments on local TV news programs. The evening that
Wyler's chauffeur had picked her up at the hotel, the camera
crews had been waiting in front of the Wyler house to record
Kai's arrival.

Since that night Kai hadn't stopped playing the role expected of her. Lately, she was photographed often, even
when she wasn't in Wyler's company. Her beauty had made
her a popular subject for the free-lancers who provided shots
to fill the feature pages on slow news days. Often they hung
around the entrance to the private high school where she
had been sent to complete her diploma. Tonight she was
being snapped by cameramen who were making rounds of
election-night parties to get pictures for tomorrow's society
pages. Though Kai usually dressed for school to disappoint
them, wearing shabby clothes and hats with broad peaks
that hid her face, she was being cooperative tonight. Wyler
had given her five hundred dollars to shop for a dress and
shoes specifically for the party, instructing her to buy something "glamorous" that would show off her legs. At Fields
she had picked out a trim black sequined sheath with a high
side slit.

On her progress through the rooms, Kai was stopped repeatedly by people who introduced themselves as friends
and admirers of Randall Wyler's. They told her how moved
they had been by the story of her reunion with her father,
asked how she was making the adjustment to life in Chicago, and praised her beauty. Many suggested she try modeling; some freely offered to use their connections to help
her.

Kai's experience behind the desk of the Crater Inn had
trained her well in making pleasant small talk. She left ev-

eryone with the opinion that she was charming and poised, and content in her new surroundings. But she had to grit her teeth through the lies. Content, adjusted? The hostility directed at her by her stepmother made each day a torment. She hadn't expected their relationship to be easily established, but it was clear from Alexandra Wyler's deliberate cruelties that the gap between them would never be bridged.

With her father the situation was better, if hardly ideal. Consumed by his work during the day and many evenings, whisked off to dinner parties or other society events on any free night, he was rarely available to any of his children. His relationship with Kai was politely cordial, but there had yet to be any real warmth or affection. Once or twice he had put an arm around her shoulder while introducing her to a friend, a possible political ally—but he had yet to give her an embrace, a kiss on the cheek, or sit down alone with her and try mending some fences. At times Kai blamed herself for having forced herself on the family from the start. And there were days when she was ready to surrender the dream of winning her father's love, to simply leave his house. Then she would remember the admonition Sylvie continued to repeat whenever they got together: there wasn't a thing Kai wanted from her father that he didn't owe her.

And something totally unexpected had happened—a strong attachment had developed between herself and little Vanessa. Alexandra had done everything possible to discourage any closeness, but the child kept coming to Kai. Vanessa was bright, sweet-tempered, and affectionate. It was easy for Kai to love her little half sister. There was a natural affinity between them. Vanessa had been born late in Wyler's second marriage, a decade after the older children. Separated by that gap in age, the younger child felt isolated, and little was done by the rest of the family to soothe that loneliness. Kai suspected that Vanessa's conception had been an accident; she wasn't truly wanted, any more than Kai had been.

A photographer stopped in front of her and raised his camera, then started waggling one hand, urging someone else closer into the frame. Turning, Kai saw her father moving up beside her along with a large man chomping on a cigar.

"Kai," said Wyler, "shake hands with Tony Banks."

Kai's hand felt dwarfed in Banks's huge paw.

"Pleasure," he said. "Mind if we take a picture together?"

Wyler seconded the request with a nod. "Fine with me," Kai said dutifully.

She smiled, the flash went off, and the photographer went away.

"Tony's just given me the good word that he'll manage my campaign."

Banks turned to Kai. "So how do you feel about your father becoming a senator?"

"Don't we need an election before I can answer that?" Kai said.

Banks laughed and nudged Wyler. "Got yourself a born politician." He glanced back at Kai. "Nice to meet you, Miss Wyler. I think we're all going to enjoy working together." He moved off into the crowd.

"Tony thinks you're going to be a big help to me," Wyler said.

"A real asset," Kai murmured.

Wyler gave her a sharp look. "It goes with being part of the family, Kai. What do you think made the Kennedys so strong? Everyone worked together. This is what you wanted, isn't it? To be part of the family?"

"And I've gone along with everything, haven't I? I just wish you could be glad I'm here for some reason besides helping you get what you want." It was the first time she had made the complaint. Her own words surprised her and she wondered if the glass of champagne she'd had was responsible.

He stared at her a second, then moved closer. "I haven't made much time for you, have I? It's been hard, you know, because Alex, she . . . well, finding out. . . ." He trailed off.

It touched Kai to see him lost for words—the silver-tongued defense attorney who had held a courtroom in thrall the first time she had ever seen him.

"I'll try to change, though," he went on. "You just have to be patient with me. I guess I haven't been much of a father to any of my kids. But give me a chance to get it right."

Then, for the first time ever, he leaned over and kissed

her cheek. From the spot where his lips touched her skin, Kai thought she could feel warmth radiating throughout her body.

But as Wyler moved away to acknowledge greetings from other guests, Kai saw Alexandra. She had returned from putting Vanessa to bed and stood across the room, staring at Kai through the shifting gaps between the crowd. To anyone else, her expression might have seemed neutral, but Kai saw the spark of intense emotion that burned in her eyes. Resentment? Hatred? No, it was something more complicated and somehow more disturbing than even those powerful emotions. Then Kai realized what it was.

Jealousy.

Kai wrenched her gaze away from her stepmother and watched Wyler working his way through the crowd, shaking hands. She had thought that what she wanted from him—just his love—ought to be a simple and natural thing for him to give. But now she realized that Alexandra would never see it that way. For her, it would always be a competition. And only one of them could win.

Chapter Eleven

Her pale blond hair newly cut in a short boyish bob, Sylvie Tremblay stood in a plain black dress at center stage in the basement cabaret and addressed the audience seated at small tables, nursing their drinks:

"Okay, let's make sure I've got this straight. I'm Katherine Hepburn, and he's Henry Kissinger." She pointed to the spindly young man with a mop of black hair waiting at a corner of the stage—the antithesis of Nixon's portly globe-trotting Secretary of State with his stiff washboard pompadour. "The style you asked for is a Tennessee Williams play, and the line you want us to start with is 'Watch out for that big hole!' "

Sylvie went into a twenty-second huddle with the young man. As they separated he pushed his hair straight back with his hands, then put on a pair of horn-rimmed spectacles somebody tossed from the wings. Sylvie pulled a chair onto the stage, sat down and opened her mouth wide. The young man leaned over her with his hand by her mouth, and began to emit a high-pitched nasal whine. Sylvie threw her legs straight out as if being jolted by pain. It was instantly clear that they were miming the roles of a dentist and his patient.

After writhing in the chair a moment, Sylvie thrust the young man away from her. "Would you kindly watch out for that big hole, Dr. Kissinger?" she said in a fair imitation of Katharine Hepburn's patrician voice overlaid with the accent of a Southern belle. "I do believe I have nevah entrusted a more sensitive cavity into your hands." Sylvie fluttered her enormous blue eyes, underlining the sexual nuance by her exaggerated innocence.

The audience laughed and applauded at the way their random suggestions had been adopted into the improvised skit.

Laying on a thick German accent, the actor playing Kissinger assumed the role of a wickedly sadistic dentist, and the lines they tossed back and forth about her "sensitive cavities" went on mining a broad vein of double meanings.

Alone at a table in back, Kai marveled at her friend's bold cleverness. Sylvie had telephoned in April to say she had won a place in Chicago's famous improvisational troupe, the Windy City Players. Though eager to see Sylvie perform, for the past six weeks Kai had been kept busy as a volunteer in her father's campaign for the senatorial primaries. It was the longest stretch that Kai had gone without seeing Sylvie. Throughout the first year she had lived with Wyler, the two friends had continued to meet regularly. Sylvie had come once to the North Side mansion, but after that visit she told Kai that the atmosphere there was too uptight, and from then on they always met in the Loop and spent their time shopping or seeing films.

Having decided to stay in Chicago, Sylvie had quickly gotten herself a job as a cocktail waitress in a downtown bar. She often accepted dates from attractive men who came into the bar, and one had turned out to be a stage manager with the national company of a hit Broadway musical who suggested Sylvie's uninhibited exhibitionism was perfectly suited to improvisational theater. The next day she went to the cabaret where the Windy City Players had been established for more than a decade. The troupe had no openings, but Sylvie talked herself into a job waiting on the tables. While serving drinks, she studied the improvisations of the eight regular cast members. Eight months later, one of them dropped out and Sylvie begged to be auditioned. From the moment she walked onto the stage, there wasn't a doubt that she was right where she belonged.

At the end of the show, Sylvie came over to sit with Kai.

"So?" she said, dropping into a chair. She had changed into a leather mini-skirt with a purple satin bolero blouse, and both her arms were sheathed to the elbow with costume jewelry bracelets.

"I don't know how you can do it," Kai said. "Always coming up with the right thing to do and say in the blink of an eye."

"You know what's even harder? Thinking up *two* things to do or say—because the first one that pops into my mind is usually something that'll get me locked up.'' She paused to examine Kai. ''I like the new look, by the way.''

At the insistence of Tony Banks, Kai had gotten her hair cut. ''You can help us with the youth vote,'' Banks had told her with his usual brusque candor. ''But if you look too much like a hippie or like some island girl wading out to greet the monthly mail boat, we'll lose just as many votes as we gain.'' Banks had arranged an appointment, and the luxuriant fall of silken copper that had reached nearly to her waist was cut to shoulder length and styled to frame her face with a loose wave across her brow.

A waiter came and Sylvie ordered a black coffee. ''Throw some brandy in it,'' she added. Kai was content to stick with her ginger ale. As the waiter left, a pair of young men approached and asked Sylvie to autograph their programs. One of them was quite attractive, and Sylvie bantered with him, suggesting he might like to stay around for the second show. When he said he was with a date, Sylvie told him to come back after he dropped the girl off. It seemed probable she wouldn't sleep alone tonight.

Kai had often seen Sylvie invite such contacts with men. In the early days of their friendship, Kai had advised her friend to try finding one man to fulfill her. ''One man could never do it,'' Sylvie stated matter-of-factly. Eventually, Kai stopped interfering.

''How about that? I'm a star,'' Sylvie said after the young men left. ''Well, what's new with you, toots? Has the Wicked Witch of the North Side put any new curses on you?''

Kai frequently poured out her heart to Sylvie about her conflict with Alexandra. ''We've learned to keep out of each other's way. The campaign helps. She's busy making the rounds with my father. I only go with them once in a while.''

''But you're also shaking hands and kissing babies on your own,'' Sylvie said. ''I've seen the pictures in the paper. You're getting almost as much publicity as he is.''

Kai laughed. ''Yeah, well now, Mr. Banks, the guy who's managing my father's campaign, thinks I can make a difference if I give some speeches at colleges, factories, places where I can talk to younger voters. But I've never done that kind of thing, Syl. I don't know how to stand up in front of people.''

"Honey, if I have any advice to give, it's just to be as natural as possible, be yourself. Let's face it, Kai, nobody's gonna mind looking at you standing up to talk for five or ten minutes. You could do the hula, for chrissakes, and you'd win votes. Truth is, people don't listen to what politicians say anymore. Voters go on looks and style and—what's that thing they were always saying the Kennedys had?"

"Charisma. Personal magnetism."

"Yeah. Well, you've got it. Banks ought to know that."

"But it scares me," Kai admitted. "When you're involved in a political campaign, everything you say or do gets put under a microscope. I worry about saying something that ends up making my father look bad, losing votes for him."

"Sounds to me," Sylvie said tartly, "like you're just afraid you might let the truth about the sonofabitch slip out."

Kai looked away into the dim corners of the basement room.

"Sorry," Sylvie said. "You've got to go easy on him now, I suppose, but I don't." The waiter brought Sylvie's coffee and she took a sip. "How's it going between you and your old man?"

"For the first time," Kai answered quietly, "he's glad I'm here."

"And that's why you'll knock yourself out to do whatever he asks. But do you really believe he's the best man to represent the people?"

"He's on the right side," Kai answered. "He's against the war, he wants to make things better. He really *is* the best man for the job."

Sylvie shrugged. "As long as you can say it like you believe it, then you'll bring him the votes." She leaned across the table. "So there's no problem, is there?"

No problem, Kai assured herself. She could speak on his behalf, make people believe in him. And if she won him enough votes, then she might win his love.

As the primaries heated up in the late spring, Kai was dispatched on a full round of ladies' luncheons, college rallies, and Junior Chamber of Commerce banquets. Not just in Chicago but throughout the state.

One reason she was being given her own schedule, Kai finally realized, was that her stepmother had ordered Banks to keep them separated. Alexandra expected to stay at Wyler's side, the image of the steadfast political wife, but she didn't want to share the same platform with Kai. Of course, Tony Banks explained to Kai that she was able to speak directly to constituencies that might not otherwise vote for Randall Wyler—younger people, ethnic groups. Accordingly, the speeches prepared for her by professional speech writers always mentioned her Hawaiian background, her mixed blood, using it as a touchstone to speak of her deep personal feelings about the evils of racism and the need for equal rights for minorities and women in America.

She was a nervous speaker at first, but she gradually smoothed off the rough edges. Soon she was inserting passages spoken off the cuff. Appearing at several state colleges, where opposition to the war and to the draft was the hottest issue, she pocketed the prepared speech and spoke movingly about seeing the coffins unloaded from the navy cargo plane, and the need to end the war so America could heal the wounds at home.

Banks scolded her when he learned she had departed from the prepared texts. "We go over everything in those speeches to make damn sure nothing can get twisted around and used against us. Shoot from the lip, Kai, and the wrong thing comes out, we could get killed. It happens in elections all the time."

"If I'm not helping, Tony," Kai answered, "then stop sending me out."

By the time she said it, she knew damn well that Banks wouldn't stop using her. At each appearance her audiences were getting larger, attracted by the publicity she was receiving on her own. Newspapers had begun sending reporters just to cover Kai. As Banks had foreseen, she was a story in her own right, earning space in the newspapers and television news programs—not just because of what she said, or where she came from, but what she looked like.

Seeing Kai becoming the darling of the press was a bitter pill for Alexandra. But she could hardly object to anything that improved Randy's chances of winning the nomination. He needed every edge. The leading contender, Paul Forrest, had already spent two terms in the House of Representa-

tives. Wyler's enormous wealth and high-society profile also
worked against him with much of Chicago's minority and
blue-collar population. As the primary came into its final
weeks, the polls showed Wyler trailing behind Forrest by
several points.

At Wyler campaign headquarters, the atmosphere was
kept upbeat by Tony Banks. In the large central room of the
office suite Wyler had rented in the same building as his law
firm, the campaign manager started every day by climbing
on top of a desk to rally the assembled staff and the growing
corps of young volunteers like a general sending his troops
to the front.

"The momentum is with us!" he bellowed at eight
o'clock on a gloomy Monday morning as the primary entered its final phase. "We've been picking up two or three
points each week. With a little extra effort, we'll pass that
s.o.b. right before election day—the perfect time to peak!"

But they couldn't afford to let down, he exhorted his
workers. More doorbells had to be rung, more people but-
tonholed on street corners, more phones calls made, more
contributions extracted.

After climbing down from the desk, Banks called Kai into
his office. She started each day by stopping at headquarters
to receive her schedule, or a new speech, and to rendezvous
with whichever woman volunteer was to chaperone her appearances.

When she went into Banks's office, her father was already
there, getting a more detailed breakdown on the latest poll
results from Al Korchak, the campaign press secretary. Wyler acknowledged Kai with a nod while he went on listening. Banks came over to her.

"You're down for extra duty like everyone else," he said,
pulling the ever present cigar from his mouth. "It's closer
than I thought, Kai. We need every vote. I'm sending you
out of town to cover new territory—rural areas in the central
part of the state. I could dress your dad in a straw hat and
send him to the farmers, but he'd look like a fish with whisk-
ers. I think you can connect, though. Hawaii's kind of rural,
isn't it? Lots of folks making their living on the land. And
you grew up on a plantation, right? See what I mean, it ties
right in."

Kai saw that her father had stopped paying attention to the poll figures to listen to her reaction.

"Farming sugarcane and pineapple isn't exactly the same as raising corn and dairy herds, Tony."

"Sure, sure, you and I know that. But how many Illinois farmers have ever been to Hawaii?"

Kai shrugged. "If you think I can help, of course I'll go."

"That's my girl," Wyler said, giving her a grateful smile before turning back to confer with the press secretary.

Tony took some papers from the mound on his desk and thrust them at Kai. "Here's a couple of new speeches—special for the hay-and-oats crowd. Now go and pack for five days on the road."

"Five days?"

"Yup, today through Friday—puddle jumping from one small town to another." The concept was to let her get close to people in smaller groups, he explained, to have her travel by car, without a big press caravan trailing her around. "The staff has already lined up a bunch of county fairs, grange meetings, 4-H clubs, churches on bingo night. Old-fashioned vote-getting, Kai. And it'll do you good to breathe some country air."

Alone on the road for five days? The trip sounded awful. And lonely.

But she saw her father eyeing her again expectantly.

She took the speeches from Tony, and he told her that a car and driver would be at the Wyler house to pick her up in an hour.

Her father blew her a farewell kiss.

Kai raced back to the house, packed, and put on one of her campaign traveling outfits, a wrinkle-proof apple green skirt and pale pink blouse. Country colors, she thought. Then she sat glumly waiting for her ride. It was all Alexandra's idea, Kai felt certain; keeping her away from the press would give her stepmother more room in the spotlight.

Livesey, the English butler, came to her bedroom door to announce that a car had arrived.

Parked in the drive was a dented, dusty Buick sedan of uncertain vintage. A tall young man wearing black pants and a leather jacket stood beside the car. He hurried to take the valise Kai was carrying, stored it in the trunk, then ran to pull open the rear passenger door.

She paused before getting in. "Who are you?"

"Michal Karlozic," he said, offering his hand.

She shook it. "Where's my driver, Michal?" She tried to pronounce his name as he had, rhyming approximately with *nickel.*

"I am your driver," he replied.

"I see that. But I mean for the trip. I was told one of the women—"

"The poor lady. She was on her way over here to get you, and had a fender-bender with a taxi on Lakeshore Drive. The office tried to get another woman, but the only one who could spare five days out of the city just had her driver's license lifted after two speeding tickets and running a red light. That left just the guys." He smiled. "Quite a few volunteered, Miss Wyler."

Kai stared at him. "You mean, *you're* taking me? I'm supposed to spend five days traveling with a man I don't know?"

"Mr. Banks gave me enough money to cover separate hotel rooms all the way, and made my duties perfectly clear. I'm your driver, bodyguard, and advance man. Mr. Banks also warned me if I wasn't a perfect gentleman every minute we're together, he'd—well, I won't tell you what he said. But it'll keep me in line, don't worry."

Kai looked him over carefully. He had dark brown hair, wavy and slightly unruly, and blue eyes hooded by very long lashes. His features were craggy rather than regular, and his complexion was marked in one or two places along the strong jawline by faint pockmarks, probably the aftermath of youthful acne. Altogether, it gave him the appealingly rugged appearance of a young man who might have been raised in the outdoors—on a farm, perhaps. Considering the violent nuts who went around these days stalking political figures and their relatives, he might be an even better escort for a long trip than a woman. Kai got into the car, not through the rear door he was holding open, but through the front door she opened for herself.

When he was behind the wheel, she said, "Michal, why did Tony pick you out of all the volunteers?"

He turned the key in the ignition and started steering down

the driveway. "He asked all of us the year and make of our cars. The other guys all had new ones, mostly sport models—you know, Miss Wyler, most of the volunteers who work for your father are from money. My car was the oldest of the American models. Just what Tony wanted."

"Why?"

"You're going on the road to tell a bunch of farmers your father understands their problems better than other candidates. Think they'd go for the line if you arrived in a Ferrari?"

Kai took his point.

They drove out of Chicago on the highway heading southwest toward the fertile central plains. According to a typed itinerary Michal gave Kai to look at, their first stop would be at a county fair outside Joliet, a couple of hours' drive.

It wasn't long before a free-flowing conversation developed against the background of varied music Michal kept popping into a tape player—Sinatra, Tchaikovsky, the Beatles, Beethoven, Elvis. And they stopped being "Miss Wyler" and "Michal." His friends, he said, called him Mitch.

He asked Kai questions about Hawaii, then about herself, though he admitted to knowing some of her story from all the publicity. In fact, he remembered the stories that had been printed when she was first reunited with her father. "I've wanted to meet you since the first time I saw your picture in the paper," he said.

"Is that the reason you volunteered to work on the campaign?"

"Wouldn't have been a bad idea," he said ingenuously, "but I couldn't give all this free time to a candidate if I didn't really admire him."

It occurred to Kai that all the while she'd been working alongside dozens of others committed to electing Randall Wyler, this was the first time she'd heard anyone speak of actually admiring him. It wasn't something she herself could have said. She was trading her support for love, Tony Banks for money, Alexandra for social ambition. Mitch seemed to be doing it on principle. "What do you admire about him?" she asked, now intensely curious.

"He was poor once, as I am. He started at the bottom, now he's got it all. I admire him for making his dreams come true."

"Not his politics?"

"A big part of politics *is* trying to make dreams come true," Mitch said. "End the war, make people's lives better. Aren't politicians always talking about dreams? I figure if Wyler can get everything he wants for himself, he's got a shot at doing it for the voters."

Kai wondered what Mitch Karlozic would have to say if he knew how her father had made his dreams come true, the lies he'd told, the lives he'd damaged. But she fought down the temptation and asked Mitch about himself.

He'd emigrated from Poland with his parents when he was three years old. Their original reason, he said, had been to seek sophisticated medical treatment for Mitch's older sister, who had been born with a congenital heart defect. But the communist government had taken so long to grant the family's request to emigrate that the little girl had been critically weakened; she had died only weeks after reaching the United States. Mitch and his parents had joined relatives in Chicago, settling in the large Polish community centered around Milwaukee Avenue. Like many Poles, his father had found a job in the stockyards.

"He works in a slaughterhouse," Mitch told Kai. "Stands ankle deep in blood and cuts the cows' throats as they come along a conveyor, hanging head down."

Kai hadn't asked Mitch to describe his father's job in detail. When he drifted into talking about it, Kai could hear his revulsion—yet at the same time a fierce gratitude for the filthy work his father had taken on so that the family could survive in America. Mitch was now attending the University of Illinois, with a scholarship earned partly for his basketball prowess. When he graduated next year, he planned to go on for his master's in business.

"I'll be goddamned if I'll ever stand in blood to feed my family," he told Kai. "I'm going to have it all, like Wyler."

Mitch talked about making "tons of money" in business, but his motive seemed to be more than mere greed. He had a vision of using money to do good works, he said. One ambition was to improve the conditions he had seen in the stockyards, take over the companies that did business there and clean things up. "These companies cut too many corners to save money," he said, "instead of thinking about the health of their workers—or even their customers."

They arrived at the first county fair, where Kai participated in judging a pie-baking contest before talking to an
audience of several hundred farmers' wives inside a tent.
Her brief speech referred to being born on a plantation and
her sympathy with the hardships of making a living from
agriculture.

"As some of you may know," she concluded. "I wasn't
able to live my early years with my father. But since my
mother died, and we've found each other, I've been able to
tell him about the problems I grew up with. He's grown to
have a special sympathy with those who live on the land,
who feed the rest of us but sometimes have trouble feeding
themselves. So on Primary Day, I hope you'll give Randall
Wyler your votes. And tell your husbands they'd better do
the same if they know what's good for them!"

There were loud cheers and an ovation when Kai finished.
As she came off the platform, she was mobbed by members
of the audience wanting to express support. She was grateful when Mitch waded in beside her and acted as a buffer.
After a few minutes he steered her out of the crowd. "Sorry,
ladies," he called out apologetically, "Miss Wyler has to
get to her next stop."

But when they left the tent, Mitch didn't head for the car.
He pointed to the big Ferris wheel at the center of the fair-
grounds. "Ever been on one of those things?"

"No."

"Didn't think so. That's what I had in mind for your next
stop."

They rode the Ferris wheel, then a small roller coaster
and some of the other carnival rides, and they went along
the booths of the midway, tossing balls at milk bottles and
darts at balloons. Several times Kai halfheartedly reminded
him that they were supposed to be campaigning, but she
didn't argue when he led her on through the tents where the
animals were being judged, farmers were showing off three-
hundred-pound pumpkins, and their wives were displaying
beautiful handmade quilts. She had never enjoyed herself so
much. Anyway, Mitch said, there was time before they had
to be at their next scheduled stop, a 4-H dinner in a town
sixty miles away. "And darned if you don't deserve some
fun," he teased. "between having to shovel so much horse-
shit."

Chapter Twelve

For five days he drove her and guarded her, brought her warm tea when her throat was raw from the constant speaking, and kept her amused as they covered the miles between planned engagements and unplanned stops on block-long main streets, in general stores, and diners with three-stool counters.

They stayed their first two nights in roadside motels, then accepted an invitation they received the third night to stay in a large farmhouse. Separate bedrooms, of course.

For the last night they found a guest house in a small farming town. As Kai rested in a hot bath in the old-fashioned bathroom after another long day on the road, she thought about how well Mitch had taken care of her.

She had been soaking for twenty minutes when he knocked on the door. "How much longer?" he called. There was just one bathroom for the guests.

"Sorry. I was daydreaming."

"What about?"

Having the door between them made it easier to speak, almost like being in a confessional. "This time together has been so wonderful, Mitch . . . the best days I've had since . . . as long as I can remember. I've been hoping it wouldn't end."

"Tony wouldn't mind if we stayed on the road. Your father has gained two more points in the polls, and the demographics show a surge in support from the farm belt." The report was up-to-the-minute; Mitch phoned the campaign office at the end of each day to get any changes in the itinerary.

"I wasn't talking about campaigning," she said. "Just . . . being together."

"I've got an idea, Kai." His voice came back with a new buoyant quality. "Let's elope."

She turned to stare in amazement at the door between them.

"We could find a justice of the peace around here, wake him up right now—"

She laughed softly. "My god, can you imagine if we did? They send you out with me for a few days, and we . . ." Her laughter turned to giggles.

"I'd do it," he said earnestly. "I'd marry you tonight."

Her laughter subsided. What had she started? "Thank you, Mitch. That was my first proposal. But I'd like to know the man I marry a little longer than four days."

He retreated from the extravagant gesture, mocking it. "Yeah, I suppose you'd need at least a week."

The mood had turned light, yet the feeling hadn't evaporated. Rising out of the tub to dry off, Kai felt suddenly chagrined by her confession. Mitch was there on the other side of the door, and they had begun to express their feelings for each other. She threw on her white terry robe, as though hiding her nakedness from eyes that could see through the door.

He remained silent, but she knew he was there waiting. At last she unlatched the door and pulled it open. He was dressed, though his shirt was unbuttoned, the tail pulled out. They gazed at each other only a moment before he leaned toward her, and she raised her mouth to his. Their lips met in a long, questing kiss. Her fingers twined in his hair while his hands clawed up the material of her robe at the rear so he could caress her thighs. Kai felt moisture between her legs and knew it was not from the bath.

They broke apart, both breathless.

"No chance I could change your mind about eloping?" he said.

"Why do you keep bringing that up?"

"Because it's the only way I can let this go any further. Remember, Tony made me give my word I wouldn't—how did he put it?—compromise you." He smiled. "The only way you wouldn't be compromised, seems to me, is if I married you."

She hugged him. "Whatever we're feeling now, Mitch, if it lasts we'll have other chances."

"If it lasts," Mitch echoed incredulously. "No doubts on my side."

The way he looked at her, she knew he expected the same assurance. Yet she couldn't give it to him. Being dependent on him for four days had sparked a certain closeness, but her feelings seemed fragile.

"Well," Mitch said with a touch of sharpness, "tonight taught me one good lesson."

"What?"

"I'll think twice next time about keeping my word." He went into the bathroom and closed the door gently between them.

A pale purple twilight sky silhouetted the skyscraper office buildings and high-rise apartments of the Gold Coast as they drove into the fringes of the city.

There had been little conversation between them on the ride back. The effort of readjusting their relationship after last night's encounter had produced a lingering tension. This afternoon's campaign stop had also left them in a somber mood—the dedication of a small memorial in a town of nine hundred people which had lost four of its native sons in Vietnam. After several days out of the glare of the press, word had traveled back to Chicago about Kai's "old-fashioned vote-getting" junket, and reporters for a few city newspapers had shown up. Impressed by the way she touched her listeners, they closed in on her after her speech and kept her busy until Mitch pulled her away.

As the city skyline came in sight, he said, "Come home with me for dinner, Kai. Meet my family."

She accepted, happy to have a rest from all the hurly-burly and forced smiles, and eager to get back on a relaxed footing with Mitch.

Before going home, he stopped on Milwaukee Avenue to buy extra provisions for the dinner. As he led Kai from the butcher to the baker, to the liquor store in the Polish neighborhood, he was given friendly greetings by the shop owners and other customers. Mitch usually stayed a minute or two, speaking Polish to them. Kai felt as though she had been transported to a village in another country. Everything Mitch bought was a Polish specialty—a round loaf of bread made of coarse brown flour, a sausage called kielbasa, a bottle of plum brandy called slivovitz. How good it must feel, Kai thought, to live amid so much of the flavor of the place they had been forced to leave for freedom. She had never felt so homesick for her own birthplace.

They drove a few blocks to a street lined with identical wooden frame houses fronted by narrow porches. Many were poorly maintained, but the house before which Mitch stopped the car instantly bespoke pride of ownership. The white paint was fresh, the windows clean, the oak front door varnished.

A cluster of small metal balls tacked to the frame jingled as they walked through the unlocked door, and a compact woman in an apron came running along the corridor from the rear. Her graying yellow hair, carelessly pinned back, shook loose as she hugged Mitch and babbled at him in Polish.

"This is my mother—Anna," Mitch told Kai. "She says the food on our trip must have been awful, I look like I've lost weight." He pulled Kai forward. "Mama, this is Kai Wyler. She's worked harder and is even more starved than I am, so I brought her home for some of your cooking." He gave her the large shopping bag, explaining he'd brought extra food.

"Welcome, miss," Anna Karlozic said, shyly tucking her hair back into the pins. Then she murmured again to Mitch in Polish.

He translated for Kai. "She says you're even more beautiful than your photograph, even if you are too thin."

"Thank you," Kai said.

"Make at home yourself," Anna Karlozic said. "We wait now for papa." She scurried off with the bag of extra groceries.

The house was cozy, a place where each worn piece of furniture and each faded photograph on the wall suggested a whole history of belonging to this family. It was, thought Kai, the opposite of the cold, impersonal luxury in the Wyler mansion. She was reminded of Mak and Lili's little plantation shack, and even—though it had its hateful memories—of the beach cottage where she had been raised. Home. Mitch was lucky to have one.

In the small downstairs bathroom, she washed off the grime of a day's traveling. Just before she finished, she heard the jingle of bells at the front door signal the arrival of Mitch's father. When she returned to the front room, he was there with Mitch, sitting in an easy chair, a grave, unsmiling man with piercing dark eyes flanking a long, straight nose, and a thick brush of a mustache shadowing his lips. His dark hair was shiny and plastered down, as though he had just showered. Kai remembered what Mitch had told her about his father's work. Yes, he must have washed off the blood of the abattoir before coming home.

"This is my father, Lech," Mitch introduced him. Kai moved forward to shake his hand, but he just issued a grunt, putting her off. Mitch looked embarrassed by his father's reaction but said nothing.

Kai also forgave it. Working in a slaughterhouse all day was reason enough to have a depressed view of life, but Kai recalled, too, that Mitch's sister had died in childhood. Lech Karlozic couldn't be blamed if he had become a blunt, humorless man.

When they sat down to dinner at the kitchen table, Anna did her best to make Kai feel welcome, heaping sausage and cabbage on her plate, and asking about the trip with her son, whom she always called Michal. She avoided political matters, though, being more curious about the sights they'd seen, events at the country fairs.

But Lech's brooding silence remained so overwhelmingly oppressive that Kai wondered about Mitch's motive in bringing her here. Perhaps he wanted to expose her to the worst aspects of his life before their intimacy developed any further.

It was near the end of the meal when Lech finally spoke. "So," he addressed his son, "have you fooled enough people into voting for this man you work for?"

Mitch threw another apologetic glance at Kai. "Papa, no politics. Kai shouldn't have to hear you tearing down her father."

"She can defend him if she wishes."

Anna tried to intervene, murmuring quietly to her husband in Polish.

"Yes, yes," Lech replied, "she's a guest. So we must be on our best behavior, eh? Like politicians—who behave so very politely when they're in our company, but screw us the minute they're out of sight."

"Maybe we should leave, Kai," Mitch said, starting to rise.

"Sit down!" Lech bellowed. "You talk about being polite, but you'd run from your mother's table before our meal is finished?"

"It's all right," Kai said quietly to Mitch, who settled back into his chair.

There was a strained silence while Anna cleared the dishes, then brought coffee and a delicious homemade nut torte.

After a sip of coffee, Lech said, "Would you be interested in knowing why I could not vote for your father, Miss Wyler?"

Anna gasped, and Mitch burst out, "Pop, why do you have to—"

"Because it's the truth!" Lech roared. "You brought her here, Michal. Did you think that would turn me into a liar?"

"No!" Mitch shouted back. "I was hoping you might even get over this crazy hatred you've been carrying around all these years if you could just meet his daughter, see how decent she is."

Kai glanced from father to son. She perceived now that something more than politics was at issue between them, and somehow her father figured in the balance. "Tell me, Mr. Karlozic," she said, "why wouldn't you vote for Randall Wyler?"

Lech fixed his dark, piercing eyes on her. "Because he defended the men who murdered my daughter."

Anna muffled a cry into her napkin.

"It wasn't murder," Mitch said tightly, evidently repeating words from a thousand past arguments.

But Kai kept her eyes on Lech as he told the rest of the story. His daughter, then seven years old, had been brought to a Chicago hospital for heart surgery soon after the family had arrived in America. She had also been suffering from a high fever for which she had to be treated before she could undergo the rigors of a heart operation. Heavy medication had only masked the condition, however, and the girl had entered the operating room in a weakened state. She had died on the table.

"I was prepared to accept it as the will of god," Lech said, staring down at the white tablecloth in front of him as though he could see the sterile white of the hospital. "But then a nurse who had seen the operation told me there were mistakes. I would never have known, except the nurse was a young woman from a Polish family, and so she felt our pain. It became a malpractice case. The doctors deserved to be punished, but there were lies told, and Mr. Wyler was very clever. He won, and no one was punished." Lech raised his eyes to meet Kai's. "You understand why I could never support him? A vote is a declaration of trust, is it not? It is, in a way, a piece of our souls."

Touched by the value placed on his vote by this refugee from tyranny, Kai nodded sympathetically.

"But my son forgets all of this," Lech added bitterly, "because he sees a picture of a beautiful girl in the newspaper, a rich girl . . . and he sees a way to serve his purposes."

Kai glanced sharply at Mitch. He'd mentioned seeing her picture, she recalled, though he denied that it had anything to do with his work on the campaign.

"Don't listen to that nonsense, Kai," Mitch said quickly. He turned on his father. "I believe in different things than you do. Why is that so hard for you to accept?"

"Because I don't see you believe in anything. You only reject what we are, what you come from. We are poor, you want to be rich, and you'll do anything to succeed, even reject your blood."

"What does that mean?" Mitch demanded.

Lech Karlozic looked away from his son as though he couldn't be bothered to reply.

Furious now, Mitch rose half out of his seat, fists clenched. "What'd you mean, damn it?"

Lech turned again to Mitch, glaring. "We are Polish and proud to be. You see your mother? Polish. And so many girls from this neighborhood, good Polish girls are here for you. Daughters of my friends. Yet you reject them and bring strangers."

"Bastard," Mitch hissed. "I bring someone I care about, and you insult her."

The atmosphere in the room was explosive. Anna cowered and whined an appeal. "Michal, please . . ."

Kai had been paralyzed by the escalating family argument, but finally she realized she had better act. "Mitch, let's go."

"Sure, I'll go." Then he pointed at his father. "After you apologize."

Lech pounded his fist on the table, making the dishes and silverware jump. "I should apologize?" he screamed, his face red with rage. "To the daughter of a man who protected my child's murderers? *His* blood—and not even pure blood at that! I've read about her, a native girl, half a savage. That's what you want while you reject your own—"

The viciousness of Lech Karlozic's words stunned Kai.

Mitch threw himself at his father, grabbing him by his shirt and pulling him up out of his chair. Anna screamed. For a moment Kai heard and saw the fight as though it was happening on the other side of a foggy window. Then her senses cleared and she bolted from the table.

"Kai!" Mitch let go of his father and ran to her. 'I feel awful about this." He grasped her arms. "I'll take you home—"

She shook loose from him. "No, I'll find a taxi. You can leave my luggage at the office."

He stayed with her as she went out, down the steps, grabbed her arm again. "Why? What did I do?"

Why blame him, too? Because he had brought her here. Because she had learned things that made her wonder if she could trust him. Because to be her father's daughter she knew she had to take sides.

"You're his son," she said, retaliating with the same cruel logic that had wounded her. "His blood. That's enough."

He let her go.

She walked for a long time along Milwaukee Avenue, trying to sort out the tangle of confused thoughts and emotions before she finally took a taxi from a rank. In the taxi she broke down. Crying not just for herself, but for her mother. Those few brutal words from Mitch's bigoted father had given Kai a taste of the wounding rejections that had whittled away Lokei's self-respect.

When the taxi arrived in front of the Wyler mansion, Kai remembered she was carrying no money. For five days all her needs had been paid out of the campaign funds handled by Mitch. She told the taxi driver to wait while she went inside.

As she let herself in, her father came into the entrance hall from the living room. He was in his shirtsleeves, holding a tumbler of ice and whiskey in one hand. He saw at a glance her reddened eyes and tear-streaked face. "What's happened. . . ?"

"I need money for a taxi," she said.

"I'll take care of it. Wait in there." He motioned to the living room.

"I'm tired," she said. "I'm going to bed."

His voice hardened. "Sit down and wait for me."

Of course, if he had been a normal father, there would be nothing extraordinary about his concern. But Kai felt strange, the idea of having a heart-to-heart with him was so alien.

Drafts of a speech he had apparently been working on were on a coffee table, a half-empty bottle of whiskey serving as a paperweight. Kai took a seat on one of the two facing sofas.

He returned from paying for the cab. "Pretty long trip on the meter," he remarked. "A campaign worker was supposed to bring you home. Why didn't he?"

"He invited me to meet his family."

"And what happened?" He came back to the sofa, poured more whiskey into his glass.

Kai's emotions flooded to the surface as she poured out the story of what had happened, repeated the racial slurs hurled at her by Lech Karlozic.

Wyler bolted angrily to his feet as soon as she was finished. "Dumb Polacks. I've half a mind to go straight out there and beat the shit out of them myself!"

It was a comfort to see his urge to protect her, but Kai could no longer stop thinking like a politician. "And when that makes the papers," she said, "you can kiss the election goodbye."

"Think so?" His hand mimed the spread of a newspaper headline as he declaimed, "Wyler Defends Daughter's Honor."

Daughter. Just to hear the word on his lips! "Never mind," she said. "I'll get over it."

"Well, I won't." His eyes flashed with fury.

Kai rose to go upstairs. Then something else occurred to her. "One reason this man wanted so much to hurt me was because of what had happened to his own daughter. She died when she was a child—during a heart operation—and later he sued the doctors.'' She paused. "He says you defended them and won the case.''

"It's possible,'' he said evenly. "When was it?''

"Fifteen years ago.''

Wyler shrugged. "I've had a lot of cases, Kai.''

She nodded. Why take it further?

He smiled at her. She felt a barrier between them had fallen. She went to him and kissed his cheek. "Thanks for listening,'' she said.

"I'm sorry it happened,'' he replied, embracing her.

"Not your fault.''

He leaned back to look at her. "It started with me, didn't it—wanting your mother? I suppose it would have been better for everyone if I hadn't. But, my god, I couldn't resist her. I've never known anyone more desirable than she was.'' Then he added quietly, "Except you. She passed it on to you, Kai, I can feel it—something like an invisible fire that's burning inside you. You're going to have to be careful with men.''

Suddenly Kai felt frightened. She didn't like being compared to Lokei or the idea that her whole life could turn out the same. She reminded him that she was very tired from her trip and said a quick good night.

Kai looked for Mitch at the campaign offices. Failing to run into him after several visits, she asked about him and was told by one of the volunteers that, on his first day back after the trip, Mitch had been ushered out of the offices by Tony Banks and told he was no longer welcome. Kai realized that the order had been passed down from her father. When she heard nothing about Mitch trying to contact her, she wasn't sure if it was because access had been blocked or because Mitch had been subdued by his own father. She thought of calling him, but the urge faded. She didn't hold him responsible for his father's ignorance and vindictiveness, but now other doubts stood in the way of any renewed intimacy. Lech Karlozic's rantings had seeded the idea that Mitch had deliberately maneuvered to meet her and get close to her, perhaps even as part of his ambition to duplicate the life of Randall Wyler.

Thinking back to the night he'd proposed eloping with her, remembering how close she'd come to giving herself to him, she warned herself not to forget her father's advice. She was going to have to be very careful with men.

Chapter Thirteen

The Wyler for Senator Committee planned a fund-raising banquet to be held in the ballroom of the Palmer House the last Saturday night before Primary Day. At the fund-raiser Kai and Alex would appear together for the first time to reinforce the image of family solidarity. But when Wyler asked Alex to apply her famous good taste to help Kai find a gown to wear, all her resentment flared into the open.

"Frankly, I'd just as soon see your little *wahine* wearing a lei and a potato sack," Alex told her husband when they met with Tony Banks.

"For godssake, Alex, I'm just asking you to help her look good."

"She's your little mistake, not mine," Alex shot back. "Want to dress up your doll? Do it yourself!" She walked out.

The next day Tony had an idea that might simultaneously net some extra publicity and teach Alex a lesson for being uncooperative. He brought a tailor to the campaign offices to take Kai's measurements. Then he asked one of his political contacts in the Kennedy camp to call Jackie Kennedy's designer, Oleg Cassini, and pass on the measurements.

The afternoon before the banquet a package from Cassini arrived at Wyler headquarters. A note from the designer said the contents were loaned with his compliments. In fact, the gown had been designed for Jackie to wear at a White House dinner—but had not been made at the time because of President Kennedy's assassination.

On the night of the banquet, it was understood that the Wylers and Kai would ride together from their home to the Palmer House. The other children, who had been less involved in the campaign, were to be brought separately by the butler. Kai was the first to be ready, and she took a chair in the foyer to wait. A few minutes later Alexandra descended. Her all-black gown, with a skirt of tiered taffeta ruffles and a low-cut cinched velvet bodice with thin straps, was elegant enough for the Inaugural Ball. The stark black made her diamond necklace and earrings appear all the more dazzling.

It took Alex only a glance at her unwanted stepdaughter to realize some first-class professional advice had been solicited. The sinuous sheath of pale apricot silk that hugged Kai's figure and left her shoulders bare was a design of classic understated elegance, perfect for her coloring and statuesque bearing. With her copper hair gathered back simply on both sides by a pair of pearl-studded combs, Kai looked suitably youthful rather than regal—still, Alex hadn't a doubt about who would be the show stopper tonight.

For a moment she had an impulse to surrender the field. If she could only embrace this exquisite girl—take pride in her—wouldn't that be easier than feeling that they were rivals?

But her vanity was too deeply ingrained to permit surrender. Stand aside for this intruder in her home? The daughter of a whore? As her husband came down the stairs to join them, it was all Alex could do not to claw the gown right off Kai, and force Randy to choose an allegiance to one of them or the other. She would have . . . but then reminded herself, as she had a hundred times before, what the prize for her cooperation would be. Alex bestowed a curt nod of approval on her stepdaughter.

But when they were being helped into their coats by a maid, Alex saw the lush white fox stole that had also been furnished for Kai, the perfect compliment to her gown. In a sharp aside to Randy as they went out to the car, she said, "You went on quite a shopping spree with your little girl, didn't you?"

"As a matter of fact, it didn't cost me a cent." He explained that Tony had obtained the clothes on loan from Cassini.

To hear that the designer who'd dressed Jackie Kennedy when she was First Lady had dressed Kai tonight was an even bigger slap in the face than if thousands of dollars had been spent on Kai. But again Alex choked down her resentment and kept her mind on the goal.

Arriving at the ballroom, greeting the assembled crowd of wealthy backers, smiling for photographers, the Wylers managed a convincing picture of family unity. Friction was kept to a minimum during the dinner, since Alex was seated at Randy's side on the dais, while Kai was several places away between two of Wyler's richest supporters.

When the meal was cleared away and dessert and coffee served, the crowd settled back to hear their candidate speak. Wyler neatly walked the fence on the hottest issue of the moment. The war couldn't be tolerated, he said, the death of one more American boy was too much—*yet* there was a price that had to be paid for keeping freedom and democracy in the world. To withdraw too soon and "run home like a pack of whipped dogs" would only encourage further communist aggression.

Wyler's views were made all the more effective by emphasizing his special understanding of matters in Southeast Asia. After all, he reminded the audience, he had done his military service in Hawaii, "that part of our own United States which has the closest kinship to the peoples of the Pacific." He felt intensely the tragedy of a war that was costing the lives of Americans in defense of an Oriental people, because within his own family—"right here tonight"—was his daughter, a blending of two cultures. Never mind the distinction that should have been made between Asiatic peoples and Hawaiians, whose ethnic roots were in Polynesia. Wyler played his kinship with Kai to the hilt. Pausing to look at her, he spoke about his good luck in having her come back into his life, her invaluable contribution to the campaign, the helpful insights she had given him into the views of young people in these difficult times. The crowd responded with an enthusiastic ovation.

As Tony watched from a corner of the ballroom, he folded his arms and smiled. This touching father-daughter act might just be good enough to play the circuit all the way to the White House. If Alex could just keep herself under control.

At the close of his speech, Wyler finally turned to his wife and expressed his thanks for her "steadfast inspiration and support." It was too little too late for Alex, who was raging inside at the greater attention accorded to Kai.

Wyler was cheered by backers who lined up to slip thousand-dollar checks to Tony Banks, then the tables were pushed off the floor so that the crowd could dance. A series of eligible bachelors took Kai onto the dance floor, one cutting in on the next. She had begun to weary of them and think of asking Wyler's permission to go home when she found herself in the arms of a man who caught her interest.

"You're looking bored, Miss Wyler," he said. "It always makes me sad to see a beautiful woman looking bored. There are so many ways you could be amused, and so many men who'd be happy to do it." He smiled and introduced himself in a way that suggested she ought to recognize his name.

Orin Olmsted. The name didn't mean anything to her, yet Kai was impressed simply by his aura. He had one of those agile bodies, tall and lithe, that seemed made for dancing. It took only a few gliding steps for Kai to know how graceful he was, how totally confident. His sleek look was carried through in his lean face: high cheekbones accentuated clear gray eyes, and his dark blond hair was worn long but expertly cut and brushed back. Kai had difficulty pegging his age. A mature thirty or a youthful forty.

"I'm not bored," she replied, careful to say nothing that reflected negatively on any of her father's functions, "just tired. Campaigning is hard work."

"You've certainly given it your all," Olmsted said. "If your father gets elected, you'll deserve a lot of the credit." He punctuated the compliment with a deft whirl.

"If Randall Wyler wins, Mr. Olmsted, it'll be because the people think he's the best man with the best ideas."

He laughed, revealing dazzling white teeth. "Don't try to fool me, Miss Wyler. If you've been in politics more than a week you know that what wins elections is everything but ideas."

"Then why are you backing my father?" Kai asked.

"Because if he wins," Olmsted said, "then his ideas *will* matter. Same reason I give money to a few dozen campaigns around the country—to do what I can to keep this country going forward instead of backward."

Kai heard a ring of genuine concern in his voice. "In what way, Mr. Olmsted?" The number ended and the band took a break, but she stood waiting for her answer.

"There's a lot of angry dissent going on right now," he said. "Free speech, we call it—and it makes some people

start wishing there were limits. We've even got people saying it might be better to censor the press and 'protect'
Americans against radical or immoral ideas. I support men
like your father because they won't go along with that. Because they're my natural allies. You see, I'm working for
another American revolution, Miss Wyler, one that guar-
antees the right to say and read and do whatever men and
women want to do in their own bedrooms. Randall Wyler
seems to be sympathetic to the cause. And I'd be delighted
to think you are, too.''

He gave her a clear-eyed, unabashed stare, but the innuendo made Kai edge away. ''Well, Mr. Olmsted, it's been
interesting—''

''Wait,'' he said, and put a hand around her arm to pull
her closer. ''I haven't made my proposition yet.''

''Haven't you?'' she echoed, openly indignant as she
pulled her arm away. ''Maybe I don't want to hear it.''

''Business proposition,'' he said quickly.

She paused. ''Oh? What kind of business?''

''Publishing. I was wondering if you'd be interested in a
job with me.''

''What sort of work would I be doing?'' Kai asked warily.

''I don't have anything specific in mind yet. But my entire
organization has been built around beautiful young women
like yourself. I don't think there'd be any trouble working
you in—right into the center of things, if that's where you
wanted to be.'' The smile he gave her had something
charmingly devilish about it.

Her curiosity was piqued. ''Mr Olmsted, just what—''

''Please,'' he put in, ''call me Orin.''

''Orin,'' she said, and she was about to continue when
Tony Banks appeared at her side.

''Sorry, Orin,'' Tony said breathlessly as he laid a firm
grip on Kai's elbow, ''but we've got a load of people here
who've been asking to meet Kai. I can't let you tie her up
all night.''

''Of course not. Good night, Kai. Think about my offer.''

Before she could say anything else, Tony pulled her away.

''Tony, what's the rush?'' Kai said as he steered her rapidly toward the other side of the room. ''You're moving as
if a bomb was about to go off.''

"It almost did," Tony said. "Why do you think I came over? It's not good for people to see you looking too friendly with Orin Olmsted, Kai." He glanced at her. "What was that about an offer?"

"A job, that's all. I was just trying to pin down exactly what it was when you came along. He did say it could be at the center of things, if I wanted."

Tony erupted in a loud guffaw. "The center! If you wanted! Oh, Kai, that's a good one."

She pulled up short and looked at him. "Why? Who is Orin Olmsted, Tony?"

He glanced at her in surprise. Then walked on, pulling her with him. "You don't know? Been in Chicago a whole year and you never heard anyone talk about him?"

Kai shook her head.

"Suppose I asked if you ever heard of his magazine—*Tomcat*?"

Kai stared at Tony. Who hadn't heard of *Tomcat*—the first and most successful of the glossy monthlies that had made it almost respectable to print photographs of nude women? Each issue featured a removable centerfold pin-up of a beautiful woman known as "Tomcat's Kitty of the Month." Kai had seen the magazine stacked openly on newsstands all over the city.

As she thought back over Orin Olmsted's offer to put her "right into the center of things," Kai blushed. Yet he hadn't been the least bit rude or pushy. In fact, perhaps she had misread exactly what he had been suggesting.

"He doesn't seem like such a bad guy, Tony," Kai said. "Maybe he was offering me a job on the editorial side."

They reached an alcove at the side of the ballroom. Tony stopped and faced her. "Listen, Kai, I'm not saying Olmsted's bad. He's certainly a whole different breed than the kind of sleazy porn merchants who used to print nudie pictures. He's turned his magazine into a corporation that takes in more than a hundred million smackers a year, and I'm delighted to help myself to the fat checks he gives us because he likes our politics. But don't fool yourself. Sex is what made Olmsted rich. Sex is a big part of his politics, that and his dependance on freedom of the press. I'd bet my election-day bonus that sex is what he sees when he looks at you. Like any publisher, he's always looking for a new angle to boost his circulation. For all we know, he's got some crazy idea to run a whole feature on daughters of candidates, all in the buff—with you as the centerpiece and some Kennedy girls sprinkled around the sides.''

Kai laughed. "Tony, you're being ridiculous. He wouldn't do anything to embarrass a candidate he supports.''

Tony stared back at her. "I'm not sure Olmsted knows where to draw the line, Kai. He's got his own ideas of what's allowable. Maybe that's why he's been so successful at pushing back the boundaries. But whether I'm right or wrong, steer clear. Okay? Don't call him, and for godssakes, don't take him up on any invites to visit the Alley.''

"What alley?''

"*The* Alley. It's what he calls the place where he lives, a big mansion he's turned into a kind of dormitory—maybe harem would be a better word—for all his kitties and whatnot. Where all the tomcats hang out, in other words. It's a hot scene, Kai. Not the kind of place the candidate's daughter should ever be caught dead in.''

"Okay, Tony," she said demurely, mocking his serious tone. "I'll be good.''

"All right. Now . . . you ready to shake a few more hands?''

Kai and her father arrived home a little after midnight. Alex wasn't with them, and the other Wyler children had been brought home earlier. Alex had slipped out of the party alone not long after the speech. The official story was that she hadn't felt well and had gone home on her own, but Kai knew from past incidents that it wasn't the truth.

As they rode home from the hotel, Kai felt badly for her father. The banquet had been a great success; he was looking like a sure winner. Yet his wife had walked out on him. Kai wasn't unaware of the irony in her feelings. Hadn't he walked out on her mother? Why feel sorry for him?

Because he was her father. Because the heart knew no logic.

"Don't go to bed yet," he said when they entered the house. It was quiet, the other children already asleep. "I told Livesey to put out some champagne—to celebrate. I knew tonight would go well.''

In the long living room, an ice bucket with a chilled bottle of champagne and crystal flutes were on the cocktail table between two facing sofas. A pair of lamps provided soft lighting. But one detail struck Kai as odd. There were two glasses, just two. Had Wyler planned to celebrate alone with Alex? Or had he known she wouldn't be coming home with them?

He popped the cork on the champagne, filled the glasses, and handed her one. "To victory," he said, raising his glass in a toast.

She drank, but then she paced away from him. "This feels wrong," she said.

"You don't think I'm going to win?"

"I mean, pretending it makes no difference that Alex isn't here. How do you think I feel knowing I've caused this split—knowing she wishes I didn't exist, hates even to be in the same room with me?" Kai dropped onto one of the sofas.

"Don't blame yourself if she's not here, Kai." Wyler drained the champagne in his glass and went to pick up the bottle. "Alex has a lover," he said calmly, filling his glass again. "More than one. Had them since before you came."

"And you don't care?"

He sat down near her and sipped at his champagne, still holding the bottle in his other hand. "Want the truth? It's a goddamn relief. As long as she can satisfy herself some-where else, then she doesn't expect me to love her—something I've never been able to do."

Kai stared at her father, shocked and disappointed. She wanted so much to forget the callousness that the past had taught her was part of him. Why did he have to remind her, even flaunt it?

He read the look in her eyes. "I know. I shouldn't tell you things like that. Except what's the point in hiding any-thing from you? You know the worst about me—knew it before you found me." As if toasting her achievement, he raised the glass, then swigged down the contents. He filled it again and put the bottle back on the cocktail table. "Lucky you came, though. Scared me at first, Kai. I didn't see how it could work, how you'd fit into my life. But now I don't see how it could work without you."

She heard his voice grow hoarse with emotion. Oddly, she felt more confused than touched. It had been wonderful when he spoke publicly of his pride in her to the crowd tonight, but this private confession made her uneasy.

She forced a smile. "I'm tired. I should go to bed."

As she leaned over to kiss his cheek, he hooked his free hand around her waist and held her close a moment. When she drew away, he said, "How long will it take?"

"What?"

"For you to forgive me."

Looking into his eyes, she saw the yearning and pain. "Daddy," she whispered, a plea to let the wounds heal in their own time. When the word sprang to her lips she realized it was the first time she'd ever said it. How strange it sounded.

He still had his arm around her. "Remember the first time we talked? I told you I wasn't sure I'd ever loved your mother?"

She nodded, trying to overcome her uneasiness. It was partly the alcohol talking, she knew. But if this was the moment he chose to connect with her, she had to listen.

"I wasn't brave enough to tell you the truth," he went on, "because it was so much worse. I did love her, and I left her anyway because I was hungrier for what Alex could give me. For this." He waved at the walls of the grand house, the symbol of the rewards of wealth. "But believe me, Kai, I've suffered for it as much as if Lokei put a curse on me. Because I could never get back what I had with her. I've had everything else, but not the excitement, the passion." He drained his glass once more and put it aside. "Funny thing is, I was so damn busy being successful, I hardly noticed what was missing." He laid his hand over hers. "Until you got here. You're so much like her—the way she was when we met, all the fire and the—" He broke off, shrugged. "It all came back then. I realized how much I'd lost."

His honesty frightened her rather than making her feel closer. "There's no way to go back," she said cautiously. "The best you can do now is try not to hurt anyone else."

"If only you'll give me a second chance." His grip on her waist tightened.

He was pleading for forgiveness again. "But that's why I'm here," she said.

"Yes," he said, "that's why you're here." A slight smile

of appreciation broke across his face, and his grasp on her loosened. She stood and said good night.

"Let me hear it again," he coaxed as she walked from the room.

She knew just what he meant. "Good night, Daddy."

The door opened in the darkness, and a figure outlined in a shaft of light moved toward her.

It was a dream, Kai told herself. But then she realized she was conscious, eyes open. As he reached the bed and looked down, the stream of light through the door caught his face. "What's wrong, Daddy?" she murmured, propping herself up on her elbows and blinking the sleep from her eyes.

"Jus' had to see you 'gain, baby. Talk s'more . . ."

The slurred words, his dark shape wavering unsteadily across the shaft of light, told her he must have gone on drinking the champagne. Glancing at the clock, she saw it was more than an hour since she'd come upstairs.

"Go to sleep," she urged. "We'll talk tomorrow."

He lowered himself to sit on the edge of the bed. "Never should've left you," he said.

His mind was still circling over the same territory they'd covered earlier. Kai felt some satisfaction in knowing it tortured him so much, yet now she wished she could give him peace. "I told you, we've got a second chance. I've forgiven you. Now, please—"

Her voice caught as he shifted suddenly on the bed, and one arm went across her body to support him as, slowly, he lowered his face toward hers. "Second chance, baby. That's all I need. There's never been anyone else like my *kaimana*."

In the split second before his mouth covered hers, Kai finally understood that he wasn't asking for a second chance as a father.

In his drunken imaginings she had taken the place of Lokei.

For a moment that seemed like forever she couldn't break out of the kiss. Then she pulled her head to one side. "Please," she panted desperately, "don't. . . ."

"Second chance," he repeated, as though it was a magic

phrase that would grant even this profane wish. His groping hands found her wrists and pinned them to the bed.

"No!" she screamed, arching her back, trying to buck him off. But she could hardly move beneath his weight.

"Don't fight me, baby," he murmured drunkenly. "Said I could have a second chance."

"Daddy . . ." she pleaded, no love in it now, clinging to the word only because it might call him back to reality. "No, *Daddy*. . . !"

Suddenly he stopped moving and rose up to look at her by the light coming through the doorway. "Jesus," he hissed softly.

She had reached him, she thought. It was a whisper of shame.

"Oh, Jesus," he repeated. But then he said, "You're so beautiful—my *kaimana*." His mouth searched for hers again. This time when she tried to twist away, he removed his hand from her wrist and clamped it brutally under her chin, not only forcing her face around so he could kiss her, but pressing on her throat, half choking her. As Kai went rigid with terror, he straddled her and used his other hand to tear away the covers.

She wanted to throw him off, but her limbs seemed to be paralyzed. She lay there staring up at him, telling herself it must be a dream after all. He wouldn't do this, had to be an illusion, wait, just wait and it would end, any second. . . .

Now he was fumbling eagerly at his pants and clawing up her nightgown.

Move! She screamed silently. Reaching out blindly to the side, her hand touched the lamp on her night table, an electrified brass candlestick with a square base. She turned her hand over so the base would be upright and closed her palm around the small shaft. She lifted it, feeling the heft of the brass.

"Please don't . . ." she tried once more, begging him not to force her to violence.

It was as if he hadn't heard. His pants were open, he had her nightdress bunched up over her stomach.

Arm straight, she arced it up from her shoulder as hard and fast as she could. The base struck him squarely in the temple. He let out a short moan, then toppled over, his head landing on the pillow beside hers.

She lay pinned beneath his dead weight, spent, waiting again to wake from this terrible dream. But in the pause his body seemed to be turning to lead, crushing down so that she could no longer breathe. In a fresh burst of hysterical energy, she heaved him off, and his body tumbled to the floor beside the bed.

Moving like a robot, unaware of time, of decision, she dressed by the light coming through the still open door. Only when she was about to leave the room and took a last look back, did she see the crumpled shape on the floor next to the bed—and remember. He had tried to rape her, and she had—

Killed him? He hadn't moved at all since the blow.

She sprang to turn on the switch for the overhead light. In the sudden harsh glare she saw his splayed body, face up, eyes closed, blood running from the gash on the side of his head. She would have cried out to him, but "Daddy" stuck in her throat. Even as an echo in her mind it repelled her.

The first time she had seen him flashed through her mind. In the courtroom. What justice could she expect—the daughter of a *hapa* whore who'd forced her way into his home? A second later she was moving again, choices made without thought—clothes thrown into her valise, the little money she could call her own shoved into a pocket, racing down the stairs.

She was halfway down when the front door opened. Alex entered, returning home from her tryst. Both of them froze. Alex's eyes flicked to the valise in Kai's hands, and for a second a smile of satisfaction touched her lips. Then her eyes went to Kai's face and her smile faded.

"Why are you leaving?" she asked quickly.

For an instant Kai had an urge to pour out the truth.

But then she reminded herself that her stepmother was the last person in the world who'd give her the benefit of the doubt.

As Alexandra began moving toward the stairs, Kai ran past her, fleeing into the night.

Chapter Fourteen

Sylvie opened the door of her tenement apartment wearing a ratty silk kimono that hung open to reveal her nakedness. "Holy shit, kiddo!" she exclaimed when she saw Kai. "Never expected *you*!"

Kai stepped into the kitchen—the front room of the railroad flat—and set down her valise. Long ago Sylvie had scribbled down her address with an open invitation to come any time, but Kai hadn't thought she'd ever take up the offer. The South Side neighborhood where Sylvie lived was one of the city's poorest and most dangerous, its rundown tenements and the streets around them known as havens of vice and drug dealing. Even duty-hardened policemen's hearts beat faster when called into the area.

With her fondness for living on the edge, Sylvie had headed straight for the worst part of the South Side when she went hunting for an apartment. The fact that it was a predominantly black neighborhood meant nothing to her. The choice, she told Kai, was purely practical. "Where else am I going to get four rooms for eighty-five bucks?" In the days when she'd worked as a waitress, there had probably been some necessity in her choice. But now that she was a regular with the Windy City Players she earned enough to live in a safer place. The real reason Sylvie was here was because she got a kick out of breaking down barriers. She liked living every moment of her life as a dare.

"Sorry to come so late," Kai said, though she realized Sylvie had probably gotten home not long ago after a late performance. Candles on saucers were burning on the kitchen table and windowsills, and Kai could see the flicker of more candlelight through a doorway leading to the back rooms.

"Late?" Sylvie said. "Honey chile, this is the shank of

the evening." She glanced at Kai's valise. "The evil step-mother throw you out?"

Kai shook her head mutely.

"Well, what do we do now, play twenty questions? Jesus, you look terrible." Sylvie pushed Kai toward a chair at the kitchen table. "Sit down, tell me what—?"

"I killed him." Kai sank down in the chair.

"Wyler?" Sylvie gasped.

"He went totally crazy, started kissing me and he tried—" Her voice gave out. She closed her eyes, and tears started seeping between her lashes.

"Oh, baby." Sylvie crouched beside Kai and hugged her tightly.

A man's voice shattered the moment of comfort. "Who the hell is that?"

Kai's eyes flew open. Framed in a doorway facing the table was a man with handsome features and the most amazing body she had ever seen. He wore nothing but a towel cinched around his narrow hips, his torso an ideal sculpting of bone and muscle, his gleaming dark brown skin catching the candlelight in pools of glowing warmth.

"This is my friend Kai," Sylvie said. "Kai, meet Dexter."

He nodded at Kai, then turned to Sylvie. "Don't like to be left cooling my ass while you and your girlfriend have a tea party." Lowering his voice seductively, he added, "She looks tasty, though. Why don't you ask her to join us inside?"

"I don't think she's in the mood," Sylvie replied harshly. "And if you can't wait to get your rocks off for just a few minutes, Dex, then you can take your ass back out on the street and pick up some piece of meat you can fuck at your own speed."

"Fine with me," he said calmly, and left the doorway.

"Hey, I didn't know I'd be in the way." Kai started to rise, a reflex of manners left over from another world and time.

Sylvie pushed her back in the chair. "Just another man, kiddo. Not worth changing my plans for."

Seconds later, Dexter strode through the kitchen, a coat and trumpet case clamped under one arm as he tucked his unbuttoned shirt into his pants. He stalked out, leaving the door open. Sylvie walked over and screamed into the hallway, "And don't come back, you horny black bastard!" She slammed the door shut with a bang that probably woke half the tenants in the building.

"I think he heard what I told you," Kai said anxiously.

"Won't matter, hon. People in this neck of the woods mind their own business, no matter what it is. As for Dex, he once spent two years in jail for stabbing a guy in a bar fight. If the cops show up, it won't be 'cause of him." She slid into a chair across the table from Kai. "Who else would know you came here?"

"I don't think there's anyone . . ." Alexandra had seen her leave the house, but Kai had never spoken to her stepmother about the friendship with Sylvie.

"Then the cops won't come until they've spent a day or two asking around. Unless, of course, you've pulled off the perfect crime and nobody's gonna think of looking for you at all."

"They'll be looking, all right," Kai said bleakly. She explained to Sylvie exactly what had happened.

"So," she said when Kai finished her account, "they're going to find the sonofabitch lying next to your bed, your fingerprints all over the whatsis you cracked him with . . . and your worst enemy saw you run from the scene. The perfect crime it ain't."

The mental blizzard that had clouded Kai's mind was finally settling. She realized she had only once choice. "Sorry to pull you into this, Syl. I was so crazed, I didn't know where to go. But I really should turn myself in."

"Forget it!" Sylvie erupted. "Go to the cops? Baby, those are the same pigs who gassed us and played drums on my head."

"I won't be able to run forever," Kai said desperately.

"You'll be okay here tonight. Tomorrow . . . there's people living up and down this street who'll drive you to another state for a few bucks, or fix you up with some new ID. Give yourself up, Kai, and you'll do some heavy time. There's nobody to make bail for you, and when it comes to a sentence you'll get *years*."

The cold force of Sylvie's warning started Kai shivering. As the shock wore off, panic was taking over. Sylvie came around the table and pulled her up gently from the chair.

"C'mon, baby, lie down. Try to get some rest. Tomorrow we'll figure it out."

Kai allowed Sylvie to lead her to a sway-backed couch and tuck her under some blankets. Then Sylvie lay down beside her and held her. "It wasn't your fault, kid," Sylvie kept saying softly in the darkness, "it wasn't your fault."

But inside Kai's head it was *his* voice she kept hearing, telling her she was going to have to be careful with men.

At last the tide of jangling energy that had been surging through her since he opened the door into her room receded, stranding her on the silent black coast of sleep.

Sylvie had already been up for an hour by the time Kai woke, and she reported that there was nothing on radio or television about Wyler's death.

Not a word about it in any of the newspapers, either, she announced after returning from a short walk. She tossed the newspapers on the kitchen table and started stowing the groceries she had purchased while she was out.

"Maybe they didn't get the story until it was too late," Kai said after riffling the papers front to back.

"Those are the late editions." Sylvie faced Kai, her hands on her hips. "Face it, duckie: you didn't kill the prick. The witch came home in time to save his life."

Kai couldn't believe it. The emotions she'd experienced, the visions she recalled, had fixed murder in her mind as the only reality. She grabbed up the telephone on the wall of the kitchen, and dialed the number of Wyler campaign headquarters. Passing herself off as a local television news reporter, she asked the volunteer on the phone for a rundown of Wyler's campaign schedule for the day. Then she hung up and let out a whoop of joy.

"Does that mean he's dead or alive?" Sylvie cracked.

"They've canceled all his appearances for today," Kai said. "They're saying he had an accident at home, fell off a stepladder. He'll be back tomorrow, keeping all his speaking dates."

"You're in the clear!"

Kai frowned. "You don't think he'll look for me?"

"Why would he—as long as you stay lost, and don't go around trying to make people believe your nasty little story."

Kai's gaze settled on the front page of one of the news-papers on the table. One story reported on Wyler's speech last night and the "war chest" he was building. Randall Wyler, said the paper, was looking more like the state's next senator every day.

"But I can't let him be elected," Kai protested.

"Honey, if you had a chance to make it stick, I'd say speak out. But Wyler and his wife will say anything to make it sound like your own sick fantasy. You want to have everything about your mother's life dragged into the open? Wyler might even try to have you put away in an institution, for chrissakes!"

"He couldn't!"

"Wouldn't he like to make you look crazy—and tap the sympathy vote at the same time? Leave it alone, Kai, or they'll bury you."

"But people should know the truth about him. Or he could be—"

"So he's a rapist!" Sylvie cried out, exasperated. "What the hell do you expect from politicians? Only difference with this one, he tried doing it one on one. The rest of 'em are trying to rape all of us at the same time."

Kai's stay with Sylvie lengthened into a week. She spent most of the time in the apartment, curiously devoid of any will to move. She found herself spending hours brooding, staring at the walls. The parallel didn't escape her: this was the same sort of mental paralysis that had afflicted Lokei in the last year of her life. It took all her determination to involve herself in even the small constructive tasks that gave her day some sense of purpose—rising, washing, shopping for food. She also contributed some decorating touches to the apartment. Sylvie had done no more than the bare minimum to make the four rooms livable, furnishing them with items bought from the Salvation Army and pieces she'd found by scouring the streets—old couches, broken chairs. As a way of showing her gratitude, Kai applied some of the housekeeping experience she'd picked up at the Crater Inn. She bought remnants of colorful fabric which she hung over rods for curtains and spread over the sofa to cover the torn upholstery. Sylvie made no mention of any of the touches, whether because she didn't notice them or didn't like them Kai wasn't sure.

The newspapers Sylvie brought home daily informed Kai that Wyler had won the primary—and that the press corps had raised questions about her sudden disappearance. In a statement by Tony Banks, reporters were told that Kai was exhausted from her strenuous efforts to help her father. "We expected too much from a kid her age," Banks was quoted. He answered all questions about where she had gone by saying, "I can't give you that information." It left the impression that she'd been sent away to rest. The groundwork was being laid to suggest she'd had a minor breakdown, discredit her if she came forward later to make charges.

Sylvie had originally told Kai to stay as long as she liked, but after a week it was clear neither one could tolerate the arrangement much longer. Sylvie brought home a different lover almost every night—Dexter reappeared once—and Kai felt awkward, bumping into unfamiliar men emerging from the bathroom, being forced to hear Sylvie's orgasmic growls through the thin walls.

One morning, having coffee together after Sylvie's latest had departed, Kai said, "You can't live this way much longer, Syl."

Sylvie surveyed the peeling paint on the walls and ceiling. "Yeah, I'm beginning to think so, too. The curtains and covers you put around only make me realize what a dump it really is. In fact, I've been to look at a couple of new places."

"I didn't mean where you live—I mean the way you live. All these guys passing through here—"

"Sorry, Kai," Sylvie cut in sharply, "I forget you're a goddamn professional virgin, and it's gonna wind you up too tight to be around somebody who's getting laid."

Kai tried to ignore Sylvie's abrasive tone, to finish what she wanted to say out of concern for her friend. "It can't be good for you to have so many guys. How can you really enjoy it if you're just letting one man after another . . . use you like that? I don't think it can be healthy to—"

Sylvie smashed her coffee mug down on the table, and the coffee exploded out of it, splattering them both with hot black droplets. "Who the hell wants to hear what you think is 'healthy'? It's me, my body. And I think it's just fine . . .

no, I don't really think that, Kai, because I don't have to *think* about it. It *feels* fine.'' Sylvie put her hands on her crotch and bit her lip suggestively, goading Kai. ''It feels terrific. I like men, I love sex. Why should I listen to someone who's terrified of both?''

Kai raised her pitch to match Sylvie's. ''Whatever my problem is, doesn't change yours. If sex is so good for you, why can't it be good with just one man instead of a whole battallion?''

Sylvie sprang up from the table. ''Christ, I don't have to listen to this—''

''I'm only saying it because I'm worried about you.''

Sylvie whirled on her. ''No! You're saying it because while you're so tied up in knots, my freedom bugs the shit out of you. Well, angel face, I don't want your fucking opinion about—about my opinion of fucking! You of all people—practically a basket case because somebody tried to get into your pants.'' Sylvie leaned across the table toward Kai. ''Okay, he was your prick father. But nothing happened in the end. You got a couple of bruises, he got a headache. So what's all the melodrama about? Maybe if you let yourself get fucked by a couple of the right guys, you wouldn't have given the wrong one the idea you were ripe for it!''

''Give him the idea?'' Kai echoed tightly, quietly, though she wanted to scream.

Sylvie stared back for a moment. She was too angry herself to apologize. ''Don't expect anything to be different around here,'' she said at last. ''It's my turf, I'll do what I want. So clear out, Miss Prim. Because I don't want to be judged, and I sure as hell don't want to cramp your high-and-mighty-pure-as-the-day-you-were-born-holier-than-thou style.'' To underline that there was no hope of anything being said to soften her stand, Sylvie abruptly raised her middle finger in the air, then stomped off into her bedroom, slamming the door.

The door to her room was still closed when Kai was packed and ready to leave. She called through it: ''Let's not leave it this way, Syl . . . I really appreciate what you did for me . . . it was time I moved on, anyway. . . .''

No answer. Kai knocked lightly on the door. ''I want to stay friends, Sylvie.''

When there was still no response, Kai peeked in. The

room was empty. Sylvie's robe lay bunched on the floor in front of a full-length mirror. Perhaps her answer to the argument had been to take a good look at herself, then go straight out and find herself the next man.

At a coffee shop in the Loop, Kai counted her money. Fifty-five dollars, the balance of the small nest egg she'd brought with her from Hawaii. During all the time she had lived with Wyler, her clothes and other needs had all been paid for, but she had never been given an allowance, never wanted to ask for one.

If she had saved enough money, she would have gone straight to the airport and bought a plane ticket back to Hawaii. But she was stranded. It shouldn't take long to save the fare, though, once she got a job—a hotel somewhere in Chicago ought to be able to use her behind the desk.

Kai took a bus to the Hilton and asked at the desk to see the manager. Almost immediately a short man with slicked-down brown hair and a mustache appeared from a rear office. "I'm the assistant manager, Mr. Hepworth. Our manager is out for a late lunch, but if there's anything I can do . . ."

"I was hoping you might have an opening for a reception clerk," Kai said. "I'll work nights."

Hepworth gave her a skeptical once-over. In her race to escape the Wyler house, Kai had taken only jeans, pullovers, and a couple of sweaters. She was suddenly conscious of being dressed inappropriately for inquiring about this kind of job.

Then Hepworth asked, "Do your parents know you're here, Miss Wyler?"

So *that* was it. Of course. It was foolish not to realize she'd be recognized after all the press coverage. She understood, too, that anyone who'd read the most recent newspaper stories wouldn't deal with her without consulting Wyler.

"Yes," she lied. "Of course, they know."

Hepworth smiled tightly. "Well, why don't you sit down while I consult our personnel files and see what can be arranged?" He pointed her toward a waiting area in view of the front desk.

Kai nodded and walked toward the seating—until she saw

that the assistant manager had gone back into his office. She had no doubt he'd try to reach Wyler immediately. She hurried out of the hotel.

Obviously she needed a job where she wouldn't be so highly visible. Waitress, secretary, salesgirl? As she passed through the stream of pedestrians on the busy sidewalks of the Loop, she became acutely conscious of passing glances, even an occasional friendly smile that came her way. It dawned on her that the weeks of attention she had received made it impossible to work anywhere for long without being identified. And once she was? Would she be forced to return to Wyler? Legally, she was under his guardianship. Or would he leave her alone and risk her willingness to keep silent about the attack?

The afternoon passed in a haze of wandering, sitting at luncheonette counters, or on the grass in the park across from where she had met Sylvie and seen the violent side of politics in America. Passing a newspaper kiosk, she paused to scan the afternoon editions laid out in stacks, wondering if anything at all had been printed about Wyler's "accident." There was nothing. She was just turning away when something else at the kiosk caught her eye: the current issue of *Tomcat*. The cover featured a gorgeous redhead standing at the center of a horse corral, wearing nothing but cowboy boots, low-slung, backless leather chaps, and a skimpy vest made of palomino horsehide. "Tomcat's Girls of the Wild West," read one of the cover lines.

Seeing the magazine reminded Kai of Orin Olmsted—and of what Tony Banks had told her about the Alley, Olmsted's mansion that was open to many of the girls who worked for him.

As a plan began to take shape, she remembered that Tony had told her it wouldn't do the Wyler candidacy any good if his daughter was linked too closely to Orin Olmsted.

At the Alley, Kai thought, she might find the answer to all her problems.

The mansion was a rectangle of brown stone with a flat roof, designed in an unadorned monolithic style popular early in the century. Not an attractive structure, but it was huge, three stories with fifteen windows across the front on each floor.

It was twilight by the time Kai passed through the gates and walked up the long drive. A big party was in progress. Thumping rock music and the babble of a crowd could be heard. In the gathering dark, all the windows of the house were aglow with light. Dozens of cars were lined up in rows across a parking area in front of the mansion, and more cars waited in line at the entrance. As drivers and passengers got out, the cars were handed over to female valets wearing pastel satin outfits cut like bathing suits. Each costume sported a long curving fur tail, and each girl wore a clip-on bandeau with a pair of pointed fur ears atop her head and a matching fur choker. The costumes identified the wearers as "kitty cats"—the term coined by Orin Olmsted for the women who worked in the profitable multi-city chain of Tomcat Clubs he had started as an adjunct to the magazine.

A beefy bouncer squeezed into a tuxedo checked each guest who passed through the entrance. He gave Kai a welcoming smile, then eyed the valise. "Come to stay?" he asked.

She was distracted for a moment by all the sights and sounds. From the marble-floored entrance hall several large rooms were visible, all crowded with people mingling under muted lighting. Kai saw dozens of attractive young women, and spotted some instantly recognizable faces. Jack Nicholson, Muhammed Ali, others she knew by sight if not by name.

"Moving in?" the bouncer prompted again, as if it was the usual thing to give shelter to any young woman who turned up on the doorstep with her baggage.

"I-I don't know. I have to talk to Mr. Olmsted."

"Can't be done, sweetheart. He's locked up for the night."

Kai stared back. Locked up? "But he's giving the party."

He laughed. "There's a party at the Alley *every* night, doll. But O.O. doesn't always join the fun. He's busy tonight, putting the next issue together."

"Could somebody tell him I'm here?" The bouncer started to shake his head. "I'm Randall Wyler's daughter," Kai declared firmly. "My father is running for senator, and Mr. Olmsted is one of his backers. I know he'll want to see me."

He looked Kai over once more, then grabbed up a telephone on a wall near the door. He spoke into it softly, then turned to Kai. "He'll see you. Go on up there." He indicated a wide marble staircase.

At the second-floor landing the house branched off into two wings. To the left a long carpeted hallway extended past a number of doorways before turning a corner. Walking toward Kai along the hallway were a couple of beautiful young women in tight, low-cut party dresses. To the right, a small vestibule fronted a pair of red lacquered double doors. Affixed to one door was a gold plaque engraved with the famous Tomcat logo, a single line swiftly drawn to suggest the head of a cat with one winking eye. Wondering which way to go, Kai was about to call to the two girls when the double doors opened and Olmsted stepped out. He was wearing green silk pajamas; a gold whistle hung from a chain around his neck.

"Hi," he said, as if he had known Kai forever, "c'mon in." The two young women nearing the stairs caught his eye. "Hello, girls," he said. "Enjoy the party."

"We'll do our best, O.O.," one replied.

"But we'll miss you," cooed the second. Kai recognized her as the girl pictured on the cover of the current issue of *Tomcat*.

Both girls flicked shy glances at Kai as they added in a coy unison, "Don't work too hard."

Olmsted chuckled as he closed the door behind Kai. "Put your suitcase down and come with me," he said.

This entire wing was occupied by his separate living quarters, Kai realized. Inside the double doors a vast gallery stretched away to a few rooms around the periphery. The space was designed in a spare modern style, floors of polished black granite, walls sheathed in panels of soft black leather. From fixtures recessed into the ceiling, islands of light shone down on pieces of modern metal sculpture.

Kai trailed Olmsted across the dark gallery toward an open door from which shafts of colored light emanated. As she passed through the door, she saw that the glow came from dozens of translucent color photographs arrayed on large fluorescent panels attached to three of the four walls in the darkened room. The photos were all of the same beautiful raven-haired woman in various poses—wearing panties, wearing only stockings with garter belts, wearing nothing at all, stretched out on a beach, taking a shower with her face turned to the spout, bending over to water some plants in a garden, lying on her stomach, on her back, one knee up on a chair, hands cupping her breasts, one hand touching the cleft between her legs. . . .

Kai stared at the multiple images until the light panels abruptly flickered out, and regular lights came on in several hidden ceiling fixtures. Kai saw now that she was in a bedroom—the most remarkable bedroom she had ever seen. The most unusual feature was the bed itself. Low and circular, it was five yards in diameter. Set at the center of the square windowless chamber on a sea of soft gray carpet, it was the only item of furniture. Curving around part of the circumference was a sort of headboard which incorporated an elaborate electronic panel covered with dials and switches. As Olmsted leaned over the panel, touching some of the switches, soft music began to play, the logs in a fireplace built into one wall suddenly flamed to life, the light boards rotated into the walls and oil paintings took their place.

Most of the bed's surface was spread with pages of printing, cartoons, advertisements, and photographs. Olmsted pushed some papers aside, making a space on the mink throw beneath them. "I can't stop for long," he said. "I have to put this issue together so the printer can have it in the morning."

"You do this work all by yourself?"

"I have plenty of editors to handle the details. But I always take care of the final layout and choose the pictures of the girls. That's the real heart of the magazine." He gestured to the space cleared on the bed. "Sit down, Kai."

She hesitated. "Why don't you have any chairs?" she blurted, thinking aloud.

"Look, I'm not going to seduce you. I brought you in here because you came to see me, and I'm working, and this is where I always work—where I really live. A bed is where we're born, where we die, where we create new life— I don't see why I should have any other furniture. But if it makes you feel better, you can stand up while we talk. Or I'll bring you a chair."

She felt foolish now for objecting. She sat on the edge of the cleared space, while Olmsted slid to an area nearer the center of the bed and crossed his legs Indian-style.

"You mentioned that you might be able to give me a job," Kai said. "And . . . I could also use a place to live. I've heard that you let some of the women who work for you live here."

Olmsted nodded and regarded her silently for a few seconds. "What's going on, Kai? From what I read in the papers, it sounded like you were exhausted, sent off on some kind of vacation. . . ."

"I'd rather not talk about that," she replied. She wasn't ready to trust Olmsted. His interests were best served by getting Wyler elected. If he knew she had the ammunition to sink her father's candidacy, would he help her?

"You must be aware," he said, "of what would happen if you start living at the Alley and the news gets around. You saw that crowd downstairs. Plenty of them are in the press—reporters, columnists. If the story gets out, it's certain to kill off a big block of votes for Wyler. After the way you've worked for him, it seems pretty strange you wouldn't think about that."

"Oh, I've thought about it," she said with a wry smile. "But Tony Banks didn't think *you* had. He didn't even want me to be seen talking to you."

Olmsted laughed. "I remember—yanked you away from me the other night as if I had smallpox."

"He thought you might ask me to pose nude for *Tomcat*," she said, her tone both accusing and questioning.

"If you did, you'd make one of the most gorgeous centerfolds I've ever had. The magazines would fly off the stands."

Kai tensed. What was Olmsted's game? He professed concern about the negative political effect of any acquaintance between them, yet he did sound quite interested in using her to sell his product.

Olmsted evidently detected her annoyance. "Forgive me if I seem presumptuous," he said quickly. "When I say something like that, Kai, I mean it as a compliment. Plenty of woman are thrilled to have their picture in the magazine."

"Well, it wasn't at all what I had in mind when I came here," she said crisply. "But maybe I made a mistake—" She rose from the bed. "I'd better go."

Olmsted scrambled up and caught her by one arm. "Wait,

Kai. You want to stay at the Alley, you're welcome. No strings attached. I do wish you'd tell me why you're at loose ends—but that's a request, not a requirement. I'd just like to know why you left your father's campaign.''

Kai paused only a second before she answered flatly, ''He tried to rape me.''

Olmsted stared at her. ''When was this?''

''The night of the banquet, after we got home.'' She couldn't stop herself now from spilling out the whole story, what had led up to the attack and the way she had defended herself.

Olmsted listened intently. ''I'm glad you trusted me enough to come here and tell me about this,'' he said when she finished. ''If you want, I'll go to the police with you.''

''There's nothing you can do, except get yourself in trouble. I just want to forget it now. To tell you the truth,'' she added thoughtfully, ''I couldn't even say it's reason enough for you to stop supporting him. He's still the candidate running against the Puritans.''

Olmsted smiled. ''We'll see. Right now, let's get you moved in.'' Abruptly he grabbed the gold whistle on a chain around his neck, put it between his lips, and gave one long, shrill blow.

Almost immediately a very pretty girl with coal black hair and blue eyes, dressed in a purple satin jumpsuit, came running into the bedroom. ''Patti, this is Kai,'' Olmsted said to her. ''She's going to be staying at the Alley for a while. Will you take her over to the Catwalk and show her around? I've got to get back to work.''

''Sure,'' Patti said. ''Hi, Kai.''

''Hello,'' Kai answered. As she took a closer look at Patti, Kai realized she was the girl in all the photographs Omsted had been appraising on his light boards. Turning to thank Olmsted, Kai saw he was involved again at the bank of switches. The music stopped, the flames in the fireplace went out, the light panels rotated into view again.

As she followed Patti out, Kai couldn't help thinking about the peculiarities of Orin Olmsted—hiding away in his bedroom to look at pictures of naked women while the party he was throwing in his own house went on without him. She wondered, too, what he really felt about women, the natural resource on which he had built his business. He had treated her with perfect respect and consideration. But it was disturbing to Kai that he would summon another woman by blowing a whistle.

The Catwalk was the name that had been given to the wing of the mansion where young women stayed as guests of Orin Olmsted. Patti explained the house rules. The twenty-four rooms were strictly off limits to all men, and each guest was responsible for cleaning up after herself. "O.O. doesn't want anyone to have an excuse for saying he lets the place be used for wild sex, or that the girls here are . . . well, not just nice, clean girls."

In a niche of a hallway was a large wooden board lined with brass hooks, a number below each one. Some of the hooks were empty, some had one or two brass cutouts of the Tomcat logo hanging on them. "This tells us where the vacancies are," Patti explained. "Take any tag you want, and take the room with that number. Whenever you move out, hang the tag up again. That's all there is to it. Is it okay if I leave you to choose your own room? O.O. doesn't like to be alone too long."

"I'll be fine," Kai said, and Patti scampered off.

Kai stood in front of the board a minute, uncertain about whether to commit herself to stay even one night.

Yet Olmsted had not made any demands on her. And where else could she go? Reaching out at random, she lifted a brass tag with the number 14.

The room was four times larger than the one she'd had at the Wylers and furnished with every comfort. Along with the two beds and dressers positioned against opposite walls, there was a fireplace, a writing desk, a television, even a professional hair dryer. There was a private bathroom and an enormous closet behind a wall of mirrored doors. A mound of stuffed animals perched on one of the beds and the clothes occupying half the closet indicated she had a roommate. Despite the rules about keeping things neat, the other girl had left underwear and towels strewn across the bathroom floor. But Kai didn't mind the mess. She was rather glad to see that Mr. Olmsted's power could be defied, even in such a small way.

By the time she had unpacked, she could hear that the party down below was going strong, the thumping dance music rising up through open windows and the floor. Allowing herself the excuse that she had nothing to wear, she went to bed. She was utterly exhausted from her day of wandering, and besides, she couldn't think of dancing and parties without memories burning in her mind, destroying any hope of frivolous enjoyment. In the darkness of this room, so many years and miles away, she could still see the bonfire stabbing at the sky and the distant undulating figure of her mother performing that cruel dance of humiliation for Harley Trane.

Chapter Fifteen

In the ten years since Orin Olmsted had acquired his huge mansion from the estate of one of Chicago's meat-packing moguls, he had installed every imaginable amusement and luxury. In addition to the main rooms, there was a movie theater, beauty salon, exercise gym, six-lane bowling alley, and discotheque. There was also an Olympic-size indoor swimming pool with one underwater glass wall where the girls were encouraged to skinny dip—providing the backdrop for a basement bar.

In almost every issue of *Tomcat*, at least one photo feature showed the girls mingling with men in these facilities. Using the house to illustrate what was known as "the Tomcat life-style" not only spiced the pages of the magazine, but also allowed Olmsted to claim that the immense costs attached to the mansion were necessary business expenses—thus tax-deductible.

Although Kai had come to Olmsted with the idea of obtaining a job, she fell quickly into the fun-loving atmosphere fostered by living among a few dozen other spirited young women. After the rigors of campaigning and the distress of her episode with Wyler, she was content to stay inside the mansion, sleep late, swim, and mix in with the young women she met.

During the first week, she didn't have another chance to see Olmsted. Kai soon learned that O.O. was a workaholic with a catalogue of eccentric habits. Though published pictures of parties at the Alley often showed him at the center of the action, the fact was he usually put in a quick appearance solely to pose. The rest of the time he spent in his windowless bedroom dressed in pajamas, working on the magazine. When not involved in editing, he conferred with his staff or devoted himself to writing installments of the long tract on sexual history and habits in America that appeared as a regular feature in the magazine titled "The Tomcat Philosophy." Olmsted lived by his whims, without any adherence to the normal routine of day or night. He worked, slept, ate, and made love whenever he felt like it. Whatever girl was his current romantic interest could always be found nearby, waiting for the sound of his whistle. His relationships rarely lasted more than a month or two. The girls, always chosen from among the Tomcat Kitties, understood that they could not hope for more. Freedom, after all, was a cornerstone of the Tomcat philosophy. Yet they felt a certain honor in being chosen for even a little while to be the current "pussycat"—as Olmsted's flame of the moment was called around the Alley.

A principal source for Kai's growing fund of information about Orin Olmsted was her roommate, Terry Cole.

On her first morning at the Alley, Kai had been woken by the sound of pitiful sobs emerging from the bathroom. Going to the open door, she saw a statuesque woman with a tumble of honey blond hair looking at herself in a full-length mirror—wearing nothing but a pair of horn-rimmed spectacles. Tears streamed down her cheeks as she used a tweezer to pluck out stray hairs to define a perfect pubic triangle between her thighs.

Kai was tall, but the other woman was three or four inches taller, putting her at no less than six feet. She had long legs tapering from narrow hips, and a tiny waist, flaring to broad shoulders. Kai rarely gave any special notice to a woman's bust, but she couldn't help realizing that this woman was spectacularly endowed. Along with the amazing figure went an adorable face with dark button eyes, a turned-up nose, and a cupid's-bow mouth.

Catching Kai's reflection in the mirror, the blonde turned to her. "It hurts so bad," she whimpered.

"Then why don't you stop?" Kai asked sensibly.

"Oh, all Kitties have to do this before our pictures are taken. Orders from O.O. Most girls use wax, but I'm allergic to it." While she ceased to inflict torture on herself, her tears abated. "I'm April," she said, smiling at Kai.

"I'm Kai Wyler. Nice to meet you, April."

The blond giggled. "No, April's not my name, that's my

month—when I'll be in the magazine. My name is Terry Cole.''

Thrown together in a situation where Kai relied on Terry—a relative veteran of the Alley, since she had arrived five days earlier—their friendship developed easily.

Terry had been born twenty-one years ago in Brooklyn to a longshoreman named Rocco Colimaretti. ''Well, I always say he's a longshoreman, but he's really sort of like . . . well, you know the book that came out a couple of years ago, *The Godfather*?''

''Your father is a gang boss?'' Kai said. They were talking over breakfast in the mansion's free coffee shop.

''No, he's not important like that. Actually, he does a little work on the docks now and then. But mainly he does odd jobs—not awful things like breaking legs—he just runs errands. Thing is, those guys are all strict in a funny way. They'll do stuff like kill people and run prostitution rings, but they really hate it if their own wives and children don't act like saints. My father's the same.''

As she talked, it became clear that she was scared of being punished by her father or his friends when she appeared in *Tomcat*.

''But then why are you doing it?'' Kai asked.

''I look in the mirror, Kai, and I know the score. I'm not real smart, and my father doesn't believe in college for girls, but just 'cause I can't be a lawyer or an astronomer doesn't mean I'm content to be a trophy on a wiseguy's arm. I want a life of my own, a career, and this is my best shot at it.''

Terry had won her slot as April Kitty after a man who ran a photo studio in her Brooklyn neighborhood had persuaded her to accept fifty dollars to let him take a few calendar shots which he'd sent to *Tomcat*. The magazine didn't buy the pictures, but Terry had gotten a call. She was thrilled. Until then she had been kept at home while her father hoped she'd attract romantic interest from someone high in the mob, maybe even the son of a boss.

''See, that's my dad's idea of making a good life for his only daughter,'' she said. ''Marry me off to some guy who keeps me pregnant while he runs around with bimbos, then gets sent to prison or found dead in the trunk of his goddamn Coupe de Ville. You blame me for wanting a career?

This is a good start, too. Five days' work, and I'll make two thousand bucks!''

"Two?'' Kai said. "I've heard the Kitties get paid five.''

"Yeah, but the photographer who sent in my first pictures wanted three, and I couldn't refuse. After all, he could get bumped off if my father gets mad about this and finds out who was responsible.''

"Listen, Terry,'' Kai said. "You did that man a favor already by posing for pictures he hoped to sell. The magazine didn't like his pictures, either. You'd be more than generous if you gave him five hundred dollars.''

Terry blinked her dark button eyes at Kai. "Gee, I'll bet you could be a lawyer. What the hell are you doing here?''

Kai developed a warm sisterly feeling for Terry Cole, a very different bond than the one she had formed with Sylvie Tremblay. Sylvie's toughness and lustful amorality had always marked off an emotional territory that was alien and impenetrable. But Terry was open and vulnerable; she aroused protective concerns in Kai very similar to those she had felt for Lokei.

Also unlike Sylvie, who was intimidating because she was so experienced, Terry seemed to share many of the same doubts and confusion about sex that troubled Kai. Though not a virgin, Terry had always felt tremendous guilt about the few boys she'd had intercourse with. Her father was constantly reminding her that she'd never be chosen as the wife of a *capo* or one of their sons unless she was "intact.'' Yet it was also her father who told her that God had given her a body that was meant to drive men crazy with desire, and if she made the most of that gift she could get anything she wanted in life.

"It's got me all twisted around,'' Terry sobbed. "Always being told I can't let this body go to waste, only any time he thinks I'm using it, he acts so insane I'm sure somebody's gonna get killed.''

But for all her fears Terry's mood was generally upbeat. She was always ready for the nightly parties at the Alley. Enough celebrities passed through Chicago on any given day to make for a large and lively company.

Kai's reluctance to join in was soon overcome by Terry's coaxing. She was pleasantly surprised to find that the mood of a Tomcat party was not the wildly permissive melee she had imagined. Drugs were strictly forbidden by O.O., and even excessive liquor was frowned upon. Ernie, the black-tie bouncer, escorted any unruly drunks straight out the door. There was a lot of pairing off between men and women, but there were also pockets of good conversation and a lot of innocent fun—charades, water polo games organized in the pool. Though numerous men asked Kai for dates, she was put under no pressure when she refused. So many alternatives were available to the roaming bachelors that they quickly moved on.

Since few of the other girls were politically aware, Kai was at the Alley for a week before anyone recognized her. But on the second weekend she ran into Jerry Vaughan, the reporter who'd helped her get into the courtroom her first day in Chicago.

"So *this* is where you've been hiding out!" he exclaimed as he gave her an approving up-and-down examination. She was wearing a fringed, beaded calfskin dress borrowed from a Cherokee girl who had stayed on to work in one of the Tomcat Clubs after appearing in the recent "Girls of the Wild West" photo feature.

"I'm not hiding," Kai said stiffly.

"Can I quote you? C'mon, Kai, what're you doing here?"

If she told him nothing, Kai thought, he'd only pry elsewhere. "Olmsted asked me to come and work for him."

"You don't say? What's your job?"

"It . . . hasn't been decided yet."

"So how should I phrase it? Say you've given up campaign whistle stops while waiting for O.O. to blow his whistle?"

The association with Olmsted's famous whistle had only one meaning. "There's no personal involvement between me and Orin," she said quickly. "I can't stop you from writing for your paper, Jerry, but make damn sure it's the truth—or you could be sorry."

Vaughan nodded. He seemed to accept that Kai had the kind of determination to make good on a threat, no matter how long it took. "Nothing but the truth," he said, raising his palm as if taking the oath. "But in this case, I think that'll be plenty good enough." He flashed another smug grin before moving away.

Kai was having breakfast alone the next morning when Patti appeared and said O.O. wanted to see her right away.

"Have a look at that," he said, tossing a folded newspaper at her as soon as she entered his windowless bedroom. Dressed in Chinese red silk pajamas, he perched at the center of his enormous bed surrounded by the dozens of editions delivered daily from cities around the world.

Kai sat on the edge of the bed and looked at the paper. Vaughan's front-page story was headed WYLER'S DAUGHTER FOUND—as if she had been the subject of an extensive search like a kidnap victim or shipwreck survivor. The scant information Vaughan had collected was accurately reported: she was living openly at the Olmsted mansion, and claimed she was going to work for the publisher. Yet a scandalous tinge had been given to these few dry facts. The mansion was described as "a notorious pleasure dome where Mr. Olmsted lives like a pasha, and one entire wing dubbed the Catwalk houses dozens of the nubile young women who nourish his readers' fantasies." Kai's denial of any involvement with Olmsted was quoted, but the suggestion was clear that business and pleasure were never separated where O.O. was concerned.

"I've already had a call from Tony Banks," Olmsted said as Kai finished scanning the article. "He thinks the damage can be controlled—if you're out of here today. Begged me to make you leave. If you stay, Wyler can kiss the election goodbye. Not too many voters will think he can be trusted to look out for their interests if he can't keep you on a tighter leash."

"Well," Kai sighed, "you said this would happen."

"What do you want to do about it?" Olmsted asked.

"Is it my decision? This is your house, and you've told me why you're backing him."

"I'm in favor of sexual freedom, not rape. The way I see it, Kai, your father's attack on you disqualifies him for office."

"Then of course I want to stay," Kai said, feeling a rush of surprise and gratitude that he would support her so unequivocally. "Except I don't want to be one of your damn catwomen—whatever you call them. I really did come here because I thought you'd give me a job. I mean a real job, on the magazine."

"Okay," Olmsted said with a good-natured chuckle, "let me give it some thought, see where you'll fit in."

"As long as you don't decide it's 'somewhere near the center'," Kai cautioned him, her tone teasing with what had become their private joke.

He laughed again. "Now go have some fun," he said. When she was at the door he added, "But don't go out unless you want to be tied up giving interviews. There's a bunch of reporters and cameramen down by the front gate ready to pounce on you."

That afternoon Kai saw several notes for her tacked up on a bulletin board where messages were routinely left for the girls. A few were from Tony Banks asking her to call campaign headquarters, others from people with connections to the media. She threw them all away. Except for one slip that said, "Call Jill Evans tomorrow," followed by a phone number and signed "O.O."

When Terry returned to the room later, Kai showed her the note and recounted the meeting with Olmsted. "So who's Jill Evans?" she asked.

As Terry sat on the floor, painting purple polish on her toenails—as prescribed for the April Kitty shots—she replied that Jill Evans was O.O.'s "right-hand man," the only person outside of himself that O.O. trusted to make decisions about his business. "While he putters around on his bed all day long, she sits at a desk in the company office and takes care of all the nuts and bolts. I mean everything. She came to the photo studio today while they were doing my test shots, and made me stand in front of her in my birthday suit. Said she wanted to see if I'd plucked myself enough. Then she made the makeup man rouge my nipples with a different color pink than he'd used the first time. Had him rouging away with one color after another until she got exactly the shade she wanted. I don't know if she's just a perfectionist or was getting a kick out of watching this poor guy touch up my tits with his powder puff."

Terry also supplied some history. Jill Evans had been one of the first Kitties back when Olmsted was just starting his magazine—and, like many others since, she had also been one of his lovers. "I think she holds the record," Terry remarked, "stayed with him for more than a year." Unlike the girls who quickly moved on when they fell out of favor with O.O., Jill had remained to work in different positions on the magazine. As *Tomcat* grew into a hundred-million-dollar corporation, she was rewarded with the position of executive editor and stock holdings that were second only to Olmsted's.

"I've heard that she's never set foot in the Alley. She doesn't want to see O.O., even though they talk business all the time on the phone. Some people think she's still in love with him—and they'll get back together the day he's ready to move out of here and live a more normal life." Terry put the finishing touch on her little toe and bent her long leg up so she could blow the polish dry. "That's about all I know," she concluded, "except for one more thing—her nickname. It shows she's come a long way since being a Kitty."

"What is it?"

"They call her The Tiger. If you're gonna be working under her, Kai, you better watch out for her claws."

In the six years since Orin Olmsted had raised the sixty-one-story building called Tomcat Tower in the heart of the Loop, it had been the butt of many jokes by Chicagoans and the subject of harsh comment by serious critics of architecture. The main offense was that Olmsted had ordered the building's roofline to reflect the famous cat logo—a curving arc punctuated at either end by two triangular points to suggest the ears. Many, considered it nearly criminal to give such a frivolous design to something as permanent as a skyscraper. But to Olmsted this attitude was an extension of the same prudery that spoiled the enjoyment of sex. He was striking another blow against puritanism with his building, which suggested—particularly at night, in silhouette—that a cat bigger than King Kong was crouching within the concrete jungle of Chicago. His irreverence had paid off handsomely. Because Tomcat Tower was so recognizable, it was as popular an address as New York's Empire State Building. Except for the restaurant and drinking club on the roof—called the Topcat Club—and the eight highest floors taken by the magazine, it was fully rented to outside corporations.

Jill Evans was standing in front of her desk when Kai walked into her office. Despite her fearsome nickname, The Tiger was smaller than most of *Tomcat*'s current models.

She wore her straight, long brown hair pulled back in a barrette, and her bright green eyes were accented with a minimum of makeup. Nor did she have on lipstick, nail polish, or any of the other beauty aids that adorned the vixens in *Tomcat* photographs. Her clothes were basic, a red angora sweater with the sleeves pushed up over a camel's hair skirt. Knowing that Jill Evans had been with the magazine since its early days, Kai calculated she must be at least in her mid-thirties, though even without makeup she looked ten years younger. She was not beautiful as much as timelessly pretty.

She pointed Kai to an upholstered chair in front of her. "Why do you want to work here?" she asked with no chatty preamble.

Looking into those penetrating green eyes, Kai saw that it would be unwise not to be perfectly honest with this woman. "I need to earn enough money so I can get back home."

"I thought your home was just a taxi ride across town."

"Not anymore. I want to go back to where I was born."

"Hawaii," Jill Evans supplied, indicating her familiarity with Kai's history. "And when you get there, what will you do?"

Kai paused. She hadn't thought about it. "I'll see a couple of people I care about and then . . ." Her voice faded as she realized that absurdity of what she was going to say.

"Then what?" Jill prodded.

"Look for a job."

"Doing what?"

"I used to work at a hotel. I think they'd take me back."

"And while you're here, what did you think you might do?"

"Whatever you need. Assistant, reception—"

"So, let me get this straight." Jill folded her arms and began to pace in front of her desk. "You want me to hire you to do an everyday routine job just so you can make enough money to quit and go five thousand miles to work at an everyday routine job?"

Kai shrugged and gave an embarrassed smile. "Put like that, it does sound silly."

"No." Jill stopped pacing in front of her. "Put like that, it sounds like you're running away."

There was a pause.

As Kai stared back at Jill, she guessed that it might not be her claws as much as her amazingly acute senses that accounted for her nickname.

"From what I've been reading about you, Kai, I think there's a lot you could do here. Nothing routine, but something that would put you out front, make use of your particular talents. But there's no sense talking about it if you've decided to quit before you start." Jill shot Kai another steely glance. "Should we continue?"

"I'm going back," Kai said, "because I haven't been happy. If that changed, I'd stay."

"Good," Jill said. "Here's the situation. *Tomcat* is in a constant uphill fight to be taken seriously because we rely openly and unashamedly on sex to make a sale. It's there in most other magazines, of course—just look at their ads—sex is being used to sell everything under the sun. But *Tomcat* doesn't pretend for a minute that sex isn't a prime attraction for our readers." She again looked squarely at Kai. "We also print the best short fiction in America, pay great reporters to cover the political scene, interview people on the cutting edge of what's happening in this country. And yet we're always battling the idea that we're just flesh peddlers, always putting up with comedians on television who joke that *Tomcat* is the magazine men read 'with one hand.' We can't let our guard down for a minute, because if we do there are plenty of people who'd turn up the heat and cut our access to the market, choke off our business any way they could." Jill leaned back against her desk. "I could use you, Kai, to help me to fight that battle."

"How? It doesn't look like I'll have any useful political connections—"

"Nothing to do with that," Jill said. "It's you, just what you are, that can help us get the message across." She reached for another chair beside her desk, pulled it around to face Kai, and sat down facing her, almost knee to knee. "Ever hear of the 'It Girl'?" she said.

Kai shook her head.

"Movie actress named Clara Bow, back in the Twenties. Got the label because she had more of 'it' than anyone else on screen at the time, a thing they weren't even allowed to call by name in those days. Same thing that put Marilyn

Monroe in a class by herself. Sex appeal. It's a mysterious, elemental thing that some people give off to an almost overwhelming degree.'' Jill paused and leaned forward, putting both her hands over Kai's, which were folded in her lap. There was nothing aggressive in the move; it seemed rather like the gentle touch of a counselor. ''You've got it, Kai. I'd gotten hints of it in a couple of clips on the TV news, but when you walked into this room five minutes ago it really came across. Your sex appeal is no less—''

Kai shifted in her chair, freeing her hands as she broke in: ''I don't see how this has anything to do with—''

''I know, I know.'' Jill seized control again, sitting back in her chair. ''It makes you uncomfortable. I see that, too, in the way you move, dress, the way you'd rather not talk about it right now. This thing is a burden for you. I don't know why, Kai, don't need to know. But I can tell you that trying to deny such a basic part of yourself could lead to a lot of unhappiness. You can't change what you are.''

Suddenly, Kai felt irritated by this woman's presumption, this assessment of her personality. ''Look, if you think all this is going to get me to take off my clothes in front of your cameras—''

Jill shook her head. ''Far from it. We've got no shortage of women to do that. What we need more is someone who has that kind of sex appeal even with her clothes on, and can think fast on her feet. That's what I saw you do while you were campaigning, Kai. Speaking out, influencing people. Gave me the idea you'd be the ideal ambassador for the company.''

''Ambassadors usually get sent to foreign countries,'' Kai observed. ''Where would you send me?''

''Conventions, schools, maybe even testifying at congessional committees in Washington. There are hundreds of opportunities for us to get across our message—that sex should be a healthy, normal part of everyone's life and nobody needs to be afraid that *Tomcat* magazine is a dangerous, corrupting influence.''

''So it comes down to public relations,'' Kai said.

Jill nodded. ''The perfect representative. Sexy as hell, but knows how to talk. We've needed this for a while—I thought O.O. would be our spokesman, but I can't get him to take off those damn pajamas long enough to go and give a speech or talk to a convention.'' She laughed amiably, and Kai laughed along with her. As the laughter faded, she asked, ''How does it sound?''

''I'm not sure. Do I know enough about this business—about this philosophy O.O. is working on?''

''I wasn't thinking you'd go straight out and climb on a soapbox. The first step would be for you to intern here—work alongside me and some of our other editors.'' She leaned closer as if sharing a confidence. ''Not to take anything from O.O.—the man's a kind of genius—but there's still a lot more to *Tomcat* than what he does on his big ol' bed.''

Kai exchanged a smile with Jill. After spending more than a week at the Alley, where Olmsted's name was always spoken in hushed, reverent tones, this was the first time she had heard anyone talk about him as merely human. Kai thought of what Terry had told her about Jill—that she was rumored to be carrying a torch for Olmsted. If so, it didn't seem to be interfering with her ability to think about him objectively. Kai had the feeling she could learn a lot from working with this sensible, intuitive woman.

''I'll do it,'' Kai said.

Jill told her to report for work the next day, and walked her to the office door. ''Oh, about your salary,'' she said, as if it was an afterthought, ''I'm giving you a thousand dollars a week.''

Kai was sure she'd heard wrong, but then Jill went on:

''It's not just salary, Kai. I expect you to spend the lion's share on clothes, shoes, accessories—whatever it takes to make the most of what you can be. That's part of the job.''

And it was the part that scared her. Looking sexy, being sexy, was an aspect of herself Kai had made a conscious effort to deny for so long. But she knew Jill Evans was right: she couldn't change what she was. The problem was how to accept it, live with it . . . and not let it destroy her as it had destroyed her mother.

Chapter Sixteen

For six weeks she circulated through the different departments of the magazine, getting a feel for the nuts and bolts of producing the monthly issues. She sat in on editorial staff meetings, where ideas for new articles were discussed, and went to photo shoots, where she saw all the careful preparation that went into striking the perfect balance between depicting Kitties as alluring sex symbols and wholesome, real young women. She spent weeks in the advertising, circulation, and publicity departments.

It became apparent to Kai that beyond the professional savvy of the people who worked with Orin Olmsted, there were other reasons for the success of *Tomcat*. Over the years the magazine had often been forced to defend itself against obscenity laws, and the right to publish had been consistently upheld. Each victory had reinforced the idea that *Tomcat* was spearheading a challenge to outmoded restrictions and broadening the definition of true freedom, and Orin Olmsted was the prophet of an age of liberation in American sexuality.

But Kai was uncertain that she could adopt the same conviction about the importance of *Tomcat* to a degree that would make her an effective spokesperson. She agreed that the magazine had a right to exist without censorship, but she thought it was grandiose of Olmsted to see himself as a revolutionary.

To acquaint herself more with his ideas, she decided to read what he had written about attitudes toward sex and their effect on American life in his "Tomcat Philosophy." The series of articles started several years ago now amounted to a few hundred pages. At the Alley bound copies of it were left in the rooms—like Gideon Bibles in a hotel. When she first picked up Olmsted's so-called philosophy, she expected it to consist of dull, self-justifying private musings, published only because Olmsted owned the presses. But she discovered it was well written and often fascinating. Starting off with a history of American sexual customs dating back to colonial times, it covered the sex habits of animals, Darwinian theories on the evolution of the species as they related to sex, and the sociology of sex among primitive tribes. A long section dealt with the history of sexually repressive laws in the United States, deriving from religious thought and practice. He detailed laws in various states that still defined it as a crime for men and women to have intercourse if they were not married, or for married people to engage in oral sex, or for people of different races to marry, as in parts of the South, where it was illegal for black men to have sex with consenting white women, but legal for white men to have sex with consenting black women. Many such laws remained on the books, even if they were not enforced. Olmsted's tract also examined the disparities between American and European sexual attitudes—for example, those that made prostitution a criminal activity in this country, while abroad it was state-licensed and regulated.

Much of what Olmsted had written touched on things basic to the roots of Kai's existence. The interest stimulated by reading Olmsted led her to many of the books referred to by him, all available in the library of the *Tomcat* offices. She read *Sexual Behavior in the Human Male* and *Sexual Behavior in the Human Female,* the two studies by Alfred Kinsey, a zoologist who had made a life's work of applying the same methods of collecting data on animals to researching this aspect of humans. She read books by Sigmund Freud theorizing about the importance of the sexual urge in determining normal and abnormal personality. She read the *Psychopathia Sexualis* of the German psychiatrist Richard Krafft-Ebbing, detailing cases of extreme deviations in sexual practice from the viewpoint of a trained medical observer.

Having recognized the value of a frank, unashamed knowledge of human sexual desires, Kai accepted that Orin Olmsted's formula for a magazine catering to the healthy interest of young males in beautiful, sexy women, combined with an appetite for literature and information, had carved out a legitimate niche in popular culture.

While she went to the *Tomcat* offices during the week, Kai continued to live at the Alley. Terry moved out after completing her photo shoot and obtained a job as a waitress at one of the Tomcat Clubs while she hoped for better things to develop when her pictures were published in the spring. Girls were generally discouraged from staying as guests longer than a month, but Olmsted told Kai she could remain indefinitely. From the time she had admitted her reason for leaving the Wyler house, he had been more protective of her than the others. He often sent messages that he wanted her to visit with him in his quarters. The visits were brief at first, quick exchanges in which he inquired how her experience at the magazine was going. But as she began to raise questions or points of discussion that occurred to her while reading his and other reference works, their conversations became longer.

"You're really studying this stuff," he noted, pleased when Kai revealed she had plowed through the bizarre case histories recorded by Krafft-Ebbing, and then asked Olmsted his own criteria for judging any sexual activity as abnormal. "It can't simply be whether it's against the law," she observed. "As you've pointed out, the law is tailored in many places to punish people engaged in even the most basic sexual practices—sometimes for having sex at all!"

Their discussion on the definition of "abnormal" sex went on for more than an hour, and was cut short only became Olmsted had to return to his editorial work. But he sent a note saying he'd like to see her the next day, and when she arrived he gave her some books—the Tropic novels of Henry Miller and *Lady Chatterley's Lover* by D. H. Lawrence—and told her to come back as soon as she'd read them. "I'm interested in knowing," he said, "whether you think they're obscene or pornographic."

Kai not only read the books, she managed to find some volumes in the office library that detailed the law cases that had gone all the way to the Supreme Court, fighting attempts to ban *Lady Chatterley* and other books labeled "obscene."

When she returned to Olmsted with her homework done, the discussion between them over what constituted obscenity and pornography lasted twice as long as their conversation about abnormality, and generated a lot more heat.

"Maybe you're right that nothing should be censored," Kai argued with Olmsted, who took the position that nothing was obscene. "That only makes people more curious about it, anyway. But there's a difference between writing about sex in a way that reminds people it's a natural human activity, and doing it in a way that depicts women as being deliberately degraded and hurt."

And what if women liked to be hurt? Olmsted said. It was obvious that he enjoyed this wrangling over the issues, and that he asked many questions purely to play devil's advocate.

His invitations to Kai became more frequent, and their meetings lasted longer, yet Kai never felt that he wanted anything more from her than the excitement of arguing viewpoints. Olmsted's live-in companion was still Patti, and it was well-known that he was absolutely faithful to his current "pussycat."

At the end of Kai's eighth week at the *Tomcat* offices, she met with Jill Evans and told her she felt ready to undertake the public-relations role originally outlined.

Jill looked across her desk and appraised Kai. "You certainly look ready."

The fitted two-piece red suit and matching heels were Kai's way of impressing upon her mentor that the apprenticeship was over.

In her first two weeks on the job, when Kai had begun making the clothes purchases allowed for in her large salary, Jill had disapproved of every single choice. Every day at work Kai would be subjected to the sort of inspection a drill sergeant might give a recruit. Dress, shoes, makeup, accessories—none of it passed muster with Jill. Too many of the things were shapeless and overlarge, she said, the designs pedestrian, the colors drab and uncomplimentary. "It's nothing less than sabotage!" Jill cried. "You are positively determined to sabotage your own sex appeal."

At last Jill had dragooned Kai into shopping with her. "If you're going to represent this magazine," she said, "I'll be damned if we'll have you looking like Old Mother Hubbard's younger sister. You've got to knock 'em dead, Kai. That's part of the job—take it or leave it."

Kai had assumed that what Jill would choose to "knock 'em dead" would be tight, skimpy, sparkly, and revealing. There were indeed some items selected—mainly for evening wear—that were slinky and clinging, with high slits and low necklines. But there were also fitted suits, slacks, tailored blouses that buttoned up high, and simple dresses with clean lines. It took a while, but eventually Kai grasped the principle. Simply looking her best—wearing what was fashionable, original, appropriate to the time and place—was as important in bringing out her natural appeal as being deliberately provocative. Looking unattainable could be as sexy as looking cheap and easy.

"A princess can be a lot sexier than a hooker," was the way Jill put it. "The essential thing is to be the most of what you are. Just don't be ashamed of it." The lesson was liberating for Kai. She no longer dressed deliberately to hide or play down the appeal she had been told so often came naturally to her.

"So where do I begin the public relations?" Kai asked Jill now.

"We've always got a pile of requests coming in from colleges, law schools, and various organizations to send someone from the magazine to appear at forums or lectures. Look through them and take your pick. I'll help you set your schedule. We might also offer a program that ties in with sex education in the city schools—make visits to classrooms, discuss the issue with kids. But one of your main assignments will be a Senate hearing coming up next month in Washington to review standards and practices relating to sex and violence on television. We'd like to be represented because O.O. wants to get involved in television. There's an experimental format called cable broadcasting that might be big someday, and has the potential to be less restrictive than the networks. Our lobbyist thinks we could get a head start on winning approval for a *Tomcat* channel if we start having a voice in Washington."

"You think I can handle that better than O.O. himself?"

Jill smiled. "Sending you is his idea. From what he tells me about these talks you've been having, you know the issues as well as he does. And," Jill added, "you won't have to worry anymore that it looks like a conflict of interest."

That was a reference to Randall Wyler's bid to become

senator. It wouldn't have been suitable for Kai to make any kind of appeal before other legislators if they were going to be his colleagues. But the past week the voters had gone to the polls and Wyler had been roundly defeated. It was generally acknowledged that the voters turned away from him when his daughter defected from his campaign to become involved with *Tomcat* magazine.

Jill told Kai that she would be given her own office and a secretary to handle the public-relations work. On her way out of the meeting, Kai paused.

"Jill, it doesn't bother you, I hope, that O.O. suggested I go before a congressional committee. I mean, that's high-profile stuff. You should be the one, if you want. . . ."

A puzzled look clouded Jill's face, then cleared. "Oh, I get it," she said. "You think I might be jealous—maybe wondering what's going on between you and the boss?" Jill came out from behind her desk. "I guess you did a little research on me at some point—that I was one of his pussy-cats back in prehistoric times and I'm still in love with him. Right?" She crossed the room to stand in front of Kai.

As always when she looked into Jill's clear green eyes, Kai felt incapable of deceiving her, even for the sake of tact. "I did hear something like that," she said.

"Well, it's true . . . as far as it goes. I'm still in love with him, and maybe always will be—but only with the part of him that's a man, and I don't mean anatomically. He can be charming, brilliant, stimulating . . . and he knows a lot about how to make a woman feel good. But there's too damn much of O.O. that's still a spoiled little boy. He wants everything his way all the time. The way he's arranged things he can even convince himself that the sun rises and sets on his schedule. That's not a way of living I'd ever want to share." Jill paused, gazing at the carpet for a long moment. "I used to hope he'd grow up one of these days, and then we might get back together and have a real life. But now I know better." She looked up at Kai. "So if you are involved with O.O., Kai—"

"I'm not!" she put in quickly.

Jill went right on. "Well, if it ever happens, enjoy it while it lasts . . . and then be damn glad when it's over and you can find yourself a grown-up man." She smiled again. "But I won't be jealous. Not for a minute."

* * *

Kai began making appearances as *Tomcat* magazine's "Goodwill Ambassador." Wherever an issue of sexual censorship arose—whether or not specifically related to *Tomcat*—the magazine's public-relations office found a role for Kai. Because she was photogenic, and had built up notoriety since her involvement in the Wyler campaign and her defection to live at the Alley, Kai was sought out at public appearances by journalists and TV camera crews. She spoke always as a proponent of the view that it was time for society to leave behind the tradition of repression that had dominated America since Puritan times. If few minds were changed where the moral positions were deeply felt on both sides, she nevertheless obtained invaluable free publicity for *Tomcat*.

And the more Kai became a spokeswoman for a liberal point of view, the more demanding her schedule became. Requests poured in from around the country to appear at college forums, lead seminars, speak at business luncheons.

As she became busier, she had difficulty keeping up any of the friendships she had formed. Terry was offered a small role in a low-budget movie by a producer who came to the Tomcat Club, and she moved away to California. Then there was Sylvie. . . .

Kai had tried numerous times to repair the break, but Sylvie remained distant. When she answered the phone at her new apartment—only a studio, but in a nice high-rise on the shore of Lake Michigan—she was cool, and always found an excuse to hang up quickly. She passed up Kai's invitations to some of the parties at the Alley. Once, when Kai had dropped in late at the Windy City Players, Sylvie had given her a quick hello before excusing herself to disappear with one of her stage-door Johnnies.

So Kai was pleased and surprised when her secretary announced late one morning that someone named Sylvie was in the outer office. "Send her right in," Kai said eagerly.

Sylvie appeared, dressed in a day-glo yellow miniskirt, pink halter top, and cowboy boots. "Quite a setup," she said, scanning the office. "You've done real well for yourself, sweetie."

Kai tried to get things quickly onto a friendly footing.

"It's so great to see you, Syl. Sit down. Can I get you coffee or—"

"I came to say goodbye," Sylvie cut in, pacing around on the thick-pile carpet. "The Players have been offered a gig in New York for a couple of months. We leave tomorrow."

While observing the sentimental amenity of saying goodbye, Sylvie continued to sound cool and agitated. Maybe she was just uncomfortable with this reunion, Kai thought, and attempted to put her at ease. "New York! That's great! I'm really pleased for you."

"Yeah, it's a good thing it happened now," Sylvie said. "I think I've run out of guys to fuck in Chicago."

There was a time it would have been funny, uttered in Sylvie's tough, wry manner. But it was obvious to Kai today that Sylvie was testing her, throwing down a gauntlet to see if Kai would level any new judgments against her behavior.

Kai came out from behind her desk. "Sylvie, I'm sorry if I hurt you. Believe me, whatever I said about your—your way of life, it was only because I care about you, and I was worried."

Sylvie stopped pacing and faced her. Her hard expression softened. "You were like a sister, Kai, you know that? I just couldn't get over it when you attacked me. I really wanted to be friends again, but you've made it so damn hard."

"I have? Sylvie, I've called a dozen times, came to see you—"

"Sure, sure," Sylvie said dismissively. "You act nice. But meanwhile you're involved with all this *Tomcat* bullshit! You know this fucking magazine encourages men to treat us all as brainless sex toys. Working here makes you a traitor to your gender!" She crossed her arms and fixed Kai with an accusing stare.

Kai was rocked back on her heels by Sylvie's assault on the magazine. It took her a second to reply. "This is why you came today—to chew me out for—?"

"Bet your ass!!" Sylvie shot back. "I wasn't gonna leave town without telling you what a fucking hypocrite I think you are. Gave me all that high-falutin' crap about how I should respect myself. Then you help sell this rag that encourages men to forget their respect.''

Kai shook her head in utter bewilderment. ''I don't get it, Sylvie. You're angry at a magazine that celebrates the beauty of a woman's body—angry at me because I think any woman has a right to choose of her own free will to share that, without shame, without pretense? And yet you've let dozens of men—hundreds, more likely, do whatever they want with you!''

Color flooded Sylvie's pale face, and her eyes narrowed to slits. ''My sex life is my business. If I want a lot of men, I'm not hurting anyone else. But that's different than making a business out of treating all women as objects with staples in their belly button. Don't you understand, Kai? The men who get off on these pin-up pictures never learn to see us as *real.*''

''I can't believe my ears,'' Kai said. ''You of all people spouting that line.''

''Well, believe it, sweetie. I had to get it off my chest before blowing town.'' For an instant there was a catch in Sylvie's voice, a dewy glimmer at the corner of her eye. ''Christ, I've missed you, Kai.''

Kai moved toward her. ''Then just be who you are, I'll do the same, and the rest won't matter.''

''No,'' Sylvie said, the hardness back in her tone. ''It won't work 'cause I don't know who you are anymore— some hypocrite to be working here.'' She flung her arm out to indicate Kai's plush office.

A spike of anger went through Kai. She had done her best to heal the breach, but Sylvie seemed determined to insult her. ''I think I'm entitled to believe something different than you without being called a hypocrite,'' she snapped.

''A hypocrite, Kai, is somebody who does one thing and says another. You talk all about what a good thing *Tomcat* does, you tell me how it's such a celebration of female beauty.'' She advanced on Kai, her chin thrust forward pugnaciously. ''But I don't see you putting your body where your mouth is. You believe this is such a great outfit you work for, then why don't you go all the way for the company—let the world see *you* buck naked?''

As a reflex defense, Kai blurted, ''I just might.''

''Yeah, sure,'' Sylvie said, ''and I might decide to become a nun." She turned and went to the door of the office. "So long, Kai. I wish I could've helped you." She went out.

The irony of her lost friend's last words echoed in Kai's mind long after Sylvie had gone. Which of them was the one who needed help? Kai had thought it was Sylvie. But now she wondered.

"I just might," she said to the empty room.

Orin agreed to see her right away, but before discussing anything else he wanted to hear her usual weekly report on the appearances she'd made on behalf of the magazine. She told him about a speech she'd made at a convention of newspaper publishers in New Orleans, some television interviews. He sat listening at the middle of his enormous round bed. His pajamas today were a deep shade of gold mixed with brown, shades of autumn.

"You're doing a great job," he said when she finished. "I'm unhappy about one thing, though."

"What?" It dismayed Kai to hear that Orin was dissatisfied. She felt she had been working especially hard, and had been very effective. *Tomcat*'s subscription role was up twenty percent since she had begun appearing in public; she couldn't take all the credit, but much of it came from colleges or cities where she had toured.

"Jill tells me there have been some feelers from *Cosmo* about luring you away to do a column for young women, and there's also been some contact from a movie company— something about going out to Hollywood for a screen test."

Kai laughed lightly. "I guess I'm getting what they call a high profile. Is that what bothers you?"

"What bothers me is that you'll take one of these offers."

Kai laughed again. "I can't act, O.O.—and even if I could, it doesn't interest me. You don't have to worry about losing me to another magazine, either. Don't you think I believe in loyalty? You really gave me a home when I needed one."

He smiled. "That's a load off my mind."

"There is something I'd like to add to my duties at the magazine, though." Kai leaned back on one elbow into the fur that covered O.O.'s bed.

"You want to try a column?"

Kai shook her head. "I want to be a Kitty."

Orin regarded Kai dubiously. "Where'd this idea come from?"

"Friend of mine said I had no right speaking up for *Tomcat* if I'm not ready to support what it stands for one hundred percent. 'Put my body where my mouth is' were the words she used."

"So that's it? A friend dared you, and you're afraid of losing face?"

"No, it's much more than that," she said slowly. "It's important to me not to be a hypocrite—not to say one thing and do another." Her father had done it to Lokei, she thought. That was why it wasn't a small crime to her, why she couldn't bear to be guilty of the same thing.

Orin was thoughtfully silent.

Kai sat up. "Well?" she prompted. "Why not?"

"I thought when I met you you'd make one of the most stunning Kitties we've ever had. . . ." He paused.

"But?" she demanded. In the absence of any enthusiasm from O.O., she felt a pang of rejection.

"I know you better now. You've already started to make your mark, to create a—a different kind of image. I'm not sure it would be a good idea for you, Kai. Remember, millions of men see those pictures."

Kai appreciated the almost fatherly concern O.O. was showing for her. But his suggestion that it could damage her "image" seemed to run counter to his own philosophy. "You're not going to tell me they'll think I'm a bad girl," she said tartly.

"No, Kai, I just don't want you to do this on a whim. You have to think about all the consequences. I give the same advice to all the women who pose for us. Look ahead to a time years from now, a time when you might be married and have children, might be a successful businesswoman—just be sure you won't have any regrets." O.O. sat up straighter and ran his hand through his hair. The gesture produced a little tuft of upstanding hair that made him look like a little boy in his pajamas. Though he was acting like a father figure, Kai was reminded of Jill's caution that there were many ways in which O.O. had never grown up.

"Here's what I propose," Orin said at last. "Don't make a rash decision overnight. If you still want to pose when

Christmas comes, we'll do the shoot at the house in Tangier.''

At regular intervals O.O. flew off with an entourage to one of his holiday homes in Aspen, Beverly Hills, Grand Cayman Islands, and Tangier, where he always went for the winter holidays. Kai had yet to be included in these festive jaunts. She'd heard rumors about the nonstop parties, wilder than anything that went on at the Alley, but she'd never felt left out. She was a serious member of the *Tomcat* enterprises, not a playgirl eager to participate in fabled orgies.

"Christmas," Kai said, affirming her commitment, "no regrets."

Chapter Seventeen

Wearing a striped silk beach robe, Kai sat on a huge rock, her copper hair streaming in the wind. Before her the waves of the Atlantic crashed on the North African beach; behind her the city of Tangier basked on its hills with the rugged Rif Mountains forming a backdrop. Soon she would remove the robe and stand nude in front of the photographer and O.O., who was personally supervising the shoot.

"Take as much time as you want," he had told her. "Nothing will happen until you're ready."

She turned her face up to the sun and closed her eyes. For a moment the sound of the surf reminded her of Hawaii. But Tangier, with its stark white buildings, its markets filled with the braying of camels and donkeys, its towers from which the prayers to Allah were called out by *meuzzins* at sunrise and sunset, was a world away from the home of her youth. The city looked bright and sparkling under the sun, but it was a place where danger lurked in the alleyways and souks.

Kai opened her eyes and saw Burt Chetwyn, the English photographer O.O. used in Europe and points east, moving some of the large silver reflecting screens to catch more of the sun. Burt, built like a teddy bear, his long hair worn in a ponytail, caught her eye and gave her a wink.

Now or never. She slid down from the rock in one liquid motion, then waded into the water, but no matter how far out she went, the depth remained the same, covering nothing but her feet and ankles. With her back to Burt and O.O., she removed the robe and balled it up in her hands.

"Catch!" she shouted as she spun to face them and launched the wadded cloth into the air.

O.O. caught it and nodded approval as his eyes roamed over her naked body. Her nipples rose and hardened as the breeze played over her skin. She felt defenseless, vulnerable, and she wondered suddenly why she had done it. Was it because Sylvie had dared her—or because she had dared herself?

"Come toward me, luv," Burt was saying.

As she walked through the water he clicked his camera rapidly. "Lovely . . . super . . . magnificent . . . fab . . . great . . ." He called out a compliment each time he pressed the shutter, never repeating himself.

Gradually she loosened up, splashing water toward the shore, playfully prancing through the waves, thinking of herself as a mermaid who'd been given the power to walk. Burt shot roll after roll of film, dancing behind the camera, twisting his body in odd positions to capture her in whatever posture she assumed on a whim.

Eventually, Kai forgot the camera. She sank to her knees to examine a pink shell cast up on the beach, then lay back in the surf and let it wash up between her legs. She arched her neck for the pleasure of feeling her hair tease her shoulder blades. Burt's cries of "sensational" and "smashing" mingled with the sound of the surf.

At last she rose and ran along the beach, overtaken by a glorious sense of freedom, though Burt was running behind her, snapping all the time. It was a surprise when O.O. appeared directly in her path, bringing her to a halt. "It's over, Kai," he said as he draped the striped silk caftan over her shoulders. "We have more than enough film. You were incredible."

In a curious daze, yet feeling triumphant, Kai walked up the beach toward the steps that were cut into the side of a cliff, leading to O.O.'s vacation house. It had been built so that it seemed almost an extension of the rock that rose sheer from the sea. Fronted by a thick grove of cypress that concealed it from the coast road, its traditional Moorish design was reminiscent of a palace from the Arabian nights. But the entire back of the house had been opened to the light and the ocean view with a wall of glass webbed in steel.

As Kai and O.O. entered the house, a platoon of servants was replenishing the candles in braziers on the walls. O.O.'s parties in Morocco were always lit by thousands of candles—tonight electricity would be allowed only in the kitchen and the servants' quarters.

Ibrahim, the major domo in charge of the Moroccan staff, rushed up to claim O.O.'s attention, while Kai continued up the curving staircase to her room, one of a dozen that lined the marble-floored corridor. Behind the closed doors, Kai guessed that guests were beginning to prepare for the Christmas party that was now only a couple of hours away. Jill had come along on the junket, and several potential Kitties—one of whom, a gorgeous brunette named Amanda, was definitely making a bid to become O.O.'s new Pussycat. A French movie star was installed in the room next to Kai's, and the room across the hall was reserved for the rock star, Tina Warner, who was jetting in from London. Mick and Bianca Jagger, who were renting another villa up the beach for a week, were supposed to appear for the party; and a Hollywood contingent, flown in and lodged at a local hotel at O.O.'s expense, would also be there. Local expatriates, business magnates, and some members of the Moroccan royal family were also invited. Even King Hassan might come—though the guests had been told he would be incognito, and anyone who recognized him was to pretend otherwise.

Laid out on the bed in her room, Kai found a magnificent Moorish caftan made of golden cloth with myriad seed pearls sewn into the bodice. A wooden box with a hinged lid lay next to the caftan. Kai lifted the lid and saw a note written in O.O.'s obsessively neat hand: "This must be returned to the Royal Museum but enjoy it tonight." Pushing the note aside, Kai saw what appeared to be a necklace of tiny golden bells. When she picked it up, their tinkling was so melodious it made her laugh with pleasure; she felt like the heroine of a fairy tale with her golden gown and magical charms.

Not until she had bathed and dressed in the caftan, her hair gleaming and loose, did she realize that the bells were not a necklace after all, but intended to be worn as a circlet around her head. As she stood before the mirror and fitted them on, she thought she truly looked like a Moroccan princess, dressed for some ancient ritual.

By the time she floated down the staircase, the lower salon was brilliant from the light of a thousand flickering candles. A sinuous, haunting tune rose from an orchestra of native musicians. One of them, a woman in a shawl, held a small drum made of animal skin and beat out a throbbing rhythm with agile fingers covered with blue tattoos. As Kai watched her, the woman lifted her head, and beneath the rim of her shawl Kai could see that her face also was tattooed. Scanning the room, Kai saw Jill, dressed in a black velvet gown that covered her in front from neck to ankle; then Jill turned, revealing the entire sweep of her graceful back open to the uppermost slopes of her buttocks. The effect was stunning. Kai wondered if O.O. had handpicked Jill's outfit, too.

Burt came to Kai's side, holding two glasses of champagne, and handed one to her. "Here's to the best model I've ever had," he proclaimed loudly so that everyone else in the room could hear.

"It was a great shoot, all right." Kai turned at the sound of O.O.'s voice. He was resplendent in a tuxedo with diamond studs in his creamy silk shirt. "And before the rest of the crowd arrives," he said to all the houseguests, "I'd like to wish us all a Merry Christmas. This evening is designed for pleasure, and I want you all to enjoy it to the hilt. We've earned it." He made a little bow in Kai's direction. "No one more than Kai Wyler, who not only represents *Tomcat* so ably, but will be gracing its pages soon."

The huge salon was soon filled with guests and the sounds of English mingled with French and Arabic. Servants circulated with never ending glasses of champagne and trays of delicacies. Kai saw people she had only read about before. An American expatriate reputed to be the richest woman in the world arrived with her teenage lover, a black-eyed Arab boy wearing American jeans. Mick and Bianca came, and George Harrison, and Jean Shrimpton, a tall, doe-eyed English beauty known more commonly as "The Shrimp," who was currently the top magazine covergirl. The native musicians were replaced with a rock band. As the guests crowded onto an outside terrace for dancing, Amanda shook her voluptuous body so vigorously that a party of local businessmen took bets on how soon her breasts would fall out of her strapless gown.

"So many beautiful women," said a voice in Kai's ear, and she turned to see a tall, handsome man in a white dinner jacket standing at her shoulder, regarding her with gleaming, appreciative eyes. "We are used to O.O. honoring us with his presence, but this evening seems special, even by his standards."

"And why is that?" Kai said.

"Because tonight I am looking at the most beautiful woman I have ever seen."

A bit heavy-handed, she thought, but she merely smiled.

"If you are free tomorrow," the man said, "it would be my pleasure to arrange a most wonderful treat for you."

"What would that be?" Kai asked. She could hear a flirtatious lilt in her voice, and it occurred to her she'd better cut down on the champagne.

"I have the most extensive collection of pornography in Tangier. Something for everyone—"

Jill was suddenly in between the man and Kai. "Excuse me," she said determinedly, "O.O. needs to see Kai." Linking her arm through Kai's, she drew her firmly away. "Hope you don't mind. I thought you ought to rescued from Dirty Donald. His porn collection isn't so bad, but he usually tries to drug anybody who goes to see it, then he brings in a bunch of boys—and lets them do whatever they want while he takes pictures to add to his collection."

"Sounds like he ought to be locked up," Kai said.

"In another country he might be. I keep telling Orin he's abusing the Tomcat Philosophy to invite a man like that."

"Then why does he?"

"He's the architect who built this house," Jill said.

Jill steered Kai into one of the many little anterooms that lay through the Moorish arches lining one side of the grand salon. This one was furnished only with piles of brocade cushions, and Jill sank down with a sigh. "Relax," she said, patting a place on the cushions beside her.

"If you'd like to be introduced to some of the special treats in Morocco," she said when Kai settled next to her, "you don't have to go to Dirty Donald's." Jill opened her tiny jet evening bag and took out two cigarettes. She held one out to Kai.

Kai waved it away. "I don't smoke," she said.

"Honey, these aren't plain old cigarettes. They're joints—filled with the finest hashish in the world. Right from the source. C'mon, try one." Again she pushed the small rolled white tube at Kai. "It'll be good for you," she coaxed. "You need to get loosened up, Kai—you've needed it from the time we met." She leaned closer, as if to confide a secret, although they were alone. "And don't think you've done it just because you've let everyone see you in your birthday suit. I think maybe that's your substitute for the real thing."

Kai hesitated. Jill had always seemed so perfectly straight and sensible. She had also given Kai so much good advice over the months since she had begun training under her. Maybe this was an experience she needed. She took the hashish.

Jill lit the joint for her with the solid gold lighter she always carried—a gift from O.O. Kai watched the way Jill smoked the hashish, inhaling deeply and holding the smoke in her lungs, and did the same. It burned her throat at first and she coughed, but soon she got the hang of it. As smoke curled off the end of her joint, Kai realized she'd been smelling the minty odor of the hashish all evening without knowing what it was.

"It doesn't seem to do much for me," she said to Jill after a minute. Yet she did feel unusually relaxed, she was suddenly aware. The music of the rock band seemed to be coming from very far away and, curiously, the flames of all the candles seemed to be wavering in exact synchrony with the beat of the music. A high-pitched shriek came from somewhere, and Kai wondered if Amanda had finally fallen out of her red dress. She started to tell Jill, but it seemed much easier to just remain silent.

Kai took another deep drag on her joint, then another.

"Go easy," Jill said. "This stuff is very potent."

It could have been five minutes or an hour later when Kai realized she was alone. When had Jill left?

Kai got to her feet slowly. When she walked, she felt as though the ground beneath her lacked solidity. She was walking on a cloud, and her vision seemed exceptionally clear. But as soon as she was surrounded by all the noise and motion of the party, she wanted silence again and she drifted up the staircase, thinking she would lie down in her room.

As she walked down the long candlelit corridor, feeling the golden cloth of her caftan moving against her legs, she had an illusion that she was truly in the castle of an Arabian prince, long ago in ancient times. Then she heard a loud groan, a sound of pain coming from one of the bedrooms along the hallway. She wheeled around, her instinct to rush in and help, but she saw too many closed doors, and wasn't sure from which room the sound had come.

Then she heard it again, a choked whimper, and she knew it came from behind the door directly to her left. Immediately she was at the door, her hand on the knob. She paused for a second, overtaken by a mysterious terror, feeling herself suddenly powerless—as though a genie had reduced her to a speck imprisoned in a bottle. But she ignored her unreasoned terror and pushed open the door.

Inside, at the end of the bed in the center of the dim chamber, Lokei was squatting naked on her haunches, her dark hair hanging over her face, her moans rising as Harley Trane stood with eyes glazed and a demonic look on his face, ramming the erect red shaft of his member into Lokei from behind.

Kai glided forward in a stupor, never questioning that the genie's magic had returned her mother to life and brought her here. "Mama?" she said in the small voice of a child.

The man and the woman turned toward her, and as the light through the doorway caught their faces, the illusion was shattered. The woman was the French movie star, the man a stranger Kai had never seen before. They paused for an instant, and then the man slowly began to move again, his eyes remaining on Kai. "Join us," he said.

"Oui, cherie," purred the Frenchwoman as she was prodded from behind. *"Venez.* Come with us."

The man gave a growling laugh. "Yes. Come . . . ."

Kai whirled and fled from the overlapping visions of past and present.

As she ran down the corridor, the flames of the candles in the wall sconces seemed to surge as she passed, reaching out for her. Ahead of her, the hallway looked as if the walls were narrowing, pressing in. Suddenly the red line on the floor that stretched beneath her feet was no longer a carpet but a river of lava. Kai jumped back. She was in great danger—the volcano was about to erupt. Panic swarmed into her throat, choking her, but with a supreme effort she forced herself to run through the river of molten lava and she felt nothing.

Without any awareness of intervening time, she found herself outside, stumbling along a road. A wind had risen, and the stars overhead seemed to be the eyes of a million *kahuna* staring down at her. Kai turned her eyes away from the frightening sky and kept going toward the lights of the city ahead. As she walked, stoically putting one foot in front of the other, her mind whirled with a tormenting tumble of images, her mother and Trane, the French actress being taken like a dog, Lewis Standish assaulting her, and then her father—that awful night and afterward, thinking she had killed him. Why was there so much cruelty and violence in sex? Where was the love?

She thought of herself on the beach only a few hours ago, letting her nakedness be photographed for all the world to see. She was no longer sure why she had done it. She had meant to free herself from old fears, but they were still with her. Confused and miserable, she stumbled on. In the darkness the only sound she heard was the low moan of the wind and the tinkling of the tiny bells in her golden crown.

Kai found herself in the *medina,* the old city, where the narrow streets converged in a jumbled maze. By day it was a hive of activity, crammed with souks and bazaars that sold everything from rugs to fine leather goods to jewelry and perfume and aphrodisiacs. Now, though, it was dark and deserted.

She glanced down an alleyway and thought she saw a dark figure lurking ahead in the gloom. Abruptly, she turned back and walked swiftly in the other direction. A new fear struck her. The golden crown of bells around her head was a treasured museum piece. If it was glimpsed by some lurking denizen of these alleys, it could easily be stolen. A quick thrust with a dagger, and her caftan would run red with blood, the crown ripped from her head. Even without the golden museum piece she realized she was in terrible danger. Moslem men would have the greatest contempt for any unchaperoned woman abroad in the streets of the *casbah* in the middle of the night. O.O. had warned her about such behavior before they made the trip, showing her a newspaper clipping about a Western woman, a tourist, who had been

stoned to death in Turkey because she was walking the
streets of a village in shorts.

Kai's heart pounded in her chest and a metallic taste of
fear filled her mouth. Turning into another alley, she saw
the thin, graceful finger of a minaret rising in silhouette
above the lower roofs of the city. A mosque, a temple. She
would be safe there. She guided herself toward it, turning
this way and that, in the labyrinth of streets. Starving cats
darted out from the shadows and ran in front of her, brushing the hem of her caftan. She thought she heard whispers
emerging from dark doorways, propelling her faster through
the night.

At last she was in the street of the mosque. She hurried
to the heavy iron door and pushed it open.

It was as deserted inside as the streets of the *casbah*. Yet
she felt safe in its cool silence. As she entered and saw the
carpets that lay edge to edge over the stone floor, Kai remembered that it was traditional to remove one's shoes. She
left her sandals by the door and took a seat on one of the
worn carpets, looking toward the front of the mosque—facing
Mecca. Gradually her heartbeat returned to normal, and her
dread diminished. She would wait here until it was light, she
thought, until the *muezzins* called the faithful to prayer.

The long flight had cleared her mind, and she realized
that all her terrifying visions had been the result of the hashish.

Several times Kai nearly fell asleep, but she was brought
awake again by her strange surroundings and the need to
make sense of things, to make decisions. She now felt a
distaste for the life she was making, and yet she had no idea
how to change it. She recognized, too, that she owed a debt
of loyalty to Orin. He had taken her in and protected her.
He had shown the sort of kindness she had hoped to find
when she left Hawaii in search of her father.

In the dome of the windowless mosque were a few small
slits, and Kai saw the light streaking through change from
a deep blue to a pearly grey as the sun rose. At last a wailing
chant rang out from the minaret, the call to prayer.

She slipped into her sandals and left her place of refuge
before the first of the devout arrived. Having departed from
O.O.'s mansion without money, she was prepared to repeat
the long walk that had brought her here.

But as she made her way out of the *casbah,* she heard her name called out from along one of the alleys. Turning to her left, she saw O.O. standing by the entrance to a souk that was just opening for the day. His hair rumpled, his eyes taut with worry, he ran toward her. She broke into a run, too.

"Where have you been?" he cried as they met, his hands grasping her arms as though worried she might break away. "I've been going out of my mind, Kai, searching all night long."

"I'm sorry, Orin." She thought of telling him that she had tried hashish and had a bad reaction, but she didn't want Jill to be blamed. "I just had to get away."

"I know. It was a bad scene. I'm the one who should apologize."

"Never mind," she said. "I wasn't lost. I can take care of myself." As she said it, she realized it was true. She had always thought that she needed someone to take care of her, that she would stay lost and vulnerable without a father. But something had changed last night. She had lived through some of her fear, and she felt stronger.

"I guess I'm the one who felt lost," Orin said.

She looked at him curiously, but he said nothing else as they turned and left the *medina,* his arm encircling her shoulders protectively.

Chapter Eighteen

In late March, advance copies of the May issue featuring Kai were delivered to the Alley. Returning to her room at the end of the day, Kai found a card from O.O. taped to the door, asking her to visit his quarters.

Though he had participated in social activities while in Morocco, O.O. had resumed his peculiar habits as soon as he was back at the Alley. With one difference. For three months there had been no "pussycat" sharing his rooms. And in his recent installments of the "Tomcat Philosophy," O.O. had declared that he was abiding by a self-imposed period of celibacy. As he explained in the column, there was a time when all men should abstain for the purpose of renewing their appreciation of the miracles of physical pleasure. He then used his personal statement to elaborate on the role of celibacy in history, and indulge in philosophical speculation on the role of self-denial in human improvement. Indeed, O.O. wrote, because there was no more important force than sex in the life of a man, it was necessary to test oneself by controlling the sexual appetite. "A fast," he wrote, "will always add to one's appreciation of the feast."

That America's leading merchant of sex should decide to abstain from the pleasures of the flesh inspired considerable comment—from those close to him as well as tabloid columnists. Until now he had been regarded by those who knew him as a genius entitled to live according to his own plan; now they wondered if O.O. was no longer merely eccentrically reclusive, but had tipped over into some sort of half-mad monkish obsession.

Whenever Kai saw him, however, nothing about O.O. seemed any different—except that he no longer wore the gold whistle on a chain around his neck. Having kept her

commitment as spokeswoman for the magazine, she continued to report to him on her activities. Since that moment
he had found her in the *medina,* there had been a special
closeness between them.

Today, when he sent for Kai, he was not on the bed
dressed in his trademark pajamas, but wearing dark slacks
and a burgundy silk shirt with an ascot.

"Why the new look?' she asked at once.

"I guess it's a way of celebrating *your* new look," he
said. He pressed a button on the console at the head of his
bed. The light panels on his wall flared to brilliant life—
and there she was, in dozens of poses, naked as Eve. Leap-
ing above the sand dunes, lying at the edge of the ocean,
the surf caressing her flesh. The honey tones of her skin
were in glorious harmony with the long, empty beach, the
sun-bleached rock, the perfect azure sky, and deeper turquoise water.

During the pre-publication period she had never asked to
see the pictures—had been afraid she would regret them,
after all. Now she stared at the images of herself as if they
were pictures of a stranger. There was no reason to feel
shame. This was a celebration of nature, timeless and elemental, and she was as much a part of it as the sand and
sea.

"Magnificent, aren't they?" O.O. said. He moved behind her and put his hand on her shoulder. It rested there a
moment, then it slipped down, past the short sleeve of the
loose T-shirt she had put on as soon as she returned from
work. His fingers played lightly along the skin of her arm.
There was no mistaking the message of the caress.

She turned to him questioningly. "I thought you didn't
want anyone."

"I've wanted you from the first moment I saw you," he
said softly. "But neither of us was ready, were we?"

Was it for her that he had been "fasting"?

"I'm ready now, though," he said, barely above a whisper. "Are you?"

Looking into his eyes, she gave him her silent answer,
and in the next moment he lowered his mouth gently to
hers.

Every doubt and fear that had kept her desire imprisoned
for so long was swept away in the flood of need released by

his kiss. Her lips opened to him, and their tongues met, speaking a wordless language of urgent longing. His mouth moved from her lips to her neck, her throat, and she tossed her head back, gasping as his hands pressed into the small of her back, pulling her tightly against him. When their mouths met again, a deep, painless ache began to rise in her. Impulsively she pushed him back to undo the buttons of his shirt. Each undressing the other, they moved across the floor to the bed. There he took complete command, pushing her hands aside as he finished removing all she was wearing, breathing warm kisses onto her skin at each new place that was bared. She was tingling everywhere as he eased her down on her back. Then he was naked beside her, and they wrapped themselves around each other, rolling in a tangle across the surface of the enormous bed as they kissed. He pulled her to a stop and his mouth began to roam, exploring her neck, shoulders, breasts. He brushed his lips across her hardened nipples, ran his tongue around them in circular motions, sending electric jolts of pleasure to her core. When his hand brushed teasingly between her legs, she arched forward, eager for him, ready to have all of him. But he gentled her back.

"Wait," he whispered.

He laid a trail of kisses down across her stomach, and then she felt his warm lips on her thighs. A moment later he was pleasuring her with his tongue. It went on and on, building in waves of sensation so intense she thought she might die if he didn't stop. At last she called out to him, "Please . . . now . . . !"

Suddenly he was there, above her, and no sooner did she lift her legs and part them than he was sliding down inside her. She clenched her legs and arms around him, and as he thrust into her again and again she felt a spear of pain that came and went so quickly she could barely distinguish it from the pleasure. The exquisite spasms became stronger and stronger, so strong she was almost afraid. Afraid that the boiling red core of her being could overflow and destroy everything around it. She felt herself trembling on the brink, as though something within her had cracked open, and suddenly a rush of sensation exploded through her body and outward, in gradually diminishing waves. It was nothing to be afraid of, she realized. A cry of joy and gratitude rose from her throat for the release he had given her.

"I'm glad I was first," he said at last. "I adore you, Kai."

She eased away to look at his face. There was something in the way he had said he valued her that wasn't quite satisfying. Was being adored the same as being loved? She wasn't sure. Or did it matter? Did she love him—or did she simply realize that there was no one better to educate her to all the sensations she now longed to discover?

She stayed with him that night, and all the next day and another night. If his fast had lasted months, hers had lasted years, and she couldn't get enough of him. O.O. was a generous and patient lover, with an amazing sensitivity to her shifting needs and moods. Soon she was eager to show her own unselfishness, and she gave herself to him in every way he wanted. They stayed in bed constantly and ordered food delivered from the Alley's kitchen. Kai began to understand the unique spell that was cast by staying within this windowless world, where the demands of a schedule were erased along with the distinctions of night and day. Where every other boundary of time was erased, it was easier to banish the boundaries of propriety. Here they were as primal as animals in a cave, with nothing to do but rest and satisfy their appetites.

On the second morning when Kai woke, O.O. was beside her in his pajamas, with the material to be edited for the next issue of *Tomcat* spread out around him. It was time for her, too, to return to work.

They took a shower together and made love once more under the sluicing hot water. "From now on," he told her when he kissed her goodbye, "you'll live with me. I'll have all your things moved in here."

It didn't occur to her to disagree. She wanted him beside her, *inside* her every moment she could have him.

As she walked the corridors of the Alley, returning to her room so she could change into clothes for the office, she was aware of the glances of the other girls and the whispers passed back and forth in her wake. Yes, of course, they had to know. Having been cloistered with O.O. for the better part of two days, she had officially taken over the role of "pussycat."

It bothered her a little to be regarded now as O.O.'s property. Yet she couldn't help feeling pride, too. Didn't they all want him? And she was the one for whom he had broken his sexual fast!

When she arrived at work, her secretary handed her the wad of message slips that had piled up during her absence. "And Jill wants to see you. Said you should go in as soon as you got here."

Dressed in a timeless black Chanel suit, her hair in a neat French twist, Jill managed to look severe and feminine at the same time. "Sit down, Kai," she said with a noticeable lack of warmth as she moved behind her desk.

Since Kai had no speaking engagements scheduled for the day, she had dressed more casually in a shirtwaist dress. Jill's elegance was a reminder to Kai of the time when she had been a mere protégé. Yet she did not feel intimidated by Jill's curt manner; the past two days had powerfully reinforced her ego.

When Kai was seated, Jill examined her carefully, almost like a doctor looking for symptoms. "He's good, isn't he?"

It took Kai a moment to understand the significance of the question. Word had traveled fast from the Alley to the tower.

Not just good, fabulous. Kai toyed with the answer as a way of punishing Jill for prying. But she didn't want to be drawn into reducing her experience to petty gossip. What she had with O.O. she wanted to keep for herself.

As Kai paused, Jill hurried to fill the silence. "Never mind. I suppose you're thinking the whole thing is too sacred to spoil by sharing it with anyone else."

Kai was surprised less by Jill's perception than by her bitter, mocking tone. Jill had always seemed so sincerely untroubled by the dissolution of her romantic involvement with O.O. Suddenly she was acting jealous and angry. Obviously she wasn't as well adjusted to loving O.O. from afar as she had claimed.

Kai pulled forward in her chair as if to go. "You've been a great friend to me, Jill, showing me the ropes around here. I'd like to keep that friendship, so I don't think it's a good idea for us to talk about anything but magazine business."

"I *am* trying to be a friend, Kai. That's why I wanted to warn you about Orin."

Kai shot to her feet. "I thought so. But is it a warning? Or is it just the best you can do to hold on—hoping that if you chase everyone else away, then someday you'll get him back?"

Jill smiled thinly. "I don't have to chase anyone away. He does that himself. That's what I thought I'd better remind you of—as a friend. Don't make the mistake of thinking it's going to last. No matter how good it is with O.O., prepare yourself for the fact that it's just temporary. Accept that right at the beginning, and it'll be easier later."

Kai bridled at Jill's attempt to cast a shadow over her pleasure. "But suppose I'm different," she snapped. "Suppose he's ready for something more than he's had before." Even as she spoke, Kai had to wonder why she was defending herself and her affair with Orin Olmsted with such vehemence. Did she hope to be with him forever?

The thin, crooked smile hadn't left Jill's face. "It always starts this way—with every single one. With me, too, I won't deny it. Each one thinks she'll be different."

"That's enough, Jill," Kai said, turning and starting for the door. "I don't need to listen to you. If O.O. wants me, then it's not just because he wants to keep his bed warm."

"You still don't get it, do you?"

The shrill pitch of Jill's voice succeeded in stopping Kai in her tracks. Kai turned back to stare at Jill as she went on. "It's the only way he wants any woman—it's his *kink*. Don't you see, that's why it's always one of the Kitties who becomes his pussycat? He's got this macho thing where he has to be taking a woman away from someone else to appreciate her. Except with O.O., it's not enough to take her away from just one man. He has to make a million other men lust for her first . . . and then, only then, he'll want her."

As Kai stared at Jill, she recalled that when she had first told O.O. she wanted to pose, he had tried to dissuade her. Was his concern only part of a pretense? "If you're right," Kai challenged Jill, "then you knew I'd get involved with him as soon as I offered to pose for the magazine."

"It was inevitable," Jill agreed.

"You didn't mention that at the time," Kai observed quietly.

"You'd have been even less likely to listen to me then than you are now. Anyway, I've never wanted to discourage you from having an affair with O.O. Frankly, I always thought he'd be the ideal man to have for your first lover."

Jill's presumption annoyed Kai. "What makes you think he *is* the first?" she said.

"We spent a lot of time together when you first came here, Kai. Do you think I couldn't see that you were still afraid of men?"

Afraid of men? She had never thought of her problem in exactly those terms. She had been afraid of herself, if anything, afraid that the intense sex appeal she had been told she possessed would cause her to be victimized as her mother had been. But, yes, perhaps it amounted to the same thing. And why wouldn't she be afraid, after having her perceptions molded from the earliest age by a man like Harley Trane—and most recently by her own father? She thought that with O.O. her fear had finally been conquered. In the rush of gratitude she felt toward him, she believed that she did love Orin.

"I guess I should thank you," she said quietly. "For saying nothing then . . . and for warning me now. But you don't have to be concerned about me, Jill. I'm not expecting anything more than I think I can have." In her own mind, Kai meant that she was still confident of being the exception; if she loved Orin, he would surely return that love.

But Jill took Kai's words to mean that she was being realistic. "As long as you're not setting yourself up to get hurt, Kai. I've been through it, and I was hoping to save you some pain."

Kai thanked Jill coolly once more and left her office. She still doubted that Jill's motive for the warning had been purely unselfish. But she was inclined to be forgiving. Jill had obviously never gotten over her affair with O.O. There was nothing sadder, Kai decided, than a woman carrying a torch for a man who no longer wanted her.

If Jill had done nothing else, she had made Kai conscious of her own feelings, and the need to have them reciprocated. But Kai would not plead for love, would not try to buy it by declaring her own. It had to be sincere. Her mother had deeply loved a man who gave her a false love in return, and it had destroyed her. So she was determined to wait for Orin to voice his feelings before she declared herself.

Their affair continued to blaze with physical passion; she lived with him, and her body hungered constantly for all the varied pleasures he knew how to draw from her nerves and flesh—at times, it seemed, from her very soul. She set no limits on what he could do with her, or what she would do for him. But she didn't believe she could regard their sexual enjoyment of each other as an expression of love until he was willing to define it exactly in those terms.

When the issue of *Tomcat* containing her pictures went on sale, there was a flurry of media attention because she had become something of a public figure through her representation of the magazine and her relationship to Randall Wyler. O.O. reported proudly that newsstand sales figures were the highest in the magazine's history.

Jill's warning was very much on Kai's mind when O.O.'s already prodigious sexual appetite seemed to grow even more insatiable in the weeks after her pictures were published. If he wasn't working on the magazine—reviewing layouts, writing, conferring with editors—then he wanted Kai. He kept her with him in bed whole days at a time. O.O. no longer wore his golden whistle—Kai had told him she thought it was demeaning—but he summoned her nevertheless from wherever she was when he felt the need to make love. The sensations were so new for Kai that her desire for him was no less consuming.

In the aftermath of each passionate interlude, Kai became more desperate to define the meaning and purpose of their coupling. Was it love or only an obsession?

O.O. was unsparing with his words of adoration. "You're unbelievably good," he would whisper as their bodies intertwined. "I worship you," he would murmur against her skin. "I adore you . . . there's no one like you . . . you're a miracle . . ."

But never those particular three words. The hunger of her body had been satisfied, but her heart was still starving.

Each spring, *Tomcat* conducted its annual readers' poll to find out which of the Kitties for the past twelve months

was "Top Kitty"—the readers' favorite. The honor carried
a cash award of $10,000, along with such lesser prizes as a
fur coat, a jeweled watch, and an assortment of designer
clothes.

When the cards were tallied in June, Kai received more
than seventy percent of all votes cast.

"That's the widest margin we've ever had," O.O. said
when he gave Kai the news. "You're the most popular centerfold in the history of the magazine." He told her then
that there would be a big party at the Alley to celebrate her
victory, and present her with her prizes. In the meantime
she would have to pose for a whole new set of shots to
appear in the September issue, when the results of the readers' poll were published. "Let's think about going someplace fabulous to take the pictures. Tibet, maybe. How about
that—you, in all your glory, with the Himalayas as a background."

Kai's excitement about winning the prizes was tempered
by the news that she would have to pose again. She had
done it once unashamedly to prove something to herself.
Doing it a second time was allowing herself to be exploited.

She couldn't express this to O.O., however. He was certainly not going to excuse her from fulfilling her obligation.
It was matter of business, as well as his philosophy. The
readers wanted to see more of Kai; there were magazines
to be sold.

She was ready to do anything he required of her, she
decided, if only she knew that his commitment to her would
last.

The night he told her that she had been chosen Top Kitty,
he made love to her with a driving intensity that seemed to
surpass even the fiercest passion he had shown in the past.
Barely had they finished once than he wanted her again.

But she held him off, the first time she had ever shown
even momentary reluctance. "What do I mean to you,
Orin?" she asked.

He shook his head in bewilderment. "Do you have to
ask?"

"Yes," she said simply.

He shrugged in a way that said he would humor her. "I
want you because you're beautiful and sexy and smart and
fun to be with—because you're desirable in every way. I

want you because you're an incredible woman who knows how to take pleasure and to give it. And I want you because . . . well, haven't I said it all?"

"No, not quite," she coaxed. "There's one more thing you might say."

He looked at her for a long moment. "Oh," he murmured finally. "This is about love." He pulled away from her and sat up, his back to her. "Of course I love you."

She started to reach out.

But then he went on. "But whenever that word gets used between people in bed, it's too easily misunderstood. Right away it becomes a clause in a contract. If I love you, then there are other things you should be able to expect." He turned to her. "Right?"

"Love ought to mean something in concrete terms."

O.O. smirked. "Concrete. That's the word, all right. Hard and unbreakable. And colorless. I thought by now you understood, Kai. Hell, you've been preaching the Tomcat Philosophy long enough. The basic idea is that we should be unafraid of pure pleasure, that we shouldn't have to make excuses to ourselves or to anyone else, shouldn't have to make deals, or pay for it, or look beyond the moment when we have it." He leaned toward her again. "Sure, I love you. I'm crazy about you. But if you want me to say it's going to last forever, I can't."

O.O.'s definition of love, she saw, was as idiosyncratic as everything else in his life. "You can't even say it'll last for another week, can you?"

"No," he said without hesitation. "And you don't have to say it, either. Just enjoy what we have now. Enjoy it each and every minute it exists."

The same advice that Jill had given her.

She gazed at him a moment, then she opened her arms, inviting him to take her again, giving herself with total abandon.

But she had already decided it would be their last time.

Later, when he had fallen asleep, she gathered her belongings and left the Alley. As always, even long into the night, there was a party going on in the downstairs rooms, and disco music pulsed in the air. But Kai felt only a twinge of regret at deserting the never ending party, and she gave not even a thought to forfeiting the honor of being Top

Kitty—along with its cash prize of ten thousand dollars. In fact, she knew she was cutting herself off from everything connected to *Tomcat,* the way of thinking as well as living. Unable to endorse O.O.'s philosophy of love, she realized that she could no longer work for the magazine.

Wherever it would lead, the choice was made. There had to be something more than pleasure alone. If she accepted nothing more, gave herself to a man who wanted nothing more, then how much better was she than a *manuwahi*?

Kai hadn't looked ahead very far to how she would survive. During the time she'd worked for *Tomcat,* most of her large salary had gone for expensive clothes. Even her fee for posing as a Kitty had been gobbled up, partly by a used car and by proudly sending a check for two thousand dollars to Mak and Lili, who were getting ready to retire from their jobs at the Crater Inn. Kai assumed she would get another job, save money, and finally take herself back to Hawaii. After all the time that had passed, she still thought of the islands as home.

She expected that her notoriety as a Kitty would give her some marketability as a model, but when she made the rounds of local agents, the only photographic work she was quickly offered was to pose again in the nude, always for magazines of lesser quality than *Tomcat.* To a degree, her one experience as a nude model had already branded her. She had lost the wholesome image that would have brought her work in catalogues or advertisements.

But then she discovered that being a former Kitty was a saleable qualification in the area of making "personal appearances." For a fee of between two hundred and four hundred dollars an agency could hire her to appear at openings of new health clubs, or supermarkets, or at conventions and trade shows. Booked for two or three appearances a week, her savings account soon began to show a healthy balance. When she had twenty thousand dollars saved, she thought, she would return to the islands; she might look for a small business—or even try to attend college.

But her plans changed suddenly. On a hot afternoon late in June, after doing a stint promoting computers for a manufacturer at an electronics show, she returned to the small residential hotel where she occupied a furnished studio with a pullman kitchen. A letter from Mak was waiting in her mailbox, forwarded from the magazine offices.

Kai had been waiting eagerly for this response to her last letter to Mak and Lili two months ago, in which she had reported proudly on her well-paid job in the magazine business and had included the check for two thousand dollars. In view of the large gift, she had been surprised not to receive an immediate answer. She decided that the size of the gift must have made it an issue of pride, and they were grappling with whether to accept, refuse, or even pretend it didn't exist. Perhaps they feared she couldn't afford it. Kai had been thinking she would have to write again and clear the air if she didn't hear from them soon, so it was a relief to have their letter.

She carried it up to her room, changed into some comfortable clothes, poured herself a glass of pineapple juice, and sat down by a window that looked out across an alley to the brick wall of an adjacent building to enjoy this small vicarious taste of life in the beautiful islands.

As she pulled the single page from the envelope and unfolded it, the torn bits of her check fluttered out into her lap. Kai smiled. So she'd been right. They wouldn't accept it.

But as soon as she began to read her smile faded. By the time she had finished, she was in tears, her heart torn by a bitter mix of grief and shame and deep despair.

Three weeks ago, Mak wrote, Lili had died. She had been ill already with a diseased heart—the reason they had decided to retire from the inn—but he believed that her death had been hastened by the shock for which Kai was responsible. After Kai had written about her job with *Tomcat* magazine, they were curious about the publication, which they had never seen. When Mak boasted to Mr. Swenson about Kai's job, the hotel owner indicated that it was a very successful magazine with pictures of beautiful women, but Mak had not quite understood until he went down to Hilo and purchased a copy. It was the May issue, featuring Kai.

They had always taken special pride in her, Mak wrote, because they believed she had resisted the moral decline that had destroyed Lokei. But now they had no reason to be proud of her. In their minds, her willingness to show herself made her no better than a whore. For Lili, the horror of this realization had been enough to strip her of the will to live. Though her dying words to Mak had been to tell him he should forgive Kai, Mak could not. He wanted never to see her again, never to hear from her, and he certainly would never touch a penny of her money. There was no point in her trying to change his mind. "They say a picture is worth a thousand words," he finished. "These pictures said enough to break our hearts."

Kai had never imagined that the photographs would have such a devastating impact. Couldn't they separate the image from the substance of what she was? They *knew* her!

But then she realized that Mak and Lili no longer believed they did know her. She had been gone too long. The pictures were more real to them than the memories, and they were simple, moral people who could not tolerate what they saw as indecent.

She made a telephone call right away and reached Francis Swenson at the Crater Inn. She asked him to intervene with Mak, to explain that the world had changed, that she had done the photographs as a statement of freedom from censorship, of pride in herself.

Though Swenson was sympathetic, he offered little hope. Mak truly believed that Kai's nude photos had hastened Lili's death. It was no more rational than the belief in *kahuna* gods that Lili had never lost—and its hold was no less strong. Mak had obliged Lili's last wish to be buried in a ceremony conducted at a *heiau* by a *kahuna* priest.

BOOK
THREE

Chapter Nineteen

Kai gazed intently through a one-way glass panel at the two young men seated in sturdy oak chairs in an otherwise bare room. One, the clean-cut sophomore in a patterned ski sweater, held a black metal box in his lap with a dial on top, a bright red button next to it. A black wire snaked out of the back of the box, down across the floor and beneath the second man's chair.

Picking up a microphone on the counter in front of her, Kai pressed a switch to activate it and said firmly, "Dave, turn the dial up another notch."

The young man glanced at a corner loudspeaker which delivered Kai's command, then turned to the man in the other chair, a balding graduate student wearing a dark suit with a striped tie. His arms and legs were strapped down, and small electrodes were visibly taped to his wrists and ankles. He remained silent; by the rules of the experiment, he was not supposed to speak.

"Are you sure?" Dave said, his eyes directed to the glass panel—though on his side it was only a mirror. His voice came again through the intercom. "The last jolt I gave him seemed pretty hard to take. . . ."

"I'm sure, Dave," Kai said into the microphone. "Turn the dial up another notch."

Dave sucked on his lip a moment, then turned the dial on the black box slightly to the right and pressed the red button.

Instantly, the man in the second chair was thrown into an apparently painful spasm. After a moment he settled back, head lolling on his chest, seemingly semiconscious.

"Jesus," Dave could be heard gasping as he stared at the second man slumped over in his chair.

Kai consulted the notes on the counter in front of her, then spoke into the microphone. "He's all right, Dave. If I thought he wasn't, I wouldn't let you continue." Encouragement and reassurance, that was the next step. In a few moments she would ask Dave to turn the dial up another notch, and if he resisted, she would remind him he had agreed right at the beginning to do whatever was necessary to help in the research.

The project, which Kai had chosen for her senior work in behavioral psychology, was duplicating a classic experiment that had been designed and carried out more than fifteen years ago by Stanley Milgrim, a sociologist at Yale University. Milgrim's work was an attempt to explain the moral failure that accounted for totalitarian control and such crimes as those perpetrated by the Nazis—atrocities carried out by ordinary people whose excuse was simply to say, "I was only following orders." To test this crucial fulcrum in human behavior—the degree to which basic morality could be overcome by a tendency to abdicate responsibility to anyone in authority—Milgrim had set up an experiment similar to the one Kai was conducting: one person in charge of an apparatus that could be controlled to administer an increasing charge of strong electric current to a second person.

Except—as in Milgrim's experiment—the circumstances were a sham. The box Kai put in the hands of her subjects was *harmless*, and the "victim" only pretended to be affected whenever a slight buzzing sensation came through the wire. The unknowing subjects, recruited at random with a notice on college bulletin boards offering to pay for their time, were told only that they were participating in experimental research.

After the Yale experiment, grave doubts had been expressed by other academics about the morality of manipulating unwitting subjects into apparent acts of cruelty. But when Kai read about Milgrim's work in her textbooks, she had been fascinated. The puzzle of how and why decent people could be made to act contrary to their own better judgment was closely related to questions that had plagued her since she was a child—when she had seen her mother "taking orders" from Harley Trane.

Her wish to understand this self-destructive behavior had sparked the interest in psychology Kai was pursuing at Jefferson University in Baltimore. Though Jefferson didn't possess the traditional luster of the Ivy League, it was well known for its fine medical school and especially strong in the sciences. After completing her high school equivalency courses in Chicago, Kai had applied and had been admitted.

Now, from the room beyond the glass, Kai heard Dave's voice coming through the speaker in the control cubicle. "Look, this is really worrying me. . . ." He was nervously eyeing the graduate student who was still slumped over, eyes closed.

"We have an agreement, Dave, don't we? You said you'd do this. You're being paid. Now don't let me down. . . ." The phrases were all from a script, designed to test the limits of conscience, honor, and personal obligation.

The young man stared helplessly at the reflecting glass. In the room, he heard Kai as no more than a disembodied voice, unconnected to any visible face or form—in effect, the pure voice of command. "I'd rather not go on," he said shakily.

In the course of the experimental sessions, Kai had seen all variations of response. Several subjects had refused to cooperate the moment they believed their actions were causing harm; the majority went on, their reluctance growing even if they never resigned from what they began to see as their "duty"; a few showed no regrets at all.

"It's not a matter of choice, Dave," Kai said. "You've agreed."

The sophomore sat in the chair, visibly trembling with uncertainty.

"I'm afraid I have to insist, Dave. You've got to do this."

At last he rebelled. "The hell I do!" he shouted, bolting from his chair. "There's no law. I don't care about the damn money you're paying. I'm finished." He ran to the door, threw it open, and dashed out.

Kai noted down exactly what had occurred—including the fact that the subject had not taken the time in his rapid exit for even a backward look to check the condition of the other man. Tomorrow she would contact the subject, reveal the true circumstances, and pay him for the time he had given to the experiment.

Through the glass panel, Kai saw the graduate student sit up. She swept her notes into a briefcase, left the control cubicle and walked along a corridor to enter the adjoining room. "That's all this morning, Jason," she said to the grad student.

Jason Metz got out of his chair. "I hope you're not planning too many more of these sessions," he said. "It's beginning to bother me, too. It's such a strange experiment, Kai."

They left the room together and walked down the corridor of the science building.

"I suppose it is," Kai said. "But it seems to provide proof that most of us cling to our ideas of what constitutes moral behavior by a very slender thread."

"Is that really worth proving in scientific terms?"

"Defining the problem is the first step to providing a solution. Maybe we take it too much for granted that people are basically good or know instinctively what's right. I agree there's something unpleasant about this research, but the hardest part is that it forces us to face something unpleasant about ourselves. Once we face it, we can develop ways to solve it, educate people better to understand what's right or wrong."

Jason nodded. "Okay, I'll stick with it a while longer." They stopped at a stairway. "By the way, a touring company of *Hello, Dolly!* is coming to town next week. How about going with me?"

She smiled. "It's a sweet offer, but I've got too much work."

The graduate student didn't press. Even before trying his luck, he'd known that the girl generally regarded as the most beautiful on campus was also famous for refusing all dates. As far as anyone knew she had no life outside of school and her studies. He told Kai he'd see her at the next lab session and went off down the stairs.

Kai looked at her watch. Not yet noon. She had a class at three, she reminded herself, the first one of the new semester's survey course in Experimental Psychology.

She went to her locker on the third floor, exchanged her briefcase for the large tote bag that was stored in the locker. Then she left the building, running all the way to the parking lot.

Fifteen minutes later, she was in downtown Baltimore, entering one of the ancient red brick buildings along the section of East Baltimore Street which had once been lined with striptease bars. In the past few years, as the once proud port city had taken the first steps to save itself from the decay that had overtaken its downtown, many of the strip joints had closed. But the building Kai entered was still occupied on its ground floor by a place called Sassy's. Even though it was just noon, as Kai climbed to the third floor of the building she heard brassy stripper's music rising faintly up the stairwell.

The dingy third-floor corridor was lined with three doors on each side. Kai went to a middle one. LARRY MEYER—PHOTO ART was stenciled across frosted wire glass pane in its upper half. She took a breath and walked in.

The windowless room inside was large with an overhead skylight. Photographic paraphernalia stood around everywhere—lights, reflectors, tripods—and a dozen pieces of mismatched furniture were heaped in a corner. At one side were two unpainted plywood doors. "DARKROOM—KEEP OUT" was scrawled across one in black marker, and a red light bulb glowed above the frame.

"Larry?" Kai called out. "It's Kai."

A muffled voice emerged from the darkroom. "Wasn't expecting you."

"I know, but I had a couple of free hours."

"All right, I'll use you. Give me a couple of minutes to finish these prints. Meantime, get ready."

Kai went through the other door into a cramped, dirty bathroom. The bathtub was filled with boxes of photographic paper and bottles of chemicals used for developing. A shower-curtain rod was being used to hang a collection of lingerie and other costumes—corsets, leather jackets, gowns with the bustlines completely cut away. A small rack squeezed in beside the sink held two dozen pairs of slippers and shoes in different styles.

Folding her clothes neatly into her tote bag as she removed them, Kai stripped naked. From a side pouch of the tote, she took out a wig of long black tresses and a makeup kit. She put on the wig and adjusted it carefully, then applied false lashes, pink lipstick a dark eye liner, and a brownish eye shadow that had the effect of dulling the brilliant turquoise of her eyes.

Quickly she rouged her nipples, then rubbed some Vaseline on the tips, then along the pink tissue of her labia. Finally she wrapped herself in a terry kimono and stepped out of the bathroom.

Larry Meyer, the photographer, was standing with his back to her, reaching up to a long roll of red cyc paper hung on the bare brick wall at the rear of his studio. Rolls in other colors hung in parallel brackets. The paper provided the background for all his shots. The photographer pulled out a length of ten yards, covering the wall and also a section of the floor, then crossed to the heap of furniture in a corner. "Thought we'd use the velvet chaise, try some stuff with a Victorian feel. Help me dig it out from under."

He was in his early sixties with thick shaggy gray hair, a pleasant face, and a paunch that hung over his belt and threatened to pop the buttons of his denim workshirt. As Kai helped him move the studded velvet chaise longue, her unfastened kimono hung open, but the photographer never looked. His attention was concentrated on the heaped furniture, making sure it didn't topple as everything shifted when the chaise was removed. Then he steered a path through all the paraphernalia so nothing got knocked over.

When the furniture was placed on the red paper, he went to a tripod on which his Rolleiflex was mounted and started to adjust the focus. "Okay, kid," he said, "up and at 'em."

Kai slipped off the kimono and went to the chaise. "How do you want me? Lying down, sitting, straddling . . . ?"

"Improvise," the photographer said wearily. "Be creative."

Her money had run out after the first two years. No matter how careful she was, she had always known it would not be enough to get her through college without working. She had looked for jobs on the campus, at the bookstore, in the cafeteria, but these were awarded to students who had been promised financial aid at the time of admission, which Kai had not.

Falling back on her experience at the Crater Inn, Kai had taken part-time work as a desk clerk in a downtown hotel, but she found it difficult to manage the number of hours necessary to earn a reasonable wage and still keep up with her course studies. Working downtown also required that she buy herself a reliable used car. The costs added up. She tried sales, waitressing, working as a guide in the Baltimore & Ohio Railroad Museum. But the problem was always to earn enough money to supplement tuition and dorm fees without leaving herself so tired it became pointless to be in college.

Early this term, after struggling to make only a partial payment of tuition, she realized it was imperative to increase her earnings. She had already decided that to make the most of her work in psychology, she had to go on to graduate school. She had to start saving, and at the same time pay off the balance of current bills. Kai prayed, too, that she might somehow find extra money to visit Hawaii. It was the only way she could ever make up with Mak. Her letters had all been returned unopened.

The idea of modeling had naturally occurred to her. The first step would be to get sample shots she could send to modeling agencies. Larry Meyer was one of the photographers listed in the classified telephone directory, and when she called to ask his charge for a small portfolio, he had given a price half that of the nearest competitor.

The minute she entered his studio for the first time, Kai was under no illusions—Meyer was certainly not earning his living with fine portraiture. She might even have walked straight out, yet his price was so low, and there was something about his mild, unhurried way that gave her the feeling he could be trusted.

He worked quickly, and when she came back the following day to collect developed prints of the poses—in the variety of outfits she had supplied—Kai could not conceal her surprise at how well they had turned out. "These are really excellent," she said. "I'll bet I land some work once I get them out to the right people." She had told him while he was shooting the film the previous day that she was a student at Jefferson, and explained why she wanted the pictures.

"I suppose," he said, sounding slightly insulted, "you thought just 'cause I wasn't charging you a fortune, I'd give you a load of junk."

"No," Kai replied. "I just never thought they'd be this good."

"You're a very beautiful girl, Miss Wyler. Any man who couldn't take good pictures of you should be forbidden by law to hold a camera."

Then, with a slight effort at introducing the subject delicately, he had offered her a different kind of work. "You told me you need money for college. I don't know how much you need or how fast, but I do know real modeling is practically a full-time job and requires a good-size investment before it pays off. You won't get any decent work until you've gone to New York to tour the agencies and do test shots—and once you get assignments, you'll have to be away from Baltimore for weeks at a time. Nothing wrong with that if you're chasing a career as a model, but from the way you talked yesterday, it sounds like you care about your studies. So I thought I'd ask if you'd like to work for me. You won't earn near as much as a top fashion model, but it'll take a lot less of your time. I'll shoot at your convenience so it doesn't interfere in any way with your classwork."

He revealed then that the bulk of his own income came from taking nude photos on a free-lance basis and selling them to girlie magazines or for promotional calendars. His models came mostly from the strip bars—though that source was shrinking as the joints closed up—but occasionally there were other reputable young women who saw him as a good source of extra income, and felt no shame at having their bodies photographed. In recent years one of his best models had been a promising violin student at the Peabody Conservatory, one of the nation's finest schools of music, founded more than a hundred years ago—in a building that now co-existed amid the seedy strip joints. With some pride Meyer added, "These days she performs in concert halls all over Europe—always dressed to the nines. But she might not have made it through Peabody if she hadn't worked for me."

Kai was inclined to believe that Meyer really meant to help rather than exploit her. However he had come to support himself in this way, he was a talented man, who seemed basically decent. "I'll have to think about it, Mr. Meyer," she told him.

"Of course. Take your time. Forgive me if I've insulted

you by asking. I can understand you might want to put that part of your life behind you.''

Behind her. It was suddenly clear that he had recognized her as a former Kitty—not surprising that he would have seen the pictures even if they were seven years old. It was his profession, after all. But she appreciated that he did not use her past willingness to pose nude as a pressure point.

She mailed the pictures to several top model agencies in New York. All replied with letters of interest and invitations to spend a few days in the city—no expenses paid. With fare and lodging, the trip would cost her several hundred dollars. And what was she investing in? Could she keep up a career as a model?

Nevertheless, she rode a bus up to New York for a day to see one of the agencies that had expressed interest. At first sight, she felt uncomfortable in the city, with its rushing crowds and dingy gray canyons between high buildings. She took the bus back to Baltimore only two hours later, after being told by the woman who ran the agency that the only way to succeed as a model would be to quit school and concentrate on the career.

For her first three hours of posing for Larry Meyer, Kai received $250 in cash. Subsequently, working just six or seven hours a week, she averaged almost two thousand dollars a month. It allowed her to cover her bills and start putting away money for future expenses.

For all the sleaziness of the milieu in which he worked, Meyer proved to be consistently fair and honorable. The money he paid represented a good percentage of what he received for his finished pictures. When he found a market that paid better than usual, he shared the extra money with her. He had a genuine concern, too, that nothing he did would interfere with her schooling or damage her reputation. Before taking the first nude shots, he had suggested she might want to disguise herself with various wigs and makeup.

Today, when she headed back to the Jefferson campus, she was three hundred dollars richer. She had spent an hour posing on the red velvet chaise, and a second hour dressed only in a leather jacket and biker's hat, holding a lion tamer's whip.

* * *

She arrived a few minutes late, however, for the introductory class of her new course in Experimental Psychology taught by Dr. Laura Cooke. As Kai scuttled to a seat in the back row of the lecture theater, she noted that Dr. Cooke was not like the other women who taught at Jefferson. Most of them bustled around school dressed very casually in slacks and sweaters and plain shoes—if not for comfort and convenience, then to send a message to students that elegance and chic were extraneous to teaching. But Dr. Cooke was turned out as if to attend a downtown luncheon for ladies of the upper crust. Her dawn pink shantung suit looked as fine as any Italian designer original Kai had ever seen on Alexandra Wyler, its knee-length skirt revealing good legs that tapered down to high-heeled shoes in matching beige leather. Around her neck hung a double strand of pearls, and a pair of polished gold earrings glittered with each movement of her head. Her shoulder-length chestnut hair was well cut, styled to catch the perfect balance between casual and formal.

As Kai settled at the back of the raked auditorium, the professor broke off her introductory remarks and darted a look in Kai's direction, a message that she did not appreciate late arrivals. Then she went on:

"The survey will cover both history and method, beginning with such early experiments on animals as those done by Fechner and Pavlov, and running through to the more recent work of Hull, Tolman, B. F. Skinner, and others. We'll also look at some of the practical applications of experimental psychology, aside from psychotherapy—for example, the role it has played in the organization and training of the military, in industrial management, in education, and pediatric care. . . ."

Kai got out her spiral notebook and a pen and jotted down some of the names the professor had mentioned. She knew about Pavlov and Skinner, not Fechner and Tolman. Before the next class she intended to check the library and do some independent reading.

As she started taking notes, a student seated across the aisle shifted to a place beside her. She glanced up to see a young man with crewcut dark hair, a bull neck, and bulging biceps protruding from the rolled-up sleeves of his dark blue sweater. Sewn to the front of the sweater was a big gray *J*—

a letterman in athletics—a member of Jefferson's football team, Kai guessed. He gave her a leering smile, then a wink. Quickly, Kai dropped her eyes back to her notebook and concentrated on what the professor was saying about the common assumption in experimental psychology that animal testing could have human applications. From the football player's leer, Kai was certain he'd recognized her from the old *Tomcat* photos—if not her more recent pictures. It had happened often enough over the years. Old issues of *Tomcat* constantly floated to the surface at colleges; some students had collections of every issue they'd bought since puberty struck.

Ignoring him wouldn't be enough, she knew; Kai also knew from experience that changing seats would only incite the "chase." Oddly, many men took certain kinds of avoidance as a signal to step up their pursuit.

It was a minute before a folded scrap of paper was shoved at her. She took the paper and unfolded it. *Busy Friday night?* he had scribbled.

I have a boyfriend, she wrote at the bottom and passed it back.

He jotted something else and held out the paper. As she looked down, intending to shove his hand away, Kai saw the single word he'd added—*bullshit.* When she threw him an irritated glance, he murmured, "C'mon, babe, give me a try."

"Will you please leave me alone?" she whispered hotly. Having left no doubt about her distaste, she thought it might now do the trick if she changed seats. But when she moved a few rows down, he followed to the seat right behind.

"Why play hard to get?" he whispered in her ear. "You could have a lot more fun playing 'get me hard.' "

She whirled in her seat and hissed at him. "Lay off right now, okay?"

When she faced forward again, she saw that the professor's eyes were targeted on her as though blaming her for the disruption. Rather than enlarge the issue, she mimed an apology and looked at her notebook again.

Dr. Cooke continued, "The experimental method as it relates to human psychology is a systematic attempt to discover the conditions which determine behavior by manipulating variables that—"

The whisper filled her ear again. "If you really don't want to miss anything, kittycat, don't lock me out. I've seen all you've got, but you haven't seen all of me. And what I've got would fit nicely into your—"

There had been dozens of times over the years that Kai had been tested by the crude passes of men who presumed too much; always she had managed to extract herself from the situation before it exploded. But today her control finally shattered. With her right hand balled tightly into a fist, she swung around with all her strength and landed a hay-maker beneath the eye of the guy who was still leaning forward to whisper in her ear. The crack of her fist connecting with his cheekbone sounded like a gunshot across the lecture hall as the football player flopped backward in a daze. All eyes in the hall were suddenly riveted on Kai. The students were looking on with amazement, Dr. Cooke with obvious fury.

"You—young lady!" she shouted, moving from the lecturn to the front of the stage. "What's your name?"

"Kai Wyler."

The football player sat up now, rubbing his eye. "All I did was ask her for a date," he called out, "and she slugged me."

"I'm not going to interrupt the class now to sort this out," Dr. Cooke snapped. "Get out of here, both of you, and be at my medical school office at six o'clock. You can explain then. And if you want to get back into this class, it had better be good."

Kai swept up her books and ran up the aisle, eager to escape before her victim, who in spite of the professor's stern warning, could be driven by his wounded male pride to attempt retaliation.

"What the hell does she expect?" snarled the burly athlete squeezed into one of the chairs facing the professor's desk. In the two hours since the class had ended, his left eye had puffed up and taken on the color of an eggplant. "I mean, a million guys buy this magazine every month, and hang that centerfold on their wall. What's any guy supposed to think if he can look at a broad practically life-size, and he knows she doesn't mind showing off her pussy to millions of—"

"Mr. Fazenda," Dr. Laura Cooke cut in, "this isn't the locker-room. Whatever you want to tell me, do it with proper language."

"Yes ma'am." He gritted his teeth and flicked a glance at Kai before continuing. "Put it this way: if Miss Wyler lets the whole world look at her without any clothes on, then she shouldn't act so damn insulted if somebody like me thinks it would be nice to, well, see it again for real under . . . more private conditions."

Dr. Cooke glanced to Kai inviting rebuttal. But Kai had already recounted what led her up to her explosion and had nothing to add. She shook her head and kept her eyes straight ahead, afraid she might lose her temper if she looked at her tormentor again.

The professor turned back to the young man. "Mr. Fazenda, I'm sure you've seen John Wayne playing parts in the movies where he has a showdown with the bad guys and shoots them dead. I don't think he ever assumes that playing the part gives everybody in the audience a right to challenge him to a real shoot-out when he takes his family to a restaurant. A line has to be drawn between real life and what's on the screen, and the same distinction applies to Miss Wyler. I have no idea why she chose to appear in that magazine. Nor do you. We have no more right to make any assumptions because of those pictures than if we'd seen her playing a part in a movie. Do you understand my point?"

"Yes, ma'am," the football player replied tightly, "I get it. But I still think any woman who shows herself that way—"

"I don't need to hear it again, Mr. Fazenda," Dr. Cooke said firmly. "What you think was made clear by your actions. The way you spoke to her is inexcusable. My own view is that Miss Wyler's response was not inappropriate, and she's entitled to your apology."

"Well, that *would* be your way of looking at it," he grumbled darkly, "wouldn't it—ma'am?" The emphatic twist he gave the final word was enough to draw the battle lines strictly as a matter of gender.

The professor bristled. "Careful, young man. I was going to let you off with no more than a reprimand and an apology. But if you want to take this to a higher disciplinary committee because you think the male deans will see your

side, feel free. I warn you, though: in that case, I believe
you will probably receive a hefty suspension, or worse.''

The football player stared back, as if weighing his chances
of actually getting a better decision from a committee of
men. At last he lowered his eyes and shook his head.

"The apology," Laura Cooke commanded. "Then you
can go."

The football player turned to Kai and muttered a few
words to the effect that he was sorry for insulting her. Then
he was allowed to leave.

"Thank you," Kai said when she was alone with the professor. "I'm not sure I deserve to be let off completely, Dr.
Cooke. I should've handled it better, I suppose, but . . . I
just snapped."

"Well, it's a lucky thing you've got such a good right
hook. If you hadn't stunned Mr. Fazenda so completely with
the first punch, he could've torn you apart."

Kai smiled. "I didn't know I had it in me." The meeting
seemed to be over. Kai thanked the professor again, gathered up her coat, and stood to go.

"I'll walk you out," Dr. Cooke said. She took a lush
lynx coat from the coatrack in her office, turned out the
lights, and they went down the corridor of the medical
school building together. As they walked, Dr. Cooke chuckled softly.

"That shiner you gave him really was a beaut. His real
punishment is going to be wearing that around for a week."

Kai joined in her laughter. "He's on the football team,
you know. Can you imagine all the ribbing he'll have to
take from the other guys?"

"I guess I shouldn't admit this," Dr. Cooke said, "but
maybe I wasn't completely impartial. There have been so
many times in my life I've wanted to haul off on some smug
s.o.b. like that."

Their laughter trailed off as they went down the stairs
through the exit. The January night air was cold as they
headed toward the parking area.

"I wonder, Kai," Dr. Cooke asked, "since you've come
to Jefferson, how often have you been harassed like that—I
mean, because you were a . . . what do they call it?"

"A Kitty," Kai supplied, and then shrugged. "Over the
past three years, there've probably been two or three times

a week I'm hassled by some guy or other. Not always this bad, though. Sometimes just a remark as I'm walking across campus . . . or a note dropped over my shoulder in the library."

"I can't blame you for finally blowing your stack," Dr. Cooke said. "It's amazing you've controlled yourself until now." She paused and turned to look intently at Kai. "With all the trouble it's caused you," the professor asked, "do you ever regret having done it?"

Kai gave the professor a curious glance. "Why are you asking?"

"I'm an experimental psychologist," she replied frankly. "It's natural for me to be interested in the reasons people behave the way they do—especially when they do things that are outside the bounds of everyday, conventional behavior."

Kai hesitated only another moment, then started to talk about the way she had become a Kitty. Dr. Cooke's interest in her immediately touched a need that had been building through the years since she had left Chicago, a need to look back, to take stock and come to terms with her own choices.

But even beginning to explain how she had become involved with *Tomcat* linked up to so much more—to Orin, to running from her father, to the search that had brought her from Hawaii, to her mother's suicide. Ten minutes into the story, Dr. Cooke had suggested that Kai might like to continue talking over dinner—as her guest, of course.

With the professor at the wheel of her sporty two-seater Mercedes, they drove from the campus to Baltimore's Little Italy, where they settled at a table in Sabatino's, a local favorite. During the ride, and through the meal, Kai continued to fill in details of her past. Encouraged by the older woman's sympathetic curiosity, relaxed by the warmth of the unpretentious family-style restaurant, the delicious food, and her share of a bottle of chianti, Kai unburdened herself freely. She felt completely at ease with the professor, who insisted on being addressed informally as Laura.

As she ate the last spoonful of zabaglione and waved off a waiter offering a third cup of coffee, Kai was finally seized with embarrassment over how much she'd been jabbering for the past two hours. "I guess that was one hell of a monologue,'' she said with a sheepish laugh. "I'm sorry, Laura.''

"Don't be. I haven't been bored for a second. But you never did answer the question that set you off.''

Kai fell silent. For a moment she couldn't remember what it was—and then it came back. "Do I regret posing for *Tomcat*?'' Kai said thoughtfully. "No. I needed to. Not to show off, as guys seem to think, but just to prove it wasn't such a big deal. It was a way of overcoming a fear I had of being . . . the kind of woman I am—or at least that other people think I am.''

"What kind is that?'' Laura asked.

Kai gave her a modest smile. "Sexy . . . so they tell me. I don't know where it comes from—it's nothing I do intentionally—but I've heard it from women as well as men. Being desirable is supposed to be great, right? But it's always bothered me because it feels a little like—like being possessed by something that's not a part of me, something I can't control. And I've worried—I hope this doesn't sound crazy—that it might take me over, the way it did my mother. Doing those pictures gave me a chance to look at myself the way others see me. I guess I thought if I could do that, I'd have some kind of control over it.'' Kai paused and smiled nervously again at Laura. "Does this make any sense?''

The professor nodded. "You'd be a lot worse off if you couldn't admit that what happened to your mother affected you very deeply, left you with a lot of anxieties.''

There was a silence. From the way Laura Cooke was looking at her, Kai felt she might have drifted across the line from being a dinner companion to a case study. Yet Kai felt there was compassion behind the psychiatrist's curiosity. "I'm still doing it, "Kai blurted on an impulse. "Posing nude. It's the way I'm paying for school.''

"Really?'' Laura said, her voice level but the surprise not totally concealed. "Does it pay well?''

"Better than anything else that still leaves time for school.'' Kai now regretted the revelation, but could not detect any sign of disapproval from the older woman.

As if sensing Kai's discomfort, Laura smiled. "It's hardly the usual way for a young woman to pay her way through college. But then again, how many have the necessary gifts and temperament for the job? Whether right or wrong, it comes down to a question of whether you're exploiting it or it's exploiting you."

Kai wanted to know if she had penetrated past the psychiatrist's professional veneer to her personal opinion. "Would you tell your own daughter the same thing?"

"I don't have a daughter. But if I did, I'm sure I'd feel exactly the same."

Kai felt tremendous relief at Laura's answer. Already she sensed that her relationship with this warm, intelligent woman was going to be important in her life, and she was determined to have her good opinion.

In fact, thought Kai, Laura Cooke was nothing less than the image of the mother she would have wished to have.

Chapter Twenty

Kai walked through the the fresh drifts of the late February snowfall, thumbing through the letters that had been waiting in her mailbox at the student union building this Monday morning. Bills from the college bookstore and the finance company for her auto loan, monthly bank statement, and a note from Mitch, recognizable by the return address of the Chicago trading firm that now employed him. Without reading it, she knew essentially what it would say. Mitch wrote every few months, never more than a few lines, to report his salary was climbing and he hoped she'd come to Chicago to help him spend it.

After the rift caused by his father, there had been a long period without any contact. But when her pictures had appeared in *Tomcat*, he had tracked her down. It made him sad, he said, to see her doing such things to support herself. He had offered then to lend her whatever she needed. Although she declined the offer, she had met with him a couple of times for coffee.

In the years since she'd gone away, he'd visited Baltimore only once, passing through on his way to New York for business. It had been a strained visit, Mitch reminding her that they could have been married—an undercurrent of seriousness belying his light tone. Kai hadn't wanted to end the friendship, but she made it clear that if there was any chance for something more it would have to wait. Since then there had been a short note from him every few weeks. In his job on the Mercantile Exchange, he boasted, he was now earning a couple of hundred thousand dollars a year. Why shouldn't he help her out? But Kai wouldn't risk taking anything from Mitch. Money meant too much to him; he wouldn't give it unless he expected something in exchange, and what he expected she was unwilling to give.

Flipping past Mitch's letter, she came to another long white business envelope, also with a Chicago return address—"Blaine, Kessel, Gerrity, and Unser," located in the city's most prestigious downtown office building, the new one hundred and ten-story Sears Tower. The unfamiliar names had the ponderous ring of a legal firm. Struck by an intuition of bad news, Kai stopped walking and tore open the envelope. The letter inside was brief and to the point:

Dear Miss Wyler:

I have been retained to act for the plaintiff in the case of *A.D. Smythe* v. *R. Wyler*. Your appearance as a witness in this case will be required. Please telephone my office collect to arrange for pre-trial deposition.

It was signed by a partner in the firm, Victor Kessel.

It sounded like her father was being brought into civil court. But who was Smythe? Why did the plaintiff's lawyer think it would help his case to have Kai's testimony?

Kai crumpled the letter and stuffed it into a pocket. She wanted nothing to do with her father. He had no place in the new life she had worked so hard to create. If she never answered—pretended the letter had never reached her—the case could surely take its course without her.

But it stayed in her mind, a hovering cloud that made it impossible to concentrate in her classes. Near the end of the day she went to a public phone in the student union and made the collect call. After giving her name, she was put through to a lawyer named Arnold Gilliam.

"I'm answering a letter from Victor Kessel," Kai said. "I'd like to speak to him."

"I'm one of the associates on the Smythe case," Gilliam said. He spoke in a clipped manner, his voice a slightly nasal monotone. "I have a copy of the letter in front of me, Miss Wyler. I assume you're calling to arrange to be deposed."

"I'm not sure I know what that means."

"A deposition is a statement made by a witness prior to trial. It encompasses the same information we seek from your testimony, but by having answers to our questions in advance of your appearance in court, we're better able to prepare our case. It's customary for each side to depose witnesses on the other.''

"But what information could you possibly need from me? I haven't seen or spoken to my father in many years. I don't even know this Mr. Smythe you're representing.''

"It's Mrs. Smythe,'' the answer came back in the lawyer's clipped, nasal delivery. ''And of course you know her: she was your stepmother. Smythe is the name of her second husband after divorcing your father.''

Kai lapsed into silence as she absorbed the news. Cut off from her father since the night she'd run away, she had no idea Alexandra had left him. But it didn't really come as a shock. Their marriage had been a shell held together only by the promise of power he would gain as senator. When that hope collapsed, there had been nothing to sustain them.

While Kai listened, the lawyer explained the reason for seeking her testimony. Alexandra Smythe, recently divorced from the man she had married on the rebound, was suing Randall Wyler for exclusive custody of their youngest child, Vanessa. Though their original divorce agreement had been a reasonable document—Wyler had agreed to pay liberal child support even though his wife was extremely wealthy, and in return had been granted liberal visitation rights—now Alex was seeking to change the arrangement and bar Vanessa from ever seeing her father. ''Whether or not she's successful in that effort,'' the attorney concluded, ''may hinge on what you can tell us, Miss Wyler.''

"Tell you about what?'' Kai asked.

"Mrs. Smythe claims that Mr. Wyler should be forbidden from seeing Vanessa because . . .''

Through the phone, Kai heard the lawyer pause to draw breath, as though he found it distasteful to continue.

"There is some indication he has been sexually molesting the child while she was under his supervision.''

"Oh, my God!'' Kai exclaimed. ''But—''

The lawyer cut her off. ''What we're interested in determining is whether Randall Wyler has exhibited a pattern of incestuous behavior. Your stepmother has told us you can provide important testimony in that regard.''

Kai's thoughts flashed back to the night she had escaped from Wyler's attack—Alexandra arriving home just as Kai was running from the house. It was Alex who must have found Wyler bleeding on the floor of Kai's bedroom, his pants unzipped and halfway off.

Yet if Alexandra had known since that night about Wyler's assault on Kai, why had she waited so many years to expose it? Why hadn't she used it to protest the liberal visitations with Vanessa the first time around?

Being dragged back into the middle of hostilities between the two people who were responsible for her greatest unhappiness was as bad as anything Kai could imagine. She should have trusted her intuition, she thought, thrown the letter away.

But she worried about her young half sister, Vanessa. If the charges were true . . .

The lawyer's voice drilled into her thoughts. "The trial is on the calendar for late March, Miss Wyler. When can you get here to give us your deposition?"

"I don't think you can avoid it," Laura Cooke said, leaning back in a chair at her dining room table. "If you don't go willingly, they can get a court order requiring you to appear. You could hire a lawyer of your own to represent you, but that's terribly expensive, and it won't change the result. Ignoring a court order is a crime in itself. I don't know what the penalty is, but you'd be running a risk."

Kai chewed thoughtfully on the last forkful of lasagne on her plate. Preoccupied as she was, the taste came through. Laura was an excellent cook. She seemed to do everything well.

"He told me I would definitely be compelled," Kai said, "unless I came to be deposed within the next three weeks." Still, Kai had ended the conversation without giving the lawyer any promise to appear at his offices. The prospect of having to confront her father was so unnerving that she had actually considered dropping out of sight, leaving school, maybe taking a trip in the car—at least temporarily, until the trial was settled without her.

She would never have done anything so drastic, however, without first talking to Laura.

In just the few weeks they'd known each other, Kai had become very close to the older woman. Kai's need for a role model had been met at last by Laura Cooke. She was attractive, intelligent, shared the same interest in psychology.

Lately, Kai stopped by Laura's office at the medical school three or four times a week, and as often as not their chats would extend to a lunch or a dinner. Two weeks ago, Laura had invited Kai to her home—one of the charming houses dating from revolutionary times that lined the cobbled streets of the old Fell's Point district near Baltimore's harbor. Apparently, Laura was a shrewd manager of her resources as well as an accomplished educator. The homes had been bargains up to a few years ago when the area was rundown, but now it was being cleaned up and houses were climbing rapidly in value. Laura's house was beautifully decorated throughout, with more space than she needed, though one whole floor was devoted to offices where she saw her private patients.

Whereas Kai had readily spoken about herself in the early phase of their acquaintance, Laura had been less forthcoming. In the nature of the teacher–student relationship, Kai had felt Laura was right to retain her privacy and had been reluctant to pry. It was only after Kai started visiting the house, where Laura lived alone, that the older woman had begun filling in more of her personal history—sharing surprisingly intimate details that made Kai feel both privileged and vaguely uneasy.

She came from an old Maryland family of seamen and merchants, Laura told Kai. In her youth she had not rebelled against the traditional role assigned to her. The family business remained the province of men, and she was expected to marry and have children. At nineteen she had been introduced to the handsome son of the Cooke family, another clan of old-line Marylanders, and she had felt lucky when he proposed marriage. She had believed herself to be in love. Not until the night of the wedding celebration, where the champagne flowed unstintingly, had she ever seen her beloved drunk. And on that same occasion she had discovered that his drinking unleashed a violent, sadistic streak. The wedding night had been anything but a tender initiation into the pleasures of the matrimonial bed. Totally without sexual experience up to that point in her life, Laura had been timid, yet eager for a gentle, gradual introduction to passion. But her new husband was concerned only with his own gratification. Deaf to her pleas, he had thrown her onto the floor, ripped away the expensive lace nightwear of her bridal trousseau, and rammed himself into her again and again, satisfying himself with no thought for his bride. He had forced himself on her in ways she had never known were part of the sex act.

"I couldn't call it making love," Laura summed up for Kai. "He took me as if I was an object to be used any way he wished, without my consent. Wife or not, I was raped and sodomized—more than once. I didn't know then there could be such a thing as rape within a marriage. I was twenty-one, this was in the ancient 1950s. One of the old-fashioned ideas I'd been brought up to believe, and no one had yet to question, was something called conjugal obligation. Whatever my husband wanted, I was obliged to accept and endure. Perhaps I would have tried to escape sooner from the marriage, but he could be kind and gentle when he wasn't drinking."

Inevitably, though, he would have too much liquor at a cocktail party or a business dinner, and it would always end the same way. Then one of these brutal episodes had occurred when Laura was in the eighth month of her first pregnancy. Her husband's treatment had been so rough that it had caused not only a miscarriage, but serious hemorrhaging that had brought her to the brink of death. After leaving the hospital, she had refused to dwell with her husband. Even then, her own family had advised her she owed her husband another chance.

"They told me it was *my* fault that the marriage failed," Laura said. "They kept quoting the wedding vows to me as if they were too sacred to break—you know, 'till death us do part'—as if I had no choice but to stay with him, even if it meant being in constant jeopardy, knowing someday he might kill me."

But Laura was determined to have independence in her life. She obtained a divorce, went to college, reconciled with her own family, and continued on through medical school. She had been alone since, she said, and content.

"I guess after that I was never able to trust a man. Not fair, I know. I wish I could solve that one for myself . . . but he hurt me so terribly. . . ." It was out of this internal search for resolution of the problem, however, that she had focused on psychiatry as her medical specialty. And in her practice she had refined her interest to deal mainly with women who were sexually dysfunctional.

Still, she admitted, her own distrust of men persisted, even though she defined it as irrational. It was Laura's honesty about this that made Kai confident no one could better understand her own intense fear of getting anywhere near her father, even in a situation where they would not be alone. If Laura was urging her to make the trip back to Chicago, Kai knew it was not being done lightly, without genuine concern or full awareness of the psychological toll it could take. As much as Kai had come to regard Laura as a substitute mother, she suspected that she also filled the reciprocal role of daughter. Laura had mentioned that the unborn baby she had lost was a girl—and that Kai was the same age the child would have been had she lived.

This Tuesday evening, after telling Laura over dinner about the summons to Chicago, Kai helped clear the dishes and they sat down again over coffee in the front parlor. The room was painted a soft yellow and furnished with an artful mix of early American pieces and comfortable easy chairs. Kai and Laura settled in the two chairs on opposite sides of the fireplace, where Laura had kindled a warming blaze.

"There's one other thing that bothers me about giving this testimony," Kai admitted. "It seems almost certain that speaking about what happened to me will decide the case against my father."

"No doubt that's why the lawyers insist on having it."

"But I'm not sure it's fair."

"Why not? It did happen, didn't it?"

"To me, yes. But does that prove he's also guilty of molesting my half sister? What I say will make Wyler look so bad he'll certainly be ordered to stay away from Vanessa. I know that's what Alexandra's counting on. But from what I remember about her, she's capable of cooking up this whole thing out of revenge—because her second marriage just failed and she's so angry and frustrated in general she has to take it out on him."

Laura took a thoughtful sip of her coffee. "That's for the courts to judge, Kai. If he's innocent, your father will no doubt have a lot of evidence presented in his defense—medical testimony, evaluations by a child psychologist—"

"But once I speak, none of that will count. You know it,

Laura. If he attacked me, they'll assume he could have taken advantage of Vanessa.''

"Not an unreasonable conclusion," the psychiatrist said. "I still think you have no choice but to testify."

They were silent awhile. Laura offered brandy, which Kai declined, but the older woman poured one for herself from a small bar and returned to her chair.

"It's amazing," Kai said pensively, staring at the flaming logs in the fireplace, "the way sex rules all our lives."

"Rules us?" Laura said. "It's a major factor, but I think it's an overstatement to say that it—''

Kai cut her off, her thoughts racing down their own track. "Look what happened to you, to my mother and father, to me. In each case we've been forced down a certain path because of sex—the desire for it, the fear of it, the inability to enjoy it, or the power it has to control us, make us act stupidly or childishly or even illegally. Maybe you can say we're special cases, I don't know. It just seems to me, almost everybody gets . . . pushed around so much by this animal urge inside us. Well, you must see it in your practice.''

"Dealing with sexual problems is my specialty. Of course I see it.''

Kai was silent another moment. "I wish I could understand more about the power it has over us.'' She sat forward, struck by a thought. "That's something useful I could be doing—sex research. Not just experimental psychology, but experimentation that could explain more about human sexuality, help give us more control over it, over ourselves.''

"Sounds worthwhile," Laura agreed. "You have any specific idea about what you'd want to learn, or how you might go about collecting the data?''

Kai shrugged; the idea was so new to her. "I just know I'd like it to be something that contributes to making people less confused and unhappy about sex—myself included. I've seen so many who are . . . well, fucked up.''

Laura smiled. "It sounds to me like a very tricky area in which to experiment. But if it interests you, Kai—if you think there's a contribution you can make—then give it more thought. Think about the kind of experiment you'd like to do, what sort of problem you'd like to study.''

Kai sorted through a number of vague notions without being able to focus on anything specific. She wondered if it had been too foolish and presumptuous to suggest sex as a subject for formal experimentation. Of course, there were observations that might be gathered from laboratory animals and extrapolated to humans. But that wasn't what she had in mind. She wanted to do something that would be directly related to humans, and directly beneficial. And how would such an experiment be designed?

"Maybe it's not possible," she answered at last. "At least not for me."

"Don't give up so quickly," Laura urged. "You'll be graduating soon, Kai. It would be good for you to have a graduate research project. If you come up with something viable, I might even be able to get some money for you, a grant to pay for the research—with a stipend for you so you could stop posing for those pictures."

Though Laura had never been critical of Kai's means of earning money, lately she had more than once seemed eager to help obtain some sort of grant that would allow Kai to support herself another way.

"Would you be willing to help with the project?" Kai asked.

"I might. Depends on what it is."

"Well, I'll give it some more thought," Kai said. "Let's talk about it again when I get back from Chicago."

Once the decision was made to cooperate with the deposition, Kai did not delay. The morning after her dinner with Laura, she made a reservation on Mid-Coast Airlines, the only carrier with a Friday morning flight to Chicago out of Baltimore. Then she called Arnold Gilliam and told him to arrange for the plane ticket.

"I don't want to miss too many classes," Kai explained. "I'm hoping you can see me Friday afternoon, and I'll stay through the weekend in case you need more time with me."

"That will be fine," Gilliam told her. "I'll have a limousine waiting when the plane arrives at one o'clock, and plan to see you around three." That would give her time to stop at her hotel, he explained, adding that her accommodations would be paid for by the firm.

After finishing her conversation with the lawyer, Kai stood

by the phone in the student union. In preparation for another call, she had already changed a few dollars into quarters in the cafeteria, but now she wasn't sure the second call would be wise. She knew that Mitch would take any desire she expressed to see him—especially if she returned to Chicago—as a sign she was ready for another try at romance. Kai didn't want to lead him on. Yet she felt it would be immature and downright rude not to honor the friendship.

She dialed the number for the commodities trading firm where Mitch worked, and dropped in several quarters at the operator's request.

"Milliken-Jessup," a female voice answered.

"Mr. Karlozic, please."

"Sorry, no one here by that name. Please check the number you're dialing." The call was instantly disconnected.

Had she made a mistake? Kai looked down at the letter from Mitch she'd brought with her to have the phone number on the letterhead. Milliken-Jessup Commodities Brokers, right there in black and white. The envelope for the letter was postmarked only a week ago. Kai couldn't believe he'd been fired; he gave her little enough personal news, but he always said how well he was doing. She glanced over the letter again—and there it was: "Just got a raise . . . could really support a wife in style."

A new girl at the switchboard perhaps. Kai decided to chance a second call.

"Don't hang up on me," she said quickly the second the phone was answered. "You just told me Mr. Karlozic doesn't work there. Could you tell me why he left? Did he quit or—"

"Nobody left, miss. I've been here six months and never knew anybody named Karlozic."

Kai's disbelief mushroomed. Was it simply a lie—sustained for all these years? "Mitch Karlozic?" she blurted incredulously. "You never heard of him?"

"Oh, Mitch!" the operator said. It had the ring of complete familiarity. "Sure, there's a Mitch here. Mister *Karel*. Think that could be who you want?"

A thin, ironic smile came to Kai's lips as she remembered her visit to the Karlozic house, the way Mitch's father had taunted him for ignoring the neighborhood girls—wanting to cut himself off from his own roots. Evidently there had been some truth in it. "Yes, I think he's the one," Kai said.

"He's in the trading pit," the switchboard girl said. "It'll be tough to get through to him down there."

"Would you try? I'm calling long-distance."

She was put on hold for so long that she had to keep dropping coins into the telephone to keep the connection. Just as she was about to give up, there was a fresh burst of noise on the phone, and a man shouted, "Hello!" It seemed to be Mitch's voice, but Kai could barely hear him. It sounded like he was in the middle of a riot, dozens of other voices screaming in the background.

She shouted, too. "Mitch! It's Kai!"

He yelled back. "Jesus, Kai! That's wonderful! Are you coming to Chicago?"

"Yes! How did you know?"

"I couldn't imagine any other reason you'd call! When will you be here?"

"Friday, and the—"

She had only started to answer when Mitch shouted over her, but almost as if he had switched into another language: "I want the contracts! Seven July soybeans, seven! And ten August!"

"Mitch! What's going on?"

"Sorry, Kai. I'm in the pit, it's really impossible to talk. But I'll be waiting for you. I'll keep myself free!" The line went dead.

She might have been annoyed at getting such short shrift, yet it was a relief that he seemed to take it rather casually, still putting business first. Maybe it wouldn't be so hard to keep her relations with Mitch strictly on a friendly basis.

Chapter Twenty-one

Kai slept fitfully the night before she was to leave, and all the while she was packing for the trip she was plagued by an anxious gnawing in the pit of her stomach. She'd never felt such a premonition of danger as she did about this visit to Chicago. She knew it was irrational, the lingering effect of terror that had been seeded the night she was assaulted by her father.

Once the plane was in the air, however, her anxiety disappeared. She had carried on her briefcase, and during the flight she brought out a pad and wrote some notes on ideas for research into human sexuality she might develop with Laura. Soon, tired from a night of broken sleep, she took down a pillow from the overhead compartment and settled in for a nap. When the plane landed for a short stopover in Cleveland, her eyes opened only at touchdown. Some passengers filed aboard, the plane took off, and she dropped back into a doze.

She was jostled awake sometime later by the elderly woman in the seat beside her. "Can't sleep, dear," the woman said. "You need to hear this."

Kai took in the look of alarm in the woman's eyes, then became aware of the rustle of activity everywhere throughout the plane. A faint acrid odor was in the air, and the voice of a stewardess was coming through the p.a. system.

". . . with the pillow on your knees, your upper torso bent forward resting on the pillow, hands grasping your knees. As soon as the plane comes to a complete stop, evacuation chutes will be deployed at the emergency exits. . . ."

"What's happened?" Kai asked.

"Someone was smoking in a lavatory and it started a

fire,'' said her seat mate. "We're near Chicago, but we'll have to make an emergency landing.''

"Oh god,'' Kai sighed. So *this* was what her premonition of doom had been all about!

The plane flew on for a few minutes, nose angled down in rapid descent, as the odor in the cabin became stronger and a haze of smoke drifted along the aisles. Two stewardesses moved past the seats, handing out pillows. Somewhere near the front a baby was wailing. Curiously, Kai wasn't frightened as much as she was angry. She didn't want to die. There was so much she hadn't done yet! She wished now that she had been bolder about everything, been braver with her heart.

In the adjacent seat she heard the elderly woman intoning some rote prayers. *Holy Mary, mother of God . . .*

And whom could she pray to? Kai wondered. She was suddenly full of the memory of visiting the *heiau* with her mother—the *hamakua* and all the folklore of the gods. Pele, goddess of the volcano, ruler of fire? Not a bad one to pray to, perhaps. *And, damn it, don't you owe it to me?* Kai demanded silently. *Didn't my mother sacrifice herself to you?*

A man's voice came through the p.a. Steady. Calming. "This is Captain Loffmer again, ladies and gentlemen. We're approaching O'Hare International, and we have emergency clearance. We're going straight in. Assume the crash position until we come to a complete stop.'' After a momentary pause he added, "God bless you all.''

Kai bent forward, pressing herself onto the pillow across her knees. She felt the rumble of the landing gear descending beneath her, heard the whine of the flaps being deployed. Thank God—thank you, Pele!—the systems seemed to be working. But the smoke was so dense, it was no longer possible to see the front of the cabin. Her eyes were stinging, and her throat felt raw.

The woman next to Kai was no longer praying. Although she was facing away, Kai heard her wheezing loudly, as though she was having trouble breathing.

Kai touched her shoulder. "Are you all right?''

The old woman turned her head around. "My asthma . . .'' she whispered hoarsely.

"Smoke's the worst thing, isn't it?''

"Oh . . . and the stress, dear," she whispered, panting shallowly, "that's . . . no help, either." Amazingly, the woman smiled, evidently intending to be light-hearted.

Though Kai smiled back, she said nothing in order to avoid extending the woman's struggle to speak. But her hand moved to grasp her neighbor's, who gave her an answering squeeze. Moments later the plane dipped and bumped down on the runway. The jet engines screamed as they reversed thrust, and the plane rapidly decelerated.

A shout from one of the stewardesses rang through the smoke: "Remain in position until we stop! Then proceed *calmly* to the emergency exits front and rear, rows nearest the emergency exits first."

As soon as the plane stopped, people tore off their seat belts. The smoke was so thick, Kai couldn't see more than the few rows around her, though she thought the front of the section was nearer. Then faintly, she saw a rectangle of light cut dimly through the haze—the forward escape door being opened. Ghostly figures moved quickly toward the light. Voices of the crew came from both ends, calling out directions—"Quickly, please—jump onto the chute—keep moving." The smoke was getting blacker at the rear of the plane, billowing forward alarmingly.

Kai started into the aisle, but then noticed that the elderly woman was still in her seat, bent forward. Kai went back to her, opened the seat belt, and hooked her arms through the unconscious woman's to pull her up. Dead weight, but at least the woman was small and thin. As Kai maneuvered in the limited space, she glanced toward the back and saw yellow tongues of flame for the first time. Some of the passengers from the rear panicked and began to rush for the forward emergency exits. People squeezed past her as she sidled along the aisle, dragging the unconscious woman like an enormous doll. Carrying the additional weight forced Kai to breathe deeper, and with each breath her lungs felt the excruciating heat. Her arms began to feel leaden, her burden too heavy to support, but Kai clung on, took one lung-stabbing breath after another, and kept moving toward the light. And then it was too much. She felt as if her legs were pushing through mud. . . .

"Take her . . . please . . ." she said as the shadowy figure of a man loomed near her. Then she toppled into a seat, gasping. She closed her eyes to shut out the burning, and waited to stop breathing, almost impatient for the pain to end.

"Hold on," a man said. Kai felt a firm, strong arm circle her waist, then gently lift her. She tried to open her eyes again, but they stung too badly. Half conscious, she felt a fast rush of frigid air as she glided down the chute—in someone's lap, it seemed—arms enfolding her. Then she was lifted up, being carried. Shouting voices and sirens were everywhere around her. She forced her her eyes open again. A blurred face floated over hers as she felt herself being set down on a cool, soft surface. She tried to bring the face into sharper focus, but her eyes wouldn't work. Indistinct as it was, though, it seemed to be a face she wasn't seeing for the first time.

"Better let me take her, mister," someone said. Then there were other people leaning over her, dressed in white.

"Tell me your name," another voice said quickly. A man. Was he talking to her?

No matter, she couldn't answer. An oxygen mask was clapped over her face, and she breathed deeply, feeling again the rawness in her throat and lungs as the gurney was wheeled rapidly away.

"Can I get dressed and leave, please?" Kai called out as she saw a nurse scurry past her cubicle carrying a box of gauze bandages. "I'm all right, really."

A cheerful black nurse who kept racing back and forth to deal with the airplane emergency paused to look in. "Honey, I'm sorry, but you have to be officially released by the doctor. Otherwise, we might get sued, you know? Now just relax, he'll get back to you soon. Best to keep the gown on, he may want to do the stethoscope bit once more." The nurse yanked the curtains on the cubicle together before she sprinted away.

Kai had already spent more than an hour in the airport infirmary, and had been quickly examined by two doctors— one the regular airport staff physician, the other a pulmonary specialist who had been on the flight himself and who was taking a special interest in his fellow passengers. Both men had judged Kai to be basically fine, except for smoke irritation of her eyes and respiratory tract.

She lay back on the examining table. Of course, she could probably walk right out in the midst of all the activity and no one would notice. But as impatient as she was to be released, she felt too drained of energy to challenge airport policy just now.

"*There* you are."

Kai propped herself up to look at the man who had pushed aside the curtains to speak to her. As he stepped inside the cubicle, she realized he was the one from the plane. He was very attractive, in his mid-thirties, she guessed. Tall, tanned, a rugged slightly weatherbeaten look, as though he spent a lot of time outdoors.

"It's a relief to see you're okay," he said. "Been such a madhouse around here, I wasn't able to get in to see you, and I was worried. Finally I just sneaked in." He paused to give her a curious little smile. "You don't remember me, do you?"

"From the plane. I guess you pulled me out."

"I did. But that's not the first time we met. We go much farther back."

She studied him, and he returned her gaze, smiling, challenging her memory. He was dressed in a tweed blazer, gray slacks, and a blue shirt open at the neck. She studied his clothes, feeling that there might be a clue there. Still, it wouldn't come. She shook her head.

He chuckled. "I ought to be insulted," he said lightly. "I remember you, Kai, as if it was yesterday. It must be true what they say about the uniform, though. That's what the women really look at."

Uniform. "My god! You?! Pearl Harbor! The officer . . . !" She couldn't find his name in her memory, but she recalled everything else clearly now—how kind he had been, his help in discovering her father's identity, the free flight he'd arranged for her.

He broke into a broad grin. "Jim Bolton," he said, putting his hand out.

She took it in both of hers. "Jim!—yes. How could I forget?"

For a long moment they stared at each other. Kai began to feel intensely self-conscious, her nakedness concealed only by the paper gown she'd been given to wear for the examination.

Sensitive to her discomfort, he said, "Forgive my barging in like this, but I just wanted to be sure you were all right before I left."

"I'm okay, I think. I feel ready to check out of here, but it seems I've gotten a little tangled up in red tape. They won't let me go until a doctor comes."

"Suppose I see what I can do to move things along."

She was going to tell him not to trouble himself—she didn't want special treatment when others were in more urgent need—but he had gone out through the curtains before she could object.

He returned in a couple of minutes carrying a clipboard. "I can spring you right now, though I shouldn't do it if you're feeling even a little woozy."

"Really, I'm fine—except my throat's still a bit raw."

He tapped the clipboard. "A release form. You just have to sign this, releasing yourself into my care."

Kai glanced at the form, then gave him a quizzical smile.

"It's not a contract for life," he said dryly. "Of course, if you prefer to wait . . ."

"Nosirree. I want to get out of here." He gave her the gold fountain pen from his jacket pocket, and she signed the form.

While he went to turn it in, Kai got dressed. She put on the ivory linen suit she'd been wearing, the skirt ripped in a couple of places and smudged all over by oily smoke. Checking herself in a mirror over a sink in the cubicle, she saw that her hair was a frizzy mess, and there were a few faint smudges on her cheeks. Only when she tried washing them off did she realize the reddish blotches were places where her skin had been seared by the heat. If she had realized she looked so bad, she wouldn't have released herself into the care of Jim Bolton. For the first time in her life, she felt a little vain; she didn't want him to be seeing her looking so awful. Especially him, a man who had remembered her after nine years.

But it was too late now.

He was standing just outside the cubicle when she emerged. Compared with how ragged she looked and felt, he seemed to be in perfect condition, not a mark on him, his brown hair neatly combed, his tweed jacket and gray slacks neatly pressed.

"There's a back way out," he said quickly, steering her away from the infirmary's main access to a side passageway. "The press are all over the front door."

They emerged into the terminal near a bank of phone booths. Looking across a span of open floor, she saw the entrance to the infirmary thronged by reporters and camera crews. "I'm glad I didn't have to run that gauntlet," she said. "Thanks." She was impressed by the way Jim Bolton had taken charge, obtaining her release with a minimum of fuss, yet without being overbearing.

"I've got a rental car waiting to be picked up," he said, moving toward one of the exits.

Suddenly Kai halted. "Wait, my baggage!" She'd want to change out of her clothes as soon as she got to the hotel. Then it occurred to her that she didn't know which hotel had her reservations; the limousine driver who was meeting the flight was supposed to have that information. Everything was in a muddle.

"This way," Jim said, changing directions.

But instead of taking her to a baggage-claim area, they approached one of the large windows that looked out across the runways. There, in the distance, lay the smoldering mass of a fuselage, the top part of the long tube completely burned away, water and foam still being hosed onto it. Only the tail assembly and the nose section were still intact.

"Our baggage didn't make it," Jim said.

Kai felt her stomach flip as she realized what a close call it had been. "Did everyone get out?" she asked.

He shook his head. "Three fatalities. But even that's a miracle, considering. When planes start to burn, they can go pretty fast." He paused, then made a low grunt of disgust. Kai looked at him and saw his jaw clenched, apparently in anger.

"What's wrong?" she asked.

"It's just so needless," he said tightly, taking her arm to guide her back toward the exit. "Someone smoking a cigarette in one of the washrooms, and you have three people dead. Smoking should be banned on airplanes. It would help, too, if the manufacturers would develop materials that don't give off toxic smoke or burn so damn fast."

As he expressed his anger, his strides quickened, almost as though he was hurrying somewhere to right these wrongs.

While Jim went to collect the car, Kai remembered to stop at a phone booth and call the law firm. An airport clock showed it was already half past three.

"Miss Wyler!" Arnold Gilliam exclaimed as soon as he came on the phone. "I'm so glad to hear from you. When I heard the news about the plane, I was terribly worried."

Worried that you had no case, Kai mused as the lawyer went on:

"The driver we sent to the airport told us you'd been injured. He left, thinking you'd been sent to a hospital."

"I'm fine, Mr. Gilliam. But I'm just leaving the airport, and I'd like to go to my hotel."

"Certainly. It's the Palmer House. There's a suite reserved in your name." Under the circumstances, he said, he understood that their appointment would be delayed so that she could rest. "Why don't you come in at six o'clock?"

"This evening?" Kai didn't know whether to be outraged or amused by the lawyer's insensitivity. "Certainly not."

"Well, Mr. Kessler plays golf on Saturdays, and he wanted to be here—"

Now it was easier to decide on an emotion. "Mr. Gilliam, I've just come pretty close to dying, and I still don't fell like traipsing around town, much less letting a couple of lawyers for a woman I don't like very much give me the third-degree. So you can tell Mr. Kessler to take his golf game and . . . and shove it up his hole-in-one. I'll come in tomorrow, not before." It was her unresolved fury at Alexandra coming out, too, Kai thought; these men were Alex's soldiers, after all.

The lawyer told her he would see her tomorrow and hung up abruptly.

Jim was waiting in a plain sedan outside the terminal. When Kai stepped out into the frigid February air of the Windy City, it occurred to her that her winter coat had burned up along with everything else stowed in the overhead compartment: her purse, her money, identification. She slammed the door as she got in the car, and sat stewing as Jim wended his way out of the airport traffic. He kept silent, too, yielding to her mood.

They were on the expressway to the city when he said, "Want to tell me what's wrong?"

She might have launched into the whole messy situation that had forced her to come to Chicago, but she held back. The one thing she didn't resent about being here was having been brought together with Jim Bolton. Looking over at him, she actually felt glad at the way things had worked out—strangely, almost glad that she'd been caught in a near disaster. They might have shuffled on and off an uneventful flight without ever meeting. It would be foolish to waste time with him complaining.

"I'll work it all out," she said, determinedly lifting the mood. "You know, I feel bad about not recognizing you the minute I saw you. I wouldn't want you to think I've ever forgotten how kind you were the first time we met."

He glanced over and smiled. "All in the line of duty, ma'am. You were going off to search for your father, as I recall. I've always wondered how that worked out."

"I found him," Kai said plainly. "But we didn't live happily ever after."

He seemed to detect that she wasn't prepared to supply details. "I'm sorry to hear that. You settled in Chicago, though."

"No. That's the funny thing about meeting you today. This is the first time I've been back here in years. And, to be honest, I would have preferred to stay away."

Jim tossed her a questioning glance. But again Kai didn't elaborate. "What about you?" she asked. "Why were you on this plane today?"

"The answer to that would be funny," he replied, "if it hadn't turned into such a tragedy. I was on a research trip."

"Research into what?"

"Mid-Coast Airlines. Over the past couple of weeks I've been traveling a lot of their routes to check operations—Washington to St. Louis, St. Louis to Cleveland, Cleveland to Chicago. . . ."

"What did you want to learn?"

He paused a moment. "Whether or not to buy the airline."

"*Buy* it?" Kai echoed, giving him a wide-eyed look.

"Not all by myself," he said. "I've brought together a group of investors—and it's a bigger step than I've ever taken before."

"Still, it's very impressive." She paused to study him

again. "Tell me, how does a navy officer turn into a tycoon in nine years?"

"I'm no tycoon," he laughed. But then he went on to provide a sketch of his life between the last time she had seen him and today.

He had gone back to Vietnam and served another year aboard a patrol boat. At first he thought he might go on serving even after fulfilling his draft requirement, but the war had left him disillusioned with the military. So he resigned his commission and went back to finish Harvard Business School. He had only just begun to think of how he might apply his business training when the war in Vietnam ended. After all the years of sending in men and materiel, the Americans virtually fled overnight. It had occurred to Jim then that while the men were gone, there were billions of dollars worth of abandoned machines and weapons that had to be left behind, some damaged, some practically new. It was likely, too, that the new communist government of the war-ravaged country might want to convert some of that surplus into dollars to be used for reconstruction. He had dropped out of business school immediately.

It had taken a couple of years of intensive effort to foster contacts and overcome the communist Vietnamese resistance to dealing with an American, but gradually Jim had been able to build up a trade in salvaged parts for planes and helicopters. His business expanded rapidly. Now, just two years since the end of the war, it had become extremely profitable.

"But there's a limit to what I can do with surplus," Jim concluded. "So I've been looking for other ways to expand. That led me to the Mid-Coast deal. Having an airline would be a good fit with the other business."

"After today," Kai asked, "are you still interested in the airline?"

"The accident doesn't change anything. I got a little more research than I bargained for, but it doesn't necessarily reflect badly on the company. The problem wasn't caused by their carelessness or bad maintenance. From what I've seen, in fact, Mid-Coast is very well run, a good deal for my investors. I think," he said cheerfully as the car rolled up in front of the Palmer House, "we'll probably make a bid."

He stayed with Kai while she checked in to the hotel, one of the city's largest and best. At the desk she was given a message slip: Mr. Karel called—urgent. Kai guessed he had heard about the plane.

As she walked to the elevator with Jim, Kai said, "I ought to let you go now. From what you've told me, I imagine you have a lot on your mind besides taking care of me."

"Nothing as important. And I've got a hunch you might still need me around."

He was flirting with her, and she liked it. "What makes you think so?" she said, matching his tone.

"Plain horse sense. For one thing, I'd guess you're going to need some clothes, and so you'll need something to buy them with, and—"

She gasped. "That's right!" She needed everything new, from underwear to hairbrush to stockings and something to wear to the deposition in the morning. And she had no money.

Jim told her not to worry, he'd lend her as much as she needed.

"Now all I need is the energy to go shopping," she said. The after effects of the ordeal were taking their toll. All she really wanted to do was climb into bed and sleep.

He had an answer for that, too. Instead of going out, they could call a couple of stores and have them send over an assortment of things in her size to choose from.

Kai wasn't sure how to go about ordering that way, but they went up to the room, she told Jim her sizes, and he handled everything, requesting an assortment of coats and other clothes and shoes to be delivered to the hotel within an hour.

"Why don't you climb in a hot bath and have a soak while we wait?" Jim said. "Best thing for you."

"Good idea." She had no sooner answered than he was in the bathroom, running the water for her. She followed him and watched as he put his hand under the tub spout, testing the temperature. It felt wonderful to have someone taking care of her, but still she wasn't comfortable handing over control. "Jim, I'll be all right now . . . if you have to go . . ."

He stood. "I don't have to," he said quietly but firmly. "And I don't want to, unless you'd rather—"

"No," she said quickly. "I like having you here."

Their eyes rested on each other's and Kai was struck by a memory. They had stood like this before nine years ago. But there was something different now. A different electricity.

He broke the silence. "Go on, take your bath," he said, and stepped outside, closing the door behind him.

The hot water leeched the tension out of her body. Eyes closed, half in a dream, she imagined his arms around her—as she recalled them holding her as they glided to safety.

At last she emerged, her head and body wrapped in the hotel's large bath towels. A colorful array of clothes was draped over sofa and chairs—suits, dresses, robes, nightwear, boxes of shoes and slippers. A rolling table had also been delivered by room service, laden with a selection of cheeses, a fruit bowl, a teapot and cups, and several covered plates. Jim, in a chair pulled up to the desk, was talking into the telephone while he jotted notes on a pad. Kai looked through the clothes, while she kept an ear cocked to his conversation.

". . . then make the offer in a week, ten days. They're blameless, but the bad publicity should make them a little nervous, maybe save us a few million on the price." He paused, listening, as she turned to look at him. He smiled at her, then said quickly, "I'll get back in touch with you, Herb. I've got an appointment now, someone I can't keep waiting." He hung up.

"You didn't have to cut that short for me," she said.

"I was finished, anyway." He went to the table. "Thought you might be hungry." He lifted a cover from one plate, revealing a large roast beef sandwich.

"You've thought of everything," she said, moving to stand by him at the desk. "But I think I'd like just a cup of tea."

"Sure." He started to pour. "Feeling tired? It's common with shock, the letdown after a surge of adrenaline."

She nodded.

He suggested she go into the bedroom and get comfortable and he'd bring the tea. Sugar and lemon, the way she liked it. Before going inside, Kai picked out a nightgown and robe from the display of clothes.

"This is heaven," she said when he brought her the tea and pulled up a chair beside the bed. She was propped up on the pillows, under the covers. She felt like a sick child, kept home from school, with someone to take care of her. She'd never really had that in her life. With her mother, for as far back as she could remember, Kai had felt it was her duty to take care of Lokei, not the other way around.

"Sweet enough?" he asked as she took her first sip of tea.

"Perfect," she said.

Again their eyes locked, and she felt grateful to fate—or was it the gods?—for having their paths cross a second time. As she sipped the tea, she wished she wasn't feeling so desperately tired; she would have liked to go out somewhere with him, go dancing. . . .

He interrupted her thoughts. "There were a couple of phone messages while you were in the bath. A secretary from a law firm said your appointment tomorrow is eleven o'clock. And someone named Mitch. Asked you to call him at home. I left his number on a pad by the phone." He paused. "He sounded bothered at finding a man in your hotel room. Full of questions about what I was doing here. I think my answers satisfied him, but I'm sorry if it creates a problem between you two."

"He's just a friend," Kai said, setting her cup down hard on the saucer in her lap. "He had no right to question you."

"That's all right, Kai. I couldn't blame any man for trying to hold the inside track with you."

Kai smiled slowly. She had an impulse to tell Jim Bolton that if anyone had an inside track right now it was him. But then she cautioned herself against being so reckless. She really didn't know him at all, and for all his kindness and compliments, with the passage of nine years he might even have found himself a wife, started a family.

As she was wondering about that unpleasant possibility, the rising wave of exhaustion overtook her. She started to push down deeper into the comfort of the bed, forgetting the teacup balanced on the covers. Jim reached out and caught it just before it spilled.

"Go ahead," he said. "Tuck down."

Like a child she obeyed, and her head was barely on the pillow before she was drifting into sleep. The last thing she felt were the covers being straightened, and then a hand, lightly smoothing her hair in the gentlest of caresses.

Chapter Twenty-two

"Now, suppose we talk a little about that night."

Victor Kessel paced the thick pearl gray carpet of his office high in the Sears Tower. He was about sixty, tall and sinewy, with full white hair brushed straight back, and a shrewd, taut face behind gold-rimmed spectacles. His black suit, cut along narrow lines that accentuated his long legs, conjured the image of a spider in Kai's mind as he crossed back and forth in front of her.

The large, elegant room bespoke his power and success as a lawyer. Of course, Kai understood, if he was going to take up a case against Randall Wyler—himself a titan in the legal field—Kessel had to be one of the best. For this morning's deposition a single chair had been placed at the center of the open space in front of the handsome desk, facing across its polished marble surface to immense windows. Beyond them, a bird's-eye view of the city stretched away. Kai felt as if she were simultaneously in a witness box and isolated on a cloud.

"Let me see if I have the facts correct on this," Kessel went on. "Along with your father and Mrs. Smythe—your father's wife at the time—you had been to a campaign dinner. . . ."

He had spent the previous half hour dealing with the circumstances that had brought Kai to live with her father, probing her general feelings about him and her stepmother during the two years Kai had shared their household. He had been courteous, putting her under no pressure. His associate, Arnold Gilliam, a bland, balding man in his forties, sat off to one side, a file folder in his lap, speaking only when Kessel asked for some detail from the file. So far Kai had felt comfortable with both of them.

She had awakened feeling fairly well recovered from the

effects of yesterday's calamity. A note from Jim propped on her nightstand said he would be unreachable during the day, but would call later. An hour after she woke, a glorious bouquet of flowers had been delivered to the room; the note read: "Isn't it great to be alive? Fondly, Jim."

Yes, oh, yes, she had thought as she picked out a stylish beige suit from the selection still awaiting her perusal.

Then right before she left for the appointment there had been a call from Mitch. He told her he had tried to get through a few times last night. "The hotel said you asked not to be disturbed."

"I was asleep," Kai told him. "Recuperating." She guessed Jim had thoughtfully arranged for her to have an unbroken sleep.

"Well, I pushed it and they finally rang through. Who was the guy in your room?" Mitch demanded.

"Just a man from the plane who drove me to the hotel."

Mitch left it at that. He told her he expected to spend the evening with her. Kai didn't know how to respond. There had been an understanding that they would get together when she came to Chicago, yet she wanted to spend time with Jim. "I'll see you tomorrow, Mitch," she said. "I'm on my way to the lawyers right now, and I don't know how long they'll keep me. I'll probably want to rest later."

Mitch grudgingly agreed.

Now, as Kai heard Victor Kessel refer to "that night," all idle thoughts about the near future fled from her mind, and she sat up rigidly, preparing to be hurled into the darkest moments of her past.

". . . Alexandra had joined some friends afterward for a drink," Kessel was saying. "But Mr. Wyler had to work on a speech, so he returned home, taking you with him." The lawyer stopped pacing and looked directly at Kai. "Is that correct?"

Kai spent a moment weighing her answer. Should she say it was more likely that Alexandra had been meeting a lover late that night than having a drink with friends? No, she couldn't know for sure.

"It's true I went home with my father," she replied. "I don't know where Alex was, or whether or not my father planned to do any work."

"But when you arrived home that night, he didn't work, did he?"

"No," Kai admitted.

"What did he do?" Kessel asked.

A slight shiver went through Kai. She recalled now that Laura had told her she was entitled to have a lawyer represent her; for the first time she wished that she had someone protecting her interests. How much was it safe to say? At what point would she compromise herself? It seemed too late now, however. *Just get it over with,* she instructed herself.

She began the account quietly, working to control her emotions. Her father had wanted to celebrate the success of his campaign dinner, so there had been champagne.

Kessel cut in. "A minor point, Miss Wyler: this champagne, did you drink it right after you arrived home?"

"Yes. It was already quite late."

"Ah, yes, you'd been out for the evening. But champagne is usually enjoyed most when it's chilled? Didn't you wait for it get cold?"

"It was already in an ice bucket," Kai explained.

"I see. Go on."

She sensed something ominous in Kessel's brief digression, then decided it was simply a lawyer's love of detail. She continued, recounting that after a glass of champagne she had gone to bed, and had almost fallen asleep when her father entered the room.

"And it was then," Kessel put mildly, "that he came into your bed?"

Kai eyed the lawyer uncertainly. Had her ears played a trick? "He came into the room and sat *on* my bed," she said.

"Very well. Then what happened? Tell me everything."

No point delaying it any longer. "He'd gone on drinking after I left him," Kai said in a rush, "and he was confused. He'd been thinking about my mother, and in that state of mind he had me mixed up with her, and he wanted . . . he wanted to make love to me. Well, not to me really, to my mother. I tried to fight him off, but he was too strong, and he was drunk. I don't think he knew what he was doing. But when he wouldn't stop—wouldn't listen—I grabbed up the heaviest thing I could put my hands on, a lamp . . . and

I hit him.'' She paused, breathing hard, almost as though she had just been through the struggle. "He—he fell down, bleeding from here." She touched her temple. "I thought I'd killed him—I was sure I had—and I ran from the house. That was the last time I saw him."

There was silence. Kessler gave her a long, curious gaze, then exchanged puzzled glances with Gilliam before turning again to Kai. "Bleeding, you say. He fell down bleeding. And unconscious?"

"I told you, I thought he was dead."

Kessel stopped pacing in front of Kai. "How long was it after you struck your father before you ran from the house?"

"I don't know, a minute or two. I took almost nothing with me. I was scared."

"And is Alexandra Smythe telling the truth when she says that as you were running down the stairs, leaving, she returned home?"

"Yes," Kai said quietly.

Kessel took a step closer to the chair and bent slightly toward Kai. His voice hardened as he said, "You injured your father so badly that you believed he was dead, yet two minutes later your stepmother came into the house, went straight up to your bedroom, and there was Randall Wyler, no blood on him, wide awake?"

"No, that's not true—"

"Oh? Were you there? I thought you ran away."

"Yes. Yes, I did. But . . . I know how I left him. He was hurt, badly hurt."

"Not according to the only witness—other than your father."

"Witness?"

"Alexandra *Wyler*."

Kai shook her head, bewildered. "But that can't be right. She must have found him the way he was when I left him."

"Indeed. And she says he was in your room, perfectly well."

For a second Kai gazed helplessly at the lawyer. Then she remembered: there was proof. "He was injured. That's why he had to cancel all his campaign appearances for that day."

"Oh, yes, we know about that." Kessel thrust a hand out toward Gilliam, who instantly extracted a packet of newspaper clippings from the folder in his lap and passed them over. Kessel glanced at the one on top. "The story is a matter of public record. He had an accident at home. But that was the next morning—"

"No," Kai said. "I did it. That story about falling off a ladder was a cover-up, a lie he told to protect himself."

Kessel moved closer, bearing down on her. "Was it? Or are you the liar? Are you the one who needs to hide your sin?"

"My—?" Kai stared back, a shrill edge of panic coming into her voice as she answered. "I don't understand. Why are you twisting it around? I've told you what happened. He attacked me, and I hurt him. I'm not trying to hide that. Why would I lie about something so terrible?"

"Because," Kessler thundered, "you know the truth is worse."

She couldn't even answer now. She could only look back at him, mute with horror and confusion as she waited for him to explain.

"You know," he went on, "by telling us you fought off an attack, you can appear to be the victim, an innocent caught by surprise—when in fact you were willingly involved in an incestuous relationship with your—"

"No!" she cried out, enraged.

The lawyer went right on: ". . . that had started long before that night. Perhaps even soon after you came to live with—"

Kai gripped the arms of the chair as though to keep herself from flying apart. "That's crazy! Why are you saying these things? You can't possibly believe they're true!"

Very quietly Kessel said, "I am bound to believe what my client tells me, Miss Wyler. I can understand that you might well deny it—might well fabricate any version of events that conceals your own part in such a profane situation—"

"I'm telling you the truth!" she insisted desperately.

Kessel ignored her. "The crux in this case is that the life of a child is at stake. And the risk to this child must be determined. Was your father just a man who lost control of himself one night, or was he a man so evil that he would use his own child totally to serve his own purposes? Our view is that Randall Wyler is not only unfit to have custody of his daughter, Vanessa, but that he should not even have access lest this young child be corrupted as you were.''

Now at last the haze of confusion began to clear. Kai perceived the vicious logic behind Alexandra's monstrous charges. To accuse Randall Wyler of making a single pathetic mistake while in a state of drunkenness might not necessarily disqualify him from shared custody of Vanessa. It was too easy to say he had been rehabilitated, or provide a sympathetic psychological explanation of one moment in which his self-control had failed. But to brand him as participating in a regular pattern of incest, that would not only slam the gate closed on any hope he had of keeping access to his young daughter, it would probably put him in jail, destroy his life. Wyler's own denial would be meaningless.

Whatever anger toward her father still resided in Kai's heart, she could not allow these lies to stand. ''I've told you the truth,'' she repeated firmly. ''Alex is the one who's lying, and I'm not going to let her get away with it.''

''The court will judge what the truth is, Miss Wyler,'' Kessel said passively. ''But I think we can provide evidence to help them reach the right decision.''

The right decision? For these lawyers that meant having their hideous lie confirmed. ''Evidence?'' Kai demanded. ''What do you mean?''

''Your own words. You told us your father lied to his wife about wanting to work that night so he could be alone with you?''

''No, that's not what I—''

''You've also said that, while he knew his wife wouldn't be returning home, he left champagne chilling for an intimate late-evening tryst?''

''Good lord, you can't really think that proves anything. He wanted to celebrate a successful evening, that's all.''

''But not with his wife,'' Gilliam spoke up.

Kai looked from one man to the other. Was this how the decision would be made, the scales of justice weighted more by innuendo and suspicion than by fact? ''You won't make it work,'' she declared fiercely. ''I'll be in court to testify. I'll make them believe me. I ran from the house that night, Mr. Kessler. I ran because I was afraid I'd killed my father. Why else would I go?''

Kessel smiled, then reached out again to Gilliam. The

other lawyer handed a large piece of cardboard to Kessler. On it had been glued the nude picture of Kai as a *Tomcat* centerfold.

"Why you went, Miss Wyler, we can only speculate. But what you did when you left is not in doubt. Before long, you were posing for pictures like this. You went straight from your father's house to become—I believe the term is "a sex kitten," a common symbol of modern-day promiscuity. And, of course, if we throw in your family pedigree on your mother's side, well, I'm inclined to think you'll have quite a hard time making any judge or jury take your word over that of a respectable woman like Mrs. Smythe.''

Shocked and defeated as she felt, Kai did her best to hide it as she rose to her feet. "You bastards," she hissed. "You think it's going to be so damn easy to knock me down? Well, you can show that picture around all you want, I'll be damned if I'll slink away. Anybody who gives me half a chance will see that there's a hell of a difference between letting people look at me naked, the way I came into the world, the way even goddamn lawyers in their fancy three-piece suits came into the world—and doing the things you say I did.'' She spun around and strode to the door. "I'll see you in court.''

She was still shaking with fury when she returned to the hotel. The tension had left her with a pounding headache. She had taken a long walk around the Loop to try to calm herself down, but it hadn't worked. She wished there were friends in the city she could lean on, but Sylvie was long gone, Jill Evans had gone to California when Orin had moved his entire operation there, and Terry was also on the West coast. For a while Kai had kept in contact with Terry, a postcard, the odd phone call. A year ago she had married an up-and-coming young actor—"that's the way I love him,'' Terry wrote once, "up-and-coming"—and since then they had lost touch.

At the hotel desk there was a message that Jim had called, but now she felt curiously uneasy about seeing him again. Victor Kessel's damaging insinuations had found their mark. In spite of herself Kai felt unworthy, soiled. What could an accomplished man like Bolton want with her? A sex kitten. A face and a body—in the eyes of many, no more of a person than that. She knew it had been empty bravado to hope she could prevail against the picture that Victor Kessel would paint of her. It was going to come down to her word against Alexandra's, and the way the deck was stacked Alexandra would win.

Her suite had been neatened by the maid service, but the fine clothes were still arrayed across the furniture. She gathered them up, intent on returning everything but the few necessities she had to replace to wear for traveling. She was eager to leave Chicago now. She doubted that she'd be called back to continue the deposition, even though she had walked out on the lawyers. Reviewing the meeting, she sensed that the real purpose of bringing her here in advance of the trial was not to get information from her, but to show their own hand—to frighten and intimidate her. Part of the strategy to win for their client at all costs.

She was about to call the stores to tell them to collect the clothes when the phone rang. She hesitated, then picked up, expecting Jim or Mitch. But the voice was a woman's. "Kai?"

"Yes."

"It's Alexandra."

Kai would have slammed the phone down, but she was virtually mesmerized by the very brashness of the approach. Surely, Alex's lawyers had by now given her a full report of this morning's meeting. "What do you want?" Kai asked automatically.

"I'd like to talk to you. I'm downstairs in the lobby."

Kai stood locked in a paralysis of indecision. With Alex she had always felt out of her depth, awed by her wealth, outmatched by her greater sophistication and cold cunning.

"I can come up," the voice prodded, "or I'll wait here. It won't take long."

"I'll come down," Kai heard herself say, feeling hypnotized. She couldn't bring herself to dismiss Alexandra, but she was actually frightened to be alone in the room with her.

The lobby was crowded with fresh convention arrivals, but as soon as Kai stepped out of the elevator, she had no trouble spotting Alex. She was standing not far from the entrance, swathed in a calf-length sable coat, a large alligator purse with bright gold fittings slung over one shoulder. A matching fur cloche was rakishly tilted above the line of a pair of wraparound sunglasses. In one gloved hand she held a cigarette in the kind of long-stemmed holder favored by movie vamps three decades earlier. In her hand, it seemed chic again rather than a faddish affectation.

She turned as Kai came up to her. The dark glasses kept the reaction of her eyes a mystery, but Kai saw the lips—painted in a dark crimson shade—part slightly in the tiniest sign of approval.

"College has been good for you," she said.

"Save the compliments," Kai replied coolly. "You won't get any from me."

Now the bright red mouth twitched with a smile, as if in praise of Kai's toughness. "Can I buy you a drink?" Alex motioned in the direction of the hotel bar.

Kai shook her head. "Let's keep it as short as possible. Tell me what you want."

They went on standing near the door, the crowd in the hotel swirling around them. "You should know by now what I want, dear," Alexandra said. "I want my daughter, and I want to be sure she isn't ever again abused by her father."

Kai stared at her stonily a moment. "Are you really concerned at all with helping Vanessa?" she asked. "Or aren't you just out to hurt Randall Wyler? I have my doubts about whether he's guilty of any abuse. So much of what you've told your lawyers is false."

Alexandra shrugged. "I've had to make some guesses about what went on between you and your father—"

"Cut the crap, Alex," Kai snapped angrily. "You've made it seem I was a willing partner when you know I fought him off!"

She made no attempt to deny the lie. "Well, it simplified a complex story. And it works so much better this way for my case, makes a much stronger, clearer argument against letting Van stay with him." Her tone hardened. "I want my child, Kai. Never mind all the reasons. She's mine and I want her, completely and totally. Since my second divorce Randy's been saying I'm not really a fit mother, threatening to seize custody. Well, this is my answer!"

"Why did you come here, Alex?" Kai said. "Your lawyers must have told you I'd fight these lies."

"I didn't think there was any harm in giving you a second

chance. Why let yourself get dragged down, Kai? Even the true story you've got to tell is bad enough. I thought we could settle things in a way that's better for both of us." Alex plunged a suede-gloved hand into the large alligator purse and brought out a manila envelope. "This is an affidavit my lawyers have prepared. If you sign it, you won't have to come back to Chicago and appear in court; there probably wouldn't even be a trial. Everything could be handled so much more quietly and sensibly. It would be much better for your father, too."

Kai looked disapprovingly at the envelope.

Alexandra thrust it forward. "Go on. Take it, and I'll be on my way. You've nothing to lose by looking at it. You can always tear it up."

Kai hesitated another second, then took the envelope.

"See?" Alexandra said. "That wasn't so hard. Goodbye, dear. I don't think we'll have to meet again."

With a swirl of her luxurious coat she turned and walked out of the hotel. Kai watched through the glass as a chauffeur held open the door of a Rolls-Royce that was parked at the curb.

She waited until she was back in her room to inspect the envelope. Inside she found three copies of the one-page affidavit, clipped together, and a plain white envelope with her name typed on the front. Sitting in the living room of the suite, she read the affidavit first, two paragraphs, starting with the conventional legalese: "I, Kaiulani Teiatu Wyler, do state and affirm . . ." The substance was in the second paragraph—an admission that she had been sexually molested by Randall Wyler on a regular basis during all the time she had lived with him. The abuse had been "against her will," in the prepared language of the statement, but she had "endured it and suffered in silence" because she was dependent on her father and feared being forced out of his house. At last it had become too much to bear, and she had fled.

The document sickened Kai. Yet she could see why Alex had thought she might sign. Unlike the story the lawyers were threatening to tell in court, this held Kai blameless. In fact, she suspected now, the real purpose of her encounter with Victor Kessel was to soften her up for this alternative. As she set the papers down on a table, she noticed the white envelope she had put aside. She tore it open and extracted the contents—a check made out to her, signed by Alexandra, in the amount of $200,000. Just looking at it took her breath away.

For a long time Kai rambled around the suite in a kind of depressed stupor. It should have been easy to define her moral responsibility and carry it out, rip up the check and the scurrilous legal documents and throw them away. The truth was the truth.

But what would she get for telling it? In the end, would she be believed? Certainly her own past and even her mother's would be dragged through the mud. And for who and what would she have fought so nobly? Her father—who had abandoned her mother and had indeed attempted to assault her sexually.

Most important, there was the fate of her half sister to consider. Suppose Vanessa was allowed to continue regular visitations with Wyler. Suppose not all of Alex's charges were merely spiteful lies. Hardly impossible. If Wyler was capable of assaulting one daughter, why not another?

And if she took the money? She would have the gift of independence. She would be able to devote herself to a few invaluable years of research. She would no longer need to compromise her dignity to support herself.

Kai didn't know how long she agonized over the choices. If only she could talk to her father, the decision might be clarified. But the gulf that yawned between them seemed too wide to cross.

When the phone rang, wrenching her out of her thoughts, she grabbed it up and answered in a strained voice.

It was Jim. Right away he was attuned to her distress. "Are you all right, Kai?" he said. "You sound very worried about something."

"You've got good ears," she said.

"A few years of navy command, you learn how to listen. Helps you take care of your men."

"You must be a good man to serve under," she said, enjoying her own little joke. Just hearing his voice revived the glow.

But he didn't pick up on it. "Want to tell me what's bothering you?" he asked. "I can be there in ten minutes."

"Yes," she said. "I'd like that."

* * *

He sat with her in the room while she went through it all. "You said you'd always wondered about how things worked out with my father," she began. It was hours later, with darkness settling on the city outside, before she felt the problem was really explained, the threat of the present linked to all the history that had led up to it.

"So what's your advice, Commander?" she asked at last. He had listened so patiently, hardly speaking except to ask the occasional question that kept her memories flowing.

"My advice," he said, "is that you let me take you out to a quiet dinner. I know a perfect little place to unwind . . . and then I think you'll know exactly what you should do without being told by anyone."

Taking the hint that the place was informal—Jim was tie-less and had arrived with a sheepskin coat over his sport jacket—Kai picked out a simple gray skirt and a blouse and a knit patterned sweater, showered and dressed, and wrapped herself in a dashingly styled red woolen coat with wide collar and lapels.

"I shouldn't be wearing some of these things, because I'll have to send them back anyway," she confessed as they left the room.

"I said I'd lend you the money."

"They're still way beyond my budget." As she gave the reply, Kai knew she had arrived at a decision. She couldn't take Alexandra's money to sign a false document.

They took a taxi from the hotel to an address Jim gave on Dearborn Street, a ten-minute ride across the Chicago River, and arrived in front of a small brick-front establishment with an old-fashioned blinking neon sign in the window identifying it as EDDIE'S PLACE. It was as unpretentious inside as out, two rows of booths along the walls, between them round tables covered with checkered tablecloths. A jovial man in a bowtie greeted them as they came through the door, made some welcoming small talk about what a cold night it was, and showed them to one of the empty booths and left them with menus. Steaks, fish, good plain food. The simplicity appealed to Kai, yet she wondered why Jim had chosen the place. Chicago was full of good restaurants, many much nearer to the hotel.

She was content with a hamburger and beer, and Jim echoed the order. When the waiter had left them alone again, Jim answered the riddle.

"My father worked here for a while—the last place he worked before he died. He did that job." Jim looked over at the man in the bowtie, who was just seating a group at one of the round tables. "Making people feel welcome, putting them at ease, creating a friendly atmosphere." His eyes came back to Kai. "It's harder than it looks. Keeping your chin up and wearing a smile even when you've worked a long day, and the boss is taking it out on you because the snow has cut business in half. I always admired my dad for the way he did that simple job."

"It must feel good," Kai said wistfully, "to be proud of the people you come from."

"I didn't say I admired everything about him. I just concentrated on what was good about him. You could do the same, Kai."

"If my father had a good side . . ."

"Maybe you should keep looking for it. If you could talk to him, wouldn't that help you in deciding what part to take in this trial?"

"I've already decided," she said. "For better or worse, I have to tell the truth and let things take their course." She reached across the table to grasp his hand. "You were right, Commander. I didn't need anyone to tell me what to do. But I did need to talk it through."

He put his other hand over hers. "Have you realized," he said, "that if some careless jackass hadn't set that plane on fire, you and I might have walked on and off without seeing each other?"

She smiled. "I have."

"And think about this: if your father hadn't been a heel who walked out on your mother and left you to hunt him down, you and I wouldn't have met in the first place."

"If you're trying to tell me I should forgive him, that certainly is the best reason I can think of."

"I'm just appreciating the fact that some very terrible things can sometimes be the source of something wonderful."

Their orders came, and they spent the rest of the meal trading stories to fill in the self-portraits they were eager to paint for one another. He told her his experiences in the war. She talked about college, her interest in psychology, and the research she was contemplating.

She found herself telling him, too, about the period she had spent at *Tomcat*. When she mentioned having been a Kitty, she discovered that he was unaware of that particular claim to fame, had never seen the pictures.

"Does it make you think less of me?" she couldn't help asking.

"Why would it? You're an extremely beautiful woman, Kai. I couldn't blame an artist for wanting to paint you, or any man for wanting to look at you. And if you were willing to let your beauty be seen—all of it—I can't see anything bad in that. You could even call it an act of generosity."

She laughed. "I don't think I ever looked at it that way. But I'm glad you don't think it was . . . cheap."

"The only thing cheap about you is the way you eat—a hamburger and beer. I'd have gone for lobster and champagne."

She had decided by the time they left the restaurant that she wanted to spend the night with him. She hadn't forgotten that moment in the plane when a crash seemed imminent, and she regretted not having taken more chances with her life. She didn't know if there was a future with Jim Bolton. But the sexual electricity was there, and it had been so long since she had wanted anybody. "Let's go back to my room," she said when he asked where she wanted to go next.

As soon as he followed her through the door, she turned and kissed him, unable to wait another second. He received her eagerly into his arms, pressing her against him as their lips met and tongues spoke in a twining dance. Yes, he wanted her, too. When the long kiss ended, she took his hand and started to lead him to the bedroom.

But he resisted. "No, Kai, not tonight."

She shook her head in baffled disappointment. "Don't you want me?"

He smiled and stepped up to embrace her again. "You think a man doesn't want you just because he's willing to wait?"

"We've already waited a long time. I remember when we met, nine years ago. The chemistry was there even then."

Jim nodded. He remembered, too. "But you were seventeen," he said.

"And you were an officer and a gentleman. But now there's nothing to stop us."

"Not nothing."

She held her breath. "There's someone else."

"No. Hasn't been for a long time. I've been moving too much and too fast for that."

"Then why not?"

"Because if there's going to be something for us, I want it to be good for us—no, not just good, I want it to be wonderful. And in my experience, it's never as good when you rush it as it is when you take your time. Don't count the nine years. We're different people now, and we've only known each other for two days."

"One day was enough for me."

"There were times it would've been enough for me, too. But not this one." He let go of her, stepping back slightly. "It wouldn't be hard for me to fall in love with you, Kai. But if it's going to happen, I want whatever we have in bed to be part of that love, not separate from it."

She smiled. "Well, that's quite a switch, Commander. Usually it's the lady who just wants to hear pretty words before she'll say yes. You're the one who needs the words."

"No, Kai. I need the feelings. Until we're both sure they're part of the picture, I can wait for the rest."

She wanted him desperately, yet he was right, it was much too soon to say that the desire was born of love rather than mere physical longing. Perhaps Jim realized that sex had always been an explosive element in her life; until the foundation for complete trust had been established between them, sex had the potential to destroy their love rather than enhance it.

"Even out of uniform," she said lightly, "I guess you're still giving the orders . . . and still a gentleman." She moved close to him, resting her cheek against his broad shoulder. "But worth waiting for."

His arms encircled her again, and they kissed even more passionately than before. She could feel him swelling against her. There was no doubt he had as much physical appetite as she did. His strong hands slid across her body, until they were gripping her arms. At last he pushed her away as though it took all his strength and resolve.

"When will I see you again?" she asked.

"I'll call tomorrow. I have to meet with some bankers about this airline deal. Depending on how that goes . . ."

They walked to the door and she opened it. He leaned over, pressed his lips gently to hers once more, and said good night.

Later, lying in the darkness, waiting for sleep, Kai could still feel his lips on hers. And she believed—too late, damn it—that for her own heart, tonight was soon enough.

Chapter Twenty-three

The Mercantile Traders League, situated on the banks of the Chicago River not far from the gigantic Mercantile Exchange building, looked more like the palace of a Renaissance prince than a club for the city's finanical elite. Eight stories of time-weathered granite were fronted by an imposing arched gateway through which the members' cars drove into a private courtyard, shielding them from the eyes of the public as they were fawned over by doormen in gold-braided livery.

Kai stepped from the long white custom limousine and accompanied Mitch through the gleaming brass doors as he boasted about his membership in the exclusive club.

"It usually takes seven years on the waiting list before you get in. But my new boss is one of the trustees, and he offered the membership as part of the package when I was hired."

Since picking her up at the hotel, Mitch had talked of nothing but the offer he had accepted to leave the commodities trading firm where he'd started three years ago to head a newly formed department at an investment-banking house. He'd crowed about his new salary—half a million dollars a year—the annual Christmas bonus that could run to another couple of hundred thousand, such extras as use of the company limousine and plane when he needed it, and privileges in the bank's executive dining room. He'd known he'd be moving into the new job a week ago, but had delayed making the announcement until this weekend precisely because Kai was planning to be in town and he wanted to celebrate with her. That was why he'd been so disappointed that they hadn't been together last night—and why, without even calling ahead, he'd come to the hotel this morning to insist she spend a few hours with him. He wasn't going to take another chance on getting no for an answer.

The club's dining room was very grand, and very stuffy. Mitch had mentioned that Sunday brunch was the one occasion during the week when women were admitted to the club, yet most of the tables in the cavernous oak-paneled room were occupied by elderly men dining alone. A blue pall of smoke from their illegally imported Cuban cigars hovered under the coffered ceiling. Many of the solitary old gentlemen lowered their Sunday financial sections to look at Kai as she stood at the dining room entrance. She was accustomed to receiving stares, but she couldn't tell whether these old men were approving or disapproving. Being a member of the Mercantile Traders League didn't look as though it provided much enjoyment for a man of Mitch's age, but of course that wasn't why he had wanted to be a member. The point, obviously, was to gain status, to impress people. That was why Mitch had brought her here, had picked her up in a limousine as big as a bus, had bragged about his salary.

But Kai wasn't impressed. In fact, she was saddened by the changes so apparent in Mitch as he flaunted his success. She thought back to the week they had spent together on the campaign trail; he's been unruly, yet amusing and sincere. On the surface now, perhaps he looked better than he had then. His hair was perfectly cut and blow-dried, he was turned out in a custom-tailored blue pin-striped suit, and the gold Patek-Phillipe watch on his wrist was probably worth nearly as much as his father had earned for a year of work in the slaughterhouse. Yet Kai found the perfectly manicured and cologned Mitch less appealing than the rough young idealist, the campaign worker who had spoken of wanting to reform the world.

She noticed him slipping a fifty-dollar bill to the dining room captain before they were guided to a choice table by a window. Kai sat down and admired the view. It was another glacial winter day in the Windy City, but the bright morning sun bounced off the surface of the Chicago River flowing past just across Wacker Drive.

"Is this all right?" Mitch asked as he sat opposite.

"Fine," Kai said. "Stop worrying so much about impressing me, Mitch." Her impatience with him was magnified by the contrast to Jim Bolton. Jim could martial the resources to buy an airline for tens of millions of dollars, yet he rode in compact rented cars and favored plain restaurants where he could admit without shame that his father had done an ordinary job.

"I'd like to hear more about you than just how much money you're making," she went on. "Your father, for instance. How is he?" Two years ago, Kai knew, Mitch's mother had died of breast cancer, and she didn't retain any fondness for Lech Karlozic. Yet she was curious to know how he was reacting to his son's success.

"He's all right. I tried to get him to quit his job, or at least get into something new. I was going to support him, maybe buy him a liquor store. But he wouldn't take the money from me."

"Maybe he just likes what he's doing."

"No. He's always hated it. He's just a stubborn sonofabitch."

Remembering Lech's grim pride and his disdain for his son's eagerness to escape his roots, Kai could guess that it wasn't mere stubbornness that kept Lech from accepting Mitch's money.

A waiter brought menus. Mitch told him to start by bringing a bottle of champagne. "The best you've got."

"A little early in the day for that," Kai remarked.

"Didn't someone say it's never too early for champagne? Liz Taylor, maybe." Mitch affirmed with a nod to the waiter that Kai's objection could be ignored, and the waiter left. "I told you we're celebrating," Mitch said. "The sky's the limit."

"Mitch, I'm glad you're doing so well. But it really isn't necessary to show off for me."

"Isn't it?" He leaned across the table. "Why do you think I've worked so hard to come up so fast? What's feeding my ambition, Kai, what's the dream?" He looked at her searchingly. "You. I can't ever forget that once we were almost lovers, almost—"

"Mitch," she interrupted, "there's no point in—"

"Let me say this," he came back quickly. "Because I've been carrying it around so long. I still want you, Kai. I never stopped. So many things I couldn't control came between us. But I knew we were going to find our way back to each other. And you're going to see how much I can give you, what a fabulous life we could have together.'' The intensity vanished from his expression, as if a brief possession had passed. ''Until then I'm glad to have the dream. Because that's what's pushing me higher and higher.''

Kai was simultaneously touched and embarrassed by his declaration. She didn't want to be the object of such a fixation. Just yesterday her heart had made other choices. But it was easy to see that Mitch's obsession would only be inflamed by telling him she was attracted to another man. What could she say to discourage his pursuit?

Her eyes wandered. At a nearby table a club member, white-haired and rotund, was staring at her. When their eyes met, he smiled—the slow, seductive smile of a very rich man testing the power of his money. Without responding, Kai brought her gaze back to Mitch. ''Aside from me,'' she asked, ''what else is part of your dream? How rich is enough?''

He smiled. ''People who want to be rich don't think in terms of numbers, Kai. They want all they can get.''

''And you think it's going to make a difference to me? I liked you when we met, Mitch. In fact, we wouldn't have met if you hadn't been interested in politics, spending your time—*giving* it freely—to work for something you believed in. You had principles, ideals.''

Mitch bristled. ''You think ideals are a luxury that only the poor can afford?'' he said sharply. ''It's always been rich men more than poor who've been able to get things done. George Washington and Thomas Jefferson had hundreds of slaves and lived in the most beautiful mansions in America. F.D.R. was no pauper, either. And what about everybody's hero, Jack Kennedy?'' He paused, and his indignation gave way to contrition. ''Look, you're right. I have gotten a little carried away by this magic carpet I'm riding. I never imagined I'd be making this much money this fast. Hell, I grew up expecting to spend my life in the stockyards. Sure, it makes my head spin sometimes. But I haven't completely lost my bearings. I still want to make the world a better place. Money will just make it easier. Kings have made more of a difference in history than beggars.''

His plain speaking won back some of Kai's respect. It didn't rekindle any attraction, but she believed he hadn't totally exchanged a dream of doing good for a dream of gathering gold.

The champagne came, she drank a toast to his new job, and he toasted to her coming graduation. They ordered eggs Benedict and corned beef hash, sharing the two dishes with each other, and Mitch asked about her plans for next year. "Think you'll be moving back to Chicago?"

"No, Mitch," she said, hoping it would bring him to terms with the impossibility of romance. "I'm going to stay in the East. I'll be going to graduate school and doing research."

"Into what?"

It seemed too charged to discuss sex with him. "I haven't exactly pinned down the project yet—something to do with behavorial psychology. I also have to get some sort of grant before I can go ahead. I couldn't afford it otherwise."

"Would it help if I give you a hundred thousand dollars?"

She smiled at the irony: money was being offered right and left, but none of it was acceptable. "Thanks for the thought. But it's a rule of good research not to finance with money that has strings attached. It might compromise the results."

Mitch shrugged. He didn't deny that there were strings, though he made one more pitch. "If you want to keep my principles alive, you ought to let me use my money for a worthy cause. I can afford it now, Kai . . . and there's going to be a lot more where that came from."

Rather than ungraciously repeat the refusal, she turned the conversation back to his new job. "Why are you paid so highly, Mitch? Exactly what is this new department going to be doing?"

"The operation is called mergers and acquisitions. It involves a combination of things. The trend in business is to build up big companies by arranging marriages between smaller ones, or having one that's already big gobble up a little guy. I'm the marriage broker. I look for prospects on both sides. If there's a big company that has cash piling up, I'll try to find them something to buy. If there's a small company that's looking for money to expand, I'll see if I can find a big brother that will buy in. When I do the job right, a hundred million dollars may change hands. And my bank gets a commission, like any broker. Do two or three of those deals a year, you can imagine how the money adds up. If I'm good at this, Kai, even the money I'm making now will be chicken feed.''

"Half a million a year will feed one hell of a big chicken.''

Oblivious to her ironic tone, he went on. "But I'll work hard for it. There are eighteen- and twenty-hour days at times. And I'll only get busier. The Democrats are in the White House now, but in 1980, if that peanut farmer can be traded in for a pro-business Republican, the rocket will really take off. I'll be doing deals hand over fist, that's my bet. I could make ten, twenty million fast.'' He paused, his eyes sparkling as his own words sunk in and he envisioned the dream becoming reality. "Millions,'' he murmured in awe. "And I'd spend it all on you.''

She gave him an automatic smile. All the talk of money was becoming tiresome. From the way he'd described his sphere of activity, however, it struck Kai that he might have some insights on a subject that did hold tremendous interest for her.

As the empty dishes were swept away and replaced by coffee cups, she said, "From the kind of business you're doing, I wonder if you've ever crossed paths with a man named James Bolton.''

Mitch sat up, as if startled by the question. "Haven't met him personally, not yet. But it happens that I've been learning a few things about him. This first deal I'm handling at the bank is representing an investment group that wants to buy Mid-Coast Air, and Bolton's one of several possible buyers who are competition for my client.''

Kai gave no indication that she knew about Jim's interest.

Mitch eyed her suspiciously. "Why do you ask about him?''

She made her best effort to sound casual. "He was on the plane with me.''

Mitch's eyes sparked. "On the same flight?'' He leaned in to look at her more closely. "So he's the guy who was in your room when I called? Are you and Bolton . . . holding hands?''

"No,'' she said emphatically. True enough, she thought—for the moment.

"Then why are you pumping me?" he demanded before she could explain any further.

"Hey," she objected, "what's wrong with asking a simple question?"

Mitch gave her a sheepish look. "Sorry, Kai. One thing we have to worry about in these deals is information getting leaked. I certainly don't want Bolton to have the benefit of any inside information. That is, if he's thinking of buying."

The way he studied her, Kai felt he was looking for a hint of Jim's intentions from her response. She did her best to appear ignorant. "Listen, Mitch, I'm not some kind of spy. I haven't asked you about the deal, have I? I only know Jim because he got me off the plane alive after I fainted. So naturally I'm just a little curious about him."

Mitch gave a slow nod, still slightly skeptical. "Well, you don't want to get too close to him," he said. "From what I hear, he's a pretty shady character."

"Oh? In what way?"

"Does business with our enemies for one thing—communists. Some of it is arms dealing, scavenging for supplies the Americans left behind in Southeast Asia, buying low and reselling to other countries at a big profit." Mitch lowered his voice. "There's even a few people who believe Bolton has connections with the CIA left over from the Vietnam war, and may be involved in some drug dealing."

Kai took the report with more than a few grains of salt. Everything Jim had freely told her could be interpreted with a negative slant if people were mean-spirited, and there was no lack of jealous back-biting among business competitors. Was it arms dealing if he salvaged and recycled surplus airplane parts? Was it trafficking with the enemy if he had sensibly opened up access to the Vietnamese communists through imtermediaries? The war had ended years ago. The Japanese had once been enemies, too, in another war.

"Whoever is telling these tales might just be jealous of his success. He strikes me as being a very decent guy."

"You *would* think that if he saved your life—and if you don't know the family history that makes him so desperate to get to the top of the heap." Mitch didn't have to be asked to start spinning out the story in detail, plainly eager to discourage any interest Kai might have. Jim's father, Carl Bolton, had been a struggling Chicago manufacturer of

plumbing supplies until World War II, when he converted
his business, Reliable Plumbing Incorporated, to manufac-
ture shell casings and grew wealthy as a major government
supplier. He had indulged his wealth by shedding a wife
who was childless and marrying a showgirl who produced a son. Some years after the war, it was discovered
that Carl Bolton had been profiteering, supplying inferior
goods at kited prices. War records indicated that artillery
shells supplied by Reliable had been anything but—frequently
blowing up inside gun chambers, with consequent loss of
life and limb to American troops. Carl Bolton had been sent
to jail for a long term and emerged a broken man.

"This old guy who'd once been a tycoon," Mitch finished the story, "ended up working for thirty bucks a week
as a greeter in some two-bit hash house in the Loop. Can
you beat that?" He laughed. "I love the gall, though—
calling his company Reliable, of all things."

Kai thought back to the restaurant where she'd gone with
Jim last night, his talk of admiring his father—shreds of
admiration he had obviously salvaged out of the shame. And
she wondered if any man who wanted to pile up great wealth
wasn't responding to forces that inevitably conflicted with
decency. She certainly didn't believe that Jim had ever been
mixed up in drug dealing. But Kai decided it was equally
naive to think that because a man had rescued one damsel
in distress, he was a Boy Scout always doing good deeds.
She wondered, indeed, if she had raised a halo over this
man simply because he had saved her life. What did she
know about Jim Bolton?

After lunch, Mitch took her in the limousine for a drive
along the lakeshore. In front of one of the soaring Gold
Coast apartment towers the limousine stopped, and Mitch
said he wanted Kai to look at a place he was thinking about
buying. He had borrowed the key from the broker for the
weekend just so he could show her.

The apartment was on one of the top floors, with a gorgeous view across Lake Michigan. Much larger than he
needed for himself alone. "This is where we could live,"
he said quietly as he stood beside Kai at one of the windows, showing her the view.

She steeled herself, expecting he might try a physical display of his desire, but it didn't happen. "I don't think I

want to live as high as you do, Mitch," she said, hoping he understood her double meaning.

He smiled at her. "Someday you may change your mind."

He drove her back to the hotel. She was booked on a late-afternoon flight, and she told Mitch she needed time to check out. He offered to drive her to the airport, but she made excuses; she was secretly hoping that Jim might call and she might take a later plane. Although Mitch had known that the reason for her trip was to meet Alexandra's lawyers, he said nothing about it until the limousine was nearing the hotel. Even then his interest seemed less sympathetic than selfish. "Is it all worked out," he asked, "or will you have to come back before the trial? If I know you're coming, I'll clear my schedule."

"I don't know what's going to happen," she said, disinclined to share all the details with Mitch, especially after her heart-to-heart with Jim. But then it struck her that Mitch might actually help resolve one aspect of the situation. "I've been wondering if I should speak to my father about it. He hasn't made any effort to contact me, and I can't bring myself to pick up a phone and call out of the blue. But maybe there's a way to break the ice. I mean, if someone who had a past connection to him could find out if he'd like to speak to me."

"Are you suggesting I call him?" Mitch said.

"Well, you worked for him once. He'd know who you are. And the way your career is going, you might even end up doing business with him—"

"That's exactly why I can't get in the middle, Kai. Randall Wyler may no longer have any appeal to voters, but he's got as much clout as ever. These days he does more wheeling and dealing behind the scenes, and less trial work. And you're right, I may need a favor from him one of these days. I'd like to help you, but if I go to him as your friend . . ." He trailed off.

"Then he won't do you any favors," Kai supplied.

"I'm sorry, Kai. I hope you understand."

"Sure," she said. "It might cost you millions."

At the entrance to the hotel, she told him not to bother coming in. She had to start packing.

"Just don't forget," he said as they stood on the sidewalk. "It's here for you, whenever you want it. And I'm betting you will someday."

He gave her a kiss on the cheek before he climbed back into the limousine and it drove off. Perhaps it helped him to believe he was doing it for her, she thought, but it was only for himself.

And what was Jim Bolton's motive? Kai wondered as she walked toward the reception desk.

There had indeed been a call from Jim, but the message slip showed it had come just after she left the hotel with Mitch, hours ago.

Riding the elevator up to her room, Kai felt terribly deflated. If Jim's desire to see her again had meant anything, there would have been five more calls, a dozen. He wouldn't have risked not seeing her again before she left Chicago.

But when she pushed open the door to her suite, her spirits revived. An enormous flower arrangement, larger than yesterday's, had been placed inside. The accompanying card was signed Jim, with two lines of printed handwriting, as though it had been dictated to the florist over a phone. "Had to go to New York to meet with my bankers. Hope to see you again soon—even if nothing catches fire."

She smiled faintly at the final words, realizing they could be read two ways.

This time as she rode to the airport and boarded her flight back to Baltimore, there were no troubling premonitions of danger. As the plane rose and Chicago faded away beneath the clouds, she knew she would be safe.

And yet, if she prayed for anything now, it was to have again—soon—those exhilarating moments when her heart and soul were fully at risk.

Chapter Twenty-four

Graduation was not the stirring emotional event for Kai that it was for most of her classmates. Having arrived at college at an age when others were graduating, she didn't feel, as most seniors did, that this ceremony represented a coming of age, a passage through a gateway to full membership in the world of adults. She had been initiated into that world long ago. Nor did she have the satisfaction of being surrounded by proud family. The emotional numbness she felt was only accentuated by the deep disillusionment that had set in when Jim Bolton failed to maintain contact with her. Leaving Chicago, she had been so sure she would hear from him soon. There hadn't been so much as a postcard—though Mitch had sent a couple of notes, and one had inadvertently given Kai a glimmer of insight.

"I met Jim Bolton, by the way. A tough customer when it comes to business. He really wanted that airline."

It sounded like Mitch and Jim had wound up on opposite sides of the deal and Jim had won. Perhaps that explained why he had vanished from her life: his business had totally absorbed him. He could allow himself time for nothing else because he was operating out of an obsessive need to make sure he did not fail as his father had. Perhaps, too, he had decided that a one-time nude pin-up girl wasn't a fitting consort for a man who had to consolidate his financial credentials. Or could it be merely that he was a charming man who hadn't been scrupulous about telling her the truth?

At first Kai wanted to go in search of the answer—of Jim—whenever she was called back to Chicago for the legal contest between her father and Alexandra. The city was also headquarters for Mid-Coast Airlines, where Jim could probably be found. But two months after her deposition, Kai received a phone call from a Chicago police detective asking if she knew the current whereabouts of Vanessa Wyler: her young half sister had been abducted by her mother. The note sent by Alexandra to the Chicago newspapers said she was taking the girl because she knew that Randall Wyler's behind-the-scenes influence in the legal system would make it impossible to get a fair judgment that would "rescue" the girl from his sexual abuse.

Kai told the detective that she was the last person who was likely to be contacted by Alexandra while she was on the run.

Without any need to return to Chicago, Kai gave up the idea of seeking out Jim Bolton to learn why the romantic spark had died.

So when graduation came, it was Laura Cooke alone who applauded Kai's achievement. The night of commencement exercises she invited Kai for dinner at any place of her choice. They went to Olde Obrycki's, a Baltimore institution where the main dish was steamed crab fresh out of Chesapeake Bay, served whole in the shell, on a table set not only with knife and fork but a mallet used to break the shells and a bucket to catch the scraps. A whole evening could be spent battling with the cooked crab, but Obrycki's had the kind of warm family atmosphere Kai preferred over stuffy formality.

"Before we start getting our hands messy," Laura said soon after they sat down, "I'd better give you this." From her purse she produced a small but beautifully wrapped package. Inside, Kai found a gold Movado watch. She was not only moved by the gesture, but embarrassed by the extravagance.

Laura brushed it aside. "There's no better way to spend money," she said, "than on the people we care about." Then she skipped past sentiment by diverting the conversation to Kai's future and the research project they were hoping to pursue.

In the last few months, Kai and Laura had continued their discussions about organizing a study of unexplored aspects of human sexual behavior. Over breakfasts, office meetings, coffee in Laura's living room, and cafés after an occasional night out together to see a movie, the conversations usually went on for hours and opinions were expressed passionately, even heatedly, though there was never rancor. Based on their separate experiences, both women felt strongly that a deeper understanding of human sexuality would yield enormous psychological and social benefits. But they had not been able to agree what the exact nature of the investigations should be, what goals would be set for the project, and what kind of methodology to apply. Laura preferred the collection of a measurable data base as opposed to the "arm's-length" approach of collecting and analyzing questionnaires. "Instead of exploring all of human sexuality," she suggested to Kai, "we could limit the field of study to female sexuality. That's something you and I are especially motivated to investigate and understand."

As for a research target, Laura had observed that there could be nothing more beneficial to women than an exploration of the very crux of all sexual experience, the orgasm. Specializing in the treatment of dysfunction had made her aware that a large majority of women either failed to achieve it during intercourse or did so only rarely. "Suppose we do a study of the mechanics of the nervous system involved in achieving orgasm," she proposed. "That could be applied to improve the percentages."

Kai had consistently argued against this approach. She didn't want to spend her efforts on the kind of research that would boil down to an article or two printed in some elite medical journals read solely by professionals who then passed it on to general public awareness only gradually through teaching or specialized treatment. Her ambition was to reach the public directly, to benefit the widest number of people possible. Kai felt almost an urgency about communicating information to correct the misconceptions and myths that had long interfered with people's happiness and satisfaction. She felt that lives might even be saved by it—that her mother might not have gone mad if she could have understood her sexuality better and come to terms with it.

"Sex represents a problem to almost everyone at some time in their lives," Kai observed. "I think we might help everyone by doing a comprehensive study of human sexual requirements." As she envisioned it, the research would attempt to answer a broad range of questions. What is the nature of the sex drive? How important is sexual fulfillment to general health and well-being? What are the parameters of sexual pleasure, and how can it best be attained? Which kind of partners achieve the best results with each other? What is the range of human sexual behavior—should anything be considered "abnormal"?

"That could take four, five . . . maybe ten years," Laura warned.

Kai wasn't discouraged. What scientific study of any significance didn't require an immense effort? Alfred Kinsey, America's pioneer in sex research, had based his findings on more than 18,500 personal interviews that had taken many years to compile and interpret before producing his books *Sexual Behavior in the Human Male* and *Sexual Behavior in the Human Female*. Originally a zoologist, Kinsey had virtually given his life to these studies of humans considered in this primal, animal context.

Yet as the ground breaker in his field, Kinsey had not dared to trespass too far beyond the sensitive boundaries of existing research. His work was now almost thirty years old, and he had died more than twenty years ago. There was plenty of room to expand the boundaries, Kai insisted. New information about sex was becoming increasingly vital in the utterly permissive atmosphere that had prevailed since the 1960s. And the rising women's liberation movement spurred the demand that women achieve sexual fulfillment instead of going without it, as Laura's practice indicated that most did.

"The kind of understanding people need is long overdue," Kai said. "Why do we have a failure rate of fifty percent of all marriages—with sexual dysfunction common even in the half that survive? Maybe we can help to change that."

Eventually Laura was swayed to the idea of a more comprehensive program of research, though they continued to battle over the issue of methodology.

"Kinsey sent out a bunch of assistants to interview a small cross section of the population," Laura pointed out. "But that's all they did, Kai—go into people's living rooms, ask questions about their experiences, prejudices, secrets. It was a survey, an attempt to paint a statistical picture. There's no way to tell how accurate that picture was because Kinsey could never be sure of his results. A lot of those who agreed to talk to his staff couldn't overcome some modesty, or a reflex to protect their privacy. So the answers they gave were sometimes half truths, even outright lies—and there's no way to tell how many of which.''

To go beyond what Kinsey had learned and to trust their data, Laura said, they would have to iron out the wrinkles in his method. ''We'll have to make sure people are telling us the whole truth all the time, no matter what questions we're asking.''

''There's only one way to be absolutely positive we're getting the truth,'' Kai said. ''The most basic requirement of scientific research is direct observation. That's what we need, Laura—actual laboratory work, to observe what we're studying firsthand. Instead of talking to our subjects in their living rooms like Kinsey did, we should watch them in their bedrooms.''

It took Laura more than a moment to accept that Kai was serious. ''There's a difference between research and voyeurism,'' she responded.

''Maybe not,'' Kai replied, ''when the subject is sex.''

The first time Kai suggested the approach, Laura flatly rejected it. But whenever they came back to discussing methods, Kai expanded on the possibility of using direct observation. ''We don't literally have to go into their bedrooms. Not as long as we create an environment that's conducive to intimacy and permits us to study what happens without being an inhibiting presence.''

''Such as using one-way mirrors?'' Laura said.

''Or television cameras.'' Observations could be recorded on tape or film, Kai said, so that they could later be reviewed. ''Of course, it would never be done without the knowledge and permission of our subjects,'' she added. ''That's the key; we have to find men and women who will consent to being studied in the act of having sex.''

Laura remained dubious. People who allowed themselves to be watched might do so only because they had an abnormal need and desire to perform, in which case they would not provide useful information about average men and women.

Once more Kai disagreed. The college community provided an ideal source of sexually active individuals and partners who could set aside their privacy for a variety of healthy reasons. ''Judging from my own experience,'' she said, ''paying our subjects would be incentive enough for many.

Loads of college kids need money. Then there are those studying psychology, or in the med school, who would participate in the research in the interest of science.'' Finally, Kai had added the obvious: there were bound to be a number of normal people who would be happy for any excuse to—as the kids put it—''get laid.''

At last, a couple of weeks ago, Laura had come around. She finally accepted that Kai's radical approach would yield the most worthwhile results. But she was doubtful that the money to fund such a controversial project could be obtained from the usual sources for research grants—foundations, colleges, government agencies.

''It's always been hard to get money for sex research, anyway,'' Laura said. ''But for this it might be impossible. The people who are responsible for distributing these funds get many requests that are equally worthwhile, and easier to accept. I'm afraid they're likely to judge what we want to do as little more than a dirty joke.''

''We have to try,'' Kai urged. ''The knowledge is there for the taking, but we've always been too afraid. Too many men and women have been relying on information that's been passed along almost as primitively as tales told around the fire by cavemen. Damn it, Laura, the Puritans haven't run this country for three hundred years. Isn't it about time we shook off their influence?''

There the dialogue had seemed to break down. In the weeks just preceding her graduation, Kai had hardly seen Laura. While her days and nights were filled with preparing for and taking her final examinations, Kai had nevertheless attempted to schedule meetings that Laura had canceled or begged off from because of other obligations. Kai had begun to suspect that Laura had changed her mind. Perhaps, for the sake of her own prestige at the medical school, she had decided to withdraw any support for the idea, and even sever personal involvement with anyone else who supported it.

So Laura's invitation to dinner to celebrate graduation and her expensive gift sharply reversed Kai's fear that another more vital emotional connection had slipped away. Indeed, it became clear that Laura's unavailability during the preceding weeks had been due to a concentrated effort she had been making to find sponsorship for their research.

"I was hoping I could set this up by now," Laura reported, "so you wouldn't feel at loose ends after graduating. Any money that comes in would include a salary for you, and financing if you want to go on to graduate school. Unfortunately, as I anticipated, there's been resistance to my proposal from every single one of the usual sources for research money."

Kai listened gloomily, already musing on alternatives for the months ahead. Would she have to keep posing for Larry Meyer?

Then Laura said, "But we might have a chance with one private foundation which has an enormous amount of money to dispense. They've always given the bulk of it to general philanthropies that are more mainstream than our project—buildings for universities, clinics for the poor, grants to artists, that sort of thing. I know the people who administer the funds, so they listened, and they didn't reject us out of hand."

"Which foundation is it?"

Laura hesitated a moment, as though she might be protecting the source of money from a rival. "The Gerron Foundation."

Kai recognized the name immediately. It was impossible to attend Jefferson University and not know about the Gerron family, who had been major benefactors for generations. Their fortune had been founded at the end of the nineteenth century by Nathaniel Gerron of Baltimore, who had started with railroads, progressed into oil, and then into banking. The fortune he had piled up put him on a par with Rockefeller, Carnegie, and Ford. Nathaniel Gerron had believed his dynasty was securely established after he fathered three sons, but two branches of the family had been cruelly cut down when the oldest boys, after a summer tour of England, were presented by their father with a trip home on the maiden voyage of the *Titanic*. Though the surviving family—descended from the third son—preferred to keep a low profile, they were today among the richest Americans, with a cumulative fortune—and the endowment of the foundation, launched many decades ago—valued at several billion dollars. Jefferson University had always been a major beneficiary because Nathaniel, founder of the dynasty, had struggled to put himself through the school before making his fortune.

"The foundation is being very cautious, though," Laura went on. "They won't go ahead with us unless we meet some conditions."

"Such as?" Kai asked warily. The idea of meeting pre-set conditions ran counter to the very spirit of pure scientific exploration.

"Not long ago they set aside a couple of million dollars to finance an extensive study of PMS. Do you know what that is?"

Kai shook her head.

"Pre-menstrual syndrome," Laura explained. "In some cases, monthly hormonal changes in women can apparently be so extreme that it results in personality changes. We're just beginning to realize the extent and the severity of the effects in a sizable group. It's a worthwhile subject for research, so it has attracted several prominent medical researchers—which means the work is being duplicated. The Gerron Foundation had allocated money for work being done in California, but they'd be willing for us to have it instead." Laura paused heavily. "The hitch is that we have to convince the man who's heading up the other research to turn his financing over to us."

Kai shook her head disconsolately. "He's not going to do that. If someone had already written us a check, would we stop and hand it over to anybody else?"

"I'll admit it's a long shot," Laura said. "But beggars can't be choosers. Most people with money don't want to be associated with the kind of work we're talking about, Kai. I had to pull every last string I have to win just this much of a concession."

"It's almost worthless, though. Why should this man abandon his work to go hunting for money again?"

"That's not quite what the foundation had in mind. It isn't just the money we have to get, it's the man himself. That's the main condition, Kai. The foundation feels that I don't have sufficient research experience to supervise something of this scope. Also, because of the nature of the subject, they don't want the work to be overseen exclusively by women. They want a man on the team, too, someone who's already made a reputation as a successful researcher."

"Who is he?"

"Paul Sinclair," Laura said.

The name sounded familiar to Kai, though she didn't think she'd come across it in connection with her academic work.

"What's he done in the past?" she asked.

"Originally he was an obstetric surgeon. Treating infertility problems led to some experimenting with aspects of human reproduction—"

"I know!" Kai sat up as she remembered. "He's the one who did all that work on in vitro fertilization." His name and picture had been all over *Time* and *Newsweek* and television after the birth of the first so-called "test-tube" baby to be born in the United States.

Laura nodded. "That's him."

Kai sighed. "Laura, why would Paul Sinclair give up his work to join us? He's already a big fish in his own pond. And he's based in California. Would he consider moving east?"

"He's already shown he's willing to move from surgery to research, from obstetrics to PMS. He's obviously a man who likes to shift gears, keep the work fresh for himself. I've spoken with him on the phone—and he's not slamming the door. He's willing to meet us and listen. If we can convince him we've got the best game around—the most interesting project—I think we have a chance. Not a big one, maybe. But sometimes you can land even the biggest fish on the smallest hook." Laura gave Kai a wily smile. "It all depends on the bait."

Laura scheduled a meeting with Sinclair on his home territory, at the campus of the University of California in Santa Barbara, where he had been given research facilities. But it was not to be immediate. Laura wanted time so that a written description of the research that she and Kai envisioned could be prepared. The document would crystallize all aspects of the project—its goals, methods, costs, and the projected schedule—and provide both the Gerron Foundation and Dr. Sinclair with a clear basis on which to make their decisions. It would be, said Laura, the intellectual bait for their hook.

The writing of the proposal was left to Kai, though Laura supplied her with a monthly stipend of a thousand dollars out of her own pocket so that Kai would have no distractions. To save her additional expenses, she invited Kai to stay in a guest room at her house.

In five weeks Kai produced a hundred-and-fifty-page proposal that she titled "A Plan to Observe Sexual Action and Interaction in the Human Male and Female." Within it she gave some historical background on the fledgling field of sex research and paid tribute to the importance of the work done by Kinsey and others. But she also called attention to its shortcomings. Having made the argument for direct observation, Kai went on to provide details of the sort of "laboratory" that would be designed, and the methods used, to collect the necessary information.

While working on the proposal in the university library, Kai also did some research into Paul Sinclair, reading articles about him that had appeared at the time he'd made his splash. The photograph of Sinclair that appeared on the cover of *Time* magazine showed a man in his mid-forties with thick, graying brown hair and a lean, intense face with warm brown eyes. Tall and rangy, he suggested a smoother, better-looking version of Abe Lincoln, a man of scrupulous character, with an element of sadness clearly etched into his features. Though the biographical sketches included in each article unfailingly mentioned that he was a private man who did not like to discuss the details of his personal life, enough was known to account for that visibly lingering melancholy. While in medical school he had married a beautiful young heiress from California who was sufficiently skilled as a horsewoman to be a member of the Olympic equestrian team in the summer games of 1964. She won a silver medal in the Show Jumping event. Then a bad spill with her horse during an exhibition only a month later had resulted in a spinal injury that left her paralyzed from the neck down. As a quadriplegic, she had been confined to a wheelchair for nine years before her death four years ago.

Associates of Sinclair's quoted in the article said that he had been deeply in love with his wife and devastated first by her accident, then again by her death. Some speculated that the failure of the marriage to produce any children was partly responsible both for his deep empathy with infertile couples and for the intensive effort he had made to develop new ways for them to realize their dreams.

Kai found herself staring at the picture of Sinclair for a long time. She was certain that he would not change his work and move across the country. The suffering was still plainly there in his eyes, the evidence of his unbreakable attachment to a memory. And the home of that memory was in California.

In fact, she was not surprised after the written proposal was completed and sent to Sinclair at the end of July that two weeks went by without an answer from him. She assumed it was an implicit rejection; conceivably, he had not even taken the time to read it.

"At the very least," Laura said, expressing her irritation, "he should have called one way or the other. He certainly owed me that much."

Laura made it sound as if there was some personal connection. "I didn't realize you knew him," Kai said.

For an instant Laura looked as if she had been caught in an indiscretion. "I don't, personally," she said. "But simply as a matter of professional courtesy, he owed us a prompt response."

Though Kai sensed that Laura was concealing something, she didn't press for an answer. As she had gotten to know Laura better, she had become aware that there were certain areas of her life she preferred to keep to herself.

When another week went by without any answer from Sinclair, Laura's annoyance turned to outrage. She told Kai that she was going to call Sinclair and demand an answer. If it was a refusal—as they expected—at least they could plan accordingly and go on with their lives.

The following evening, when Laura returned home after a day at the medical school, she informed Kai that she had reached Sinclair. Kai was astonished when Laura said Sinclair had read the proposal right after he'd received it and he had found it "intriguing."

"Intriguing?" Kai echoed. "Then why did he just toss it aside and never bother to give us an answer?"

"Because he hadn't made up his mind what he wanted to say—whether or not to accept it."

Kai's eyes widened. "You mean, he might be willing—"

"He's thinking about it. It's time for one of us to go to California and talk to him personally."

"Not both of us?"

"He's on the fence, Kai, that was obvious. If it's two-on-one he could feel we're ganging up, pressuring him too much, and that might tilt him the wrong way."

Kai nodded. Laura was wise to consider the psychology of the situation. "When are you going?" Kai asked.

"I'm not," Laura said. "You are."

Kai stared back. "But you're the senior member of the team—"

"This is your project even more than mine, Kai, your vision." Laura paused and smiled. "Besides which, didn't we always say that hooking the fish would depend on the bait?"

For a moment Kai was shocked by Laura's suggestion that the ammunition of her youth and beauty should be brought to bear in persuading Sinclair to join them. But then it struck her that the whole point of the exercise was an investigation of the physical interaction between men and women.

This might only be the first phase of the research.

Chapter Twenty-five

Emerging from the arrival gate at Los Angeles Airport, Kai scanned the group waiting for friends and relatives. She had been told an assistant of Paul Sinclair's would meet her to drive her up to Santa Barbara, where she would stay while conferring with Sinclair, but no name or description of the assistant had been supplied. No one appeared to be looking to rendezvous with Kai, no one held up a sign with her name on it. She waited until the crowd at the gate had completely dispersed. Some sort of mixup with schedules, she guessed as she set out toward the car-rental desks.

Just then a young woman came racing toward her. "Miss Wyler!" she called. "Here I am . . . Miss Wyler . . . !" She intercepted Kai in the middle of the terminal floor.

She was short and slightly overweight, with a fly-away mop of curly light brown hair, lively dark eyes under thick brows, a wide mouth, and a tapering chin with a hint of weakness. Her face was so animated by energy and eagerness, Kai couldn't say if she was pretty or not, but she was instantly appealing. The oversized sweatshirt stamped with the U. of C. emblem she wore over jeans enhanced her gamine quality.

"Elsie Roth," she panted, thrusting her hand forward. "From Dr. Sinclair." She jabbered cheerfully as Kai shook hands, and they started moving in the direction of the exits. "I was stuck on the freeway in the worst tie-up. Should've given myself another hour to get here. Thank god you didn't leave. I'd catch hell if I screwed this up. Dr. Sinclair hates to keep people waiting."

Kai smiled reassuringly. "No harm done, Elsie. At least with everyone else gone, you had no trouble recognizing me."

"Oh, that was never a problem. Dave Gelly—one of the

other grad students assisting Dr. Sinclair—he got hold of some of your old boob shots, and he was showing them to every—'' Elsie froze in mid-word, struck by the realization that Kai must feel horribly compromised to know the old pictures had been passed around.

Kai laughed lightly. "Relax, Elsie, I'm used to it. The damn things never stop showing up somewhere.''

"Well, it's nothing to be ashamed of. Of course, the strict feminist position is you shouldn't let yourself be a sex object. But I'd be tempted to show off, too, if I had a bitchin' bod like yours. I mean. . . .'' She shrugged, mired in embarrassment again. Elsie Roth seemed to be one of those people who were always getting tripped up by their own boundless sincerity. "My car's this way,'' she said quickly as they stepped out to the sidewalk.

An airport policeman was just starting to write a ticket for the rusty green Volkswagon convertible at the curb. With an angry yelp Elsie ran over and, apparently drawing on feminist speeches she had heard in the past, called the hapless policeman a "typical macho bully who uses his goddamn ticket pad to beat women into submission.'' The cop calmly continued writing the ticket, slipped it under the windshield, and sauntered off.

As they drove away, Elsie still fuming, Kai mused on the contrast between the first impression made by Dr. Sinclair's assistant and the personality revealed by the incident. For all her bumbling appeal, Elsie Roth was overflowing with a determination to fight the feminist battle at every opportunity.

On the drive back to Santa Barbara, Elsie offered information about herself. Though she had attended college at Berkeley before moving to Santa Barbara to do graduate work in biology, she had grown up on the east coast in a suburb of New York City. Her father ran a dry-cleaning business, and her mother had given up a promising career as a research biologist to spend more time raising Elsie and a younger brother. Elsie candidly acknowledged that seeing her intelligent mother forced to sacrifice a promising career to be a housewife was the reason she had chosen Berkeley, with its famous tolerance for radical activists. In college, Elsie had been very involved in fighting for women's rights. "I don't want to have to give up *my* career,'' she explained, "that is, if I ever get one." She was twenty-eight years old now, and working for her Ph.D., though she confessed to being uncertain as to whether biological research was the right thing for her to be doing. It had occurred to her she might be acting out the idea of picking up where her mother had left off.

"The sad truth is I'm lousy in science," Elsie said. "I only got into grad school by working my tail off. Whenever I think of giving it up, though, I remember that the alternative is going home to work in a dry-cleaning store while I listen to my mother telling me I missed my best chance to get married by not grabbing a guy in college." She glanced at Kai. "I guess your mother never worries you about stuff like that."

"No," Kai said simply, hoping to divert the conversation from herself. But Elsie made no effort to hide an intense curiosity about what it was like to be so sexy and beautiful. Though Kai found Elsie winning and sympathetic, she finally became impatient with the interrogation about how and why she had become a Kitty, and what it had meant to her life.

"Let me sum it up for you, Elsie. Maybe some women find it makes things easier, but I'm not one of them. I'm not so different from you. I'm fighting to make a life for myself that won't depend on whether the right guy comes along, but I'd rather be alone than be anybody's pet kittycat. I've been in college the last four years, and living like a nun the whole time. Does that answer all your questions?"

Kai's outburst stunned them both to silence. Elsie switched on the radio, and Beethoven blasted through the air.

It was a balmy California day, and they drove up the coast with the top of Elsie's little convertible open to the bright sun of early afternoon and the cloudless blue sky. As Kai felt the sunshine on her face, and realized that the palm trees dotting the landscape were the first she had seen in ten years, she looked across the coast road to the ocean, and wondered when and how she might find her way back to Hawaii again. She was halfway there now, but it was still more than she could afford—in money and in pride—to go the rest of the distance. Mak's rejection still hurt too much

for her to go and plead for acceptance until she could bring
with her a record of achievement beyond that of a notorious
nude centerfold. For the first time it struck Kai that if Paul
Sinclair could be persuaded to join her and Laura, the potential reward was not just the excitement of the research
itself or the knowledge it would yield. At stake now, Kai
thought, was no less than all the achievement she hungered
for to heal the wounds of the past.

As they drove, Elsie admitted that there had been some
rumors around the lab that Kai was luring Sinclair away to
join another research product. "You don't have to tell me
what it is," Elsie said. "I'd just like to know if it's true—
if Paul, I mean, Dr. Sinclair is leaving here. . . ."

A touching wistfulness came through in her question. For
all Elsie's feminist determination to be independent, Kai
suspected she might be a classic case of the graduate student
who got a crush on her mentor. "I'm going to try to per-
suade him to come to Baltimore," Kai admitted.

Elsie nodded seriously and fell silent again.

Two hours later, the sprawl of Spanish-style houses with
red tile roofs so common in Santa Barbara came into view.
But instead of driving into the city, where the university
campus was located, Elsie took a turn off the freeway and
headed up through the oak-covered canyons of the Santa
Ynez Mountains. Was she intending to provide a sightseeing tour?

"I'm supposed to meet with Dr. Sinclair as soon as I
arrive," Kai reminded her.

"I know, but he wanted me to bring you to his ranch.
You'll be staying there."

Kai had expected to find a hotel for herself; she wondered
now if it would be wise to decline Paul Sinclair's hospitality.

Elsie drove on for another six or seven miles through the
rippling green foothills of the Santa Ynez, and then took a
turn off the main road through a gate in a long stand of
wooden fence posts. As they continued on a dirt road, Kai
saw no sign of a house, only vast sloping fields of pale green
sun-dried grass and occasional stands of trees. A pair of
hawks circled in the cloudless sky.

"Where's the ranch?" she asked, wanting assurance that
the student hadn't lost her way.

"We're on it." Elsie waved her hand around. "It's huge—a couple thousand acres."

Kai recalled that in the articles she'd read about Paul Sinclair, his late wife had been described as an heiress. "I always thought of a ranch as a place with herds of animals," she said, scanning the empty fields.

"There may have been some cows grazing around here once. Right now the doc keeps only horses, about a dozen—used to be his wife's. You know about her?" Elsie glanced across at Kai.

Kai nodded.

"Poor guy," Elsie said softly. "I wonder if he'll ever get over it." If ever he would, she seemed to be saying, she'd be ready and waiting.

The dirt road crested a hill and then dipped into a shallow valley. A quarter of a mile ahead, Kai saw a large house built in the style of a Spanish hacienda, with a roof of terra cotta tiles and an arched loggia extending over a patio beside a pond, shimmering blue with the reflected sky. Around the central house a number of outbuildings were scattered, and beyond them a corral and a pasture irrigated by a broad stream so that the grass was lusher and greener than in the surrounding fields. Horses grazed across the pasture. Vegetable and flower gardens filled the spaces between buildings, and a grove of lemon trees was visible beyond the house.

At the sight of Paul Sinclair's home, Kai resigned herself to failing in her mission. Why would he ever want to leave this paradise?

As Elsie stopped the car in the driveway in front of the house, Kai spotted a number of touches that made it appear more homespun and less grand that it had from a distance. An old-fashioned well, marked by a brick cylinder, stood off to one side, a watering trough for horses beside it. The front door was a slab of unfinished oak planks rather than carved panels shellacked to a high polish, and the wooden tubs of flowers that were spaced between the windows were merely sawed-off barrels that were splitting from age and weather. Cracks in the stucco and the warping of the green shutters that flanked each window gave further evidence of casual neglect.

Kai got out of the car and stood enjoying the tranquil

scene. The warm air was so still that the sound of horses clomping and whinnying carried clearly from the large pasture. Then she noticed that Elsie was removing her valise from the backseat of her car. Kai abandoned any doubts about staying. It was so lovely here—and Sinclair had invited her.

Elsie walked straight through the front door. While Kai lingered outside the house, she could hear the student inside calling: "Doc—you here . . . ?"

She reappeared after a minute. "Can't find him, but I know he's expecting you."

Just then a plainly dressed middle-aged woman with jet black hair and burnished brown skin scurried around a corner of the house. "Senorita Elsie!" she called out. Elsie hurried over to speak with her then returned to report to Kai as the woman dashed off to the vegetable garden.

"That's Rosa, his housekeeper. Says he had to take care of a problem, but he'll be back soon." Elsie's gaze rested on Kai, and a look of defeat passed over her face. If she had harbored some naive romantic dream, she seemed to be accepting that it wasn't likely to survive Sinclair's meeting Kai. "I hope you won't mind if I don't hang around to keep you company," she said quickly. "I ought to get back to school."

Rather than wait for Sinclair in the house, Kai strolled around toward the pond. As she turned a rear corner of the house onto the loggia, she heard the faint sound of rapid hoofbeats. Standing under one of the arches of the loggia, she looked across the fields and saw a man on horseback galloping in the direction of the house. As they neared the pond, the rider reined the horse to a stop and dismounted. Leaving the horse to drink, the man started up the incline toward the patio. Kai recognized then that it was Paul Sinclair. Wearing jeans and a Western-style shirt, his graying brown hair blown down over his forehead by the wind, he cut quite a different figure than in the news photos, where his lanky frame had been draped in a long white lab coat and every hair had been in place.

She wasn't sure he had seen her, so she stepped out from under the shadow of the arch. Still twenty or thirty yards away, he waved, called out a hello, and quickened the stride of his long legs. As the gap between them shrank, he smiled broadly, the lines radiating suddenly across his face etched sharply by the high sun. With every step nearer, he looked more dashing and vital. No trace of the sadness in his pictures.

"Miss Wyler," he said, extending his hand as he came up to her, "Paul Sinclair. Sorry I wasn't here to meet you. I had to fix a break in some fencing out by the road."

She put her hand in his. There was a timeless moment as their eyes rested on each other. "Well," he said finally, "I should be glad, after all, that Dr. Cooke talked me into letting you make the trip."

"Talked you into it?" Kai said, retracting her hand. "I wasn't told you'd put up any resistance."

Sinclair looked chagrined. "Oh, dear. There I go. I'm afraid I'm one of those people with a mouth and a foot that seem made for each other. The last thing I'd want you to think is that you're not welcome. In fact, I meant to say that having you here, meeting you . . . I'm really pleased to have this chance, even if we won't be working together."

"Won't be?" Kai echoed in dismay. "I never imagined that it was pointless for me to come. Is that what you told Dr. Cooke—that your decision was already made?"

"Well, you know I'm engaged in doing other work," Sinclair said apologetically.

Kai bristled with consternation. Obviously, Laura had withheld the truth believing that Kai could exercise her wiles to bend Sinclair to their will. The irritation she felt with this petty deception was so great that if Elsie Roth hadn't already driven away, she would have turned right around and left the ranch.

Sinclair perceived her annoyance. "Look, you're here now, and I'm glad. Really. So why don't we start fresh? I did read your proposal with great interest, and I have no doubt the research can make a very important contribution. There were some personal reasons I didn't think it was right for me, but suppose we leave all that open to debate. We'll sit down together and talk it out. I'll tell you what my reservations are, and you'll say whatever you want to counter them. I promise to listen with an open mind. Okay?"

"I'm not about to refuse," she said, smiling to take the edge off. He ambled toward the house, and she stayed beside him. "I don't mind telling you that you're the last chance. Unless the money you got for your PMS research is reassigned to us, our project is dead.''

"I doubt that," Sinclair said.

"Why? You must realize how controversial this will be."

"But the Gerron Foundation is one of the biggest—nearly a billion dollars in its endowment. Even if I keep what they've given me, Laura shouldn't have trouble getting them to provide separate funds."

"I don't think so. She told me she's already gone the last mile just to swing this transfer."

Sinclair emitted a thoughtful grunt. "I suppose her brother's the problem. He's a banker, much more conservative than Laura."

"Her brother? I don't understand."

"Andrew is chairman of the family foundation. He's the one who has final authority over how the money is spent."

Kai went on another few steps before the words finally sank in. Brother. Family. Then she halted and spun to look at Sinclair. "Laura is one of the Gerrons?"

"Didn't you know?" Sinclair gazed at her in astonishment.

Kai shook her head mutely.

"Damn. Foot meets mouth again." They had reached a set of open French doors that led into the house from the outside loggia. Sinclair paused at the threshold. "I think she even said something about it on the phone—that she hoped I wouldn't mention it. For godssakes, don't tell her I let it slip."

"I won't," Kai assured him, her mind whirling over this latest and biggest of Laura's deceptions.

Entering the house, Sinclair led Kai through a gigantic beamed living room furnished with mission oak tables and chairs, Indian rugs on dark wide-plank floors, and a concert grand piano on which a score of photographs were displayed in silver frames. Kai could see that a few of the photographs were of horses caught in mid-jump over the barriers, a young woman leaning tautly forward in the saddle. She guessed it was the same slender, very beautiful red-haired woman who, regally posed in a white evening gown, dominated the room from an oil painting above the fireplace.

"I'll show you where you'll be staying," Sinclair said as they passed into the foyer. "After you have a chance to get settled and rest a bit, we can sit down to a serious meeting about the project.''

He took her up the broad staircase to one of several guest rooms, furnished comfortably in a rustic Mexican style.

"Don't go riding off into the sunset again," she said. "I'm eager to get to work."

He smiled. "I'll be waiting for you in my study," he said. His workplace at home, he explained, was in a small separate building next to the stables.

Kai unpacked, showered, and exchanged her traveling clothes for jeans and a denim shirt that would match her host's informal attire. As she moved between her room and the adjoining bath, she pondered Laura's behavior. Perhaps it was not so strange to conceal the family connection. Laura must have wanted to establish her professional standing without giving anyone cause to think she'd only climbed the ladder by buying each rung. Especially since the Gerrons were prime supporters of the same university where she taught, the family's name attached to several major facilities.

Sinclair's accidental revelation explained instantly, of course, Laura's expensive lifestyle—the Fell's Point house, the personal largesse she had extended to Kai so far, and her access to one particular foundation when all else had flatly turned them down.

Yet she wondered why, since Laura had been so careful about keeping the secret from her closest colleagues, Paul Sinclair had been allowed to know.

Kai had no trouble finding the one-room barn wood cabin near the stable building where Sinclair had his study. The cabin had a Dutch door, and the top half had been left open. Kai leaned in. He was seated behind a desk positioned cater-corner to face the door. Bent over a pad, he was writing with intense concentration.

She waited until his pen stopped moving. "Ready for me?"

He looked up. "Sure, c'mon in." Dropping the pen, he came out from behind the desk as she entered. In front of a stone fireplace was a sitting area with a table and a couple of easy chairs. The proposal Kai had written was lying on the table, open to one of the middle pages. Kai saw notations scribbled in the margin. Not a bad sign; he'd evidently given it some thought.

They sat down, and for the next hour he turned the pages of the proposal, passing along his reactions to what he had read. He acknowledged that direct scientific observation was the only way to fill a gap still existing in the complete understanding of human sexual behavior. Yet he had not been able to satisfy himself that if it was all reduced to absolutes of technique, all quantified and measured as in any experiment, there would be more gained than lost. Wasn't there anything in nature that ought to remain partly a mystery?

Beyond philosophical reservations, he also foresaw practical problems to successfully carrying out the research. One involved confidentiality. While those working within the project would see it as scientific inquiry, to anyone outside it was bound to be regarded as purely sensational. As soon as the nature of the project became public knowledge, it would attract so much attention—not to mention so much inevitable criticism—that continuing the work would become impossible. It was essential, therefore, to keep the project secret until it was completed. Within the discussion of methodology included in the proposal, however, no thought had been given to this requirement.

Kai understood his point, but she countered that the project could not be totally closed off and isolated since the only way to gather sufficient data was to be able to bring in a large pool of men and women.

Sinclair accepted her argument. "That's another problem you have to solve—making sure *they* keep the secret. Science or no, if word of this research gets out and it's misunderstood, you'll have a public uproar. However you defend it, I think it would be shut down. The police and the courts could get into it. The university could be damaged for its association with something so controversial. All of that is of principal concern for me, because I wouldn't want to start something I couldn't finish."

Kai agreed that not enough thought had been given to the need for confidentiality. But she was sure that could be fixed. As for his philosophical doubts, she could only say that no matter how much might be learned about sex, the basic mystery would never be spoiled.

"We don't need science," she said, "to tell us that sex

at its best is an expression of love. And love is the core *human* element. Why and how people fall in love is the mystery, and that will always remain. We're not trying to break down that part of the equation. But knowing more about the nature of physical pleasure may even help people stay in love rather than drifting away from each other. If I wasn't absolutely positive that the results would be beneficial,'' Kai concluded, ''I wouldn't be interested in doing this work.''

The fervent conviction in her statement prompted Sinclair to bring up the most serious obstacle to his participation. It was obvious, he said, that one needed an inner motivation to pursue certain research, a drive formed out of one's own experiences and priorities. No one could commit himself fully to a study that could last for years without that kind of emotional fuel. His own personal drive was directed toward the PMS research he was about to begin.

''Do you mind telling me why you picked the subject?'' Kai asked.

''Not at all,'' Sinclair replied.

The reason for his interest in pre-menstrual syndrome, he said, was that he believed it had affected his late wife, Elizabeth. In general, she had always been gregarious, fun-loving, easygoing and emotionally well balanced. But he had noticed that during the time just preceding her monthly cycle, she would become agitated and often aggressive. To some degree, a higher level of irritability wasn't uncommon in women during hormonal peaks—just as men, too, had cycles when their behavior was affected by chemical changes. But the changes that occurred in his wife could be extreme.

''With the horses,'' he said, ''Beth was always exquisitely gentle. It was an absolute talent of hers, an ability to communicate silently but firmly. As her cycle approached, though, it would leave her. She'd get short-tempered, more demanding and less tolerant.'' Sinclair fell silent for a second and looked down pensively as he added, ''I think it's what ended her life.''

Stunned by the words, Kai couldn't bring herself to ask what he meant. He went on staring at the floor for a minute, then looked up and continued. It was on one of her bad days that his wife had ridden in the exhibition and suffered the paralyzing fall. Her horse had balked twice at jumping over a barrier that had been adjusted to a high setting, but Elizabeth had berated the horse and raced toward the barrier again, using her crop to force the animal into the jump. That was when she had been thrown.

"Her life—our life—really ended that day," he said very quietly, his eyes moist.

It appeared he wasn't over it yet, Kai observed.

But in the next second he determinedly shook off the melancholy. "That's what got me interested in studying PMS," he said. "I suppose it sounds foolishly sentimental, but I like to think if we can find out more about the chemical mechanism and develop ways of correcting it, quite a few other people can be saved some heartache. My last project, the in vitro stuff, was also a kind of memorial to Beth. I always wished we'd had children, but it wasn't possible. I could identify with the pain of couples who were looking for help to conceive."

There was a knock on the door, and Kai looked around to see Rosa balancing a tray with a pitcher, a couple of glasses, and a plate of crackers. She set it down on the table, exchanged a few phrases in rapid Spanish with Sinclair, and left.

"Lemonade," he said, "from our own lemons. Like some?"

Kai nodded.

"I should have thought of offering you a drink," he said as he poured her a glass. "But Rosa knows I'm not much of a host, and she takes up the slack." He gave a self-conscious smile. "She's especially glad to see me entertaining a pretty woman."

Kai felt herself flush at the flattery. He seemed to notice as he handed her the glass. Abruptly he returned to business. "Your turn now," he said. "Where does your need come from? Why this research instead of something else?"

Kai had always believed she knew and understood that her interest originated with the destructive confusion about sexuality she had observed in Lokei, intensifying with the need to come to terms with her own powerful natural appeal and the situations it had led her into. But it wasn't until she answered Sinclair that she found herself coherently linking together all the separate strands. To have been the daughter of a woman whose life was defined and dictated by sex, to have been denied a father because of a scandal centered on sex, to have found her choices being affected constantly by the sexual urges of men—until she became herself a symbol of the new sexual standards that were sweeping through society—all of it fueled her motive. Perhaps by bringing sex into the laboratory, she told Sinclair, she hoped finally to bring under control a force that had been so dominant in her life.

As she finished, she was amazed to notice that the last golden rays of sun were slanting low through the open Dutch door. She and Sinclair had been talking for the whole afternoon.

"Well," she sighed at last, "has anything I've said changed your mind?"

He gazed at her, as though truly weighing his reply. "Tell you this much," he said, "I'm not quite so damn sure as I was that it would be the wrong thing for me to do."

And there they left it. Sinclair said he had to finish the letters he'd been writing when she came in—a Senate committee was waiting anxiously to receive his opinion on whether any legislation ought to be enacted specifically to cover in vitro fertilizations. In the meantime Kai was welcome to enjoy the ranch any way she wanted, saddle up a horse and take a ride, or have a swim in the pond.

They agreed to meet for dinner at seven, and she left him in his study. As she walked back to the house, Kai was struck by the sense of anticipation she felt already about seeing him again in just an hour or two. She hadn't been so attracted to a man since Jim Bolton. But the realization came mingled with guilt. She had come to win over Paul Sinclair, and there were signs she was succeeding. She couldn't tell, though, if he was being tempted by her, or if he was becoming interested in the work. It wasn't hard to see that he had yet to free his heart from the memory of his dead wife. Yet he was all too ripe and ready, Kai thought, for her appeal—vulnerable for a physical adventure, if not for love. Had Laura counted on that, too, when she insisted Kai make the trip alone? With the stirrings of an emotional concern for Paul Sinclair, Kai was even more repelled by the idea of doing anything that could be interpreted as taking advantage of him.

Tired from her journey, she preferred to nap in her room while she waited for the evening. In a restless half sleep, she dreamed of a door opening and a man entering, advancing on the bed, and lowering himself onto her, his hands tearing at her clothes. His weight was smothering and she had to fight for air.

She came awake with a start, gasping as though the apparition had truly stolen her breath. In the purple light of dusk, the room was quiet and empty. Still, it was several minutes before the tide of ancient fears receded.

Prepared for nothing more than a couple of days of serious discussion, she hadn't brought along any special outfits, but she dressed up a white silk blouse and a navy skirt with a multicolored Hermès scarf left over from the days when Jill had taught her how to shop and dress for an attractive, professional image. She also applied a bit more than the perfunctory dabs of Arpege she customarily used, and not only to the pulse points on her neck but to her wrists and between her breasts.

Perhaps it was because of the dream—a need to purge that dark illusion of her father with a kinder reality—but she could feel herself being overtaken by a desire for Paul Sinclair, all her reservations falling away. Whatever reticence had given Jim Bolton the freedom to leave and so quickly forget her, she wouldn't let it happen again.

When she went downstairs, he was reading a newspaper in the living room, sipping golden liquid from a delicate crystal glass, the music of a solo Spanish guitar playing through a stereo. She was almost disappointed when he stood to receive her; the domestic scene was so pleasing, she would have happily sat and watched him.

He gave her a glass of sherry, and they talked for a while—about everything but the work. Then he took her out to dinner. They drove over the hills in an old English two-seater sports car, an MG, which he said had belonged to his wife. The car was kept in mint condition, Kai noticed.

It occurred to her as they drove to ask the question about Laura that had nagged her since he'd mentioned her family connection. "Laura has been so discreet about belonging to the Gerron family, why didn't she mind telling you?"

"She never told me, Kai. I've known Laura a long time—known about her family—because she was a friend of Beth's.

They met at boarding school together, one of those east coast places where the girls wear white gloves to class, and they remained close. Beth was maid of honor at Laura's wedding, and Laura returned the favor at ours. Then they drifted apart. Beth always thought Laura had trouble staying friends with her after she married me because her own marriage had been such a failure, and it made her too jealous to see how happy Beth was. I'm not sure that's fair to say. It wasn't easy for Laura to keep up the contact.''

"Why not?''

He paused imperceptibly, as though editing his answer. "Well, we lived on opposite sides of the country . . . and Laura was busy pursuing her career.''

Kai had the sense he was holding something back. Or perhaps it was only that in defending his wife's old friend, he was being a gentleman, hiding his real anger that Laura had withheld friendship at the time of his wife's greatest need. Paul's comments caused Kai to reflect on that curious reserve she had also experienced in Laura. The close personal relationship they had started to develop had stopped at a certain point. Kai wondered now if it wasn't part of the secrecy Laura had been forced to adopt because of the notorious wealth of the Gerrons. Hearing that she was a long-standing acquaintance of Sinclair's also put a new perspective on Laura's insistence that Kai make the trip alone. Had she stayed away because her jealousy had survived even the death of her friend, or because she was hoping to foster a new romance for the grieving husband?

In a small town called Los Olivos, Paul parked in front of Mattei's, a restaurant that had been built as a stop for the stagecoach that had traveled through the region only ninety years ago.

"Funny how time changes things,'' he remarked as they sat down at their table. "A century goes by—it really isn't that long in the history of the world—but stagecoaches don't even exist anymore. Here you and I are, talking about launching the sort of close study of physical magic between men and women that would've gotten us both hung if we'd done it a couple of hundred years ago.''

You and I, he'd said. Kai savored the words. It seemed he might be moving beyond merely keeping an open mind. What could have altered his position since their discussion this afternoon? She could think of only one reason. He must be in the grip of the same desire that had seized her. Yet they were both holding back, staying within the strict boundaries of a professional association.

The exquisite tension lasted through the whole dinner. Several times when she saw his hand resting beside his plate, she was tempted to reach over and touch it. Several times she wished he would touch her. But the invisible barrier remained in place.

While he answered her questions about his earlier research, she started to fantasize about making love to him. She didn't think she had ever been so aroused simply by being near a man—so aroused that she didn't quite trust the feeling. Was it something other than a pure attraction? Was it so much talk about sex . . . or a reaction to the dream . . . ?

Whatever the reason, Kai thought she'd go crazy if she had to restrain herself. She was on the brink of speaking aloud when, abruptly, Paul stopped eating and put down his fork. "I'm very tempted, Kai," he said. "Right now, looking at you, all I keep thinking is that if I say yes, and agree to join in your project, then I'll be able to stay near you for all that time. Days, months, even years."

"Years," she echoed in a whisper, encouraging his confession. At the same time their hands came together across the table.

"I—I'm suddenly feeling swept away by you, your beauty, your charm, and—forgive me, but you can't be unaware that it's part of you—your incredible sex appeal. Frankly, I'm a little scared by what's happening."

"You think I don't feel the same?" she said softly.

"It doesn't seem . . . sensible," he went on. "And I'm not sure I'm ready for it. I've been mourning Beth for four years. I haven't wanted another woman, not once. I guess I've been dead in a way, too, feeling I wanted to die with her. Even when she was paralyzed, I . . ." Shaking his head, he lowered his eyes. "I loved her so much, I suppose it was my way of sharing what happened to her, giving up those sensations."

Kai squeezed his hand, and he looked up again. "Do you think there's something wrong about feeling them again?"

"There shouldn't be. Maybe it's the circumstances. You

come here to talk about doing research into adult sex, and all at once I'm vibrating like—like a school kid having his first wet dream." He grimaced with embarrassment at his candor. "I ought to tell you that it didn't just start tonight, or even this afternoon. After I'd read your proposal, I gave one of my research assistants a chance to look at it. When he saw your name, he recognized it. The next day he brought in a copy of this magazine he's been collecting since he was a kid."

"Elsie told me," she said quietly, trying to let him know she wasn't ashamed.

Yet Sinclair still wore a pained expression. "Look, I didn't bring this up because I think there's anything wrong with it on your part. The problem's with me. The minute I saw those pictures, it triggered something. I couldn't wait to meet you, Kai. But it wasn't about the work anymore. I can't even say it was about you as much as about what you represented. Sexual freedom. And I wonder now if it didn't happen just because it's been so long. . . ."

"It doesn't matter to me, Paul. I want you, too—and I'm not asking myself why. Want a confession to match yours? Laura asked me to come out here alone because she hoped something like this would happen. She practically told me I ought to seduce you. I almost didn't come because I didn't like being put in that position." She leaned closer across the table. "And now I wouldn't want to be anywhere else."

He lifted her hand to press her fingers to his lips. His eyes closed for a moment, as though he wanted to shut out everything else but the feel and smell of her. Then he said, "If we let this happen, then what's the future? For the work, I mean."

She understood his concern instantly. Involved with each other—not knowing yet whether it was love or merely sexual obsession—how would it affect their scientific objectivity?

"Right now," she said, "I don't give a damn."

He stared at her another moment, his eyes bright. Then he turned and called for the check, his voice ringing out through the restaurant almost as urgently as if he had shouted "Fire!"

Riding back to the ranch, they held hands, the electric tingle of desire traveling through them, the impatience for

release building steadily. They glanced occasionally at each
other, but neither spoke. It was as if they were together in
a hypnotic trance that neither one wanted to risk shattering.

But once across the threshold, all constraint fell away. He
seized her and she fell into his arms, and they kissed hungrily, ferociously, clawing at each other's clothes.

It was impossible to tell whose pent-up longing was
stronger, but it was Kai who stepped back from him suddenly, conscious of the wanton race for release, and needing
tenderness, too. She didn't want to make love here on the
floor in a tangle of half-clinging garments; she wanted all
his skin against all of hers, his heat, his smell, against the
contrast of cool, fragrant sheets. Slowing the tempo, yet
losing none of the pounding urgency, she preceded him up
the stairs, her body half turned so that her eyes never left
his. At the top of the stairs, he urged her toward his room,
but she slowly shook her head and pulled loose to move
toward the room where she was staying, beckoning him to
follow. And he realized then that she was right. They could
not make love where the ghost of his wife still hovered.

In the guest room, with light pouring in on them and the
bed from the hallway, they finished undressing as they
kissed, each unbuttoning the other's clothes. They clung
then in an embrace, as their hands roamed over the ripple
of flesh and muscles, into the warm valleys and across the
rounded terrain of their bodies. And then, slowly, he sank
to his knees in front of her, like a worshiper, his prayer in
the touch of his mouth on her nipples, her stomach, his lips
gently teasing the downy triangle below. She felt him inhaling her, and then his tongue traced slowly along the labia
before he began to dart it into her. Moaning, she tossed her
head back and wound her fingers into his hair, whispering
his name again and again. The thrills rose through the center of her weakened legs and then she too was sinking down.
Her hands resting on his shoulders, she pushed him back
gently until he was lying on the carpeted floor. She turned
herself around so that while he continued to drink from her,
she took him in her mouth, remembering as she did that he
had suffered the same drought of loving she had, wanting
to give everything to him that he gave to her.

The quickening rhythm of their movements, the changing
music of their sighs and moans, the strengthening pressure

of their hands, spoke clearer than words that the time of release was near, and as if a message had passed along the nerves, they slid around so that they could be joined completely. For a moment, as he hovered over her, he stopped to look at her body, stretched out in that shaft of light pouring through the doorway—and she was aware that he was seeing her as though her photograph had come to life.

"You're magnificent," he whispered.

Her reaction came not in words, but the quick reaching of her hand to seize his hard shaft and fit it into her. She didn't want to be idolized, not now. She wanted to be woman with man, nothing more. When he was inside, plunging, her arms went around him, and she pulled him in, harder, harder, urged him deeper with her arching back and reaching hips.

Then he was so deep, touching a core of feeling that Orin never had—indeed, perhaps because her last lover's technique had been so perfect that she'd never been able to go far enough beyond the appreciation of his gift to let her emotions come into play. Here and now, though, she wasn't just receiving, she was giving, and somehow that opened her within, sensitized her as never before.

As he made contact with that untouched depth, a dam holding back a reservoir of sensations seemed to burst, and they rushed through her in a torrent. At the same moment he thrust himself down one more time, harder and deeper still, and then he exploded into her. She cried out and clung to him, gasping, half afraid the flood of ecstasy would overwhelm her, that she would be lost in it forever . . . and then the flood crested, and she floated along at the peak for a few more moments, and at last it receded. She lay in his arms, cooling in their mingled sweat, her heart slowing down again.

"God," she murmured, "how did we do that?"

He smiled at her. "We're going to try to find out," he said, "aren't we?"

It went on all night—a feast of sex to satisfy the famine that had preceded it. Dawn was tinting the sky, the black corners of the dark room shading to gray when they fell asleep at last.

At noon she woke, her head resting against his chest. The touch of his nakedness along the length of her was unfamiliar. By the bright light of day she felt an odd surprise at being in bed with him. She realized then that whatever had brought them together in this tempestuous need for sensation, love was not part of it. Respect, sympathy, appreciation—and of course physical attraction—had provided the trigger for their innermost hungers. If it was love, she doubted that she would feel as she did now. Satisfied, without shame, and yet surprised—thinking back on the incredible night just passed with mere curiosity.

Raising herself up on one elbow to look at him, she found that he was awake, too. As soon as she looked in his eyes, it was absolutely clear that he was having the same thoughts. He needed her, would need her again. But his heart was still inhabited by the ghost of another woman.

And he could see that she knew.

"Do you still think we should work together?" he asked.

"All the more," she said, and he smiled with understanding as he raised himself over her again. They had exactly the chemistry they hoped to explore.

Chapter Twenty-six

Baltimore, 1979

In late autumn the first notices appeared on the bulletin boards of Jefferson University, asking for volunteers of either gender, graduate and undergraduate, to be interviewed for possible participation in a scientific study. Those who qualified and agreed to be involved would be compensated at a rate of twenty dollars per hour.

The more than four hundred young men and women responding to the notice were winnowed down in an initial screening process to a few dozen before the exact nature of the research was revealed. To these select few, the project and its purposes were fully described; they were told that their role in the research would be to engage in sex with an existing mate or partner of their own choice, under conditions that would allow them to be regularly observed in the act. This initial statement was greeted with a variety of reactions—raucous laughter, shock, disbelief, indignation. But no one shrugged.

When the serious intent finally sank in, a core group of twenty heterosexual men and women between the ages of nineteen and twenty-seven remained willing to cooperate. Some were married, some unmarried but involved in stable relationships; in these cases, both partners had to consent to participate in order to join the study. Adding spouses and regular sex partners to the core group made a total of thirty-two. There were, too, a matching number of single men and women who were agreeable to being "assigned" to similar-minded subjects of the opposite sex.

Of the numerous criteria for selection, one of the most important was the degree to which each subject was judged capable of preserving confidentiality. Others included psy-

chological stability, good physical health, basic attractiveness, and good sexual adjustment.

There had been studies in the past concerned principally
with examining the basic physiology of sex, or understanding and treating various dysfunctions; but the purpose of the
Sinclair–Cooke project (as it was officially known) was to
focus primarily on the conditions necessary to achieve maximum sexual satisfaction. The results depended, therefore,
upon having participants who were fully functional, with
healthy sexual appetites, observing which among them had
the most fulfilling sexual interactions, and recording their
techniques. In another departure from past studies, interest
in effective sexual activity was not focused only on so-called
"normal" means of stimulation, but the subjects were encouraged to engage in whatever practices they usually enjoyed and found beneficial in achieving sexual fulfillment.
A few were chosen, in fact, because their orientation was
to more adventurous, even atypical practices.

Following Paul Sinclair's arrival in Baltimore to join the
project, there had been months of discussions devoted to
planning. Having decided how the research could be most
effectively conducted, a good part of the foundation money
Sinclair had brought with him was then applied to the preparation of the necessary facilities.

To create a comfortable and conducive environment—
similar to that in which sexual interaction would usually
occur—a large vacant house on two acres was purchased in
a suburb of Baltimore not far from the university. Five bedrooms were decorated in a variety of styles—the functional
modern of a typical motel, the opulent gaudiness (complete
with mirrored ceiling) reminiscent of a frontier bordello,
and the oriental simplicity of a windowless chamber furnished only with padded mats on the floor and a vase of
fresh flowers. The two other rooms were designed to duplicate the tasteful coziness of a master bedroom in a fine
private home. All had small private baths. There was also
one enormous, separate bathroom with an extra large tub
and shower and large floor areas. A small, well-equipped
gymnasium offered another environment to inspire variations. On each occasion when couples were to be observed,
they were allowed to select their place of performance. The

sybaritic bathroom and gym turned out to be popular favorites.

Along with the bedrooms, the project headquarters was furnished with a conference room where the staff could hold their meetings, a large, comfortable living room and dining room where they could relax or hold informal discussions, a kitchen, and several small projections rooms.

It was agreed early on that the means of observation should be by film. Any method of witnessing directly and immediately the activities between partners, as by one-way glass or television monitors, was deemed too inhibiting and intrusive. The existence of automatic and unmonitored cameras, on the other hand, was a factor that all the participants felt they could comfortably ignore. Accordingly, all bedrooms were equipped with several cameras at different angles of vision, invisibly recessed in ceilings or otherwise disguised. These operated in conjunction with sensitive sound-recording equipment. Special terminals to connect other forms of electronic-monitoring equipment were also installed. This would allow such physiological reactions as heart rate, nerve and muscular activity, and even hormonal levels to be measured by means of electrodes affixed to the bodies of the research subjects. This was planned for a later phase of the study, depending upon which subjects had become acclimated sufficiently to accept it without finding that it prevented performance.

By winter of 1980 the research facilities were completed. But the costs involved in the unusual preparations had absorbed much more of the available money than had been budgeted. The expense of running the operation was also considerable. As one of the nation's leading researchers, Sinclair alone was receiving a salary of a hundred thousand dollars—though this was less than he had been paid in California. Kai was receiving forty thousand, allowing her for the first time to be independent of any other work. The young subjects were also being paid generously for their time, an inducement which served to bind them more tightly to the oath of confidentiality they had taken—since anyone who broke it stood to forfeit substantial earnings. With each subject averaging two hours per session, and two sessions per week—not counting periodic interviews—the total monthly payroll for the group of thirty-two ran to well above thirty thousand dollars.

Finally, there were ten other staff members who had been taken on, including two computer operators. Computers were just beginning to be manufactured in a form that could be easily operated in a small office, and their application to keep records and collate and analyze results was expected to shave years off the time needed to produce a report when all the data was collected.

The crisis created by the shortage of money was solved when more funding came from the Gerron Foundation through Laura's intervention—though she did not depart from the outward fiction that she had to go through regular channels. Kai never mentioned to Laura that she had learned the truth about her family, and if any word of it ever passed between Paul and Laura, it happened only when they were alone. The research staff consisted of six postgraduate students enlisted by Laura and Paul, one of whom was Elsie Roth. Elsie had no sooner heard that Paul was moving his research base from Santa Barbara to the east coast than she had asked for a job. Paul confided to Kai that he was aware of Elsie's crush, but since she had never pressed him to reciprocate in any way, he saw no reason to refuse her request. Elsie might not be a natural scientist, but what she lacked in natural aptitude, she made up in hard work and the desire to please.

Subject couples began arriving at project headquarters at different times throughout the weekdays to spend an hour being filmed making love. Following each session, a male member of the research team would debrief the male subject in the couple, a female researcher would take notes from female subjects. These interviews were transcribed and the information weighed as it corresponded to the filmed record.

For all the sensational aspects of the project when considered in the abstract, to the researchers it became a matter of daily routine. Every morning they gathered to appraise the data that was being collected. Studying people was little different to them after a while than studying any other species. No wonder that Kinsey had begun his career in science as a zoologist.

The data piled up quickly, indicating which practices and

techniques produced the best responses, allowing for physical and psychological variables. Within months the core group was varied to include older subjects and a wider ethnic sampling. As new participants joined the project, others fell away. Some moved from Baltimore, or finished their education at Jefferson; others developed an aversion to being watched, or became involved with non-participating partners.

Still, over the first and second years of the study, the cumulative total of observed sexual activity amounted to more than sixteen thousand hours. With the computers to speed the process of analyzing data, Paul projected that a total of four years—relatively short in terms of comprehensive research—would be sufficient to publish results that would stand up as authoritative.

Since Paul Sinclair had arrived in Baltimore, Kai's affair with him had continued, though they did not live together. Paul leased a sizable house bordering Mount Vernon Place, the city's most aristocratic enclave; he had brought his Mexican housekeeper along to keep order. Kai found a charming apartment in one of the renovated buildings that had turned the Inner Harbor area from a rundown waterfront to a showcase neighborhood.

While maintaining separate homes, they saw each other three or four nights every week. Occasionally they stayed together for a few days. The affair was regarded with a curious objectivity by both. They respected each other, enjoyed each other's company, had some of the same tastes in books, art, and music, yet neither could say that they were drawn together by the bonds of romantic love. On Paul's side, he acknowledged that he was still not liberated from the intense feelings he'd had for his wife.

"There are people who think it's neurotic that I can't get over her," he said to Kai. "But is there really something wrong with loving someone so deeply, so profoundly, that when she's gone your heart goes with her?"

On Kai's side, she was less sure of exactly what kept her from becoming emotionally engaged in the affair. It wasn't just Paul's private mourning. She believed that if her heart had been set on it, she could have made him love her, could have overcome whatever obstacle stood in the way. But she

was content to leave things as they were. What she had with
Paul—what had been and remained the foundation of their
connection—was a uniquely powerful sexual chemistry.
When she was with Paul, she felt an appetite for pure carnal
sensation that seemed almost demonic. She wanted him,
every part of him; wanted him to take her in every way, and
give as freely in return. She had spent years resisting her
sexuality, terrified she might become its captive as her
mother had. But with Paul the terror fell away. The could
spend hours in slow, delicate explorations, or plunge into
frenzied demands for quick release. Whatever their desire,
whatever their need, they always seemed able to express it
without words.

Because of the work they were doing daily, they appreciated the miracle of this special chemistry even more. The
constant, dispassionate examination of the films and transcripts of research subjects could have easily produced an
inability to separate from observation to immerse oneself in
the experience. But as much as Kai was studying the sex
lives of others, as much as she was analyzing the techniques
and practices that produced the best results in research participants, when she was with Paul it was all effortless, instinctive, and completely satisfying. The longer they were
together, the more sensitized she became to him. Usually
she had multiple orgasms, a series of cosmic jolts that would
make her feel as though she was shattering painlessly, ec-
statically, into separate molecules of golden fire. They would
then coalesce again into a single glowing form, cooling to
reappear as her body.

"It's like a drug," she said one night in his bedroom
when they were done. "I'm addicted to you." It was not a
lover's compliment; her voice carried a tone of real concern.

"Better me than something that makes you see double,
or gives you hallucinations."

"This comes close."

"It can't kill you, either."

"There must be some sort of bad effect from an over-
dose."

He pushed back to look at her. "Think you've had one?
Are you trying to tell me you want to stop sleeping together?"

"No. But that doesn't mean I'm not always asking myself if we should."

He shook his head and chuckled. "Doesn't that strike you as funny? We've organized this gigantic effort to provide knowledge about this basic impulse because it gives so much trouble to so many people—but you and I don't have any problems with it. And that's our problem. It's too easy, too good. So you think something must be wrong with it."

"It's not a matter of wrong or right. I just can't help wondering if the reason we haven't fallen in love after all this time is *because* of the work. We don't see sex as an expression of love anymore. We're so involved in studying it, we don't connect it to anything else. It's an isolated phenomenon. We see it that way, and keep it as something isolated in our lives."

"Or is it the other way around?" Sinclair said. "It's something about us—about being people who keep love out of our lives—that makes us able to concentrate on this work."

His suggestion troubled Kai for days afterward. Was she keeping love out of her life? Was she so afraid of being used and hurt as Lokei had been that she would allow no man to possess her completely, body and soul? Looking back, she saw nothing that reassured her. When she had taken Orin as her first lover, she knew he would move on sooner or later—that was his pattern. And Paul? She had been told even before meeting him that his heart was captive to another. Perhaps that was why she felt liberated with him.

On Monday mornings the research team met in the conference room to discuss findings, compare notes on observations of different couples, and schedule the week ahead.

On a Monday in the first week of October, with the project going into its third year, Laura led off the meeting by informing the staff that they were faced with a new financial crisis. Kai had previously been told by Paul that the existing funds were getting short, but he had sounded no alarm. Laura might let things go down to the wire before she arranged a rescue—perhaps she enjoyed this as a way of inflating her own importance—but she would always be able to pry out another million or two from her family's foundation. After all, the Gerrons had billions.

Yet this time the situation seemed more serious.

"If we want more funding," Laura told the assembled staff, "we'll have to do a presentation for some of the officers of the foundation, people who vote on the appropriations." The staff was instructed to spend the next week preparing a concise sampling of the films and other data to present to the foundation board along with a progress report and a précis of the work ahead, with an estimated time for completion and publication. "We've been at this over two years, and five million dollars have already been spent. Now it's time to show our benefactors what they've been buying."

The data would be presented to important members of the Gerron Foundation, Laura said, over the coming weekend in a seminar at her country home in Maryland's Tidewater country, on the shores of Chesapeake Bay. The foundation officers were also expecting to meet the research staff, so they were all invited as guests.

Later, thinking about the morning meeting, Kai was intrigued by Laura's behavior. In making her report, she had said nothing to depart from her guise of being unrelated to the Gerrons. Yet she had also invited the entire staff to her country home. Did she expect to play out a charade in which the truth remained concealed? Or was she ready to expose this truth about herself that she had always worked so hard to keep hidden?

Chapter Twenty-seven

Late Friday afternoon, Elsie and Kai drove out of Baltimore following detailed directions to the southern Maryland peninsula that Laura had provided. Paul had gone to New York for the day to confer with a textbook publisher about updating a book on his in vitro work that he had written several years ago. He would get to Laura's weekend house late that night.

As they drove, they talked about the funding crisis that had spurred the weekend meeting. "It could really be the end this time," Elsie said. "If these money people are tired of paying the tab, I can't imagine their minds are going to be changed by sitting through our little movie show." A two-hour compendium of filmed records had been prepared for Laura to show, with live narration that would clarify how they were used, along with other data to illuminate human sexual activity.

Kai didn't say that Laura had an inside track; it wasn't up to her to break the confidence she had agreed to keep. "It may not be easy," she sighed. "But unless you're looking for the cure for cancer, did any scientist ever have an easy time convincing laymen their research makes sense? Pasteur, the Curies, Sigmund Freud, none of them got much help. We're lucky we've gotten this far."

"You really believe what we're doing can be put on the same level as discovering radium or pasteurizing milk?" asked Elsie.

"What was it worth," Kai said, "when Freud began examining people's dreams as a clue to treating their phobias and anxieties? Remember, he believed the mental problems he was trying to cure were caused by problems with sex. Those ideas were resisted because nobody wanted to confront the things we'd rather dream about than talk about.

Maybe that hasn't changed enough where sex is concerned.
But if we can bring the things that still aren't completely
understood out of the darkness, I think we'll be doing something just as important.''

They had reached the rolling tidewater country of St.
Mary's County, not far from the end of their journey. It was
a perfect Indian summer day, with just a hint of a snap in
the crisp autumn air. Vistas of low green hills stretched
away to the Patuxent River, where vast plantations had stood
in the days when this was an English colony. Indeed, the
nation's oldest plantation still in continuous operation was
situated along the banks of the Patuxent. In the fields around
farms and scattered residences visible from the road, black-
eyed susans decorated the autumn in mile-long blankets.
V-shaped flights of Canadian geese passed high overhead as
they arrived for their stay on the Chesapeake during the cold
months. Kai was lost in appreciation of the setting when
Elsie spoke again.

"I wish I was as sure as you."

"About what?"

"What we're doing. There are times I can't tell if it makes
sense or not. Or maybe I'm just not sure it makes sense for
me." Kai heard a catch in Elsie's voice and turned to look
at her. "It's too painful sometimes," Elsie went on. "I
know it's my own fault—I'm too goddamn choosy about the
men I'm willing to spend my time with. But I'm still alone,
and while I am, it gets tougher to sit day after day and take
notes on all these people making love . . . then go home
night after night to sleep alone."

In Elsie's two years in Baltimore, Kai knew, she had not
gone completely without involvement with men. If she still
harbored an infatuation for Paul, there was little sign of it.
It certainly hadn't interfered in forming a friendship with
Kai—or with trying to develop relations with other men. She
could make herself attractive when she wanted. With one
man—a real estate agent she had met through finding her
apartment—the involvement had lasted five months; others
had survived only a few weeks.

But each one had ended after a confrontation over some
issue of feminist rights raised by Elsie. The real problem
was not Elsie's point of view, Kai thought, but that she
stated it in a way that frightened men off. Afraid she might

end up completely subordinated like her mother, Elsie loudly stated early in any relationship that she had no intention of letting that happen. Even men who might be sympathetic to the issue were likely to be alienated by being treated as if they had been put "on notice."

Kai decided against suggesting that Elsie tone down her militancy. They had argued before over feminist issues, not because Kai disagreed with any of the basic positions, but because she felt results in attaining equality would not come through a pitched battle with men, but by an ongoing peaceful negotiation.

"You haven't always been alone," Kai said at last. "There's no reason to think you always will be."

"Except that maybe I want to be," Elsie declared. "That's the problem I can't solve. Damn it, I need a man, but I don't like the idea of having to surrender myself to get one."

"Why do you have to think in terms of surrender?"

"Kai, you've been watching the same pictures I have. The way I see it, when the male and female of the species get together on the most instinctive level, the man is the agressor, and the woman has to submit. She has to play by his rules."

Kai didn't agree but didn't argue, since this very point had already been discussed in numerous project staff meetings. True, the pattern in the majority of cases was for men to appear to be the initiators and dominators in the early phase of a sexual act. But this had been determined to depend on the physiological fact that male arousal was quicker, the need more immediate. Women almost invariably had a slower crescendo to the point of ultimate satisfaction. Consequently, for both partners to be satisfied, it was often necessary for a woman to yield to the man's pace in the early stage—though equally necessary that the man yield willingly to the woman's demands thereafter.

When Kai remained silent, Elsie went on. "There's another reason the work has been getting harder for me," she admitted. "I haven't really been able to focus on studying the problem of getting pleasure out of sex, because frankly that isn't what I'd want out of it myself right now." She threw a self-conscious grin at Kai. "The only thing I think about when I watch all these people fucking is getting pregnant, having a baby. Don't ask me why it's on my mind so much. I'm only thirty-one, but I feel as if the biological clock is striking midnight. Whatever brought it on, suddenly it's all I think about. Isn't that nuts? I can say I wouldn't mind living without a man, but the idea of living without a child is really starting to bother the shit out of me.'' The Volkswagen lurched forward as her foot went down harder on the accelerator in an expression of impatience.

''Don't take this the wrong way, Elsie, but it sounds to me like you might be a lot happier if you left the project.''

''I might,'' Elsie said ruefully, ''if I had something to do besides go into the dry-cleaning business.''

''Just don't let the pressure of staying with it become too much for you. There's usually some strain attached to doing research—whether it's taking the knocks from all the people who think you ought to leave well enough alone, or the difficulty of the work itself. We couldn't have gotten to the moon if there weren't people ready to go through the g-force—the strain of resisting gravity. Not everyone's built to take it, though.''

The sheet of driving directions said to turn off the public road at a gate marked Bluefields. They were still in the Patuxent region when the gate appeared, a tall wrought iron portal in a high brick wall that had been running beside the road for almost a mile.

Elsie took the turn, and immediately they were forced to stop at a barrier by a small stone gatehouse. A uniformed guard stepped out of the house and checked their names off a list before he raised the barrier so that Elsie could drive through.

''What is this place?'' she said. ''I thought we were going to Laura's country home.''

Kai said nothing as she gazed out the car window. The road emerged from a screen of trees and began winding gently through a series of sights that produced growing incredulity. Could all this actually belong to Laura? On a cleared flat area was a small private landing strip where two corporate jets were parked. Farther on, a golf course extended across acres of rolling hills, landscaped perfectly with stands of specimen trees and ponds. The road crested a ridge, and far ahead an enormous white mansion fronted by a long portico with a dozen soaring pillars was seen atop the next ridge, half a mile away. In between were gardens, stables, bridle paths, a lake with a glass pavilion beside it, and an Olympic-sized pool surrounded by statuary.

"What the hell is this place?" Elsie repeated. "Some kind of resort?"

"Looks like it, doesn't it?" Kai said, no longer even sure she had the right answer.

They were met at the front entrance by a uniformed butler who welcomed them, took the valises they had packed for the weekend, and conducted them through the huge, elegant rooms of the mansion.

Elsie kept whispering to Kai: "You don't think she could really live here. This couldn't be hers. . . ."

The butler guided them out to a large rear terrace looking out over sloping lawns that ran down to the banks of the Patuxent. Members of the project were already milling around a buffet table, being served tea, pastries, and sandwiches by uniformed servants. From the looks their coworkers flashed at Kai and Elsie, it was obvious that finding themselves in these breathtaking surroundings was a shock they couldn't quite absorb.

Laura, chic and comfortable in tailored white slacks and a red silk blouse set off by a gold chain necklace, broke away from the group and headed over to Kai and Elsie to welcome them. Tagging along with her was a man in his mid-thirties dressed rather formally for the casual at-home gathering in a black cashmere blazer, pearl gray slacks, white shirt, and rep tie. His narrow face, under a sleek, expertly barbered cap of light brown hair, was so handsome as to be almost pretty. The expression he wore as he moved across the terrace conveyed his certainty that he could command the attention of most women, if not all. Kai heard Elsie sigh as he neared them, though his eyes were already targeted strictly on Kai.

Laura welcomed them and made introductions. "This is my brother, Andrew Gerron," she said.

"Andy," he corrected as he performed a polite little bow to Kai, then Elsie.

Elsie sucked in her breath. "Gerron," she echoed, and

turned wide-eyed to Laura. "Your brother. So you're . . . ?"
Her voice failed.

Laura shrugged and smiled. Clearly she had no intention
of getting into a discussion of why she had not revealed it
until now. Part of the entitlement of being so vastly wealthy
was never having to explain herself or her whims.

Elsie gulped. "So this, all this is really your . . . house?"

"Elsie, dear," Laura said, "come and have something to
eat." She hooked a hand around Elsie's arm and steered her
away to the buffet table. The maneuver was plainly meant
to leave Andy alone with Kai.

The two appraised each other a moment. He spoke first.
"Laura's been telling me about you for quite a while."

"Odd that she never mentioned you to me," Kai answered.

He realized it was said tongue-in-cheek; Andy knew that
his older sister disliked advertising her stupendous wealth,
and had never previously invited professional associates to
the family estate. "You shouldn't hold it against Laura if
she isn't always completely open about some things. Being
wealthy often makes it necessary to put some walls up.
Laura's always been afraid that being famous just for being
rich would get in the way of . . . just being. She found a
way to deal with it that lets her lead a fairly normal life,
and not get completely trapped in all this." He made a
gesture that took in all the beauty and luxury around them.

"Quite a trap," Kai said. "And you? What's your way
of escaping from your golden prison?"

They were ambling across the terrace toward the buffet.
"Me? Promise not to tell. . . ." He lowered his voice. "I
get dressed up in a cape and a mask after the sun goes down
and go forth to fight the forces of evil." He swept an imag-
inary cape across his face and glowered at her theatrically
from beneath lowered eyelids.

Kai laughed. "Is that all?"

He stopped clowning. "Wealth affects us all in different
ways," he said blithely, as though it was a condition everyone was forced to cope with. Then he fixed her with a direct
look, his eyes the same cool China blue as the October sky.
"With me, it makes me hungry."

She cocked her head inquisitively.

"For anything," he went on, "that I think will be a challenge to own. There's so little I can't have."

He kept staring at her, and Kai wondered if there was anything she could say that wouldn't just make him more determined to own her.

Before any words came to mind, Laura was at their side again, having fobbed Elsie off on another group. "I'm glad you two had a chance to get aquainted. You know, Kai, Andy's very involved with the foundation. He's the one who insisted that it was time we had a get-together to show him and the foundation board what we've been doing behind our closed doors." She gave him an acid smile. "He needs to be sure his money is being well spent."

"It's not my money the foundation spends, Laura," Andy told his sister coldly. "It's just my responsibility to see that not too much of it gets thrown away on crackbrained ideas."

The climate in this little corner of the world has turned decidedly chilly, Kai thought. She would have excused herself to let the siblings argue their differences in private, but Andy moved first.

"I look forward to seeing you later, Kai. Right now I ought to do some homework. Laura's brought me a lot of material about the new data, and I want to be sure I get through it all."

"He wants to close us down," Laura said sharply as soon as he was out of earshot. "That's what this is really all about."

"But surely he doesn't have the power to do that by himself." Kai knew that charitable trusts with assets in the billions like the Gerron Foundation were overseen by boards of directors and run by professional administrators.

Laura confirmed that, in theory, her brother didn't have total authority. But he was the chairman of the board, and the other directors were all conservatives like Andy. In practice, he could control the flow of funds whenever he wanted. Laura's other brother, Charles, who spent half his time abroad where he had business interests, had given his proxy to Andy.

"So if he decides not to give us another transfusion, that will be the end. The project will die here and now," Laura said gloomily.

Kai dared to suggest the obvious. "It doesn't have to. You have plenty of money of your own—"

"You don't understand, Kai. My argument with Andy isn't simply about where the money comes from. The issue is power in the family. The men have always thought they have the right to make the important decisions. They don't think I should have the same right to do exactly as I please."

"But how could Andy stop you?"

Laura didn't answer. She was looking off toward a patio door at a group of men who had just arrived, and Kai wasn't sure whether she was distracted from the question or deliberately ignoring it. "Those people are from the foundation board," she said after a moment. "I'd better go and make nice."

Watching Laura walk toward the new arrivals with a welcoming smile pasted on her face, Kai was amazed that this intelligent, independent woman who had such vast resources of her own should actually feel so insecure and threatened. It seemed that the damage done by the subjugation and abuse she had suffered in her early marriage had never been completely erased.

Tomorrow was planned by Laura as a work day, when the researchers would make their presentation of the results so far achieved and the work still ahead. Tonight was a chance to build some bridges through friendly contact. Dinner was served in the grand mirrored dining room of Bluefields. Having been advised that evening wear would be formal, Kai had brought a black shoulderless dress with spaghetti straps, which she wore with a single strand of pearls. On impluse she plucked a white peony from the flower arrangement in her bedroom and pinned it to her upswept coppery-gold hair. The entire staff—minus Paul, who hadn't yet arrived from New York—was joined by all the board members from the foundation and eight of the executives paid to administer the funds and grants. The total of thirty-eight people sat down at a single long table set with the same china and crystal and silver that Nathaniel Gerron had set out for dinners with Morgan and Vanderbilt and Astor. A pair of enormous crystal chandeliers hovered high over the table, their multiple tiers of flickering candles providing a romantic glow. The atmosphere of kingly extravagance was carried through in the four liveried footmen who stood still as statues in the corners of the room when they were not serving food or carrying away empty dishes.

Having always seen Laura as a modern, practical woman with sophisticated but not overly lavish taste, Kai could have been confused by this display of old-fashioned opulence. But in the guest room where she was staying—her clothes all unpacked and neatly put away by a maid—she had found on a shelf a small, privately printed book about the history of Bluefields. Among many other details about the construction of the house, the materials, and artisans who had been brought from around the world, the book also recorded the fact that when Nathaniel Gerron died he had left an enormous endowment with orders that it be used to maintain the house on exactly the same scale as in his lifetime. For the past hundred years no compromises had been made to changing times. After reading the book, Kai suspected that the reason Laura disliked inviting strangers to Bluefields was that she was embarrassed by the level of conspicuous luxury. She must be holding the weekend conference here—unveiling her family connection—only to appease Andy, who clearly seemed to the manor born.

At dinner, where seats were assigned by pre-arranged place cards, Kai found herself sitting next to him. He was excellent company, well informed politically, with a ready stock of amusing anecdotes gathered in world travels and from meeting celebrities and international leaders to whom he had easy access through his bank, the foundation, or merely the name Gerron. His conversation also left no doubt that he intended to extend his acquaintance with Kai beyond the weekend. Every time she responded with interest to any story from his travels—the beauty of wildflowers and birdlife he'd seen on a river trip down the Amazon, the fascination of a photo safari on the plains of Kenya—Andy would suggest flying her on his private jet to see these sights herself whenever she wished. Two or three times he pointedly tossed in references to a wife he had divorced four years ago, making it perfectly clear that he was currently unattached.

Kai had to wonder if Laura hoped that her brother would be enticed to cooperate with the project in the same way that Paul had. Nor could she help speculating about what it would be like to accept one of Andy's invitations. After all, she was not really attached, either. For two years Paul had been her lover, but he had never made any demands on her, had never declared his heart to her. It had always been understood between them that if romance ever beckoned either of them in another direction, they would be free to go.

She circulated after dinner, shaking hands and chatting with other foundation officials. But when the older, stuffier guests started drifting off to bed, Laura brought the rest of the party to a large solarium filled with a jungle of tropical plants that had also been equipped to function as a disco, with a magnificent hidden sound system, a smooth stone floor, and flashing lights hidden among the foliage. Kai let Andy monopolize her on the dance floor, where he proved to be as good a partner as she'd ever had. As they moved to the pounding music that played through the botanical jungle, she felt a quickening excitement, a growing desire for closer physical contact with Andrew Gerron. She danced with more abandon, pulling the pins that had held back her long copper tresses so that when she spun to the music it flared out and lashed across his shoulders and face like a skein of silken whips. In the pulsing light their locked eyes sent the message back and forth. Other staff members who had been dancing stopped to look at Kai, and the floor cleared. The gap between her and Andy shrank so that their bodies touched teasingly as they undulated to the driving beat. When a song ended and they were left standing on the floor alone, his hands moved to her bare shoulders and stroked down, warm and strong, along her arms. He was ready to take ownership, she thought—and abruptly she stepped back, knowing that for Andy Gerron, who could own almost anything, there would be no value in possessing her without a challenge.

The moment she moved away, she noticed that Paul was standing at the entrance to the solarium. Had he just arrived, or had he been watching her dance with Andy?

Excusing herself, she went over to Paul. Though their relationship was not unknown to the rest of the staff, it had always been a rule for them never to show any sign of intimacy in view of the others.

"Have a good trip?" she asked.

"Fine. I'm tired, though. I'm going to bed. See you in the morning."

She heard tension in his voice, not fatigue.

After a second she said, "No, I'll go up with you."

His eyes flicked to where Andy stood, still alone, as if waiting for Kai to return to him. "You don't have to," Paul said.

"I know I don't." She put her arm through his, and they exited the room.

Behind her, she heard the music start again. Glancing over her shoulder, she saw Andy still in the middle of the floor. Then a woman moved out from the shadowy fringes to join him, and he let himself be invited to dance. In the flashing colored lights, Kai could see that Andy was still gazing after her, even while he pulled Elsie into his arms.

Paul said nothing as they entered her room, but he seized her immediately and pulled her into a deep, demanding kiss. There was a rough urgency in his passion that he had never shown before, but she didn't object. She was still aroused from the dance—and in Paul's craving to possess her instantly, to erase her interest in Andrew Gerron, she recognized his first declaration of an emotional claim. After being with him all this time and thinking that it didn't matter if he ever loved her, she found herself responding with even more ardor at this sudden omen of love.

Wordlessly they clawed at each other's clothes, leaving them in a trail as they hurried to tangle their limbs around each other on the bed. As often as she had been with him, there seemed to be a greater energy behind every touch, every caress. She felt it in herself, too, a deeper longing to take him in, devour him, become one with him, than at any time in the past. Her arms commanded him, pummeled his back as he thrust down again and again. And when he exploded into her, she felt herself catapulted over the crest of a wave of pleasure and then glided away on a long, long rippling flow of incomparable sensations.

In the morning, as they lay together before rising, he said, "Until I saw you with him—ready to give yourself to him— I didn't know how important you are to me. I've had one loss, and I almost didn't get over it. If I lost you, Kai, I'd never recover.''

She had been too long without love, and wanted desperately to believe that they had found it at last. ''Even if I'd spent a night with him, that doesn't mean you'd have lost me.''

''So, you *were* ready to sleep with him.''

She was honest. ''For a night—if you hadn't come then? I think so. And I think I know why.''

''His money.''

''No.'' It was only now, as she explained it to Paul, that Kai understood what might have been propelling her into the flirtation with Andrew. Dancing in the darkness, surrounded by tropical foliage—the scene had brought back buried memories of the night her mother had been humiliated by Trane, forced to do his bidding. Kai suspected that the unfulfilled desire for revenge against the rich man who had enslaved her mother had been transmuted into a wish to capture and control Andy Gerron.

''Or maybe,'' she added at the end of her story, ''I thought I should sleep with him in the name of science. Laura's terribly afraid Andy's going to kill the project. She seemed to be hoping I might charm him into writing a blank check.''

''The way you charmed me,'' Paul said lightly.

Kai passed over it. ''What I can't figure out is why Laura should feel on such shaky ground. She's got so much money of her own.''

''But she doesn't have full control. Everything has to be approved by her brothers. It's all in trusts that are controlled by the male heirs. It's been that way since the first Gerron wrote his will.''

''Can't she fight it? That doesn't even sound legal.''

''She's tried. Unfortunately, wills are fairly inviolate. Laura has to toe the line.''

Kai felt a rush of sympathy for Laura that reminded her of how close they had been in the early days of their friendship. For all her material security, Laura had one thing in common with Kai's mother: only by yielding to the control of men could she live securely.

* * *

The presentation was made over the course of the next day and a half. Hours of flatly lit black-and-white films were interspersed with short lectures by Paul and Laura about the goals of the work, and the progress made to date in charting human sexual interaction. From some of the stodgier members of the foundation there were audible murmurs of shock and distaste as the first images of naked young couples engaged in foreplay and intercourse appeared on the large projection screen set up in the ballroom of Bluefields. But as the films were interrupted repeatedly for descriptions of common physiological reactions associated with sex, and displays of charts related to body temperature, heart rate, hormonal balances, or measurements of encephalographic activity, the prurient effect of the films faded away. What had seemed pornographic at first became only images of light and shadow coordinated with bar charts in black and white.

During the informal meals between lectures, Kai saw Andy Gerron, but he made no effort to speak to her. Instead he spent time with Elsie. Kai was pleased to see that her friend was receiving some attention, though she couldn't imagine that there was any chance of the weekend acquaintance developing into anything long-term.

On Sunday, after all the material had been presented, Laura made a closing statement, pleading once more that research into sex not be shut away again in a closet, but allowed to take its place with research into all other aspects of human biology and behavior.

The conference ended without any formal decision being taken on the funding. The researchers were told that the foundation board would meet during the following week to consider whether or not to make more money available.

Kai felt that the conference had gone well. Remarks made by most of the board memebers seemed to indicate that they had put aside any puritanical prejudices to recognize the legitimate scientific intent of the work. That mattered less, however, than if Andy Gerron was willing to continue supporting his sister's work. In his closing statement to the group, he hadn't shown any encouraging signs. He had merely thanked everyone for coming, and told the researchers their efforts were appreciated.

But as Kai was going up to her room to pack, Andy caught her alone. "It's really a shame you and I didn't have time to get better acquainted. We made such a good beginning."

"There should be plenty of other times," she said, "if you don't cancel the project."

He gave her a slow smile. "That just might affect my vote. Though I'd be even more favorably disposed if I was sure that after you've found all the answers about sex, you'd do one more of these demonstrations"—he leaned closer—"a private one, though, just for me. I find it difficult to concentrate on the information with all those other people around."

"Andy," she said sincerely, "I don't think I'm available."

"Didn't seem that way the other night when we were dancing."

"I'm sorry if I . . . led you on. I think I belong with Paul."

He nodded thoughtfully. "As long as it's something you have to think about, maybe I still have a chance."

"First you've got to give Laura her chance. Then we can think about yours."

Ten days later, Laura jubilantly delivered the news at a staff meeting that the foundation had approved an additional four million dollars to cover costs for an additional two years.

Later, Laura summoned Kai to her office and told her there was no doubt the decision had been influenced by Andy's attraction to her. "He told me he didn't want to put you out of work. He's also putting this money down as a bet that you and Paul won't last through another two years of working together—and then the door would be open for him."

"He may lose that bet," Kai said, not liking her relationships turned into a game.

"But I won't tell him that," Laura said. "At least not until after we've cashed the check."

Chapter Twenty-eight

In the weeks leading up to Thanksgiving, it seemed to Kai that her life had finally fallen into place. For a long time Paul had been her lover, but now he was something more—the man who loved her. He had finally said he couldn't bear to lose her. Feeling his need bound her to him made her feel wanted in a way she never had before.

She had renewed the lease on her apartment only a few months ago, but now she gave up spending nights there and moved in with Paul. They made no effort to hide their affair, though their behavior was strictly professional when they were together at project headquarters.

On weekends Paul planned long trips into the Maryland countryside. They drove to Annapolis and spent two mild days in early November cruising the Severn River on a sailboat Paul had rented. Another time they took a ferry over to Smith Island, the largest island in the Chesapeake, a place that seemed almost untouched by time since Captain John Smith had given it his name before going off to marry Pocahontas. On the island they stayed in one of the local homes—there were no hotels—and walked the beaches, and Paul introduced her to the pleasures of bird-watching at the vast island sanctuary. Sitting quietly together, they watched through binoculars as blue herons, snowy egrets, cormorants, black-bellied plover, glossy ibis, and dozens of other species flapped over the marshes set aside as rookeries. Sharing such quiet moments, Kai realized that until recently there had been nothing to unite them beyond their work, and the tireless and uninhibited sex they enjoyed together. At last they had moved beyond that to sharing a fuller life; Paul was beginning to reveal facets of himself that he had kept hidden, as though they belonged to his dead wife and could not be shared with anyone else.

For the Thanksgiving holiday, he arranged for them to spend a few days at a lovely colonial inn in Virginia. The inn, near Middleburg in the so-called "horse country," included a stable on its grounds and featured horseback riding for its guests. Those who were qualified could even ride in the local fox hunt.

On the first morning after they checked in, Paul signed Kai up for riding lessons. At first she felt uncomfortable on the horse, and she might not have mastered the activity, but she recalled that the first time she had seen Paul, he had been galloping toward her on horseback. If they were going to stay together, it might be wise if she shared this, too. So she persisted, and later took a trail ride with him out into the forest and across the hills. Soon she was enjoying it, feeling less afraid when the horse broke into a canter or a gallop. She gained confidence from Paul's steady encouragement.

But on their fourth morning at the inn, when they went to the stables and mounted their horses, he led her out into a field where a barrier had been set up, and told her he was going to teach her to jump. She protested: it was too soon, she didn't feel confident enough yet. Anyway, jumping wasn't a skill she was impatient to learn. She could wait—indeed, she might remain content with relaxed trail riding.

But he became more insistent. The time to learn, to be more daring, was while the sport was fresh for her, before she had settled for a boring routine of the ordinary skills. The more she resisted, the more he cajoled, until it threatened to become an argument. At last, with the barrier set at a height of only a few feet, she tried a jump. She felt unready and terrified, but she sat tight and landed without mishap, feeling rather proud of herself. But when he told her he was going to move the barrier up a notch for her next jump, she finally lost her temper.

"I don't know why you have to make an argument out of this!" she shouted. "I tried it, maybe I'll try again sometime. But it scares me, Paul. The jumping scares me . . . and *you* scare me when I see it's more important for you to prove something, to get me to do what you want no matter how I feel." She wheeled her horse around and galloped full speed back to the stable—amazed at how well she managed to stay in the saddle.

She returned the horse to a groom, and was stalking furiously back to the main building of the inn when the realization struck, the reason it had been so important to him. He was trying to remake her into the woman he had lost.

As she entered the inn and climbed the stairs to their room on the second floor, she searched her memory. Had he ever really spoken of loving her, or had he only confessed to the fear of suffering another loss? Suddenly her feelings for him were in turmoil. Perhaps it was no more than the longing to be loved by *someone* that had made her believe her future was with Paul. In a sense, he was still a married man, cheating on his wife.

In the room, she began to pack, purposefully, without anger. The misunderstanding was no more his fault than hers. She had fooled herself into thinking he was free. And of course there was their compatibility in bed. She had permitted that to be a substitute for a full emotional commitment.

He came in as she was emptying drawers, moving her clothes to the suitcase on the bed. He didn't ask why she was packing. He had evidently come to his own realization. "I'm sorry," he said quietly.

"I know. It's nothing you could have prevented, Paul."

He moved up behind her, and his hands gripped her shoulders gently. "I care so much about you, Kai. I wish . . ." His voice failed.

She didn't need to hear it said to know the wish was hers, too. Tears filled her eyes. It was such a terrible, senseless thing that they should have so much together, and yet love had never become part of it.

He let go of her and moved away to a window. "It's being too kind to me," he said, "to say it's not my fault." His anguished tone of confession made her move to console him.

"How could it be?" she said, turning from the bed. "You can't force yourself to forget. We don't let people into our hearts on a passport that expires on any set time and date."

He went on staring out the window at the Virginia hills. "I should have told you, though. A long time ago I should have told you why I haven't been able to—to let go."

Through a long silence she said nothing. He meant to tell her now, she realized, and he was only gathering strength.

"It was so hard for her," he began at last. "It's not that

she didn't have the courage or spirit to survive anything, but she was an athlete, that was how she defined herself. The accident made her a prisoner, not just in a piece of machinery—inside her own body. Aside from her head, all she could move was a couple of fingers on her left hand.'' His voice had taken on a choked quality, as though his grieving was still fresh. ''Beth fought despair, fought it every day—god, how she fought it. But it was a losing battle, a little bit of ground lost every day as even the inner parts of her that survived the accident started to deteriorate. Lungs, kidneys. Finally`. . .''

He paused and Kai noticed his hands gripping the windowsill in front of him, the knuckles dead white. She thought of saying that he didn't have to go on if it was too hard for him, but then she realized he shouldn't be stopped. Whatever he had to say had been bottled up too long, had dammed up a river of feelings that needed to flow before he could let himself love again.

''She asked me—she asked me—she asked—''

As he stumbled over the words once more, Kai thought she knew what was going to come. She moved closer and reached out to him, and her touch seemed to jog him on, as if a needle stuck in a groove had been set back in its track.

''—asked me to help her . . . end it,'' he said at last. ''I told her no, of course. Help her? Could it be called helping? She couldn't move. She wasn't going to die unless I did it. You couldn't call that anything but murder, could you?''

Yes, yes, you could, she thought. Or had she whispered it? If so, he hadn't heard.

''But once she started asking,'' he continued, ''she never changed her mind. If I loved her, she kept saying, then I'd help her to die.'' He thrust his hands into his pockets and gave a tight shrug. ''How do you know which is really the truest expression of love? Would it be to refuse, to try making her believe in the value of her life? Or was it doing what she asked of me?''

The sun through the window caught the sparkle of tears as they spilled from his eyes, and Kai cried silently with him.

''I did what she asked.'' He looked inward, away from the prettiness of the view to the grim picture of the memory. ''I held the water glass and gave her one pill after another, then the glass to drink from. She could swallow . . . that was all she could do to help herself, so we did it that way. Anything else would have been murder.''

He wiped a hand over his eyes, took a deep breath, and at last he turned to Kai. ''Of course, in the eyes of the law it *was* murder. In mine, too, sometimes.'' He forced a thin smile. ''So there it is—that's why I can't . . . bury her, why I keep her alive in here.'' He pounded his clenched fist over his heart. ''Because half the time, half of me thinks I made the wrong choice, and I can't bear to remember that. . . .'' Once more his voice failed, and this time she knew he wouldn't find it again, not for this story.

She stood holding him for a few minutes, but they both knew that even with his confession made, he was not magically freed from the life sentence he had passed on himself. His heart would always be the prisoner of a memory.

She went back to live in her apartment. No longer did she spend any nights with Paul. She could not reconcile herself to extending their relationship purely as a sexual convenience. It had worked on those terms in the past, but perhaps only because she imagined that eventually love must flower from all the heat they generated. She knew now, though, that it was a vain hope.

There was no bitterness between them. To the contrary, she remained close to Paul. They worked well together on the project, and they often had dinners out where they confided in each other and spoke freely of their worries and confusions as they never had when they were lovers.

On a snowy December evening a week before Christmas, Kai arrived at her apartment building after an early evening with Paul to see Elsie's Volkswagen parked near the entrance. Elsie was sitting inside, the soft-top car barely warmed by its small heater. Hunched down in her collar, she didn't see Kai coming along the street.

Kai knocked on the car window; Elsie saw her and got out. Kai instantly invited her upstairs to get warm. ''How long have you been here?'' she asked as they entered the lobby of the small walk-up building, a charmingly converted warehouse for maritime supplies.

Elsie shrugged. ''An hour or so. I had an appointment

after work, and as soon as it was over I came right here and waited. I hope you don't mind.''

"Of course I don't mind. What's wrong?'' Kai peered at her friend's face; though Elsie had behaved as though there was an emergency, she didn't appear especially upset.

"Nothing's really wrong,'' Elsie said. "But I need a sounding board, Kai. I have to make some decisions quickly, and I didn't know anyone who was likely to give me better advice than you.''

Kai's top-floor apartment was a large brick-walled loft with a kitchen that had been split off behind a low counter of varnished pine, and a separate bedroom walled off in one corner. A pair of skylights and a wall of industrial-sized windows made the space a reservoir of light in the day, and at night there was a fine view over the rooftops of lower buildings to the inner harbor a few blocks away.

Kai offered to make hot buttered rum or provide some other liquor to warm Elsie up, but she just wanted herbal tea. As Kai put a kettle on the stove, Elsie sat down on one of the high rattan stools that were lined up on either side of the counter. "I'm quitting the project,'' she said abruptly. "I might not even come in tomorrow.''

Elsie had mentioned her doubts about the work, yet her action was being taken so precipitously, it had obviously been triggered by something new.

"Why?'' Kai asked. "Why so fast?''

Elsie took a breath. "I'm pregnant.''

Kai leaned across the counter. Automatically words of congratulation rose to her lips; after all, this was what Elsie had spoken of wanting so desperately. But then it registered that Elsie's announcement hadn't been delivered in a tone of jubilation or relief.

"How—when—who—?'' Kai stammered.

Elsie smiled thinly at Kai's flustered response. "In a way I have you to thank.''

"Me?''

"Remember that weekend a couple of months ago we all went to the country? You got Laura's brother so revved up, he'd have gone to bed with anyone after you walked off the dance floor.''

Kai remembered. As she had left with Paul, she had seen

Elsie move right in to take up the slack. "So you've been seeing Andy Gerron—he's the father."

"He's the father," Elsie confirmed. "But I wouldn't say Andy and I have been much of an item. There was only that weekend. Two nights." She looked away and her voice sank. "He never called me afterward."

The kettle began to shriek. Kai poured the water into a pot, threw in a couple of tea bags, and put two mugs down on the counter. She pulled over a rattan stool and sat down, facing Elsie across the varnished wood surface. "And did you call him?" she asked.

Elsie nodded. "A couple of times—after the tests came back."

"What has he said?"

"He didn't take my calls," Elsie replied flatly.

Kai reared back. "The son of a bitch. If he thinks he can just pretend this isn't—"

Elsie put out a hand and seized Kai's arm. "I don't hold him responsible," she said. "I wanted this to happen, didn't I? He didn't use me any more than I used him."

"But he can't just completely walk away from it."

Elsie picked up the pot from the counter and poured the tea. "He hasn't."

Kai gave Elsie a puzzled look. "But you said he wouldn't talk to you."

"People like the Gerrons have their own way of dealing with these things." Elsie slid off her stool and walked over to the tote bag she had dropped by the door on her way in. She fished out an envelope and returned to the counter. "I got a call at work today from a lawyer who asked me to stop at his office when I left work. He gave me this." Elsie dug some folded papers out of the open envelope and held them toward Kai.

Kai took the papers, unfolded then. It was some sort of legal document, she saw at once, drawn in triplicate, two pages each. As she began to read, she was aware of Elsie watching her intently over the rim of her steaming teacup.

As Kai scanned the paragraphs, her initial indignation at Andy Gerron turned to outrage and then to disgust. Within the document, Elsie—as the proposed undersigned—"did state and affirm" that she was incontrovertibly renouncing any present or future claim of paternity against Andrew

Gerron, and agreeing that she would henceforth "respect his privacy" and make no further attempt either in person or by any other means to contact him on behalf of herself or "any third party" for the purposes of making such claim. In precise and detailed legal language, the document went on to stipulate that certain other conditions would also be met: Elsie Roth would permanently sever connections to any company, institution, organization, or "other such group" that had any ties or affiliations of any kind to the Gerron family or its members; and would establish residency for herself and "any of her children" at a distance of at least five hundred miles from Andrew Gerron to insure that any association with him was discouraged. There was, finally, a confidentiality clause, requiring Elsie to guarantee she would never speak to anyone about the paternity of her child—or even divulge the existence of the written agreement.

In return for meeting these terms, the document stated, the sum of $50,000 would be paid to Elsie, free and clear.

When Kai raised her eyes from the paper, Elsie was still looking at her, waiting for her reaction. There was something in her expectant expression that made Kai think Elsie's choice was to accept the offer, and in fact she had brought it tonight merely as a matter of prudent review before she signed on the dotted line. She wanted someone to tell her it was all right.

Kai couldn't do it. "It's monstrous, Elsie," she said, tossing the document on the counter as though ridding herself of something tainted. "Can't you see that? He wants to wipe away every trace of responsibility—thinks he can go so far as to make you give up your work, and then tell you where you can or can't live."

Elsie went straight on the defensive. "He's also ready to pay me almost as much money as I'd earn in another two years of working as a research assistant."

"But that's where it ends. Elsie, you're not just going to be taking care of yourself on this money. You'll have this child to feed and clothe and shelter and educate—for the next twenty years. And you'll have to manage it all alone."

"I'm not objecting to that, Kai. I wanted a baby. I can't pretend I didn't get exactly what I asked for. I mean, every man I was with lately, I was always hoping . . ." Elsie paused, picked up her mug again, and stared down into it. Then she went on in a rush. "I told you it was on my mind a lot the past few months. But there was more to it than thinking about it. There were men I hardly knew at all that I slept with just because they were nice-looking, or they seemed smart, and I thought . . . their genes would be okay." She flicked a guilty glance at Kai.

"Oh, Elsie," Kai sighed sympathetically. "So you think Andy may not really be—"

"No!" Elsie broke in. "I'm sure he's the one. I'd swear to it in court. There hadn't been anyone else for months before that weekend. But the point is, Kai, even if you think he's being a prick about this, it could've been so much worse. That's what I keep thinking. I'm getting this money, and I don't have to worry about what kind of family he comes from . . . and I'll have what I wanted most. Maybe it's not fair to expect more."

Kai still couldn't stifle her anger at Andrew Gerron. His haste to dissociate himself from Elsie, to totally cut himself off from any further responsibility for the child, struck a nerve because it mirrored what her own father had done twenty-nine years ago.

"You're leaving something out," she said. "The Gerrons are one of the richest families in the world. The money Andy's offering represents no more of a drain on their billions than if you or I gave away fifty dollars. It's not enough, Elsie." Kai tapped the paper. "Does Laura know about this?"

Elsie's eyes widened with alarm. "No. She mustn't. That's why he wants me to leave the project. Andy's lawyer warned me that if I talked to Laura, the offer would be automatically withdrawn."

Kai thought for a moment. Had Elsie come to her only because she needed someone to rubber-stamp her dubious choice? Or because she was in a vulnerable state and simply couldn't fight her own battle? "Don't settle for this, Elsie," Kai said at last. "It's wrong."

Elsie had started to tremble. "What else can I do? If I don't accept what Andy's offering, he'll fight my claim. He doesn't have just one lawyer, Kai, he's got teams of them. I'd end up with nothing."

It was becoming more apparent that what Elsie really

wanted and needed was a champion. "Don't give up yet, Elsie," Kai said. "Stay here, stay with the job. Let me talk to Andy."

Elsie stared at Kai, then gave a small nod. Yes, he would surely see Kai. After all, it was Kai he had really wanted that night.

The Chesapeake Guarantee Trust Building, thirty-six stories sheathed in brushed aluminum and green-tinted polarized glass, was one of the recent additions to Baltimore's skyline that had spearheaded the city's thriving renewal phase.

It was only after Kai's phone call had been promptly returned by Andrew Gerron's private secretary to say that Mr. Gerron would be pleased to grant her request for a meeting, and would see her tomorrow at noon in his offices on the top floor of the C.G.T. building, that Kai realized the bank must be part of the Gerron empire. Coincidentally, it was a C.G.T. branch where Kai had opened and maintained a checking account since the time her nude posing for Larry Meyer had started to bring in a fair amount of money. As she crossed through the gleaming modern lobby, dressed strictly for serious business in a severely cut dark blue suit and dark sunglasses to mask her eyes, Kai mused idly that it might have been a wise precaution to transfer her bank account elsewhere before coming here. She intended to be very tough on Andy. Who could say how far he might go in retaliation?

Yet it was clear from the greeting Andy gave her that he hadn't the least inkling she was coming on an errand of anger. Rising as she entered his large, bright office, he walked out from behind his desk and crossed the thick dawn gray carpet, smiling broadly. "This is a nice surprise," he said. "The way you ditched me at Laura's, I never expected to hear—"

"It's not a social call, Andy," she said shortly, and veered from his path to take the chair facing his desk.

He appeared stunned as he retreated silently behind the desk again. It wasn't until Kai pulled the folded papers from an inside pocket of her suit jacket and tossed them across the desk that a look of comprehension settled on his features.

"Too bad she showed it to you," he said. "That automatically cancels the offer."

"So what? She hasn't lost shit, Andy. What you wanted to give her was nothing compared to what she deserves."

"Deserves!" he echoed in a sharply mocking tone. "For what? Going on a trophy hunt? She went after me, Kai. She saw you leave me high and dry, and she moved right in. If you hadn't left me so mixed up—putting stars in my eyes, then turning your back on me—this wouldn't have happened. All things considered, I'm being generous."

"Whatever led up to it, Andy, you're the father. You owe Elsie—and the child—a lot more." Kai kept her voice low and even, but she was trembling with fury.

Andy studied her. "Why are you getting into this, Kai? Elsie Roth was ready to take the deal. It would have been good for her, and for me. Why stir it up?"

"I just can't let you do it to her. It's not fair." It was enough of an answer, she thought, though she realized that the rage burning inside her was as much against her father as Andy Gerron.

He looked coolly across the desk for another moment. Then he opened a side drawer of his desk, pulled out a manila folder, and laid it in front of him. Flipping it open, he picked out a sheet of paper. "This is a report from a private investigation agency. Do you know how many different men your friend Elsie Roth has slept with in the past six months?"

"I know there have been several. But—"

He cut her off. "Sixteen. Close to a rate of three a month." He glanced at the report and smirked. "Seems there was a certain time of the month she went kind of nuts—sort of like a werewolf. For all I know, the investigation missed another dozen, since they had to hunt down this information long after the fact." He floated the sheet of paper across the desk to Kai. "Don't talk to me about what's fair, Kai. This woman was out of control, and she ran me down."

Kai didn't bother to look at the report. There was no doubt it was true, though the degree of Elsie's promiscuity was worse than she had indicated. Still, Kai didn't yield. "She swears she wasn't with anyone for two months before you."

He shrugged indifferently.

Callous as the reaction was, it made the point. Whether or not she had been pregnant at the time of her encounter with Andy, Elsie's behavior would certainly be held against her if she ever attempted to assert a claim on him. Given the high-powered legal representation Andy could muster, there was little chance Elsie would prevail.

Kai was bluffing now when she said, "We'll fight all the way. Not just for her—for the baby. Your baby."

His mild expression underwent a subtle change as the last warmth leached out of it. "You can imagine, I'm sure, that I wouldn't be happy having this matter fought over in public. But don't think it's only my reputation I'm concerned with protecting, Kai. Think of how it will look for Laura— or even you and Dr. Sinclair, for that matter—when Miss Roth has to testify about the work she was doing during this period when she . . . started running wild—went sex-mad, I guess you could say. The project will no doubt be seen as a corrupting influence. In fact, before it gets that kind of negative publicity, I'll have to be sure it won't reflect badly on the foundation. It'll be too bad to shut things down, but—"

"You bastard," Kai erupted, rising out of her chair. "You have to punish everyone for *your* mistake."

Andy stood, too, staring back at her. "I like you, Kai. You're very beautiful and very gutsy. I even admire your loyalty to a friend." He picked up the legal papers Kai had brought with her and held them out. "Because I like you so much, I'm ready to give your friend another chance. Take these back and tell her to sign. It'll be easier for all of us."

Kai let the papers hover in the air as she gazed contemptuously at him. Could she risk going forward against him? If it was only herself on the line she would. But she couldn't allow her own outrage to cause Elsie to be left with nothing.

At last Kai raised her hand and, in an angry swipe, grabbed the papers from him. "The really sad thing," she said, "is that Elsie was glad you were the one—coming from good stock and all that. I hope she never has to know what a real monster the father of her child is." She whirled and walked toward the office door.

Behind her, Andy laughed. "It's too bad you're not the one having the baby," he called after her. "I'd make an honest woman out of you in a minute."

She slammed the door as she went out.

Chapter Twenty-nine

Kai held back the truth about her meeting with Andy, knowing Elsie might simply surrender if she knew the extent of his threats. She told Elsie that Andy was considering a more generous arrangement and would make his decision in a few days.

Meanwhile, she kept trying. The day after the meeting, she found a moment alone with Paul at work to explain the problem.

"It's sad," he agreed. "But I doubt there's anything I could do to change Andy's mind."

"You could talk to Laura about it." Kai would have done it herself, but the curious distance between her and Laura that had grown after their initial friendship seemed to be widening.

Paul refused. "If Laura goes against him, he can still pull the foundation money out of the project. We've all devoted too much time to this research to have it fall apart now."

Kai was surprised by Paul's selfish stand. "There's a principle involved, Paul. What's being done to Elsie is wrong."

"It's not a perfect world," he said. "Too many bastards have too much of the money. But neither of us can change that, Kai. You said Elsie would have settled with Andy if you hadn't stopped her. Well, that's probably the only way she'll come out ahead, and she'll be a lot better off if you step out of this."

Maybe he was right, Kai thought afterward. But each time she was on the brink of telling Elsie nothing more could be done, she would remind herself that a version of the same scene had probably been played almost thirty years ago in a navy barracks. She imagined her mother's fate being settled by a bunch of officers gathered around assuring one another there was no reason a pregnant Hawaiian whore shouldn't be left to fend for herself.

Still, she realized the simmering fury of her private grudge mustn't be allowed to subvert Elsie's best interests. Lying awake, reviewing the conversation she'd had with Paul earlier that day, she decided that her crusade was lost, and she would have to report the truth of her failure to Elsie.

The phone call was part of a dream, she thought, inspired no doubt by her waking preoccupation. Her hand floated out to seize the ringing telephone beside the bed even before she was really awake. The familiar voice at her ear drifted down into her consciousness—only making her more certain it couldn't be real. "Kai . . . is that you, Kai?"

"Mmmm," she answered sleepily.

"Sorry to call you now. I guess I knew it would be a lot easier if your defenses were down."

She said nothing, her sleep-fogged mind groping for the meaning of the words.

"Do you know who this is, Kai?"

She knew. She let the word come since it was only a dream. A little girl's dream. "Daddy."

"Kai, wake up. We have to talk."

Another moment passed, and suddenly she was fully conscious, staring into the darkness.

"Why are you calling?" she said quietly, slowly pulling herself up, looking out the window at the harbor by night to fix herself in reality. "What do you and I have to talk about?"

"You haven't heard . . . ?"

"Heard what?"

"Vanessa's been found."

"Where?" She had a moment of dread, fearing from his grim tone that he was breaking bad news rather than good. After years of being on the run as a fugitive, perhaps Alex had gone beyond the crime of kidnapping to some further insanity against her own child.

But Wyler had no tragedy to report. Alex and her daughter had been found living in Florida, discovered when they moved from one community to another and Vanessa's change in schools had resulted in the exposure of some irregularities connected to her transcripts due to the assumed names Alex had adopted. From checking a national register of children illegally abducted by divorced parents, Florida police had been able to determine their true identity, and Alex's arrest and extradition to Illinois had followed. Vanessa had been placed in a temporary foster home by social services.

"I want to get her back," Wyler said then. "She shouldn't be living with strangers. She's been hurt enough by the past few years. I want a chance to take care of her—and I need your help."

Kai was struck dumb by his request, his presumption in thinking she would comply. As rash and vindictive as Alex had been, the charges she'd leveled against Wyler of abusing his youngest daughter had never been proven false. If Kai used her own experience as a guide, she couldn't even give her father the benefit of the doubt.

"I'm sorry," she said. "I can't do any—"

She got no further before he started to plead. "Kai, you don't have to agree to anything now. All I'm asking for is a chance. It's been more than ten years since . . . you were here. Don't judge me by what happened in the past."

"I have nothing else to judge by."

There was a silence. Then he asked, "If I come to Baltimore, will you see me?"

Words failed her again. At the prospect of facing him, she began to shiver under her blankets.

He went on, "Please. I want you to know me as I am now—not as I was. I've changed. Let me show you."

The phone in her hand felt as dangerous as a live grenade, set to go off the minute she let go. While she fought with herself to give him an answer, he went on with his plea. "I'll be there the day after tomorrow. I'll call when I get in and we'll pick a place to meet. Please, Kai. Just for an hour. Please say yes."

The first time she'd ever seen him, she remembered, he'd been exercising that talent he had to make juries return the verdict he wanted. Would she decide he was innocent if she let him argue his own case in front of her?

"Yes," she said quietly, and quickly cradled the phone, eager to be free of that voice in the darkness.

* * *

It was to show her he'd changed that he wanted to meet her, he'd said on the phone.

But when she spotted him waiting for her, she saw no signs of change that mattered very much. The hair was grayer, the lines around his eyes etched a bit deeper. But he was still handsome, still had all the presence of a man who counted on winning his verdict every time. Whatever hardships and losses he had suffered, it had left no trace of humility in his aura. She approached him with caution. In her mail the morning after his phone call, there had been a letter from Alex's law firm informing her of developments in "the Smythe case," and advising her that she might be called to Chicago again in connection with mounting a defense.

They hadn't spoken again to arrange the meeting. She'd been given a message this morning by someone at work who'd answered the phone before Kai arrived. "Your father called—said he'd buy you lunch at Connolly's at one o'clock." That hadn't changed either; he called the tune.

Connolly's was another of the rickety old crab restaurants on a part of the Baltimore waterfront not yet swept away by the urge for renewal. A noisy and unpretentious establishment with paper tablecloths and battle-ax waitresses, it was famous for one gimmick unmatched anywhere else—a large, brilliant-hued parrot with clipped wings that was allowed to waddle around the floor, squawking out the non sequitur wisecracks it had absorbed over years of mingling with humans. It surprised Kai that Randall Wyler should express a taste for this funky atmosphere; she had anticipated he would choose someplace quiet, expensive, and exclusive. In fact, she had dressed on that expectation in an elegant dark blue silk suit she had found in a discount outlet—a Chanel, she thought, though the label was torn out.

Perhaps his choice of this place was one sign of change.

Distracted by the waterfront view from his table, he noticed her only when she was beside the chair opposite his. Then, clearly stunned, he rose to his feet as his eyes scanned her slowly up and down.

"You're more beautiful than she was," he said at last.

Kai ignored the compliment and seated herself. It was his inability to separate her from the memory of her mother that had caused the problem in the first place.

He lowered himself again into his chair. "Thanks for coming," he said.

"I'm your daughter," she replied flatly, a pledge of duty.

From somewhere nearby came a mocking squawk. "Too bad, sucker." Looking around, Kai saw the parrot strutting between the tables, and she laughed.

"I guess he knows what he's talking about," Wyler said when she turned again to the table. "Too bad you got stuck with me for a father."

She smiled thinly, unable to disagree.

They fumbled through a few strained minutes of studying the menu and ordering drinks. The parrot lingered in the vicinity, constantly squawking out rote phrases that preserved the illusion he was actually engaged in some back-and-forth with the customers. "Watch your step, big boy." "Takes one to know one." "Your table is ready, sir." The amusement provided by the bird was a welcome relief from the inescapable tension Kai felt with her father.

"I didn't think this was your kind of place," she observed as the parrot meandered on to another part of the restaurant. "I'm surprised you even knew about it."

"It's been here a long time. Before I was sent to Hawaii, I had a few courses at the Naval College. I used to come here from Annapolis a couple of times a month."

The navy reference brought Kai's anger surging back. Try as she might, she couldn't pretend this was a cordial reunion, just a chance to get better acquainted. Abruptly she said, "You wanted me to know that you've changed. Tell me how."

He sat back and appraised her again, appreciating the take-charge style that had come with maturity. Then he put his menu aside and took hers out of her hands. "We've never had a chance to talk about that night—"

"That's not what I asked," she cut in. "I don't want to talk about that."

"But we have to," he said. "Because that's where the change starts." He paused, as though to give her another chance to protest. Then he went on.

Not long after he had assaulted her, he said, he had realized that the act couldn't be explained away as one night's drunken confusion. "The fact is, Kai, I had feelings for you that were grievously wrong for a father to feel for his daughter. It was lucky they stopped where they did—lucky you fought me off. And it's just as well that my political career also ended right there. I was sick," he said. "I had to admit that to myself and do something about it."

He had entered into a long period of intensive psychiatric treatment, he explained. As soon as his political hopes were dead, Alex had left him, and she had remarried. The one bright spot in his life was his continuing relationship with Vanessa.

"I didn't believe I could ever restore a relationship with you," he said earnestly to Kai, "but I thought there could be some sort of—of redemption if I could be a good father to at least one of my daughters. It was working out, too. I was helped a lot by my treatment. I started to understand things in my own upbringing that had confused me about love—the way I'd seen my father mistreat my mother—things that kept me from loving you, loving anyone, in the right way."

As Kai listened, she felt her sympathy stirring. But she steeled herself against being won over too easily. She was a jury of one, and he had always known how to manipulate juries.

"But there was never a problem between me and Vanessa," he continued. "I swear to you. Alex invented the whole thing to keep from losing Vanessa."

"Losing her? But you were sharing custody."

Wyler frowned. "It wasn't working out—but not because of me. Alex's second marriage fell apart, her husband left her for someone younger, and then she started going to pieces. The other children were sent off to college. Half the time Vanessa was alone, making meals for herself, while Alex spent nights out. Vanessa would turn up on my doorstep and tell me her mother hadn't been around for three or four days. I would have liked to petition the court for sole custody, but I knew I was in a bad position to fight Alex. I expected her to use you against me." He shuffled some silverware around on the table. "I let Vanesssa keep coming to me, and I took her in as often as she wanted. Then Alex started raising hell. Got jealous, really. She made up that stuff about me molesting Van so the court wouldn't let her near me."

"If it wasn't true, all Van had to do was deny it."

"She did—of course, she did!" Wyler said with pained

emphasis. "But she's still a child, Kai. When Alex claimed that Van was denying it because she was afraid of me, it raised enough doubt to keep the case alive. I'm still not in the clear. Alex broke the law, but there are still plenty of people who believe her and sympathize with her. My worry now is that Van will end up with no one. Alex may go to jail for a year or more—and I'll be denied custody, so Van will stay in foster care.'' He leaned forward and reached across the table to grasp Kai's hand. "Don't let that happen. You of all people, you should know what it would mean for her to be with me, to have her father."

Kai couldn't imagine a crueler irony. He wanted her to remember the pain of being abandoned by him to keep his other daughter from suffering a similar fate! She slipped her hand out of his.

"What do you want me to do?" she asked. Not for him, but for the half-sister she remembered with deep affection.

"If you're summoned to testify at a custody hearing, don't come. You'd have to talk about what happened between us, and that would kill my chances."

"But the facts are known anyway," she argued. "They've already been mentioned in a deposition—"

"It's only hearsay, inadmissible until you tell it to a judge."

"And can't I be forced to testify—charged with obstructing justice if I refuse?"

"This will be a hearing, Kai, not a trial. You can avoid it if you want, find excuses that keep you in Baltimore, and submit an affidavit saying you can't think of any reason I shouldn't be allowed to have my daughter back."

She stared at him. So here it was. He wanted her to lie for him. She shook her head. "I won't do it," she said quietly.

"For Vanessa," he pleaded. "It's the only way I'll get her back."

"You'll get her if you deserve her. If you can prove you've changed."

"Judges aren't always wise enough," he said. "Your story would be just too damaging."

She stared back implacably. Whatever the damage, it was his doing, not hers. If she was asked for the truth, she would supply it.

A waiter had been hovering nearby, eager to step in and take an order, but Wyler waved him away. "I guess I should warn you then," he said. "If you line up against me, Kai, then I'll have to shoot you down." Responding to the alarm that flared in her eyes, he added quickly, "Oh, not with bullets—just facts."

As she eyed him warily, he ran through a summary of the information received from an investigative agency he had hired a couple of years ago to keep track of her, in case he ever needed extra ammunition. It was all about the Cooke-Sinclair project, about Kai being one of the original organizers behind a controlled effort to closely study the sex lives of a number of men and women—a total of seventy-four subjects at last count.

"I suppose there's a way to talk about this work you've been doing that makes it sound sensible and scientific. But there are also ways that might make it seem . . . well, perverted. Put that together with some of your past escapades, and you wouldn't come out of it looking very good. Neither would your research, for that matter."

Her growing shock had frozen her tongue until now. "You haven't changed at all," she said. "If you'd use that against me—"

"You don't understand. I wouldn't have to. If I've been able to get this information, then Alex's lawyers will have it, too."

"But why should they want to discredit me? If they want my testimony—"

"The idea would be to show that your moral character evidently suffered from living under my roof."

She gave him a grudging nod. "Maybe they've got a point. Maybe it's even suffering a little more from sitting down to lunch with you." She pushed back her chair. "I won't lie for you, no matter what kind of pressure you put me under."

As she stood to leave, he leapt up and grabbed her by the arm. "Damn it, Kai, I'm just trying to spare you an ordeal—and save Vanessa, too. Please believe me. All I want is a chance to be a good *father* to her."

She wrenched loose from his grasp. "If only you could have said you wanted to be mine, too, maybe I'd have listened."

His lips parted as if to speak, but no answer came. The answer was in his eyes, though. It was too late to be her father, he had decided. Perhaps he was right.

With each step on the way out, she almost relented and turned back. She knew the pain of growing up and confronting the world without parents. What would it do to Vanessa?

Was he asking so much of her? Did she dare to believe him?

As she left, she heard the parrot squawking somewhere in the background. "Too bad, sucker."

Chapter Thirty

Finally Kai gave Elsie back the scurrilous document drawn up by Andrew Gerron's lawyers, and confessed that she had failed to gain any improvement. Elsie expressed gratitude for Kai's efforts, then signed the paper in front of her, and sealed it in an envelope to mail to Andy's lawyers. As soon as she received her payment, she planned to leave town.

"You don't seem bitter about this," Kai said with amazement.

"I'll be leaving with something much more valuable than the money," Elsie said. "I'll have my baby."

Yet Kai couldn't stop brooding over her friend's predicament. Having grown up without a father intensified the feelings she had for Elsie's unborn child.

At sunrise the following Saturday, after a sleepless night, Kai set out on a drive south to the tidewater country.

It was only a few minutes before eight o'clock when she arrived at Bluefields, where she knew Laura was spending the weekend. Despite the hour, the chiming doorbell was answered promptly by the butler. "I don't believe Mrs. Cooke is expecting you," he said stiffly, making no move to allow her to enter.

Before Kai could add anything, Laura strode into the foyer dressed in jodhpurs and boots, a tweed vest covering an ivory linen blouse. Her chestnut hair was tied back with a ribbon. Evidently she was planning to take a morning ride. "It's all right, Nelson," she said to the butler. "I'll see Miss Wyler."

Kai had expected Laura to be irritated by the intrusion, but she was pleasantly cordial and welcoming. "Had breakfast yet?" she asked, leading Kai into the house.

"No, I've been driving."

Laura's amber eyes glittered with curiosity. "So you got

out of bed at dawn and came right here. Better tell me what's wrong." Laura led her into a small solarium, where a round table was set for breakfast. They sat down, and a maid was told to bring another table setting. "Well?" Laura prompted when coffee had been poured for Kai.

"It's about Andy," Kai said.

Laura gave no hint she'd been forewarned of a problem.

Kai went on, starting her account with the weekend of the conference when Elsie had gone to bed with Andy.

"So what did you think I could do?" Laura asked tartly when Kai had concluded with an account of her failed attempt to help Elsie. "My brother won't behave any differently because I ask him. He never gives more than necessary, and always takes as much as he can get. That's what makes him a good businessman."

"And a rotten human being. He can afford to be more generous."

"He didn't want this child, Kai. Elsie did."

"I hoped you'd see this from the woman's point of view."

"I'm not Andy. My brother and I don't agree on very much—politics, lifestyle, work, charity. Any influence I had with him, I used up getting him to back this project. But he has too much money to worry about what anyone else thinks of his own choices, me included. Also, he's a man—and men have always been given the balance of power in the Gerron family."

"But you have money of your own," Kai observed.

"Yes," Laura replied guardedly. "What about it?"

"I've given up on the idea of getting Andy to do more for Elsie. But I thought you might add something to the settlement so that the baby would be fairly provided for."

"Out of my own pocket, you mean?"

Contrary to the annoyance Kai thought her request might provoke, Laura's response was mild, almost bemused. "You've got pretty deep pockets," Kai observed, taking advantage of Laura's mood, "and you're going to be this child's aunt."

Laura smiled. "So just how much did you think I should toss into the collection plate?"

"Enough to insure there's a secure upbringing, plus a good education through college. And maybe something to compensate Elsie for the trials of being a single mother."

"In dollars and cents," Laura insisted.

It wasn't just Elsie she wanted to speak for, Kai realized. She was thinking of her own mother, wishing she could have had Harley Trane here to extract a penalty from him, too. "Half a million dollars," she said.

Laura calmly raised an eyebrow and took a sip of her coffee, her eyes gauging Kai across the rim of the cup. She settled the cup back in its saucer. "I suppose you think I can easily afford that much. And if you're only talking about money, maybe that's true. But in another sense, Kai, it's much more than I can afford." She rose from the table, moved to the windows of the solarium, and stared out at the endless vista. "So many times, I've been the one who paid Andy's way out of some mess. Andy would have happily let the roof cave in rather than prop it up by paying a little extra money. Other women have gotten pregnant—though they didn't want the children, so there were abortions, very expensive abortions that I paid for. I've laid out money to the police after Andy's been arrested with hookers—because he'd dare them to lock him up rather than pay bail or give them a little hush money. It's a kind of rich man's sport for him, you see, to push things to the limit, see how much he can get away with, how tough he can be in the pinch. He'd rather go to war than settle anything on any terms but his own." Laura came back to the table and sat down. "Until now I've been the one who buckled under and paid because I couldn't bear to see the family name get dragged through the mud. I paid, even though Andy always treated me the way he treated every other woman—with contempt—the way all the men in the Gerron family have always treated all the women. But I can't do it anymore, Kai. I won't just play the woman's role and clean up after the men make a mess." She gritted her teeth and shook her head, ratifying the decision with some private inner vote. "Don't misunderstand, Kai. I feel sympathy for Elsie. But Andy has to pay the price himself this time, whatever it is."

"It's Elsie who'll pay—and her child."

"She can launch a paternity suit. I won't interfere."

"Andy will beat it."

"He's won already if she hasn't got the guts to try. Either way, it's their business, not mine. I'm sorry, Kai. But because I have a lot of money, it isn't fair to expect me to spread it everywhere as a blanket to put out other people's fires.''

Kai gave up. She was deeply disappointed, but she couldn't reproach Laura for her position. Remembering the way Laura had guarded the secret of her family name, Kai realized that for all Laura's accomplishments, her wealth had fostered an abiding suspicion that money was the only thing that attracted people to her. Perhaps that explained, too, why she had retreated from the friendship they'd shared.

A memory of that affection sparked an impulse to close the gap. ''I hope you won't think I came here just hunting for a hand-out,'' Kai said. ''There was a time I would have talked to you about any problem, anything that was worrying me. You were the person I turned to for advice—'' She stopped on the brink of saying she had regarded Laura almost as a mother. ''I don't know why that closeness faded away, but I wish we could have it again.''

Laura's expression softened. ''Then you're not angry because I've refused to help?''

''You have your reasons. I was afraid you'd be angry at me for asking.''

Laura shook her head and smiled. The gap between them had narrowed already.

Kai stayed for breakfast, and afterward Laura suggested she spend the day, take one of the horses, and ride with her.

Kai welcomed the chance to recover their lost intimacy. Laura outfitted her with riding gear, and they went on a long trip on horseback through the miles of bridle trails that had been laid out generations ago. Kai had not been on a horse since that last painful day with Paul, but she enjoyed it now. Where the trails emerged occasionally from the woods onto vast open fields, she and Laura urged their horses into a headlong gallop. And while they walked their horses, cooling them down, she and Laura talked freely and openly as they had years ago.

They returned hours later, hot from their ride, the musky smell of the horses clinging to them. Laura urged Kai to take a shower, gave her a plush bath towel, and sent her upstairs to use the bathroom in her master suite.

The tiled shower stall in Laura's luxurious bath was as large by itself as most conventional bathrooms. As Kai stood under the torrent of hot water, she felt that the morning's exercise was easing away all the tensions built up from taking Elsie's problem on her shoulders. Would the renewal of friendship last, she wondered, or disappear as mysteriously as it had the last time?

She was startled to see a shadowy figure materialize suddenly behind the steam-fogged glass door.

"Laura?" she called out anxiously.

"Yes, it's me," the voice came back. In the next second Laura opened the shower door. She stood framed in the opening, naked.

As Kai went on staring, Laura stepped into the stall and closed the door.

"No, Laura . . ." Kai said calmly. She had too much experience to feel shock or panic.

Laura grasped her shoulders. "Why not?" she murmured, barely audible over the hiss of the shower. "Please, Kai . . . I've wanted this for so long. . . ."

Kai could have easily stepped out of the shower, but she stood still, staring at Laura through the curtain of water pouring down around them. *Of course,* she understood now, this was the reason their intimacy had withered. Laura couldn't maintain it without revealing herself, and she had fought against that, certain she would be rejected during the time Kai was involved with Paul.

"Here, baby," Laura said, grabbing a cake of soap from a shelf. "Let me wash you." Her soap-slick hands glided over Kai's skin, her shoulders first, then her arms, moving inward to her breasts. "There," she said, "isn't that nice?"

Kai stood motionless, unprotesting. She had never felt any confusion about her sexuality, never felt a desire for sex with a woman. Yet strangely, she was slow now to reject Laura. While Laura washed her, cooing "baby" over and over, Kai was cast back to an illusion of being small again, being coddled and cared for by her mother. Closing her eyes, she enjoyed the slow caresses.

She felt Laura's lips lightly touch hers and almost pulled away, but Laura's mouth was already roaming down across her shoulders, her throat. Then Laura was sucking her breasts, her tongue flicking across her nipples.

Standing in the hot, sluicing water, Kai gave herself over to the sensations. Laura had sunk to her knees. As her face pressed into the warm cleft between Kai's legs, one hand stole around the curve of Kai's thighs, then moved into the cleft of her buttocks. With her other hand she stimulated herself. The water seemed to magnify every tingle that rippled through Kai's body, shooting up from her core to the sensitized surface of her skin. Then a flood of delicious spasms overtook her, and it didn't matter that it was another woman who had brought her to this peak. Laura, too, was at climax. Kai sank down beside her, and they embraced as the waves of feeling swept over them, then receded.

It was Kai who moved first, stepping out of the shower, wrapping herself in a towel and going out to the bedroom. She dressed quickly and was standing at a full-length closet mirror, brushing her hair by the time Laura emerged wearing a bathrobe.

"I tried not to," Laura said contritely.

"That's why you grew distant from me, isn't it?"

"More than that, Kai. It's why I sent you off alone to meet Paul. I thought if you fell in love with him, that would help me get over it. While you were with him, I was resigned. But then you came here today, and . . ." She shrugged helplessly.

Kai turned from the mirror. "Don't blame yourself. I let it happen, too. I'm not ashamed . . . and you shouldn't be."

Laura smiled. "Oh, I'm over that stage. You're not the first, Kai. After my marriage, I was always afraid of men. It seemed easier with women . . . less of a fight." She moved closer. "Do you think there's any chance at all we might . . ."

She didn't finish the question, but Kai knew what it was. "No, Laura. It's just not my choice."

"I see," Laura murmured. Abruptly she stepped to a mantel in the bedroom and pressed a buzzer beside it. "One of the servants will see you out."

Before leaving the room, Kai paused by the door. "I'll always need the kind of advice you used to give me, Laura. If we could be friends—"

"I doubt that's possible," Laura said as a maid materialized to lead Kai to the door. "Though you've certainly shown you're a very good friend to have."

On the drive back to Baltimore, and through several solitary hours in her apartment, drinking wine and staring out at the harbor as evening came, Kai reflected on the afternoon's incident. The phone rang a few times, but she left it unanswered, needing time to puzzle through what had happened. She could have easily rejected Laura, she thought. Why had she yielded?

It occurred to her at last that she had been ready to experiment because sex had become nothing more than a subject for research; she had dealt with it for so long as a process to be studied in a laboratory that she was beginning to regard herself as one more subject, her own experience as additional data. But while knowledge was being gained, it seemed she had lost her bearings. She had wanted to understand more about sex because it had been such a powerful—and often destructive—force in her life, in the lives of the people she knew; but the force was not diminished by however much she had learned. And she worried now that by focusing on the physical phenomena, she had somehow become less accessible to those mysterious forces of the heart and soul that were more important between lovers than even the most perfect technique. Sex was everywhere in her life. But where was love?

Her thoughts were interrupted by the buzzer of the apartment intercom. It was Elsie. "I have to see you!" she shouted.

She barged through the door, a paper bag cradled in her arms. "How did you do it?!" she screamed raucously. It took Kai a second to realize it wasn't a scream of anger, but jubilation.

"Do what?"

As if it was some kind of explanation, Elsie pulled a bottle of champagne from the paper bag. Kai shook her head.

Elsie chattered on as she shed her coat and went hunting for glasses in Kai's small kitchen. "I got a call from a guy who said he's a lawyer for the Gerron family. Tells me that he's been instructed to pay over funds in the amount of—get this!—*one million dollars*, half clear, the other half in trust for the kid. All I have to do is sign a new set of papers stating I'll keep it confidential and make no further claims. Can you beat that? Andy changed his mind. And I'd already mailed in the other papers. He didn't have to—"

"It wasn't Andy," Kai said. "I went to Laura."

"So this money is coming from her?"

Kai nodded.

Elsie popped the cork, poured champagne into a couple of juice glasses, and handed one to Kai. They clinked and drank to the baby.

"Jesus, Kai," Elsie said, stalking excitedly around the floor. "I'll never be able to thank you enough. A million dollars! How the hell did you get the nerve to ask Laura for that?"

Kai took another sip of champagne and smiled. "Actually," she said, "that wasn't the amount I wanted. But she turned down what I asked for."

"Well, don't feel bad," Elsie said, and gave her a hug, "you did great."

A week later, Elsie left Baltimore. The transaction had been completed, the money paid. She took Kai out to dinner the night before she left, and happily talked about how she planned to live now that she could afford whatever she wanted. Having no ambition to continue with any form of research, she had decided to try her hand at being a painter.

"I was always pretty good at art," she said. "But I never kept at it, because I knew it was such a crazy way to try making a living. Now that won't matter."

"Where will you go?" Kai asked. She knew that the agreement Elsie had signed still required her to live at a distance.

"I'm going to take a look at New Mexico. You know the paintings of Georgia O'Keefe? Crusty old dame who paints these enormous pictures of flowers that are so sexy you want to fuck 'em, and bleached cow skulls she picks up in the desert. She lives out there—and she's my favorite painter— so I figured maybe I'll give it a try, too. I'll let you know when I get settled, and you can come out and visit anytime you need a vacation. You know," Elsie added, "I think there's something about this project that could make us all a little crazy."

Of course, the research had produced important results already. The physiological stages of sexual interaction and intercourse had been thoroughly charted, and a greater understanding had been achieved of the physical needs of women in order to achieve orgasm. By recording and examining the encounters of numerous couples, it had been possible to produce a factual, statistical basis for a report that would end once and for all certain myths that had caused misunderstanding and unhappiness between men and women for centuries. No correlation had been found, for example, between the size of a man's organ and his ability to bring full satisfaction to his partner. For women, the notion of frigidity in those who failed to achieve vaginal orgasm during intercourse had also been disproven. While there were women who occasionally climaxed in this way, it was in the nature of feminine physiology to require stimulation of the clitoris. And although the time of arousal in women was slower, it was also longer lasting. The impatience of men who quickly achieved orgasm, only to leave women unsatisfied, had fostered the idea in too many women that they were incapable of finding the same pleasure. Kai was certain that when the results were published, they would provide a basis for improving the self-image of many women, eliminating sources of tension between lovers.

In the wake of Elsie's departure, however, Kai found it harder each day to concentrate on her work. One mistake that had been made in setting up the project, she realized, was in failing to insist that all the researchers be involved in stable relationships. It was simply impossible, she thought, to be observing and charting the sexual process, while going home to sleep alone each night.

As winter melted into spring, several other letters came from the law firm representing Alexandra Smythe, informing Kai that she would be expected to appear at a custody hearing as soon as a date was set. As dissatisfaction with her work increased, Kai decided that when the time came to make the trip, she would also leave the project. Perhaps she would stay in Chicago. Where else did she have any attachments? Meanwhile, she went to work each day, made her observations, wrote up her notes, and participated dutifully in staff meetings.

At the beginning of April, a plain envelope arrived in her mail—without a return address—containing two columns of newsprint clipped from the *Chicago Tribune* of two days earlier. The article reported that Alex had been exonerated of the charge of unlawfully abducting her daughter in view of a court ruling that it was in the child's best interest to remove her from any contact with her father. A footnote reported that a petition for sole permanent custody of Vanessa had been granted to Alex after Randall Wyler decided not to contest the petition.

She wondered if it had been sent by her father—a silent postscript to imply the blame for his loss, since there would be no hope of defeating Alex as long as Kai was determined to testify against him. Or was it Alex who had sent it as a final boast of triumph?

Now there was nothing pulling her back to Chicago. Yet here she felt at a dead end.

She had already decided to ask for a meeting with Paul to say she was planning to leave the project, when he called her at home to ask if she could meet with him the next morning.

When she arrived at his office, Laura was already there. Kai detected a curious tension in the air.

"I guess there's no easy way to do this," Paul said as soon as Kai was seated. He exchanged a glance with Laura, a bit of silent communication in which they seemed to be deciding who should speak the next words. Kai had the feeling some very bad news was about to be delivered. Was she going to be fired? Had her work become so unsatisfactory? Maybe she should speak first, tell them she was ready to go.

But then Laura said, "We wanted you to hear it from us, before the formal announcements—Paul and I are going to be married."

For a moment Kai stared back, then she had to fight down an impulse to laugh. These people who had both made love to her—whose hearts were both shackled by their ghosts and their secrets—they were choosing to make their lives together!

"Well, that's—that's wonderful," she sputtered.

Paul and Laura both smiled, sympathetic to her confusion and embarrassment.

"I'm sure it seems strange to you," Paul said. "But we've both realized there's a lot we can give to each other, and we don't want to be alone."

He almost seemed to be saying, thought Kai, that they

were united because she had spurned them both and there
was no one else they wanted.

"It will be good for the project, too," Laura added.

Perhaps, Kai thought then, they had simply come to the
same conclusion she had—that it was too difficult to be
probing the mysteries of the most intense kind of human
connection without having some emotional anchor of their
own. Kai remembered, too, they had known each other for
a long time, that Laura had been a friend of his wife. For
Paul, that might be one more way of keeping in contact with
his beloved ghost.

She thanked them both for telling her personally, and
wished them every happiness. "I have something to tell you,
too," she said then. "I'm planning to leave."

Both leaned toward her with concern. "I'm sorry if it's
because of this—" Paul said.

Kai smiled. "It isn't. I hope you'll always be my friends.
But doing this work is becoming too difficult for me. I know
how important it is. And I've learned so much about what
happens between men and women—why our whole lives may
turn one way or another based on the impulses we've been
studying. But I'm afraid . . . it's beginning to numb something inside me. . . ." She shrugged, unable to explain further.

Laura smiled back at her. "It isn't hard to understand,"
she said. "For all you've found out about sex in the interest
of science, you still need to look for love to satisfy your
heart."

"Yes," Kai said. That was exactly right.

BOOK
FOUR

Chapter Thirty-one

New Mexico—March 1986

There was no airport in the nation's oldest state capital, Santa Fe. As Elsie had instructed, Kai flew to Albuquerque, and now she sat waiting in the terminal for her friend to arrive. The plane from Dallas had landed just after noon, Kai had already collected her baggage, but Elsie had yet to appear. The sense of *déjà vu* was inescapable—Elsie bustling in late to the airport in Los Angeles years ago.

How many airports there had been since then! Kai had spent three nomadic years since leaving Baltimore, never coming to rest for long in any one place. When she applied the insights she had gained through her study of psychology to analyzing her years of wandering, she realized that part of her was still searching for something she could never find, not because it was lost, but because it didn't really exist. The child who had gone in search of a father so many years ago would never be satisfied because the man she had found was not the loving parent she longed for. Perhaps that had finally made it difficult for her to trust any man, so she always kept on moving, searching for love.

Not that the travels of recent years had been empty or aimless. They had been given a purposeful structure by an assignment Laura had offered: to gather extensive notes on sexual customs and preferences in other parts of the world, which would be used in the text as background to the American research. Kai had happily taken it on.

Without doing any sort of study in depth, the assignment had ultimately freed Kai to spend months at a time in places which provided the greatest contrasts—in parts of the Middle East, for example, where harems still existed and husbands could order their wives to be surgically altered so that they were incapable of achieving orgasm; in Southeast Asia, where young women were still sold as chattel at auctions, sexually enslaved for the rest of their lives to the men who paid for them. Paul and Laura had drawn extensively on Kai's notes for their text, giving perspective to the American viewpoint and making the research more applicable to other cultures and countries.

As she waited for Elsie, Kai browsed in the airport shops, windows filled with Indian jewelry and pottery, beaded shoes and vests, a gallery showing the work of a local photographer—vistas of the desert with long shadows cut in the brightness by jutting rock formations. Would this be the place where she finally put down some roots? She looked forward to this chance to rest from all the constant motion and make some decisions for the future.

She came to the airport bookshop, and a smile of satisfaction touched her lips as she saw the window display, a pyramid of thick volumes stacked up under a sign that read #1 BESTSELLER. *The Nature of Human Sexual Interaction* had been at the top of the list since its publication three months ago, and continued to sell out printing after printing.

Kai felt no resentment at all whenever she looked at the book cover and authorship credited to Paul and Laura Sinclair. The book as it appeared in print had been written by them. Nor had they been ungenerous in sharing praise for the work. In a special acknowledgment at the front of the book, Kai Wyler was mentioned as having been instrumental in conceiving the project, and her contributions to the text were noted. In addition, when the publisher had assembled a publicity tour, both Paul and Laura had urged that Kai be included in the round of television appearances, either with or without them. Her personal odyssey from sex symbol to sex researcher provided an angle that made television interviewers and news digest shows eager to have her, and her appearances on such shows as *Sixty Minutes* and *Donahue* and even with Johnny Carson had certainly been a factor in pushing the sales even higher. Last night Kai had completed her scheduled publicity tour in Dallas, and she had headed straight here.

As for the massive royalties the book would reap, Kai had been offered a minority share, but she had agreed along with Paul and Laura that all the money could be funneled back into an institute for the study and treatment of sexual dysfunction that would be established at Jefferson University.

Kai heard her name being called and turned from the bookshop to see Elsie, arriving on a frazzled run. Kai's delight was doubled by seeing the little girl scampering along beside Elsie, her daughter by Andy Gerron. Now two and a half, Casey was a miniature carbon copy of Elsie, except that her mop of hair was redder and her blue eyes rounder. At the time of her birth, Elsie had contacted Kai abroad to ask her to be the child's godmother. The similarity between mother and daughter was emphasized by their almost identical pale blue tent dresses. In Elsie's case, the abundant dress was essential since she was in the seventh month of her second pregnancy. This time there would be no problems with the father. Two years ago Elsie had married a professor of anthropology at the University of New Mexico who specialized in Native American culture.

The friends came together in a long embrace that was finally pried apart at the knees by Casey, who cried, "Me. Hug me."

Kai picked up her little goddaughter and hugged her.

The child returned her affection instantly. "Mommy say you more pretty of Barbie," she said.

Kai laughed.

"I don't know if you'd call that a compliment," Elsie said, "but it's the absolute tops for Casey."

"Barbie dresses better, though," Kai said wryly. She was wearing the jeans and a striped madras shirt from India that had become her regular traveling costume.

They made their way out of the terminal, Casey clinging to Kai's hand while Elsie offered up apologies for arriving late, explaining that she was going eighty miles an hour on the road from Santa Fe trying to make it on time, and had been pulled over for speeding by the state police.

When Kai saw the car Elsie was driving these days, a sleek fire-engine red Porsche, it was easy to understand why she had attracted a speeding ticket. "It's my only extravagance, I swear," Elsie said as she strapped her daughter into a child seat in the rear of the car. "Don't go thinking

I went hog wild and spent all my money recklessly on expensive toys.''

"I never thought that," Kai said. "And you don't owe me any explanations.''

"Don't I? Baby, if it wasn't for you, I wouldn't have my car or my house or all the things that have made my life out here so good. Hell, who knows if Mike would've married me if I didn't have such a healthy bank balance." With absolute seriousness she added, "I'll never forget how much I owe you, Kai.''

It was because Elsie felt this debt so keenly that she had prevailed on Kai to visit Santa Fe as soon as her schedule of publicity appearances had been completed. From their contacts in recent years—the scores of postcards Kai sent from so many places—Elsie had realized that her friend still needed a place to put down roots.

As the Porsche breezed along the road toward Santa Fe, with Casey contentedly humming to herself in the backseat, Kai enjoyed the scenery: sprawling tan flats of desert fenced in by distant mountains with deep shadowed ridges that looked purple under the contrast of bright blue sky.

"I don't know how soon you'll want to think about practical stuff like a job and a place to live," Elsie said, "but I've already tested both markets and got some good things lined up. There are a couple of great little adobe houses outside of town for rent cheap, and the university is dying to have you on the faculty." Her husband, Mike, had spoken to the head of the psychology department, she reported, and there was no question Kai would be offered a position as an associate professor with the promise of a promotion after only a few years.

"That's great," Kai said. "But give me a chance to catch my breath, Elsie. I just got here.''

"Sorry," Elsie said sheepishly. "You're certainly welcome to use our guest room and cool out as long as you like. I'm just so eager to set things up because I really want you to stay here, Kai. It'd be good for you, I know it would. You'd like the lifestyle, slow and easy, and . . . well, you'd have a built-in family.''

Though Kai had never said anything specifically to indicate that she was lonely, Elsie had come to her own conclusions from a correspondence that had noticeably lacked any mention of romance. It was astonishing to Elsie that Kai, by far the most beautiful woman she knew, had failed to form any lasting attachment with a man. In a letter more than a year ago, there had been a couple of brief sentences that hinted at a romance with someone named Gerard—"when I finish my work here, I may go to spend time with Gerard in Paris"—but the name had never reappeared.

The home Elsie had bought for herself when she moved to Santa Fe was a comfortable modern adaptation of the traditional adobe house set on two acres west of the city, with a large garden facing toward the Sangre de Cristo Mountains.

Kai settled into the guest room and while Casey took a nap, the two friends sat on a patio with a pitcher of sangria and plates of guacamole and talked in greater depth about the separate paths they had followed.

At last Elsie's curiosity got the better of her. "Who was Gerard?" she asked.

Kai replied matter-of-factly. He was a Frenchman, a correspondent for a Paris newspaper she had met while working in Saudi Arabia. He had followed her all over the Middle East, and then asked her to go back to Paris with him when he returned home on leave.

"I suppose I thought at that point I was in love with him. I'd begun to daydream about what it would be like to marry him, settle in France, and have a brood of little French-babbling children." Kai gave a little shrug. "The problem was Gerard already had the wife and three little French-speaking children living in a house in a suburb of Paris."

"The bastard," Elsie gasped. "He lied to you."

Kai smiled sadly. "Worse. He never had to lie because I never asked—never even suspected—and he just let me go on believing whatever I wanted."

"But when he asked you to come to Paris, didn't he realize it was bound to come out? Was he planning to leave his wife?"

"No. By then I guess he probably thought it didn't matter to me one way or the other. He imagined I'd be willing to stay on in Paris as his mistress. When we got there, he told me quite casually after our second night that the next day he was going to have to let his wife know he'd returned. It was the first time he'd ever mentioned her. He seemed genuinely surprised when I looked at him like a bomb had gone off.'' Kai shrugged. ''I blame myself as much as I blame him. I set myself up for it. I'd chased a lot of men away, but a point came where I didn't want to be alone anymore, and he was the most charming and amusing man I'd met . . . and so I invented a fairy tale about him.''

Elsie shook her head, moved that her beautiful friend should be so starved for love, and so deprived.

After Casey woke from her nap, Elsie suggested taking a drive to the place where her husband was excavating some Indian ruins. Though Santa Fe had been a research center for the study of Native American culture for decades, Mike Cogan was still making fresh discoveries that put him in the forefront of American prehistory. ''He's doing a new dig about twenty miles from here. I'd like you to meet him, and it's the best show in town.''

''I'd love to go,'' Kai said.

''I've been taking Casey out to the dig a couple of times a week,'' Elsie said when they were on the road. ''She thinks Daddy's just like a kid, playing in an enormous sandbox.''

''I like the movie, too,'' Casey piped up from the back.

''Oh, that's an extra added attraction,'' Elsie explained. ''For the past ten days there's a movie company shooting some scenes for a comedy just over the hill from where Mike is working. Casey thinks it's fun to watch. There're no big crowds in the desert, so they've been nice about letting us on the location. Casey's even been adopted as a kind of mascot. The stars let her sit in their chairs, take her into their trailers—''

''The lady in the tree is nice and funny,'' Casey said.

Again Elsie interpreted. When they had been watching the shoot the other day, the woman star had gotten stuck in a tree trying to get away from a couple of thugs. ''The woman's a great comedienne, I'll have to admit. And gutsy, doing her own stunts, hanging from this tree branch twenty feet in the air—though maybe that's crazier than it is brave. But that's the kind of stuff Sylvie Teer always does, isn't it, these parts for goofy dames who wind up hanging from flagpoles or standing on window ledges?''

Sylvie! A nostalgic pang gripped Kai, a feeling she'd often had when she heard Sylvie's stage name or saw it on a

theater marquee or in a newspaper ad for a new film. As
her career had taken her from the stage to television to movies over the past years, Kai had often noticed crowds for
Sylvie's films even at the theaters in foreign cities. Her brand
of comedy, relying on zany visual slapstick and the mugging
of her expressive face, played well in any language. Yet
because it was painful to think of their lost friendship, Kai
had always avoided seeing Sylvie's films. Until last year in
Paris. After learning the truth about Gerard, she had decided nothing could make her feel worse, so she had drifted
into a theater showing Sylvie's enormous global hit, *Ensign
Evans,* about a society deb who gets accidentally drafted
into the navy and becomes a daring "frogman." Kai had
never laughed so hard as she did at such Chaplinesque rou-
tines as the scene where Sylvie ended up doing a water
ballet with a pair of seals and a penguin during an Arctic
training exercise. But in the aftermath of the laughter there
were, after all, melancholy memories of the foolish arguments that had ended their closeness. She wasn't sure now
whether she would want to see Sylvie again or not.

The excavation being supervised by Elsie's husband lay
several miles off the main road, down a flat sandy track that
led to an area of towering stone outcroppings that sprang
abruptly out of dry ground where only scrub and cactus
grew. As Elsie pulled up to the site, Kai saw that it wasn't
a major project, nothing more than a half dozen shallow
pits that had been dug at the base of one of the stone pillars.
Within the dug-out areas, fifteen undergraduate students
were working along with Elsie's husband in groups of twos
and threes.

At the sight of his wife's red Porsche, Mike Cogan hauled
himself out of one of the pits and walked toward the car.
He was tall and gangly with thinning brown hair and a narrow, attractive face masked at the moment by dark sunglasses. First to reach him was Casey, who dashed across
the open ground the moment she was released from her
safety seat. Her father scooped her up and nuzzled her as
he continued toward Elsie and Kai. His easygoing nature
was apparent from the way he let Casey pull the sunglasses
off his face and start doodling with them without the least
objection.

He leaned over to kiss his wife, then gave Kai a shining smile.

"Hello, Kai," he said warmly, without even waiting to be introduced. "It's a relief to have you here at last."

"A relief?" Kai echoed. "I didn't know you were worried."

"Oh, I wasn't. But my dear wife has talked so much about you ever since I met her, being able to get to know you for myself is going to mean she and I will finally have time left over to talk about a few other things."

"Oh, Mike," Elsie complained playfully, giving him a painless swat on the arm.

"She was worried about you, too," Mike said. "Thought you might go on orbiting the earth forever like a satellite. We're real glad about the possibility you might settle down here."

"Thanks," Kai said flatly. The idea of settling anywhere still aroused a curious nervousness. Quickly changing the subject, she glanced over at the excavated area. "What sort of things are you digging up?"

The question immediately sparked an enthusiastic lecture. Handing off Casey to Elsie, Mike escorted Kai over to a tarpaulin spread out at the center of the excavation, atop which hundreds of small shards of pottery were laid out in rows. One of the female students appeared to be cataloging them, carefully writing a number on each shard and then recording it in a book. Several young men, working shirtless under the hot sun, were painstakingly whisking small camel-hair brushes over the shards to remove the last remnants of sand.

"Of course, right now it doesn't look like much more than somebody's kitchen after an earthquake, but we've carbon-dated some of these fragments and placed them among the oldest remnants of the Anasazi culture ever found, going back several thousand years. What's even more significant, though, are the designs on some of this stuff. They are patterns identical to designs we've seen on Aztec pottery, which could mean one of several things—" He stopped abruptly and checked Kai with a glance. "Sorry, I have a tendency to run off at the mouth when you get me on this subject."

"I'm not bored," Kai said. "Go on."

"Well, the Anasazis are the forerunners of the Pueblos, who most recently populated the region. Their mythology says they lived in an underworld beneath the earth's surface—a horrible, damp, dark place—until they finally found their way out into the light through the earth's navel. You can still go to some of the sacred pueblo dwellings, and you'll find a small hole in the ground they call the *sipapu*, which represents the place where the Anasazi emerged. And that's about as much as we really know about where they came from. Anthropologists have been working for a long time to pin down their origins. That's what makes the stuff we've found here so exciting. It could mean that they were an offshoot of the Aztecs—maybe a group of outcasts—that drifted north from Mexico. Or it could mean that at least the Anasazi traded with the Aztecs."

Mike Cogan was one of those educators who had the ability to infuse a subject with interest by virtue of his own enthusiasm. Elsie was lucky to have such a man, Kai thought as she followed him to the edge of a couple of the shallow pits and watched his students brushing sand away practically grain by grain so as not to damage any of the fragile relics that might yet be unearthed.

They hadn't been at the excavation more than ten minutes before Casey began to whine.

"She wants to watch them shoot the movie," Elsie said as she joined Mike and Kai after putting Casey into the car.

"Oh, christ," Mike hissed hotly, the first crack in his shell of amiability. "I wish those goddamn Hollywood people would finish up and go back where they belong. You know their goons barged in on us again this morning? It's all we can do to keep them from tromping around the dig, stepping on all this stuff we work so hard to preserve."

Elsie turned to Kai. "Apparently Sylvie Teer is one of those temperamental types who never gets to work on time and disappears off the set. They've got a couple of guys who get paid just to keep an eye on her, but she always gives them the slip."

"Why do they think she'll come here?" Kai asked.

Mike lowered his voice, evidently concerned about being overheard by the nearby students. "The whole movie outfit came over for a look the first day they were here—just tourists, y'know—and she took a shine to Matt, one of my crew.'' As discreetly as possible, Mike directed Kai to look toward one of the shirtless young men cleaning fragments with a camel-hair brush. He was extremely handsome, Kai saw from this angle, with black hair, pale blue eyes, and a muscular build tanned by the sun. "Naturally, he was bowled over by the attention from this sexy movie star. She invited him over to her hotel and apparently spent the night with him—then cut him dead the next morning. He was pretty upset by it, not likely to want to see her again. But now her bodyguards—keepers, whatever they're called—check us out every time she's AWOL. They think if she doesn't go after Matt again, she'll hook up with one of the other guys. The woman's evidently sex crazed, a total nympho.''

"That's not the right way to talk about it, Mike," Elsie put in. "She's sweet and talented—and she's got a serious problem. It's really tragic.'' She turned to Kai. "There's a story around that she went into a downtown bar the other night, picked up a guy, and took him into the men's room. That gave a couple of other guys ideas, and it was the only bartender giving her people a quick call that kept her from getting gang raped.''

"Well, people love to spread rumors about movie stars," Kai remarked. "But I wouldn't take it as gospel.'' She didn't want to pop out with the fact that she had once been Sylvie's friend, yet she felt obliged to offer some defense.

"The story came from the girl who did my hair," Elsie said. "And she's married to the owner of the bar.''

Mike stared at his wife. "That does it," he said. "We shouldn't be letting Casey get anywhere near this whore.''

"C'mon, Mike," Elsie scoffed. "She's been so sweet. Last time she took Casey into her trailer, sat her down at one of those lighted mirrors, and had her hairdresser and makeup man do a whole big number—''

"No! No more. A slut like that, I don't want my daughter anywhere near her, being made up to look like her, none of it. If Casey wants to leave here then take her home. But I won't have her hanging around that woman anymore!''

Mike had worked himself up to such a fury that Elsie knew better than to protest. She kissed her husband on the cheek to signal her acquiescence and smooth over their rift.

"I'll see you at home later," he said, forcing an amiable tone back into his voice. "You, too, Kai. I'm glad you came out."

On the way back to the house, Elsie drove past the movie location. A long line of trucks and trailers was parked along the edge of the road, and beyond them in a landscape of magnificent cactuses, Kai could see a cluster of tall light poles, a camera crane, and a crowd of people. But the center of the action was too far away to discern if a scene was actually being shot, nor could she pick out anyone who looked like Sylvie.

Casey wailed as the car passed the movie location, but Elsie did not stop.

The next morning Kai left the house telling Elsie she wanted to look around town on her own. She spent an hour at the Plaza, the lovely tree-shaded square that had been the center of Santa Fe since the Spanish had colonized it four centuries ago. She bought coffee from a cart and sat on one of the benches near the Palace of the Governors, the adobe building that had been built by Spanish settlers a decade before the Pilgrims landed at Plymouth Rock.

Why not here? she thought. Santa Fe was a place where things seemed to have a reassuring permanence. What better place to stop her restless wandering and settle?

But it wasn't just sightseeing and exploring that was on her mind this morning. After finishing her coffee, she went to an automobile rental office, got a car, and drove to the movie location.

Overnight, she had done a lot of thinking about Sylvie. Waking suddenly in the darkness as if coming out of a bad dream, Kai had found herself reliving the argument that had blown up when she advised Sylvie to do something about her voracious sexual appetite. Looking back, Kai wished she had been more persistent and persuasive. The friendship had not failed, she thought now, as much because of Sylvie's rejection as her own timidity; she had not been sure enough of herself at the time to break through Sylvie's defenses and give her the support she had needed. And apparently needed still. From the stories Kai had heard, Sylvie was obviously out of control, flirting ever closer to self-destruction.

At the desert location, there were no security people guarding the perimeter. Kai waded through a milling throng of men moving lights and camera dollies, and stopped at random a burly man in a T-shirt stamped with the head of a roaring lion. "Can you tell me where to find Sylvie Teer?"

"Damned if I know, sweetie-pie," he answered and laughed gruffly. "Right now that's the sixty-four-thousand-dollar question around here."

He leered at her then, and Kai moved on quickly. Scanning the crowd, she saw a pleasant-looking young man holding a clipboard, a sign of some authority; he seemed to be acting as a traffic cop, holding quick, harried conferences with people who came up to him, pointing here and there to indicate their duties.

Kai went and stood nearby as he finished an exchange with an older man holding a black case somewhat like a doctor's bag. "How do I know when, George? Right now I hear the head office is talking about closing down completely. Just wait in her trailer, okay?"

The older man grumbled and walked away.

Kai stepped up to the man with the clipboard. "Hi," she said, "I'm a friend of Sylvie Teer's and—"

He seized her arm in a frantic grip as he interrupted. "You are? Do you know where she is?"

"No. I was going to ask you where to find her. And," she added, with a sharp glance at his hand, "that hurts."

He stared at Kai as though suddenly aware of her loveliness, and in the next instant he released his grip on her arm. "Jesus, I'm sorry. We're all going a little nuts at the moment. As usual, little Miss Sylvie is hours late coming on the set, and it looks like the studio is running out of patience—" He cut himself off. "You said you're her friend. And you don't have any idea where she might be?"

Kai shook her head. "Actually, I haven't seen her in years. We were friends once, and when I heard she was making this movie, I thought I'd visit her."

"Well, you should have picked a better day. Sylvie's done her famous vanishing act again, and this time it might be for good. The studio can't go on wasting money every time she's late." He glanced at his wristwatch. "If she doesn't show by noon and take a blood oath to toe the line from here on, production's shutting down."

"Then what happens to the movie?" Kai asked.

"Kaput. We've shot too much to start over with somebody else. The studio will shelve it, write it off . . . and your little friend's career will be dead."

It was as bad as she suspected, Kai thought. Preoccupied, she turned away, wondering how she might find Sylvie, what she could do to help her.

The young man stayed beside her. "Hey, I'm sorry if I hurt your arm," he apologized again.

"It's fine, don't worry."

Walking with her as she headed back toward her car, he asked her name and introduced himself as Dave Lauder, the first A.D., or assistant director. Kai could tell that he was leading up to asking her for a date, but she was too concerned with helping Sylvie to talk about anything else. From the answers Lauder supplied, Kai got a much more detailed picture of Sylvie's behavior and its consequences. Her lateness was almost always connected to going off with a strange man the night before. The problem hadn't started with this film, either. Sylvie had long ago earned a reputation for unreliability. The studios had been tolerant of it in the past because the problem had been far less severe and costly than at present; more important, her pictures had made a lot of money. But the last two had not done so well, so she was being given less rope.

"On top of which," Lauder said, "Century-Lion, the studio backing this picture, is up for sale, so they're making a special effort to get their act together and run the operation more efficiently. Sylvie's hijinks are really driving the studio up the wall because a big wheeler-dealer who's interested in a buy-out may be coming today to look over this part of the operation—you know, a typical film in progress. But if he takes this as an example of the way the studio does business, the deal is pretty likely to fall through. And there's about a billion dollars involved."

Having politely answered all her questions, Dave Lauder did ask her how long she'd be in Santa Fe and if she might like to have dinner with him.

She smiled at the invitation. "How old are you, Dave?" she said.

"Twenty-six."

She thought about it, then shook her head. "Thanks for the offer, though."

"No sweat. I'll always be one of your fans, anyway."

Fans? Then it hit her. She let out a throaty laugh. "You recognized me," she said.

He grinned and nodded. A few months ago, before she'd returned to the country, *Tomcat* had published its thirtieth anniversary issue—featuring reprints of the "Ten Favorite Kitties of All Time"—and she'd been one of them. Since the magazine had come out before she returned from abroad, she hadn't even known about it until Phil Donahue brought the reprints out while she'd been on his program, in front of the cameras.

One of the film crew rushed up and asked Lauder whether it was true the production was being canceled. He said goodbye to Kai and excused himself to deal with the tide of rumors sweeping the location.

Walking back to her car, Kai wondered what she could possibly to do help Sylvie. Could she find her? Bring her here? Perhaps the chance to help had been lost years ago.

As she reached the car, she saw a long silver stretch-model limousine gliding up the road toward the location. She stood watching, thinking it must be Sylvie arriving at last. A fresh chance, after all.

But when the limousine pulled over, two men in sunglasses got out of the rear compartment. They stood talking, one with his back to her. From their sleek look, their expensive car and clothes, and the expansive, proprietary air with which they surveyed the area, Kai suspected that one of them must be the potential buyer for Century-Lion pictures who was expected to put in an appearance.

And then, as the taller and more distinguished of the two men turned and headed toward the center of activity, Kai got a good look at his face.

The man was Jim Bolton.

Chapter Thirty-two

The war of conflicting impulses seemed to last for an eternity. Get in the car and drive away, or put herself in his path and see if he remembered. Had it been nine years since their last meeting? In all of eighteen years they had spent only three *days* together! How much meaning and value could there be to any of the pretty words they'd last exchanged? He'd left . . . and they had gone on with their separate lives. Did it make sense to strike up that old acquaintance—was that why fate kept putting them in each other's way?

She thought then of what he had become. Another money-hungry deal maker like Mitch Karel, here on the hunt for his latest killing. What if they had another day or two together, followed by another disappearance as he went off to close the next big deal? She reached for the handle of the car door.

Perhaps fate wouldn't let her go. At that moment Jim's glance came around in her direction. Across the distance between them their eyes locked. A visible change came over his body, almost the look of someone who had been engaged in a strenuous search for something and had just found it. Kai moved out from behind the car and he came toward her, walking slowly, even carefully, as a desert traveler might approach a mirage. The gap closed to a few yards, and they stopped, leaving a zone of caution between them. He spoke the first words:

"Where were you going?"

"Going?" She didn't comprehend, the context lost in memories of another time. He was the one who had gone away.

He glanced toward the car. "You were about to leave."

He must have guessed she'd wanted to flee from an encounter. Flustered, she said, "Oh, I—I'm staying with friends in Santa Fe. They might be expecting me back."

He moved nearer. He looked little older than when she'd seen him last, a few more lines around the eyes, but they only made him more attractive, his hair showing the faintest wisps of gray at the temples. Dressed in silver-gray slacks and a black blazer with a white shirt and silvery tie, he conveyed a very different air than the casual ex-sailor in a sheepskin jacket who had once taken her to a burger joint. An aura of absolute power surrounded him, more than the mere confidence of a one-time military commander. James Bolton was used to having things his way on every kind of battleground.

Yet he spoke to her as a supplicant, not a superior officer. "Don't leave, Kai. Please. I have to spend just a little while here, then I'll be free. Will you have lunch with me?"

Why had he disappeared after Chicago? She wanted to know. "I'll wait," she said. What was half an hour? Seeing him, she realized that she had already been waiting years.

Jim took the wheel of her rental car, having dismissed his luxurious limousine along with the corporate lawyer who had been accompanying him. While they drove, they avoided the minefield of old emotions that might explode into re-crimination and regret, and simply brought each other up to date. Most of the time Kai was kept busy answering his questions. She recounted that she had left her full-time involvement with the project in Baltimore, then had contributed to the recently published book through the notes collected during her travels. She explained, too, how and why she had come to be on the movie location this morning.

"And what were you doing there?" she asked then.

"I thought you knew. It's a business opportunity—and, as you might remember, I don't buy into any business without looking over the operation at close range."

"I meant," she said, "how do you get from owning airlines to buying movie studios? They're such different businesses."

"I never did buy that airline," Jim told her. "I got out-maneuvered." He glanced at her. "But I thought you knew."

"Why would I? I never followed your adventures in the business news."

Jim was silent, as though he thought it better to drop the subject. Studying him, Kai saw his expression set in a puzzled frown. Curious about what was going through his mind, she might have coaxed out an answer, but just then they turned off the road and arrived at the Bishop's Lodge, a luxurious inn located at the foot of the Sangre de Cristo Mountains. Surrounded by a thousand private acres, a quiet resort of beautiful gardens and orchards of fruit trees, its nucleus had once been the retreat of a Catholic bishop who had overseen the missions of Santa Fe a hundred years ago.

A measure of Jim's importance was immediately apparent in the way the personnel at the lodge deferred to him, from the boy who took the car, to the captain of the dining room, who led them to a table by a window looking out at the mountains. Observing this mirror of the wealth and power he had accumulated, she was reminded of the story Mitch had once told about Jim's father, the dishonest dealings that had ruined him and put him in jail. Was it a hunger to erase the stigma of his father's crime that drove Jim, made him want to accumulate so much wealth that he could never be broken and humbled? Or was it simply in the blood?

When they were seated, sipping white wine and waiting for their food, she brought him back to the subject of his business. "You were telling me how you got from airlines to movies," she said.

"Don't we have more interesting things to talk about?"

"Are there things that interest you more than how you make your money?"

The edge in her remark was unmistakable. He gave her a sidelong glance, but then he shrugged it off. "Okay," he replied, "If that's what you want to hear. After the Mid-Coast deal fell through, the investment group I'd assembled were left with sixty million bucks they still wanted to put to work. No more airlines were available in our price range at the time, so they asked me to look at other opportunities. The best thing I found involved a different way of sending stuff through the air—radio stations. Bought a group of five out in the Midwest. They hadn't been doing well, but we turned them around, made them very profitable, and picked up several more. Once I was into communications, I expanded to cable-television franchises. It was a risk in those days, but cable's turned out to be the biggest earner. The problem has been providing enough product, filling all those hours with something for my customers to look at. That's the link to movies. If I buy an established studio like Century-Lion, part of the package will be their whole catalogue of old films, almost two thousand. That'll fill up a lot of airtime. Makes it very valuable to me.''

''So I hear. The price is supposedly more than a billion dollars. It's hard to think of one man having that kind of money.''

''It's not my money, Kai. It's banks who want to lend it to me. I pay them to use it.''

She hoisted her wineglass as if in a toast. ''Well, you've certainly done well for yourself, Mr. Bolton.''

''Why do I get the feeling you are distinctly not impressed?''

She paused, weighing how honest to be. ''The last time we met, Jim, I got the feeling you cared about more than just piling up wealth. I liked that about you, frankly. And . . . I guess I wonder if it can still be true.''

''What makes you think it isn't?''

''You have so damn much money. How can you have time for anything else?''

He didn't seem to know what to say. He reached out and covered her hand with his.

His touch was electric. It brought back all the feelings she'd had in that hotel room in Chicago. But why had he left without a word? She slid her hand out from beneath his.

''You're not married?'' she blurted out.

He shook his head. ''Guess I've been too busy getting rich to meet the kind of woman who'd love me even if I wasn't.'' Now he was the one putting a little edge in his words.

Kai regretted her candor now. ''I'm sorry if you were offended by what I said.''

''About my wealth? I'm not offended, Kai. If I'm touchy, it's because it's hard to hear you criticize me for something you accepted so easily about others.''

''Others?'' she echoed. ''Who?''

''Mitch Karel.''

"Mitch," she murmured, puzzled that he had dragged him into their conversation.

"If there's anyone who puts making money ahead of everything else," Jim said, "it's Mitch Karel."

"I didn't find it attractive in him, either."

"That didn't stop you from having an affair, did it? Or from giving him information that cost me that airline deal."

Stunned by the charge, Kai rocked back in her chair, her mouth agape.

"Not that I should really complain," Jim went on. "Airlines have been a lot less profitable than my radio stations and cable franchises. So maybe you and Mr. Karel did me a favor—"

"Wait a second!" she erupted. "What's all this about an affair, and giving him information? Where the hell did you get ideas like that?"

"Where else, Kai?"

"Mitch," she expelled the name again.

"When he bought Mid-Coast out from under me that weekend I met you, I was caught off guard. I was very curious about what had made him push the deal through that quickly, so I called him and confronted him on it right away. I thought I'd kept such a tight lid on the fact that I was definitely planning a bid."

"I never said you were," Kai protested. "I was very careful about that."

"Not careful enough. He told me the two of you were very close, that you'd been together and you'd tipped him off. He certainly had to know something to start the wheels in motion on a Sunday afternoon."

Sunday. She remembered they'd seen each other on a Sunday—the one day that the club where he'd brought her admitted women. So Mitch had gone directly from being with her to activate a deal. "All I told him," she said, "was that I'd met you on the plane, and you'd saved my life. It came out when he asked about the man who'd answered the phone in my hotel room."

Jim looked away, his eyes narrowing pensively. "Jesus," he whispered to himself, "the clever son of a bitch." He turned to Kai again. "Must've figured the only reason I was flying that Mid-Coast route would be to check out the operation before a bid."

"But you thought I'd betrayed your confidence."

"Oh god, Kai, I . . ." His voice failed.

After a moment she said, "He lied, too, if he said I'd ever gone to bed with him."

Jim shook his head and stared down at the tablecloth. "To be perfectly honest, I can't remember if he did or not. Maybe I just put it together that way because I . . . well, I wasn't thinking straight about anything after I thought you'd sold me out."

They both fell silent, overwhelmed by the loss of what might have been.

The waiter came and slipped the spicy Mexican chicken salads they had ordered in front of them. The food sat untouched. Neither one had any appetite.

At last, staring down into her lap, Kai said quietly, "I always wondered. I was so sure that there was something stronger between us."

Hoarsely he murmured his own confusion. "I felt so let down when I thought you'd helped him."

"So you just backed away." Her anger was rising now. "Why didn't you call *me* instead of him? Damn the torpedoes, full speed ahead—isn't that what you navy men say? How could you let him sink *us* so goddamn easily?"

"Being an officer and a gentleman again," he said wryly. "I thought you were spoken for."

For another moment the fury held its grip on her. At him for his mistrust. At Mitch for his deceit. But then she wondered if it was fair to blame them any more than herself. Could she just as easily blame herself for a failure of belief? She had made her own assumptions and waited all these years to call Jim to account.

And he was here, now, and with him came all the emotions that had lain dormant since then. Unless she let go of her anger, Kai realized, she would only compound her losses.

"Didn't business teach you," she asked, "that it doesn't always pay to be such a gentleman?"

He smiled, perceiving the lighter mood behind her question. "I guess it has. But you weren't business."

"All the same, maybe I wouldn't have minded a takeover."

"I'd rather try for a friendly merger." He took her hand

again, and this time she didn't pull away. "You hungry at all?" he asked then.

She gazed at him directly. "Not for food."

No more needed to be said. They had lost so much time already.

He signed the bill and led her out of the dining room and across a garden to the private bungalow he had taken for his stay.

As soon as they walked out of the bright sun into the cool interior, he pulled her into his arms—only to be interrupted by the jangling ring of a telephone. He broke from her reluctantly and crossed the large central living room of the bungalow to a desk. Grabbing up the phone, he barked a hello, then shot back a couple of quick replies. "Yes . . . yes . . . fine. See you in New York." The call ended. "One of my lawyers," he said to Kai as he punched a button on the phone to reach the hotel switchboard. "Hold all my calls," he said abruptly.

"Sorry." He grinned. "Won't happen again."

For one more moment they held back from each other, while the silent debate of hearts and minds determined whether they meant to proceed. Then his lips came down onto hers.

In the first instant of the kiss, she damned him again—damned herself—for all the lost years. Then every last doubt, every thought, was swept away by the flood of sensations.

Devouring each other with kisses, they reeled across the living room of the bungalow, leaving a trail of clothes. As soon as they were both naked, he picked her up and carried her into the bedroom. He set her down on the bed gently, as if laying her on an altar, then knelt before her and worshiped her body with fiery kisses. She writhed with pleasure at the touch of his lips on her neck and shoulders, her breasts, her stomach and thighs, while his strong hands slipped down her back, then slid sensuously beneath her, down the smooth, tender skin of her long legs, gently parting her at last so he could taste her.

Her breath quickened as an exquisite rush of pleasure spread from her core, shooting electric waves to the tips of her limbs. She moaned with pleasure. Panting rapidly, she could hardly summon her voice to say how much she wanted him inside her.

"Jim," she whispered, "Jim . . . now . . . come to me. . . ."

He raised himself over her, and she felt him plunge down inside, channeling himself to her depths and bringing a sense of completeness she had never felt before. There had been physical satisfaction with Paul, but ecstasy? Never. She wrapped her arms around his back, and held on as their rhythm quickened to a frenzy of pounding impact that went on and on until at last they came together with a shattering totality.

"Never," she said quietly, when her voice returned, "it's never been like that."

"I think I knew," he said, "the first time I saw you. . . ."

As they lay side by side, Kai mused on the irony of the years they had been kept apart by gallantry and misunderstanding. What if he had taken her when she was only seventeen? Would she have become the accomplished, traveled, independent woman she was? Yet what was her claim to fame? Her research into the means of achieving sexual satisfaction. And here it was, delivered complete without any need for scientific understanding. All the answers came down to connecting with the right man. What a glorious comedy life was.

Her belief in Jim was not totally unalloyed by uncertainty. A vague nexus of doubt still hovered in her mind. But whatever its source, it receded as his hands gripped her, and her desire for him began to build again.

They made love through most of the afternoon. Finally, as the sun lowered and slanted down through the drawn blinds of the bungalow, Jim rose from the bed. "I have to make some calls," he said, "before business shuts down everywhere."

He showered quickly and threw on fresh slacks and a pullover, then went into an adjoining room. Still lying in bed, Kai could hear him making one call after another. His voice changed as he managed his business, the tone becoming harder, the words more clipped. At one point she heard him loudly expressing dissatisfaction with someone on the other end of the line: "If you can't do better than that, maybe someone else will have to take over!"

She realized then why his wealth was the thing that might

keep them apart. It was a wealthy man who had victimized her mother, who had thought that a woman was nothing more than another possession among all the other things his money could buy. She argued with herself, told herself that Jim was a very different kind of man than Harley Trane. It was absurd to lump them together.

And yet what did make commerce more important to a man than teaching, or healing, or creating? Could she love such a man? Or, if she loved him already, could she trust such a love to last?

She had showered and dressed by the time he came back from the adjoining room. "What are you going to do about Century-Lion?" she asked at once. "Are you buying it?"

He looked at her askance. "If that's the biggest thing on your mind after the way we've spent the afternoon together, we could be in big trouble."

"You were the one who left me in bed to take care of business."

"Touché," he said with a bemused smile. "Mind telling me why you're asking?"

"After I have your answer. And don't worry," she added, "I'm not passing information to your rivals."

"Hey, that's a low blow. I won't ever suspect you again."

"I'm sorry."

He held his arms out, and she went into them, and they kissed. The heat began to rise almost instantly. She pushed him away, needing her question answered, a way of dispelling her doubts. "Tell me," she said.

"I like the deal. I'll be going ahead. Now, why does that interest you so much?"

"Someone at the movie location told me you might be scared off the deal if you didn't like what you saw there today."

"I wouldn't have been happy if I saw them pissing money away," Jim confirmed.

"But you were reassured. Because they shut down the film to convince you the company isn't being badly managed."

He nodded slowly. "What's this about, Kai?"

"I told you Sylvie Teer used to be a good friend of mine back in Chicago, that I went to the location hoping to renew the acquaintance."

"And you couldn't, because she wasn't there. Do you know the film's being scrubbed because she's been late on the set since day one—has raised the budget by more than a million so far?"

"I know," Kai said, then paused. Jim kept looking at her, intently curious. "I was wondering if you could keep that film from shutting down for another day or two. Give me a chance to find Sylvie, and see if I can get her back on track."

He went on studying her curiously. "That's quite a request, considering you haven't seen her for sixteen years. It could be a disaster for the company."

"It's not just for her," Kai interjected. "It's for *me*. Because I need to find out—before you and I go any further—if you ever put the problems of people ahead of dollars and cents."

He frowned slightly, then turned away and walked thoughtfully out to the bungalow's main room. When Kai followed, he was standing by a desk, flipping through some papers in his hand. "It costs more than forty thousand dollars," he said, "for every hour that crew stands there, waiting for Miss Teer."

"What's a life worth, Jim? If she blows this, she'll probably never work again."

He tossed the papers down. "Damn it, Kai," he said as he began to pace the room. "Why in hell do you have to mix up love and business? I don't even have the authority to make a decision like this, not until after a lot of paper has changed hands. Even then I need the loyalty of the executives who will stay in charge—experienced men who'll question my judgment if I overrule them to make a dumb decision."

She wasn't deterred. "You may not have the authority, Jim, but you have the influence. And you won't look dumb if Sylvie starts to behave, and the picture gets finished and makes money."

He paced several more times across the floor, then grabbed up a phone from the desk and punched a series of buttons to make a long-distance call. When the connection was made, Jim announced that he intended to proceed with his buy-out of Century-Lion. "But I don't want the Sylvie Teer picture shut down, not yet."

Even from across the room, Kai could hear the voice at the other end of the line burst into an argumentative squawk. But Jim cut through it with his clear, commanding tone. "I'm buying the company," he said, "and that's what I want."

He hung up and looked at her. "One extra day. That's all."

But whether or not Kai succeeded, he revealed then, he wouldn't be around to see. Getting his bank financing required him to be in New York early tomorrow morning; he would fly there this evening. After spending a couple of days in the city with lawyers who would hammer out the final papers for purchasing the film studio, he would be flying off to Europe. He was expanding his cable network into satellite operations, and there were partners in France and West Germany who needed to be consulted.

As if he had read her thoughts, he said, "Of course, you could come along. I'd love to have you with me."

"But first I have to help Sylvie," she pointed out.

He came and took her in his arms once more. "It won't always be like this, darling. Now that I've found you again, I'll start planning things differently. So we can be together."

He would be gone for three weeks, he said, but then he'd be flying back to California.

"More movie business?" she asked.

"No. I'm going to San Diego, not Hollywood. And there won't be any business, just pure play. You know the America's Cup?"

She nodded, thinking to herself how little she knew about this man she was ready to spend the rest of her life with. "The boat I'm sponsoring will be having its first sea trials in San Diego in three weeks. Will you come and meet me there?"

As entranced as she was by Jim Bolton, Kai had to battle against a lingering fear of constant disappointments. She didn't want to be hopscotching around the world, clinging to him while he lived his high-voltage life; she was looking to belong somewhere, belong with someone—who would stay.

Yet he said it wouldn't always be like this. Maybe next time . . .

"I'll be there," she said.

* * *

As Kai drove up to the film location, she saw very little activity. The large crew that had thronged the area this morning was gone. The camera cranes and huge lights still stood around, but no one was attending them, and there seemed to be fewer trucks and trailers parked along the edge of the road. Was the production being dismantled, after all? Jim had sworn he would make sure the production was reinstated. But perhaps his influence wasn't enough to change policy.

She scolded herself. How could she doubt him? She could still feel the glow of the afternoon, and their farewell kiss when he had left for his flight to New York.

Among the few people still circulating around the location, Kai found Dave Lauder.

"Hey," he greeted her energetically, "you came back! Had second thoughts about our date?"

She smiled and passed over it. "I thought Miss Teer might have turned up at last."

"Yeah, she did. She's in her trailer." He pointed to a long bus-like vehicle.

"But you stopped production, anyway?"

"She came too late," Lauder said. "By the time she got here, we'd already heard from the head office that production was closing down. Knocked Sylvie on her ass, all right, she never thought they'd do it. She went inside to collapse, cry it out. Damnedest thing, though. Just ten minutes ago, a new order came through from California. They're giving Sylvie one more chance."

Bless him, Kai thought.

Lauder chuckled snidely. "Don't know why they bothered, though. For her it's just one more chance to fuck things up."

"She might surprise you," Kai tossed over her shoulder as she strode toward Sylvie's trailer.

A row of four windows ran along the side of the long vehicle with a central door that could be approached by several fold-down metal steps. Kai saw that curtains had been drawn across all the windows. She stood outside the door for a moment before she knocked softly. There was no answer. Gingerly she tried the door handle. It was locked.

She knocked harder.

"Get the fuck outta here!" a voice came back.

"Sylvie?" Kai called. "It's Kai Wyler." Curiosity alone, she thought, should get a more receptive response. But nothing happened. "Don't you remember me, Syl?"

"Sure, I remember."

"Well, open the door."

"Why?"

Kai almost laughed. "For old time's sake. It's been sixteen years, Syl. C'mon, open up. I want to see you."

"Then buy a ticket to the movies."

"I would," Kai said after a moment, "but it may be hard to see one of yours—unless it's a revival."

She was answered by silence. The door stayed closed. Kai wavered between persistence and surrender. What hope was there of helping Sylvie if she had become so emotionally cold? But then Kai raised her fist to knock again, unwilling to give up so easily.

Before her knuckles connected, the trailer door swung open. Sylvie looked out, wrapped in a black silk kimono. Her large blue eyes were bloodshot and bleary, her short blond hair was wildly tousled. She still looked like a kewpie doll, but one that had been lying for too long in an attic corner.

"What are you doing here?" she said.

"Hey, is that any way to say hello?" Kai was determined not to be put off by Sylvie's attitude. "I'm here because you are—because I remember how much we meant to each other once. And," she added at last, "because you need a friend."

Sylvie gazed at her dubiously for another moment, then turned away from the door. Kai took it for an invitation to enter. She climbed the steps into the trailer. Inside, it was furnished as a comfortable dressing room. A large couch, a lighted makeup table, a couple of soft chairs, and racks of clothes. Sylvie had moved to the far end of the room. She spun around to confront Kai.

"Shit, Kai," she said, "what did you expect I'd do? Throw my arms around you and say how wonderful it is to see you? Christ, don't you realize it hurts? It just hurts to go back and think about . . ." She shook her head and turned away.

Kai went toward her. "Me, too. I wish we hadn't argued. That we hadn't lost touch—"

Sylvie wheeled on her again. "Hell, that's not what bothers me. I just don't want to think about when I was young, when everything was ahead of me instead of behind, when life was all hope, the excitement of the unknown. . . ."

"Everything's not behind you, Syl. And there's still plenty of hope."

Sylvie made a sour face. "I can't do it, Kai," she declared. "Go back and tell them I can't!"

"Tell who?"

"The studio execs. They paid you to come here and get me straightened out, didn't they?"

"No," Kai objected, surprised by Sylvie's paranoia. "I was visiting friends in Santa Fe, and I heard about the movie."

Sylvie peered at her suspiciously. "You're not getting paid for this? Scout's honor?"

"Cross my heart."

Sylvie walked to the dressing table, pushed aside a couple of scripts, and picked up the thick book lying open underneath. As Sylvie came over to her, Kai saw that the book was *Human Sexual Interaction*. "You did the research for this thing, right? I saw you with Johnny Carson, talking about it . . . ?"

Kai nodded.

"The big sex expert," Sylvie said. "I know that's why you turned up here."

Kai shook her head.

Sylvie tossed the book aside onto the couch. "See, it wasn't a total surprise when you knocked on my door. Dave, the A.D., he told me you'd been around asking for me. Right off, I thought you must've been hired as some kinda consultant to get me under control. Hell, I know all about your work, Kai. That goddamn book is everywhere—went out and bought a copy as soon as I heard about it. Don't you think I'd like to—to find a way to be . . . satisfied?" Sylvie's angry tone took on an edge of hysteria. "I know what's at stake, Kai. But I can't change!"

"You can," Kai said forcefully. "I can help you."

"Why would you?"

Kai smiled. "Got nothing better to do at the moment."

For the first time Sylvie smiled, too. Then she crossed the gap between them and looked closely into Kai's face. "Jesus, you're still gorgeous," she said. "If I looked like you, I wouldn't be worried. Of course, I am an old bag of thirty-nine, my days are numbered." In the next moment her arms went around Kai, and she hugged her and began to sob hysterically. "Oh, jesus, Kai, things are so bad . . . I'm so screwed up."

Kai held her consolingly. "I'll help you," she repeated.

Sylvie's sobs gradually subsided. Abruptly she pulled back to study Kai again. "You still a virgin?" she asked.

Kai laughed. "Not for a while."

"Then maybe," Sylvie said, "there's hope after all."

Chapter Thirty-three

Those few hours when Sylvie had thought the movie was canceled had filled her with greater terror than she had ever known. Once the film companies wrote her off as a bad investment, Sylvie knew she'd be unemployable. And that wasn't all. The studio would surely sue for millions—to recoup the salary she'd been paid and other costs—claiming she was solely responsible for all losses. It would be a claim hard to fight. For years she'd been recklessly testing the limits. It didn't matter how often she was warned by her agents and managers that the day of reckoning would come. Didn't matter how often she told herself it was time to act responsibly. The damn problem was she just couldn't help herself. For her, the craving for sex was no different than the craving for food so common in others. She went hunting for a man as casually as a binge-eater went to the refrigerator for a snack, or an alcoholic lapped up whiskey. It was her only pleasure, her reward for all the crap she had taken early in her life . . . and her way of temporarily forgetting that no matter how many men she'd had, she was still alone.

Not that she blamed anyone but herself for being alone. Why stay with one man? She needed something new all the time.

Year by year, though, the craving had become more intense, more uncontrollable. She gave herself whatever excuse she needed in order to satisfy it. As long as there was a man who wanted to make love to her, then there would always be an audience who loved her, too.

But the bankers didn't love her, or the executives who had to account for their decisions. So they had pulled the plug.

Or so it had seemed, until the word came through that she could have one more chance. One more day. And as long as she showed up on time, and did her work like a pro, and did the same thing the next day, and the day after that, she could go on working. But if she slipped once more, they'd drop her once and for all, no reprieve. That would be the end, the death of her career.

The terror Sylvie felt at losing everything had finally made her receptive to help. Though she had been angry and defensive when she believed Kai was hired by the studio bosses, those feelings disappeared as soon as Sylvie accepted that Kai's interest was personal, born out of sincere affection.

"Just tell me what to do," Sylvie said when they finally sat down together in the trailer that first afternoon. "Tell me, and I'll do it."

"To start with, you've got to give up sex."

"Anything but that," Sylvie shot back, half serious despite her comic delivery.

"Look, that isn't the whole problem," Kai explained. "It's only a symptom. In fact, there's nothing wrong with liking sex—or loving it. But what you're doing, Syl, doesn't really have much to do with how you feel about sex. It's a way of saying how you feel about *yourself*. If you cared about yourself—if you believed a man could care about you—you wouldn't keep repeating this pattern."

"Pattern is a pretty fancy word for it," Sylvie said. "It doesn't feel like anything more than getting screwed."

"Oh, it's a lot more complicated than that. What you're doing each time, I think, is looking for something that's missing in yourself. You're expecting these men to make you complete somehow . . . and each time I think you're hoping for true love."

"Geez, Kai, you wouldn't say that if you saw some of the men I picked up."

"Oh yes, I would," Kai said, deliberately ignoring Sylvie's flippancy. "You're looking for love—but simultaneously looking to convince yourself that it's going to be a disappointment, and not really worth looking for. Jumping from man to man, even picking some completely unlovable types—gives you the chance to hope and fail all at the same time."

"Wow, Kai. How do you figure these things out?"

"You're not the first woman who ever had the problem. And there is a way out of it. If you can believe you're worth loving, you'd give one man a chance to know you, stay with you. Until then you've got to go on the wagon.''

For the next five days, Kai stayed with Sylvie, giving her friendship and moral support while the production moved to various locations around Santa Fe. She explained the situation to Elsie and Mike, and moved out of their guest room to stay at Sylvie's hotel; she had her meals with Sylvie and kept her company on the set.

''Why are you doing this for me?'' Sylvie asked.

''I've often thought about years ago, not helping you then. But I didn't have the knowledge, and you didn't have the will. Now that we're both in a position to do something, I don't want to let the chance go by.''

Sylvie kept asking, though. At last Kai closed the issue by saying simply, ''Because we're friends.''

The discipline she ordered for Sylvie involved more than sexual abstinence. Kai also advised meditation for two or three short periods during the day, and taught Sylvie the techniques. Desensitized by the years of rough handling she had endured, Sylvie had admitted to Kai that she was now incapable of being satisfied. Meditation, Kai said, was a way of putting her in touch with her body again, and making the connection with her mind and heart.

The combination of Sylvie's internal terror, and the regimen imposed on her, showed immediate results. She arrived first on the set every morning. Lines always memorized. No complaints about tedious retakes, which was especially appreciated under the circumstances. The story of the film revolved around a dancer in Las Vegas who breaks the bank at a casino with a system given to her by a timid computer scientist; the couple gets chased cross-country by various gamblers, mobsters, and government agents trying to steal the money or the system. The final scene Sylvie had to shoot before the location work was finished called for her to climb a tall prickly cactus to escape a hit man. The prop men had removed a majority of the large cactus thorns, but the humorous scene required Sylvie to get snagged in the derriere, so some thorns had to be left. She wound up scratched and bleeding, but she never objected to the director's call for one more take. When the sequence was finished, the crew gave her an ovation.

''How about that?'' Sylvie said to Kai as crew members

smiled and gave her high-fives as she walked back to her trailer. "Suddenly I'm the sweetheart of Sigma Chi."

"If you hadn't worked so hard to piss them off," Kai said, "they'd have loved you from the start. Fact is, Syl, you *are* lovable."

"Yeah, yeah. What I really am is a meal ticket, and a warm place to park their dicks." She stopped and turned to Kai. "But now that we've wrapped it up here, maybe I'll give one of 'em a bonus. Don't you think one night out of five—?"

"You're headed back to the studio for another six weeks of shooting," Kai cut in. "I won't let you throw away the gains you've made."

"But I'm horny as hell, Kai! I've got to have a man." Sylvie rolled her eyes theatrically, but Kai caught the edge of real desperation underneath the playacting.

Sylvie had made a similar plea almost every night, and Kai's response was unvarying. The kind of sexual stimulation Sylvie was looking for, she might as well give to herself. She would probably be satisfied as long as she knew how to touch herself.

"For chrissakes," Sylvie complained, "a finger isn't exactly the same thing."

"Right. But if you learn to be a little nicer to yourself, then you might understand what you need from a guy to be happy." Learning how to be sensitive to her own needs, Kai said, discovering what she enjoyed and the time she required to reach orgasm, was an essential step to restoring satisfaction. When she knew how to give herself pleasure, Kai told Sylvie, then she would learn to expect it, and she would be able to accept it from a man.

As a limousine took them back to the hotel after they had done the final location work, Sylvie said, "You're gonna love being out at my beach house, Kai. It's—"

"Slow down," Kai broke in. "I'm staying here. I hardly got a chance to visit with Elsie and my goddaughter, and—"

Sylvie's enormous blue eyes were instantly ablaze with panic. "Jesus, Kai, I'll never be able to keep this up unless you're with me."

"But, Syl, I have to make a living, too."

"For godssake, if it's money you want, that's no problem."

"I can't let you pay for friendship."

"So you're going to drop me cold instead? Shit, kiddo, losing this gig would've cost me gazillions, and I was gonna blow it for sure. Without you, I couldn't have lasted even these five days—and it's a sure thing I'll crash if you're a thousand miles away."

The measure of Sylvie's gratitude was that it came even without knowing the whole truth. Kai had never revealed that the production was saved because she had persuaded Jim Bolton to intervene. Since the task was to build Sylvie's self-esteem, Kai saw no reason to revise the idea that the movie company had independently deemed her worthy of one more chance.

"Please, Kai, I'm beggin' you," Sylvie said. "You'll be paid—no argument about that. This is supposed to be your occupation, isn't it? Doing sex-repair jobs?"

Kai laughed. "I never thought of it quite that way, but I suppose it is."

She couldn't ignore, either, that Sylvie might indeed backslide if she didn't have constant support. On top of which, she had agreed to meet Jim in San Diego in two weeks.

Making a snap decision, she promised Elsie she'd visit again and left for Los Angeles that night with Sylvie. Despite her protestations that she didn't want to be paid, Sylvie continued to insist, and Kai agreed to keep whatever amount Sylvie thought appropriate.

Sylvie lived in a modern beach house in Malibu, a cube of white concrete, glass, and chrome perched on a bluff over the Pacific. No sooner did they arrive that evening than Kai knew it was fortunate she had come. They were met at the door by a handsome young man dressed in a white tunic who greeted Sylvie in Spanish and took possession of their baggage. Before he carried the bags upstairs to unpack them in the bedrooms, Sylvie introduced him as Pancho, her Mexican house boy. With smooth coffee skin, jet black hair, and beautiful onyx eyes, all strikingly set off by his white tunic, the young man was irresistible. Though he was properly circumspect in the presence of Kai, she detected the charged air that flowed between him and Sylvie.

"He's got to go," Kai said when Sylvie led her outside onto a rear deck to show her the view of the ocean.

"Oh no!" Sylvie wailed. "He's a treasure. Gets my white things whiter than anybody. Irons like a dream. And he gives the best goddamn head I've ever—"

"Pay him off tonight," Kai commanded. "It won't work otherwise. Do you want to get straightened out or not?"

Sylvie took a deep breath, then disappeared into the house for a couple of minutes.

"I hope you're happy," she pouted when she came back. "Cost me five thousand bucks in guilt money."

"As you said yourself, you'll earn it a hundred times over by saving your career."

Within the next week, Sylvie stopped her constant complaining about the restraints Kai had placed upon her, and began to crow about how well she felt, to extol the virtues of her healthier lifestyle. In the evenings, after a day of shooting, she didn't pace around restlessly like a caged animal. Rather than having to be coaxed into the long runs along the beach that Kai prescribed for exercise, she began to enjoy them. She ate healthy food, laid off the alcohol, and went to bed early.

"I think I get it," she said one evening when as they jogged along the sand at sunset. "Sex is just another form of exercise. You don't miss it much if you've got another way of working out."

Kai laughed. "That may be a slight oversimplification. You don't miss it right now because you're starting to like yourself better, and because you're enjoying your work more."

That was the biggest change in Sylvie. She had rediscovered the pleasure in her work that she had known at the beginning of her film career. She no longer moaned about the way she was treated on the set, the hostility of the director, the incompetence of the producer and crew members. Now that their star was behaving responsibly, they were eager to extend their friendship and even went out of their way for her.

For the first few days in California, Kai went with Sylvie to the studio and watched her work as she had in New Mexico. But the making of movies was a tedious process, tiresome to watch, and as Sylvie settled into her routine, Kai became restless. She went to the Getty Museum, took a long drive up the coast to Big Sur, strolled around Rodeo Drive one afternoon. But she began to feel at loose ends, just waiting for Jim's arrival. It was a glimpse of what her life would be like if she didn't find work of her own.

She had received several phone calls from Jim since their parting. Whenever he said he loved her and wanted to spend the rest of his life with her, she longed to be with him, always. But each call had to end, and when he phoned the next time it was usually from a different place. She imagined that he would always be moving around the world, busy increasing his empire; there would always be long-distance phone calls and lonely absences. She was especially shaken when Jim called from Europe and said he would have to delay their rendezvous in San Diego an extra week because he was going to Australia to tie up a deal to extend his satellite news network.

The delay underscored Kai's decision to go forward with her own life. As soon as Sylvie was finished with the film, Kai thought, she ought to head back to Santa Fe and secure a teaching position.

Near the end of the second week in California, another idea took shape. It began during her regular evening jog along the beach with Sylvie. On each run they went farther than the last one, and this time they had gone almost three miles, passing rows of beach houses they had not seen before. As usual, Sylvie pointed out those that belonged to other celebrities and included any current gossip about them. This evening they jogged past the house of an actor whose police action film was currently the biggest moneymaker in the theaters.

"I went out with him a few years ago, right after his fourth wife left him," Sylvie said nonchalantly. "He was a flop in bed. Couldn't get it up then, probably still can't. You think I got problems? This guy gets his only kicks these days with hookers. Hires 'em by the handful, and likes to put 'em in a circle, then take a golden shower—let them piss on him."

At last, as they slowed down to catch their breath, Sylvie said, "You know, Kai, so many people out here are incredibly fucked up. You'd be real busy if you wanted to help them the way you've helped me."

Kai thought about it overnight. If motivated only by professional obligation and not the friendship she had with Sylvie, would she be able to produce the same results?

As she considered what she would bring to a full-time
practice of treating people with unhealthy sex lives, Kai
realized that the urge to succeed would always stem from
something deeper and more powerful than simply doing a
job. In one way or another, every path she had taken in her
life was part of a continuing need to understand the com-
pulsions that had driven and destroyed her mother, to forgive herself for not having known how to save her, and to
make sure she didn't fall prey to the same destructive impulses. There would always be an energy and dedication
behind her work that could benefit others.

The next day Kai called a real estate agent. When she
said she wanted an office suitable for the practice of psychotherapy, she was shown a series of large spaces in
gleaming new buildings, all with rents from $5,000 a month
up to four times that much. "I can't afford these," she explained to the agent, a chic woman in her fifties.

"You're a psychologist," the agent remarked. "How can
you expect people to take your advice if they aren't convinced the minute they look at your office that you're a big
success?"

"I guess I'll have to fall back on results," Kai said wryly.

The space she rented after two more days of looking
through the classified ads was one room on the second floor
of an older building on Sunset Boulevard. It amused Kai to
think it was the sort of office that private detectives always
seemed to have in the old movies. She agreed to pay a thousand dollars a month, the first three months in advance, and
a month's security.

"Whatever you give me," she told Sylvie, "I can put it
toward the rent, and we'll call the balance a loan."

Sylvie wrote out a check. "I won't need to lend you the
balance," she said, handing it over.

The amount Sylvie had written in was twenty thousand
dollars. "That's way out of line," Kai said as she prepared
to tear up the check.

"Hold it," Sylvie said sharply. "Just tell me: what are
you going to charge to help people with their problem?"

"Seventy-five dollars an hour is about standard."

"And you've been with me more than two weeks already, nursing me along every step of the way. That makes each twenty-four hours worth eighteen hundred bucks—over twelve thou' a week. I'm already ahead, and you've got time to go before you can give me my discharge slip. So take the money."

Kai stopped arguing. Later she could repay it. For now it would certainly be useful not only for her office, but renting an apartment, getting a car, and seeing herself through the first few months. She didn't assume that a line would form at her door overnight. Sylvie said she would spread the word at the studio that she owed her "return from the dead," as she called it, to Kai Wyler's counseling. But when it came to people admitting they had problems with sex—and especially famous people, who feared exposure—Kai realized that acceptance would only come slowly.

She spent the few days before she was scheduled to meet Jim fixing up her office. She bought furniture and window blinds and carpeting. She chose paint colors for the landlord to apply. She had bookshelves and telephone installed, and she had cards and letterhead printed.

When it was all done, she sat in her tastefully decorated thousand-dollar-a-month office and wondered how she was ever going to get clients to come.

Jim had told Kai that during his stay in San Diego, except for the time they spent together, he would be working to get his boat ready for the America's Cup race trials. They planned to meet on the last Friday in April at the yard where the boat was being built.

On Friday morning, Kai took the three-hour drive down the coast and followed directions to Shelter Island, a man-made resort island in the middle of San Diego Bay, lined along its shores with boatyards, marinas, and hotels. The Viking Boat Company yard occupied a small peninsula on the island, facing out to the Pacific. As soon as she drove in, she saw the long, sleek racing yacht tied up at the end of a long pier beyond the yard buildings. Several men were moving around the deck of the boat, but Jim wasn't among them.

She left her car in a large, empty parking lot and walked out onto the dock. Now she noticed the boat's name, painted

in large red letters along the side of the white hull—*Reliable*.
It brought back instantly the story Mitch had told about
Jim's father, the swindler who had produced faulty artillery
shells that had cost American lives. Kai recalled that the
name of the company which had manufactured his defective
ammunition—almost as if chosen to help dupe his buyers—
was Reliable, Inc.

The men on the boat, all fairly young workers and tanned
by their outdoor work, stopped to look at Kai as she reached
the dockside. Though she had dressed simply in jeans and
a gondolier pullover, expecting that she might be taken sailing, she looked especially beautiful, her honey skin burnished by weeks in the western sun, the contrast heightening
the glow of her turquoise eyes.

"Mr. Bolton around?" she asked.

"Not yet, miss," answered one of the men, who was
shirtless, revealing his sinewy frame. "We hear he's coming
today, but we've been told he was expected before, and he
didn't show."

"I'm supposed to meet him here."

"If he's meeting you," the young man said with a pleasant smile, "I have a hunch he'll be here soon. Want to come
aboard and look around while you wait?"

"No, thanks." She guessed that Jim would want to be
the one to introduce her to his prized possession. She didn't
mind passing the time with a stroll, a look around the city.

But as she turned to walk off the pier, the loud racket of
a helicopter engine broke into the tranquil scene, and she
looked up to see the enormous machine hovering over the
yard, then floating down to land in a large open space at
the head of the pier. A ramp opened from the side of the
fuselage, and Jim bounded down the stairs. He waved and
jogged toward her. Whatever uncertainties had troubled her
since they had last been together were blotted out by the
rush of joy at seeing him. She welcomed him into her arms
and gave herself to a passionate kiss that they broke off in
mutual embarrassment when they became aware of some
good-natured cheers and whistles directed at them from the
boat workers.

He took her aboard the boat and introduced her to the
other men—most of whom, she discovered, weren't simply
boatyard workers but members of his racing crew.

"Let's take her out for a drill," Jim said to the crew after
all the introductions had been made.

·Within ten minutes they were under sail, knifing toward
open ocean through the waters of San Diego Bay. Jim had
given Kai a spot at the corner of the cockpit to the side of
the helm and told her not to move. She could soon see why.
The crew started darting around the deck, working in practiced synchrony to raise and lower any of the dozens of
different sails required for varying wind conditions, and
perform all the other split-second maneuvers necessary to
get maximum speed out of the boat during a race. As she
observed Jim at the helm, shouting commands as the maneuvers were executed, she could see what made him a
leader, the sort of man who had been able to build a financial empire.

When at last the boat relaxed onto one long, thrilling
tack, pounding through the waves sharply heeled over on
its side, he had time to tell her about the challenge and
purpose of the race. At the last series of races in 1983, the
Australians had won the America's Cup. That victory had
snapped a 132-year continuous winning streak by American
yachts. Now a number of boats were being built from which
one would be selected to represent America in an attempt
to win back the trophy. "I've got some serious competition,
but I'm hoping to be the guy who gets the cup back."

As he stood at the helm, with his hair blown by the wind
and a faint crust of salt from the evaporation of sea spray
frosting the bridge of his nose and the strong line of his jaw,
Kai thought she would never see a more appealing man. But
was he a pirate or a crusader? she wondered. Building and
sponsoring a boat like this, he had said, would cost thirty
million dollars out of his own pocket. She wasn't sure how
she felt about a man who spent money that way. And was
it petty of her to note that it wasn't simply to see her that
he had traveled halfway back around the world, but to con-
duct the sea trial of his boat?

At the conclusion of the sail, he took her into the helicopter with him. They lifted off, swooped away from the
boatyard, and flew along the coast. Soon they were flying
over an enormous, picturesque white wooden building with
a turreted roof that rambled along a large stretch of oceanfront. They descended onto a patch of empty parking lot

that had apparently been cleared in advance for their landing. Jim told her they had arrived at the Hotel Del Coronado, and that when it had been built in 1888, it had been the first hotel in the world equipped with elevators and electric lighting.

"Thomas Edison himself supervised the electric installation," Jim said as they walked, arms around each other, toward the entrance. "Couldn't think of a better place for us to have a rendezvous—because I want our electricity to go on burning just as long."

She laughed and tightened her arm around him. "I didn't know we were heading straight for the hotel, though," she said. "I left my suitcase with all my clothes in my car at the boatyard."

"I'll have one of my crew bring it over." At the entrance he paused to take her in his arms. "But it'll be a while before we need any clothes."

As aware as she was that he meant no more than seductive repartee, she felt a flash of concern about the way he perceived her, always haunted by the fear that she would not transcend what her mother had been, a rich man's plaything.

Yet her doubts were almost instantly forgotten as they entered the hotel. Conditioned by their previous lovemaking to expect a feast for the senses, she was no less eager than he was, and as soon as they were in their luxurious oceanfront room, they joined in a hungry rush to release the pent-up desires of the past few weeks. Once again, while she clung to his lean, muscular body, pulling him deep inside her as she licked away the dusting of fine ocean salt that still lingered at the base of his neck, the pleasure she felt surpassed what she had known with any other man.

They came quickly to one shared, shuddering explosion of passion. After lying together only briefly, the need started to build again. The second time they took it slowly, resisting completion to explore each other more thoroughly. She climbed over him finally, riding him in a growing frenzy as he kissed her and sucked her breasts and whispered her name adoringly, until they crested a wave of pure ecstasy even more cataclysmic than the last.

Neither of them wanted to leave the room. Jim ordered champagne from room service, and they lay in bed, talking about the way they had spent their time apart. Kai was interested to hear about the people he met through business—he had been entertained by government leaders in Germany and Australia—and she was fascinated by the vision he displayed in explaining his eagerness to invest in assembling a global satellite network. "The technology's available," he said. "There's no reason we shouldn't link the whole world together. As soon as all countries can watch each other regularly on television, all the barriers will fall. We'll learn each other's language, be more tolerant of each other's customs."

But she was disappointed at his reaction to her news.

"You rented an office?" he said, propping himself up on one elbow to look down at her. "You're going into business?"

"It's not exactly a business. It's a profession. I can put my experience to work helping people."

"I'm sure you can. But why start now . . . here?"

"It seems the right place for what I want to do."

He shifted closer, embracing her, and she felt his warm nakedness along the length of her body. "Kai, I want us to be together. Don't you want the same thing?"

"I think so," she said candidly, her hand tracing the line of his jaw. "But on certain terms. Call it old-fashioned, but if we're going to be together, I want it to be pretty close to a hundred percent."

He pulled back again, studying her. "I can't offer more than everything. I'm ready to marry you."

Touched as she was, she couldn't keep her doubt from surfacing. "And after you marry me, are you ready to *be* with me?" His expression tightened with confusion, and she went on quickly, "I don't call it a marriage if I spend half the time waiting for you to arrive from some far corner of the world."

"It isn't always like that."

"I never would have seen you again after the first time if you weren't always traveling, looking at companies to buy."

His face relaxed. "We don't have to be apart. You'll go with me everywhere."

"On *your* business," she observed pointedly. "And what will I do? Jim, I don't want to be just a decoration, sitting around hotel rooms, or strolling through fancy shops in all the capitals of the world while you're off somewhere closing deals. I need a life, too. I can't just be . . . waiting until you have time for me.''

Jim nodded as though he understood. But he was still deeply preoccupied. He sat up on the edge of the bed. "How do we solve this?" he said at last. "My business is communications, Kai, it's all about connecting people and places—a damn important business, I think, if we're going to hold this world together. But I have to lay down a path for those connections, go to the places, meet the people. Otherwise I can't keep building my business.''

She looked at his strong back, the muscles faintly accented by the muted light coming through filmy curtains at the windows. She wanted to reach for him again, to hold him. Yet she couldn't settle for that temporary satisfaction. "Why do you have to keep building?" she asked. "Isn't what you've got now already big enough? Radio stations, cable franchises. Do you really have to add a movie studio, or go off around the world to put together a satellite network? Aren't you more than rich enough?''

"It's not about money, Kai—''

"Then what *is* it about? What's driving you?''

He didn't answer right away. He stood from the bed, shaking his head, slipped into his trousers, and walked across the room to the window. "I'm not always sure myself," he replied, pushing back a curtain to gaze at the ocean.

After a long moment she said, "I think I know what it might be." He turned to her. "You have to keep proving that what happened to your father won't ever happen to you.''

He laughed slightly. "That's got nothing to do with it. I don't just work for myself, you know. I've got a responsibility to shareholders.''

"Sure, that's part of it. You feel a debt to them because of what your father did to cheat people. He did his time in prison, but you're still trying to repay a debt to society, redeem a piece of lost honor—even enlist in a fight for your country's sake, spend yourself and your money to pay back what he took. It's there in everything you do . . .''

"Where'd you get ideas like that?''

"From the name of your boat.''

"Reliable," he said. "It's just a good name—"

"It was good, too, for a company that made unreliable artillery shells."

Jim stared at her. Then put a hand to his forehead. "Jesus. You know, I never thought of that." After a second he smiled. "Still, a damn good name for a boat." He crossed back to the bed and sat down. "Listen, darling. However you want to analyze me, it doesn't change the situation. Was it Freud who said a good cigar may be a phallic symbol but it's also a cigar? You're the psychologist here, so maybe you're right. But wherever my ambition comes from, that doesn't change the value of what I do. And I won't stop— not for a while, anyway. It seems easier to ask you not to start something new—not yet."

Kai slid out from under the sheets and started to dress. "Even easier is not to ask each other for anything," she flung over her shoulder.

He looked at her in amazement. "You're leaving? Kai—"

"Right now I don't feel like I have a choice. My psychological insights didn't start with you, Jim. Remember how we met? I was chasing the man who said he loved my mother, married her, and then left her. And I was running away from what she'd become—what killed her, in a way— being a woman who had no life, no identity, but to wait for those moments when a rich man desired her. I can't accept that position. It isn't even worth trying."

"Christ," he said hotly, "you don't think we have more than that?"

She glanced at the rumpled bed. "I've never felt with anyone what I feel with you." She looked up. "But if it doesn't add up to much more than what happens between the sheets, then it's not enough for me."

He came around the bed and seized her. "Well, maybe you've spent so much time looking at sex under a microscope for your damn research, you can't feel the magic that happens when it's really love. We're unique, Kai. What we are together, you won't find it with anyone else."

"I'm not looking for it," she said. "But I'll wait to be with you until you want my company more than any company you can buy."

He knew it was pointless to try stopping her now. He

watched as she went to the door and opened it. "I love you, Kai," he said.

"I love you, too," she said.

But neither one had any words of surrender before she walked away.

Chapter Thirty-four

A man in a tan cashmere jacket paused in the doorway of Kai's office, and glanced back at the small reception area. It was near the end of the day, and the part-time receptionist had left hours ago. "Is this the whole setup?" he asked.

"This is it," Kai said airily. She remembered the rental agent warning her that some people would assume she couldn't help them if she couldn't afford a better office.

The man let out a somewhat disapproving grunt before proceeding through the door. Kai had decorated her office simply, with several comfortable chairs, a coffee table, and a wide sofa—not the kind of couch supplied by analysts for patients to recline, but easily long enough if they ever did have the urge to lie down. The man took one of the chairs. He was slim with gray hair in a military brush cut and skin weathered to a leathery tan by years in the California sun. In his mid-fifties, he still had a youthful, athletic aspect.

Kai took the other chair. "I thought you were going to bring your wife, Mr. Marden," she said.

"She wouldn't agree," he said flatly. "Said the whole idea is bullshit—pardon my French."

"From what you told me on the phone, I won't be able to help unless I can see you both together."

"Yeah, yeah. I know, I know," he said irritably.

Joel Marden was a television producer. He had made a fortune over the past ten years supplying television networks with a number of popular weekly comedy and dramatic shows. Weeks ago, after bitching about his personal life over lunch with a friend in a studio commissary, he had been given Kai's name as someone who might help; the friend happened to be the producer of Sylvie's recent film. Marden had finally decided it was worth trying.

When he telephoned Kai, he explained that he had been

married for seventeen years, but he and his wife had fallen out of love, had ceased having sexual relations, and he had begun an affair with a young television actress. The sex he enjoyed with this young woman was "incredible," he said, and he was planning to get a divorce so they could marry.

"I don't quite understand what kind of help you want from me," Kai said when he called. "Sounds like you need a divorce lawyer, not a sex therapist."

"I've already talked to my lawyer. And he told me there's no way around the community property law—splitting up everything I've acquired during the time my wife and I were married. Which means, Ms. Wyler, if I want this divorce I'm going to have to part with about thirty million bucks. Now, a good lay is worth a lot of money. But thirty million? Before I bite that bullet, I thought I just might see if there was any way to wake things up again with the wife. We used to be pretty good together. I don't know how we lost it, and if we could get it back . . . well, all that money! Whattaya think, Ms. Wyler, any chance?"

"You've certainly got the incentive," Kai had said. "But if you don't love her anymore—"

"I don't know if I do or don't. All I know is, I loved her plenty when we first got married—and maybe I could love her again, if she'd do for me what the new one does."

Kai made an appointment for Marden to come to the office with his wife.

Yet now he had shown up by himself.

"Mr. Marden," Kai said, "I'm perfectly willing to spend this hour with you if there's any way you think I can be of help to you alone. But if the purpose is to revive your sex life with your wife, there's no way we'll succeed unless she's willing to be a full partner in the process."

"She might be," he said.

"Good. Then bring her back with you whenever—"

"She won't come here."

"But I've just told you—"

"That she's got to be a partner, I understand." He paused and squinted at Kai. "Ms. Wyler, do you make house calls?"

Kai had never seen clients anywhere but in her office. It struck her now, however, that there was no reason to make a rule about it. Perhaps Mrs. Marden was handicapped. "Depends on the circumstances," she said.

"I told you some of the circumstances. Carol—my wife—doesn't believe you can help us, and she's also real pissed off at me. She knows about the other woman, and she's thinking maybe she'd rather have half of every penny I've got than work to put us back together. She did say one thing, though, that left the door open a little. . . ."

"That she'd talk to me if I went to your house."

"Not exactly. She said if anybody thought they could help us, then they ought to come and watch us in bed together—and that would prove how totally hopeless it was."

"And that's why you asked about a house call?" Kai said after a second. "You thought I'd come and watch—"

Marden broke in, nodding. "Hands-on treatment, so to speak."

"I'm sure your wife didn't mean it literally. It was a way of expressing her doubts."

"Could be. But that doesn't mean I have to play it her way. I'll throw the dare right back at her, tell her I've arranged for someone to do just what she wanted. Then we'll see who blinks first." He smiled at the thought of his imagined victory. "I have a hunch she'll take the bait. I mean, we could end up in bed, and you could give us an on-the-spot diagnosis."

With some bemusement Kai leaned back in her chair, mulling over the proposition. It was outside the bounds of any conventional standard of sex therapy. General practice might involve listening to the complaints of married couples, and providing advice and instruction to be tried in private. Yet the whole idea of sex therapy had been considered outside the bounds of medical or psychiatric treatment not too long ago. The rules were still being made, and the goal would always be the same. To help people, to ease their distress, and restore balance to their lives. The object in this case was not to save this man his money—even if that was his initial spur—it was to save a marriage.

She made an appointment to go to Joel Marden's house on the next Saturday night.

"Come for dinner," he said. "Then you'll watch us in bed."

* * *

In the first few months after Kai had opened her office, there had been few clients. At every opportunity Sylvie told the story of how she had been helped, but it created no great rush of interest. Sylvie's rampant desire for men was common knowledge in Hollywood circles; if she had managed to rein it in while she was shooting a picture, no one necessarily assumed that it was the result of professional help rather than a determined effort to keep her career from going down the drain. The test of what had been achieved would come when she wasn't working and had time on her hands. Would she be able to have a real relationship with one man? The betting was that Sylvie would jump right back on the sexual merry-go-round.

There was also, as Kai had anticipated, a natural reluctance for people in general—those in a public arena particularly—to submit themselves to scrutiny, especially when it came to their sexual kinks and hang-ups. Those who did decide to seek help usually turned to general psychotherapy, and because Kai knew that sexual problems could almost always be traced to situations buried in the past, she believed that general therapy was often the most useful approach. The individuals who could benefit most from the sort of therapy she offered were less concerned with finding root causes in the past than simply modifying something that troubled them in their sexual behavior. Marital discord due to sexual issues and tastes, inability to achieve orgasm, impotence, premature ejaculation, or simple ignorance of sensitive and satisfying techniques, these were problems Kai felt equipped to solve.

When calls came in, they were mostly from people who had heard one of the occasional radio interviews she was still asked to do in connection with the book. Joel Marden was the first important member of the large movie and television community who had followed up directly because of what Kai had done for Sylvie.

It could be a turning point, Kai thought. If she was able to help Marden and his wife, she would have taken a big step toward gaining the trust of others of similar stature. The odds were against her, though. She had agreed to become part of a dare that husband and wife were playing off against each other, but she knew there was practically no chance that problems built up in a marriage over many years

could be solved by one-time intervention. Her best hope
was that once she had the opportunity to be with both members of the couple, she could convince them of the value in
committing to a more conventional course of therapy that
would heighten their sensitivity to each other. She puzzled
over what she could do to move them onto a realistic, constructive course.

When Kai arrived at the producer's home in Beverly Hills
on Saturday night, she brought with her a large black valise.
Both Marden and his wife, a svelte brunette dressed in red
chiffon, inquired about the contents, but Kai would say
nothing more than "It's for later . . . you'll see."

A dinner for three was served, as if the evening was to
be no more than an intimate social gathering. But an atmosphere of tension prevailed as both husband and wife
waited to see if the other actually meant to follow through,
and what role Kai would play. Several times, with increasing anxiety, one or the other asked Kai about what she had
brought along. "You'll see when we do the treatment," she
said. For the rest of the time they worked to maintain a
polite atmosphere as Kai asked questions probing the history of their marriage, how they had met, when they had
ceased to enjoy the physical side.

As the dinner went on, the tension heightened until finally the underlying feelings flared into the open.

"I don't know why I ever agreed to this," Carol Marden
said abruptly in the middle of the meal, letting her fork fall
to her plate with a clatter. "There's no hope for us. Joel,
you know that as well as I do."

It was the opening Kai needed. "Seems to me, Carol,
that you're the only one who's given up. Joel thought it was
worthwhile coming to see me, persuading me to come
here."

"Sure. Because he wants to keep all his goddamn
money!"

Uncertain how to defend himself, the producer tossed a
helpless, guilty look at Kai.

"It's certainly one of the reasons," Kai said. "But if it
was his only reason, he wouldn't have brought me into this.
He'd let things stay as they are, stay married, fool around
on the side, and forget about the rest. I believe he wants to

get back the feelings you've lost for each other. And if you stay married, all the benefits of the money are still yours."

"That's right, Carol. If we could just be the way we were, I won't want anyone else. Maybe it's not possible, but it can't hurt to try."

Carol Marden pouted for a minute as a servant cleared plates and prepared the table for coffee and dessert.

"What'd you bring in that big suitcase?" she asked finally, as though she expected it to determine whether or not she should entrust her future to Kai.

"After coffee," Kai said.

"Fuck coffee. Let's find out what you can do for us."

"Okay," Kai said. "Shall we go up to the bedroom?"

Marden and his wife glanced at each other, searching for any hint of retreat. But both shrugged, and they all left the table.

Kai told the couple to proceed to their second-floor bedroom and "get ready" while she went for the valise.

She found them sitting stiffly on separate sides of their king-size bed, both wearing robes. Walking straight to the end of the bed, she placed the valise flat and flipped open the top.

Arrayed within were dozens of items that Kai had purchased that morning from a sex shop called Hot Times. Dildos, handcuffs, a bullwhip, bottles of lotions and ointments, leather masks, neck collars, studded bracelets, and other exotica. Kai had loaded up almost indiscriminately on samples from all the shelves and display cases in the store.

Husband and wife both stared wide-eyed at the jumble of paraphernalia. "What are we supposed to do with all that?" Carol asked.

"Try it out," Kai said.

"All of it?" Joel asked.

"Just pick out whatever appeals to you. We'll stick with whatever works."

Carol turned to her husband. "When you said sex therapy, I didn't know it came down to trying out all this junk—in front of a stranger, no less!"

Joel shrugged, nonplussed. "I didn't know either."

"Well, my approach would be very different ordinarily," Kai said blithely to Carol. "But I understand you want quick results. It's taken years to develop the problem, but you expect someone to fix it overnight with a kind of shock therapy—''

"I didn't say that."

"Wasn't it your idea to let me into your bedroom like this, show me the way you and Joel make love?"

She was silent a moment. "I guess," she said quietly. "I thought he'd never go through with it. Or you, either."

"But he would," Kai said. "Because he really wants it to work."

"And you?" Carol challenged.

"If it's the only chance you'll give me, sure. If you want to give it the best shot, though, this isn't the way."

"What is?"

Kai explained the process by which couples might rediscover sexual pleasure lost over years in which the excitement of intimacy had turned gradually into boredom bred by familiarity and repetition. In joint visits to her office, both partners would frankly discuss their sexual preferences, their fantasies, their disappointments with the performance of the other. Based on an assessment of what they told her, drawing on her knowledge of effective techniques derived from the physiological research in which she had participated, she would make recommendations for different things the couple should try. The process of rebuilding sensitivity to each other could probably be accomplished over two or three months.

"So that's all there is to it?" Carol said when Kai concluded. "We talk to you, and you tell us what to do? Doesn't sound like anything we couldn't figure out on our own."

"Have you ever told Joel exactly what you like in bed?"

Carol hesitated. "I always thought if you have to talk about it, what's the point? He ought to know what makes me feel good."

"Maybe I just forgot," Joel said poignantly.

For the first time that evening Kai saw a spark of sympathetic affection when the couple gazed at each other. She closed up the big suitcase. "Call the office Monday morning," she said. "We'll set up a series of appointments."

Joel carried the suitcase downstairs for her. At the door he thanked her, then he said, "What about all this stuff? You think maybe we should try it out?"

"It's like simple arithmetic, Joel. Let's just see if we can put one and one together and make two before we try the fancy algebra.''

He handed over the valise. "You never really meant to use it, did you? You just wanted to shake up Carol.''

Kai left him without an answer, only a smile.

Driving back to her Westwood apartment, she wondered whether she should try to get a full refund from the store tomorrow, or which stuff might be worth keeping for some future client.

The story of Kai's "dinner" with the Mardens was soon buzzing along Hollywood's grapevine, starting with Joel's reports to his cronies in the studio commissary, and Carol's sessions with her friends at the hairdresser's or over lunch.

Even though Kai had yet to succeed in restoring the Mardens' marriage, her gutsy willingness to make the house call and the clever improvisation that had gained Carol's cooperation brought approval from other men and women eager to inject a new element into relationships that had lost their original romantic fizz. Kai's appointment book began to fill. As those who brought fairly conventional complaints responded to her combination of common sense and a recognizably sincere empathy for anyone coping with the confusion and unhappiness arising from sexual problems, her reputation spread.

From her experience with the Mardens, Kai was encouraged to be more daring and inventive in her approach to each individual problem. With couples who were embarrassed about candidly describing their sexual activities, she discovered it was a helpful icebreaker to show pornographic videos, using them as a reference point. And she began to use sex surrogates to help in certain cases. The large number of aspiring actors, along with other students, provided a pool of attractive and intelligent young men and women who needed supplemental income and were willing to cooperate under Kai's supervision in a limited amount of sexual activity specifically designed to provide relief to her clients. Having found, too, that mere academic description of effective loveplay—or illustrated diagrams of sensitive parts of the anatomy—created a classroom atmosphere that turned off certain clients rather than awakening them to the excitement they were seeking to rediscover, Kai hired a man and woman to come to her office and physically enact some recommended techniques in front of clients.

With her acceptance in the Hollywood community, Kai was eventually contacted by men and women seeking to overcome more unusual sexual afflictions. One male star of action-oriented films had a taste for sadomasochism that had involved him in increasingly life-threatening adventures. After making advances to the girlfriend of a Hell's Angel in a bikers' hangout, he had been beaten up so badly by gang members that there was some doubt about whether his face would ever again tolerate the scrutiny of the cameras. Months of skilled plastic surgery had restored him so that he could be photographed again—though there were one or two forbidden angles—but the star realized he had to be cured of the urges that made him contrive to put himself in danger, or the next time he might well be killed.

In treating her clients, Kai knew she could never promise one hundred percent success. The roots of some forms of bizarre behavior remained mysterious, and occasionally resistant to therapy even where patient psychological probing revealed origins in parental treatment or environmental patterning. But those who consulted her had already exhibited the most important element in any potential cure, she knew, the courage to expose their flaws and weaknesses for the sake of changing and improving. She felt confident in promising that she could help the large majority of her clients.

Within several months Joel Marden was boasting to his cronies that his marriage had been miraculously resuscitated, and Sylvie—who continued to see Kai not only socially, but for a number of conventional visits—had entered a happy, stable relationship with an assistant cameraman she had met on a past film. He had been fond of her for years, but had resisted all her attempts to get him into bed until he had seen her recent rehabilitation.

"You give a new meaning to the words *satisfied customer*," Sylvie told her.

Soon Kai's practice developed to the point that she had little time for herself. Many of her evening hours were given over to clients who couldn't come earlier, like television performers who were occupied with the hectic schedules of making weekly series.

In fact, work became a welcome relief from the emptiness

of her personal life. Kai had hoped at first that Jim would respond to her need for more of his time. Looking back, she realized she had expected too much by hoping he would give up most of his traveling, yet she had known it would never work between them if she couldn't count on much more than playing second fiddle to his love of business. If he had made even a token concession to the unreasoned anxiety that gripped her when she thought of falling into anything like the kind of passive role her mother had played, they could have built on that. But Jim had continued to be heavily involved with his enterprises and preparing for the America's Cup trials. When he called her to suggest getting together to work things out, the time allotted was never more than two or three days, never open-ended, and always had to be scheduled in between other demands. Longing to see him, she did agree to another meeting, and he came up from San Diego after overseeing adjustments to his yacht at the boatyard. They had a lovely evening together, dinner in his bungalow at the Beverly Hills Hotel, and a wonderful night of lovemaking. But when he left, she could only insist again that she needed a more constant, reliable involvement.

He sent her flowers daily over an interim of a few weeks, and then he called again from San Diego. He was there for the official trials of his boat. He would be racing against another American boat to determine which would move on to a semifinal heat to choose the main contender. He invited her down to watch the races. "It's exciting stuff, Kai. You won't be bored, and we'd have the nights together."

The nights, not the days. She wanted to go to him, ached to be touched by him—and yet again there was the irksome feeling that she would be there for his pleasure, the *manu-wahi* receiving at his leisure the lover who was otherwise busy with his rich man's sport.

"I'm not free," she said. "Maybe afterward—if you can come up here and stay a little longer."

He called again when the trial races were over. "My boat lost," he said matter-of-factly.

"I'm sorry," she said. She knew how much it had meant to him.

"It was fun while it lasted. Anyway, I'm dying to see you, and I've got a few days before I have to be in—"

She didn't need to hear more. "It's not good enough,

Jim. I need someone who stays. It's as simple as that.''
Until he could think about staying with her, she told him
flatly, not always being so much on the go, she preferred
not to see him again.

He didn't argue with her; he had already explained that
he couldn't meet her terms.

As time went by, Kai's feeling that Jim Bolton was a special man didn't dwindle, yet whatever she felt about him,
she reminded herself constantly, it was based on very little:
the grand total of time spent together was now six days in
eighteen years.

With the steady increase in her clientele, and her dedication to helping them, Kai soon lost track of the time since
she had last heard from Jim. Was it two weeks . . . a month
. . . could it really have been six months? Ironically, as she
spent more and more of her time helping to repair the vi-
tality and satisfaction in the sex lives of dozens of men and
women, her own was moribund. She accepted dates occasionally, she met many attractive men, but there was no
spark. Taking a page from the philosophy of Orin Olmsted,
Kai practiced chastity as she waited for an enduring love to
return.

Chapter Thirty-five

By the end of her first year of practice, Kai was overdue for bigger offices. One secretary now worked full-time, taking phone calls, keeping track of appointments, and typing up her notes; another came in part-time for billing. In addition to room for the secretaries, she needed a quiet waiting room and an office for herself. She also planned to set aside space for what she would call "loving rooms," places decorated and lit to be conducive to intimacy, to be used for demonstrations of lovemaking or supervised sessions with surrogates, or where couples could be left alone to practice the lessons they had been taught. Bedrooms at home, Kai realized, were often too filled with the memories of past failures to provide the necessary atmosphere of freedom in which to try fresh approaches.

After an extensive search she moved to a floor on a new professional building in Santa Monica. She liked being able to see the ocean from her windows. The view of waves breaking on the beach was a reminder of constant renewal as well as the eternal and enduring, a symbol she found reassuring, and perhaps even beneficial to her clients. Soon after completing the office change, Kai bought a house, too, a stucco cottage dating from the Twenties. It was modest but comfortable, not even a pool in the backyard. But it was near the beach and just a ten-minute walk from the office.

She raised her fees to cover the expense of the move, but there was no decrease in demand. Sylvie had been telling Kai since the beginning that she was charging too little. "You know there are shrinks all over this town who charge three hundred an hour, and most of them are quacks."

Arriving for work one morning, her secretary gave Kai a message that Joel Marden had called. It had been eight months since she had seen the television producer and his wife. At the time they had been in the full flush of a second honeymoon. Immediately after ending their visits with Kai, they had embarked on a three-week trip to the South Seas, where, Joel said, they planned to live like natives, "wearing fig leaves, eating bananas off the trees, and screwing eight times a day." Kai received his message now with some regret. She hated to think the rekindled flame had flickered out again.

When she reached Marden on the phone, he sounded so instantly upbeat, Kai realized he wasn't calling with a problem.

"Kai, how much do you know about cable television?" he asked after they had exchanged greetings.

She knew it had made a fortune for a man she had once loved. "Almost nothing," she said. "I hardly have time to watch."

"The important thing," Joel said, "is that the guidelines for what can be broadcast are pretty lenient. There's stuff on cable channels you'll never see on the networks. I think it's the future—bigger than networks—so I've just made a deal to supply programming to one of the more respectable cable channels. They want quality stuff, but since there's leeway in what we can show, I thought we might break some new ground. There's always been call-in advice shows on the radio. There's a little German woman who's got one now, takes calls from people with sex problems. She sounds like a female Sigmund Freud, and there's nothing she won't say—tells women to masturbate with cucumbers, you name it. But what I'm talking about would be for television, visual, and with the way you'd look on camera, you'd be a natural."

"Slow down, Joel. You're proposing that I do an advice show on television?"

"Right. Same stuff you do now in private. Meet people with problems, do demonstrations with surrogates, throw in some interviews with other sex experts, the whole megillah. Only instead of an audience of one or two in your office, I'll give you one or two *million*—for starters."

Kai wasn't immediately enthusiastic about the idea. Already she had as much work as she had time for. But when she resisted, Joel said it could be organized so that she'd only have to give the program whatever time she was on the air and just an hour or two to prepare.

She remained leery. "I know there'll be an audience because there's a sensational value in anything to do with sex.

But I'm interested in helping people, Joel. I don't want to turn what I do into . . . show business.''

"Kai," Marden argued, "you ought to realize that in one way or another, everybody's a little mixed up about sex—at least at some time in their lives. Whether it's teenagers, married couples, old farts who've lost the urge and are trying to find it again. There's no one you couldn't help. Don't turn me down flat. Let me do a presentation, bring you in to meet the people at this cable outfit.''

"What's the name of the cable company," Kai said after a moment, "and who runs it?''

"Allstate Communications," Joel answered. "The head honcho is a guy named Daniel Hillman.''

"All right," she said, "I'll meet him.''

She felt no excitement after she hung up, only a sting of disappointment. If fate could have brought her and Jim together one more time, she thought, then they might have made the effort to hold on to each other.

Heatwaves, as Joel named the program, went on the air in the autumn of 1988, weekly at two o'clock on Wednesday mornings. To start, there was nothing like the audience of millions he had promised. Allstate Communications Corporation had been reluctant to depart from its staple of sports events, movies, and reruns of old sitcoms for a show that their executives categorized as sex education. "Sex is great," said Daniel Hillman, the chief executive, "and so is education. But when you put them together, it's a turn-off.'' People wanted to see naked women, all right, they wanted porn, too. But they didn't want to hear their sex problems talked about as if fixing them was no less a matter of mechanics than getting a tune-up for their car engine.

The counter argument made by Joel Marden (though not when Kai was present) was that the educator in this case was a gorgeous lady who looked like she really knew what she was talking about when it came to what happened when people took their clothes off. At last the company had agreed to try the program, though they hid it in the schedule at a late hour. Kai went along since it interfered minimally with her practice.

Heatwaves quickly reaped a large portion of the limited audience in its time slot, many of them precisely those who would be best served by the advice Kai had to offer—lovers lying awake in bed after a sexual encounter that had proven somewhat disappointing; single men and women restlessly awake, wondering why they were alone; couples who had given up on sex as a late-night activity and were constantly switching channels on the television sets seeking something to fill the vacuum.

Kai Wyler's frank answers to call-in questions, her informative exchanges with such experts as Paul and Laura Sinclair, the use of provocative visual material allowable on the cable channel, and even celebrity guests, like Sylvie Teer, who agreed to talk about past problems alleviated by therapy, was a mix that appealed even to viewers looking strictly for entertainment and diversion rather than information. Of course, Kai's personality and the sexual magnetism she projected were the main draw.

Only two months after its debut, *Heatwaves* was moved up to a midnight time slot, and a second program on Saturday night was added. With more exposure, and growing word of mouth, the audience boomed. As modern sensibilities and freedoms collided with the strictures dictated by a deadly new sexually transmitted disease, *Time* magazine featured a story on new attitudes about sex in America—putting "Sex Therapist, Kai Wyler," on the cover. Having gone from being a *Tomcat* kitty to prominence as a sex therapist, while remaining single and experiencing some of the same difficulties in establishing a permanent relationship that troubled other attractive, successful career women, Kai was depicted in the accompanying article as the very embodiment of the past two decades of sexual evolution in America.

A day after the *Time* story hit the newsstands, three dozen yellow roses were delivered to her office. "It's not getting any easier," said the enclosed card, which was unsigned.

There was both comfort and pain in knowing that Jim was still thinking about her—and that now she was no less responsible than he was for violating the conditions she had set down. Would she give up the career she was building for love?

Some weeks later, two more responses reached Kai that she might not have had except for her newfound prominence. First, a telephone call that came to the office from her half sister Vanessa. After living with Alexandra, she had broken away on her own a few years ago. Now twenty-three, she was living in Florida, earning money by topless dancing. Already she had lived with a series of men. Kai's heart ached as she listened and recalled the sweet child whose life had been thrown into a downward trajectory by the vindictive wrangling of her parents.

"Come to me, Van," Kai urged. "You can live with me, and I'll help you get your life straightened out."

"I was hoping you'd say that, Kai. When I read about what you do, it really gave me hope. I will come someday soon."

"Why wait? Come now. I'll send you the fare."

"Soon," she repeated. "There are a few things I have to do first."

Kai didn't press. It was obvious from what she heard that it had been an act of courage for Vanessa even to make the initial contact. From the description of her present life, Kai guessed she was using drugs, and her goal was to beat the habit before a reunion. Kai asked for a mailing address and ended the call with words of encouragement and love.

A week later a letter came from Georgette Swenson. Until seeing the story in *Time,* she wrote, she hadn't known where Kai was living and how to reach her; she was sure Kai would want to know that Mak had died the past year and had been buried beside Lili and Lokei. They had never gotten their house by the beach, but they had spent their money for a lovely plot in a cemetery overlooking the ocean.

Heatwaves had been on the air fourteen months when Joel Marden informed Kai that he planned to renegotiate with All-state Communications. "There's still almost a year to run on our current deal, but with the ratings you're racking up, we should both be getting paid much more, and they know it."

At the start Kai had accepted just $500 per show. She had looked on her participation more as a public service than a source of income, and had guessed there would be little profit for the cable station in a program broadcast at an hour when the audience was limited. Now that the show was becoming a profit center, the company was selling many more advertisements at higher rates.

Joel also advised Kai to obtain an agent or a lawyer to represent her interests in improving her compensation. "The right guy can get you a bundle," he said.

The notion of obtaining representation had already occurred to Kai. Offers to do magazine columns, books, lecture tours, even to appear in television sitcoms and films, had begun pouring in. With time already so limited, she had turned them all aside. Occasionally she thought about the few words Jim Bolton had last written to her; they could be taken as a challenge to limit her own opportunities—as she had asked him to limit his—to leave room for the possibility of another attempt at romance.

Yet she felt now that the help provided to people through her television "practice" was no less valuable than what she accomplished with clients in her office, and she was anxious to continue. She accepted Joel's recommendation to see a lawyer named Eric Gimbel, who specialized in entertainment contracts.

The lawyer, an avuncular man with a goatee whose large law firm occupied its own jewel-box building on the fringe of Beverly Hills, happily agreed to add Kai to his star-studded list of clients. "I'll call Danny Hillman. We'll get him to tear up the old contract and make a new one."

"I want to continue doing the program," Kai told him. "I'll accept any reasonable amount of money."

"That's what you're paying me to do, dear," the lawyer said, "help your employers understand just how much is reasonable."

The next day, he called Kai to tell her there would be a delay in the negotiations. Hillman wanted to hold off on making new commitments because he'd just had an offer to sell his company.

"Who's the buyer?" Kai asked.

"Hillman wouldn't tell me any more at this stage, but he's pleased about it. He wanted to sell a couple of years ago when the buy-out frenzy was at its peak, but then the bottom fell out of the stock market. Now merger activity has bounced back, so he's getting even more than he would have before."

"How much?" Kai said.

"Three hundred and eighty million. There's still a few wrinkles to iron out, but when the deal goes through—which could be any day—the new management will be making decisions on your contract. And you'll do well, Kai. Hillman says the success of your show was one of the elements that attracted the buy-out."

Two days later, the lawyer called again to say the sale had gone through, and he would start negotiating with the new owner.

"Did you find out who it is?" Kai asked.

"Yeah. He's a billionaire from the Midwest, one of these hot rods who's been buying things up right and left the past few years. Name is Mitch Karel."

It was not what she had hoped, though she felt a curious lack of surprise, as if she had known Mitch, too, must reenter her life someday.

"The negotiations may be harder with Karel," Gimbel went on, "because he's not already familiar with the ins and outs of broadcasting. He's been in dozens of other businesses—airlines, hotels, meat-packing plants—but not communications. Without a background in broadcasting, it may take him a little extra time to realize just what a valuable asset you are."

"Maybe not as long as you think," Kai said. She suspected, in fact, that she might soon hear from Mitch Karel herself, and he might even propose certain conditions under which a new contract could be settled instantly.

Over the years since she had last seen Mitch, he had remained at the fringe of her awareness. She knew that he had married during the time she'd been on her travels, not because it was news at the time, but because last year it had been widely reported when the marriage ended that Mitch Karel had agreed to one of the largest divorce settlements in history, worth a hundred million dollars in stock, property, and jewelry. The publicity given this rich arrangement had catapulted Mitch into the public eye, though he had evidently tried to keep a low profile in the past both for reasons of personal safety and because he preferred to do business without being known as one of the richest men in the country.

The facts widely reported at the time of the divorce were that Karel had built a fortune estimated at more than two billion dollars, and that during his eight-year marriage to a wealthy Chicago socialite, he had fathered two children. Reading about the marriage, Kai recalled how Mitch had once claimed to admire Randall Wyler. Perhaps he had even chosen his wife to duplicate exactly certain aspects of Wyler's life.

Surprisingly, weeks went by without any direct word from

Mitch. Eric Gimbel opened contract talks, but he dealt entirely with the firm of lawyers that represented Karel.

"It's going well," he reported back to Kai. "We've agreed to a salary of half a million dollars annually."

"Did I hear right—half a million?"

"That's for the first year, and it's only a base. Depending on ratings and the way syndication arrangements work out, you may get another million or two."

"Eric," Kai said with concern, "is this really in line with what I'm worth?" She couldn't help thinking that Mitch might use the offer to coerce a sense of obligation. After all, he was unmarried again.

"Listen, dear," Gimbel replied. "If the program goes into syndication—being bought by networks or independent stations—revenues to Allstate could be twenty or thirty million annually."

Kai felt reassured that Mitch was not trying to buy *her* along with her services. Yet she wondered at the odd silence that persisted.

"There are just a few small wrinkles left to iron out," Gimbel continued, "and the contract will be ready for signing. But his lawyers won't tell me what they are. Mr. Karel wants to settle the last points personally."

"When will you see him?"

"Oh, it isn't *me* he wants to talk with. He wants to resolve the final issues with you, Kai—you alone. He'll be coming out here any day."

Having been so close in the past, she couldn't understand why he hadn't called her personally by now. Should she pick up the phone herself? No, it was his move, she thought. Already she sensed he had drawn her into a sort of chess game, and if she didn't wait she would already be at some disadvantage.

On the following Monday, a woman called at the office, and identified herself as Mr. Karel's private secretary. Kai was told that Mr. Karel would be coming to Los Angeles the following weekend, and hoped to have breakfast with her Saturday morning in his penthouse apartment at the Beverly-Palace Hotel, which he owned. Kai was tempted to reply that Mr. Karel ought to call her personally to make this appointment, but she just confirmed that the time and place were fine. Perhaps this was the way Mitch did business. Perhaps it was another part of the chess game.

She went to sleep Friday night filled with curiosity about the reunion to come, her head filled with memories of young Mitch that made her smile—campaigning together, their near elopement.

The ringing phone jarred her awake. As she picked it up, she saw the lighted clock of the dial reading ten minutes to four.

"Ms. Wyler," a man said gruffly when she answered, "this is the Los Angeles police. We've got a patient of yours here at the Hollywood precinct. Because of the nature of the crime, we felt it might be best to release this man to the custody of his therapist. If you'll come down and take responsibility—"

"Who is it, Officer?"

"Mitch Karel."

Kai was speechless. Mitch? A patient of hers? She wondered for a second if it was some kind of crazy practical joke. On the eve of meeting to talk business—after not seeing him for years—she was being asked to bail him out?

"You do know him, don't you?" said the cop, sensing the bafflement in her silence. "The billionaire?"

Kai sat up, wide awake. "Yes, I know him. What's he charged with?"

"Had a woman in his hotel room earlier tonight and roughed her up a little. She happens to be the kind who gets paid to give it but not take it, you know what I mean? Their games got a little out of hand somehow, and she didn't like the way things went. She left and swore out a complaint for assault—has the black eye to back it up, so we took Karel in. Will you come and get him?"

"I'll be there soon," she said, throwing back the covers. Good lord! she thought, what a hell of a reunion.

From additional details given her by the police before Mitch was brought up from his holding cell, Kai learned that the woman he'd assaulted was a dominatrix, already listed in the vice-squad files. For a hefty fee she hired herself out by the hour, day, week, or even by the month, to men whose greatest sexual fulfillment was achieved when they were being subjugated in one way or another—whipped,

spanked, shackled, or treated as slaves—there were dozens
of scenarios.

A policeman finally brought him out to meet her. She
took him in at a glance. His dark hair was touched all over
with gray and had receded slightly, but he was still slim.
Over the years all the rough edges had been smoothed out,
yet he had as much the aura of a gangster as a tycoon, so
smooth that it seemed a calculated effort to hide the flaws.
Under the circumstances, Mitch and Kai had only the most
restrained greeting. He tried to force a smile and failed,
then murmured something about it being "a hell of a way
to meet again" before lapsing into silence as she signed for
his release.

Yet the moment they left the precinct and he was out from
under the eye of the police, he became markedly more ef-
fusive, telling her how wonderful she looked, thanking her
again for coming—so blithely that it was as if she had turned
herself out in the pre-dawn hours for a party rather than an
arrest. For all Kai's experience with the extraordinary tastes
and habits that people could keep concealed beneath an out-
wardly normal surface, she had difficulty comprehending
Mitch's behavior. It seemed incredible that he had exposed
himself to her this way instead of calling a lawyer. Was it
all some elaborate setup, a practical joke? Another move in
the chess game?

She drove to an all-night coffee shop on Wilshire Boulevard. He had asked her back to his hotel, but she didn't
want to be alone with him until she understood the dimen-
sions of the problem.

She got the first glimpse into the workings of Mitch's
mind as soon as they were in a booth, sipping coffee, and
she asked why indeed he had lied and told the police he
was her patient.

"I'm going to be prosecuted on this assault charge," he
said frankly. "I know it'll score points in court if I've already recognized I've got a problem and I'm getting help.
And who else would I ask for therapy? You're the most
famous sex doctor in town, Kai. What's more, we're almost
in business together."

She flared with anger at the idea she was only being used.
"I came down here out of friendship, Mitch. But I'll be
damned if I'd ever perjure myself for you. If you want con-

sideration from the court by telling them you're in treatment with me, you'll have to make the lie into a fact.''

''Sure,'' Mitch said ingenuously. ''I know I need help.''

''Do you have any idea why you're doing this?''

He thought for a moment. ''I guess it's a way of keeping things in balance.''

''Balance is a strange word to use. Most people would say it's a pretty unbalanced way to act.''

''Most people don't have what I have—more money than I'll ever know what to do with. Believe it or not, Kai, it's almost more than I want.'' He smiled as he saw her doubtful look. ''Sure, I always dreamed of being rich. But it took me over, the money kept coming in, and yet I still wanted more, until there was no time for anything else. That's when I started paying for women. I could buy exactly what I wanted, and once I paid, I didn't owe them anything else— not my time or my feelings. At first it was just the ordinary stuff I wanted—well, fairly ordinary. But the more money I had, the more people there were around me ready to give me anything, do anything, take my orders, take whatever shit I handed out. And I'd keep pushing the limits. How much could I get, how hard a bargain could I strike, how much of a bastard could I be? Didn't seem there was any limit with most people, as long as I had the money.'' He paused, as though privately reviewing some of the worst of his sins. ''I guess I thought I ought to be punished for some of the things I did—the way I took advantage of people, things I did in business. So I arranged my own punishment, in a way that gives me pleasure.'' He looked away and his voice fell. ''Tonight that bitch was enjoying it a little too much . . . and I snapped. Gave it back to her—which isn't supposed to be in the rules.'' His eyes came back to Kai, a startlingly honest, open look. ''Christ, who knows how I've gotten so fucked up? I'm not complaining, though.''

''Maybe you should be, Mitch. Sounds to me like you don't get all that much pleasure from the money. You've lost a family, the only kind of relationship you have with a woman is the kind you pay for—and you'd rather have them whip you than kiss you. Maybe you're not complaining, but I think your soul is.''

He stared back at her, and in the dark center of his eyes she saw a spark of realization. Suddenly he reached across the table to take her hand. "It could have all been so different . . . if we'd taken that moment. Remember? If you'd married me, I wouldn't ever have—"

"Please, Mitch," she said gently, pulling her hand away. "There's no point talking about it now."

He leaned back and shrugged philosophically. "But you'll still treat my problem?"

"Yes. I'll try."

There was a pause. "Well, I came to town to talk business," he said brightly. "Might as well get that out of the way, too."

Again she had the feeling of being disoriented. Mitch found it so easy to dismiss this crisis in his life and turn to everyday matters. Though perhaps nothing was ordinary in his high-octane existence.

It was past five in the morning. Kai would have suggested deferring their business talk, but she was here now, and she preferred to limit the contact with Mitch except for what might develop on a professional basis.

"You know that I'm prepared to pay you a great deal of money," he said, opening the discussion.

She nodded warily.

"There's only one reason, Kai—and that's because I know you can help the company earn it back many times over. You have to be willing to play ball, though. I need to be sure that you'll accept my being one hundred percent in charge, and not fight me on the changes."

"Changes?" she said. "I hadn't heard about any changes."

"If we're going to expand your audience, they'll be absolutely necessary. Your producer, Mr. Marden, has already agreed.

That made Kai feel better. Joel had conceived the show in the first place; she trusted him. "What are they?"

He talked for ten minutes, laying out not only the new format, but explaining the reasons. The show's image as being primarily a source of therapeutic advice was limiting the market, making it seem too dry and educational, a news-service type of show rather than something entertaining. He couldn't afford to sacrifice the greater advertising revenue to be earned by delivering a much larger audience. That would be done by playing up the entertainment value, exhibiting more of the strangest, most sensational aspects of sex and sexual deviation in a way that had dramatic impact. If it was done right, Kai would be able to appear on television even in daytime hours. The idea was to use her differently—not as a therapist to individuals, but as a host who would receive and question panels of troubled people, such as children of incest, wives whose husbands had been stolen away by their best friends, girls whose mothers had stolen away their boyfriends, celebrities who had troubled marriages or problems with drugs. "There's already a huge market for shows like this."

What he was talking about, Kai realized, was putting her in a format to compete with Donahue, or Geraldo, Oprah Winfrey, or Sally Jesse Raphael.

"I can't do that," she declared.

"Of course you can. You're as smart as anyone doing it now, and much better-looking, sexier . . . plus, you have the professional credentials."

"I mean, I can't give up what's important to me. I'm not interested in doing a program just to show how strange or miserable people can be. The program I'm doing now helps people—that's the point of it."

"It all helps," Mitch said. "People with problems feel better when they can turn on the TV and see other people with problems."

"They get that from me, too. Maybe they even get entertained. But I'm doing something more. Anyway, it's what feels right for me."

Mitch's face set in a hard mask. "When I pay you, Kai, I'm the one who gets to decide what's right."

"Can't you see the purpose of what I'm trying to do—you of all people, who can use this kind of help?"

"I'm ready to pay for my therapy. But not to let you give it away free—especially if it means taking lower profits."

Kai shook her head. What a sad, hard man Mitch had become to be guided so much by the quest for profit when he had more money than he could ever use. Or was this really about money? What he wanted, perhaps, was simply to show her he made the rules. Had he shifted his business in this new direction simply to own a broadcasting company, or to own her?

She had to stake out her independence. "I can't do what you want, Mitch."

"Then there won't be a new contract."

She slid to the end of the booth, preparing to go. "I'm sorry we can't agree."

"Nothing to be sorry about, Kai. You're not going to leave me and work for someone else—"

"I will if I can't do my work in my own way."

"You're forgetting something. I was willing to discuss a new contract, but there's still time to run on the old one."

He spoke softly, but there was iron in his threat. He meant to enforce his rights, to keep her from doing any broadcast unless it was done his way.

She stood up. "About your treatment, Mitch. The way things are between us, I think it'll be much more productive if I refer you to someone else."

He smiled thinly. "I won't go to anyone else."

"Mitch, you need—"

"I know what I need," he cut in. "You might even say I'm a sick man. But if you won't treat me, I'll just go on as I am." His eyes glinted maliciously.

It was the essence of his warped need, she knew, to manipulate people, control them—and then need to seek retribution. And now he was controlling her. Could she turn him down, let him sink back into his sickness? On the other side of the question, could she truly help him when so many other issues cluttered their relationship?

She stared at him for a long moment before she decided. "Call my office for an appointment," she said, and walked away.

He seemed sincere about wanting to be helped. Though he traveled constantly for business, he came back to the city at least a week out of every month and always scheduled two or three sessions. At the office he behaved scrupulously. Occasionally he spoke of wanting more than professional contact with Kai, but it was no more of a problem than she had experienced with any number of male clients. Dealing with the adoration of patients was a familiar problem for all therapists, and Kai was practiced in deflecting it gently.

In Mitch's case, the foundation of his treatment was first to probe the influences that had formed his idea of love, and had deformed it into a need to be hurt and punished. He had to be made to look at himself in the psychic mirror and see the beast he had become before he could change. The early sessions were conventional therapy, listening to him, drawing him out about his past.

It didn't take very long to confirm that the seeds of Mitch's problem had been planted by what had happened with his father. The dark, brooding man that Kai had once met was only a relatively placid surface masking a far more horrific brutality. In Lech Karlozic the ferment of grief and anger over his daughter's death, the crude, bloody work he did daily in the slaughterhouse, and the temper unleashed by too much alcohol combined to produce a loss of all human perspective. Mitch had regularly been beaten as a child, and had also been a witness to the terrible mistreatment his mother had suffered at the hands of her husband. As a child, trying to absorb and rationalize this, his perceptions about love had been all the more complicated by a genuine admiration and reverence Mitch felt for his father, despite the man's worst excesses. After all, Lech had brought his family out of tyranny and had endured his bloody work to make a home for them and give his son a fine education. Mitch loved his father—had wanted to love him, anyway—but the yearning for reciprocal affection had been met instead with physical punishment. This was the root of Mitch's twisted definition of how to relate intimately to a woman. To receive attention in the form of a beating was, in his mind, to make love.

Once this much was brought into the open for Mitch to examine, it was time to reeducate him about love and physical pleasure. This was where a surrogate became necessary. Mitch needed to be with a woman who wouldn't go along with his sick need, but would patiently redirect his urges to a normal experience of tenderness and intimacy.

When Kai explained the surrogate technique to him, Mitch said, "I won't accept any stand-in's. I want you to teach me."

Of course, this time she couldn't yield. "I still want to help you, Mitch, but only within the bounds of my professional duty. I've arranged for a surrogate, and she'll contact you directly to set up appointments with you. It'll be your decision then whether or not you want to take your treatment any further."

Later, Kai had received reports from Annie Raines. She

was seeing Mr. Karel regularly whenever he was in Los
Angeles, and he was responding well, learning to obtain
sexual satisfaction without resorting to the domination
games and masochistic rituals he had compulsively needed
in the past. Mitch was making progress.

And yet it had done nothing to soften the personality he
brought to his business dealings. Paradoxically, all the time
that Kai was determinedly applying her expertise to recast
his ability to feel a more benign spectrum of emotions, he
continued to negotiate with unforgiving harshness in regard
to her program. The new contract was put on the back
burner, no concessions were made to changing the old terms
still in effect, and lower-level executives who administrated
the cable station—following orders that obviously came
down from Mitch—made excuses to cut down on the amount
of airtime, then move it back to a later, less desirable hour.
Kai observed a strict rule never to raise any complaints about
these matters in their sessions, passing them along to her
lawyer, who made little progress. Time and again Kai had
to grit her teeth and remind herself of the seriousness of
Mitch's disorder. He was, Kai thought, a borderline split
personality; so the more progress she seemed to make in
adjusting him to normal interpersonal relations, the more
contrast there was with his brutal behavior in business. She
could only hope that would change, too, when his therapy
was complete.

And then, on a summer's eve, the call came that told her
it was a futile hope. Whatever progress she had made with
Mitch was gone in a single act of violence. She wondered,
indeed, if he had ever really made any progress. Perhaps he
had only been playing a part, hoping he might possess her
someday—if he could only fool her into thinking he had
learned how to love.

Chapter Thirty-six

Eric Gimbel raced to the police station to arrange Kai's release still in a tuxedo, having come straight from a Beverly Hills soiree.

The district attorney, a hawk-faced man named Stanley Webb, had also come to the station to tell Kai his plans for her: she was going to be charged with procuring, and more seriously, with "reckless endangerment of human life"— justified in theory by Kai's sending a defenseless young woman to rendezvous with Mitch Karel despite prior awareness that Karel had a history of bizarre sexual behavior and had turned violent in past encounters. The charge of "reckless endangerment," Webb said—willfully exposing another person to serious bodily harm or death—meant Kai could be tried for manslaughter in the death of Annie Raines.

Nevertheless, the district attorney released Kai with no more than a warning she might be brought in again at any time. "But you won't be charged," Webb said, "if you'll cooperate with the prosecution."

"What sort of cooperation do you want?" Kai asked.

"Mitch Karel is going to be caught and put on trial, Ms. Wyler, I promise you that. Since you've known him such a long time, whatever testimony you give about him will carry a lot of weight. If you tell us more about his perversion, help us build a picture we can use in front of a jury of a depraved—"

"Anything I know about my clients is privileged information," Kai protested.

"Your client is a murderer, Ms. Wyler: he killed a young woman who regularly had sex with him at your recommendation. Now, if you were a doctor or a lawyer—even a newspaper reporter—you might get away with claiming your knowledge is privileged. But you're none of those things. You talk with people about sex, and try to help them enjoy it a little more, right? If you avoid giving us information by trying to claim privilege, contempt of court will be added to the other charges. So go home and think about what you want to do.''

As Kai left the station with Gimbel, they were surrounded by a huge crowd of reporters and television news teams. One of the ten richest men in the country was on the run, a fugitive for murdering a sex surrogate supplied by a glamorous sex therapist. The Hollywood media hadn't been thrown a juicier news item in this vein in the thirty years since Lana Turner's gangster lover had been stabbed to death in her bedroom by Lana's teenage daughter.

Gimbel's advice to Kai was to talk to the press, be relaxed and informative, express her own shock, do nothing that smacked of having anything to hide. But the reporters weren't easily satisfied by a few reasonable answers. They fenced Kai in and kept shouting one lurid question after another. Was it true her practice was a front for a call-girl ring? Had she actually been in the room at the time of the murder, part of a threesome that led to a lethal quarrel?

In the end she had to shove her way angrily out of the crowd, leaving the most absurd questions unanswered. No doubt the pictures where she looked grim and frazzled—not the earlier ones, where she'd been calm and cooperative— would be the ones printed in all the morning papers.

''My mistake,'' Gimbel said as he brought Kai back to her house in his limousine. ''I should have kept you away from those jackals. The truth is I'm a whiz at negotiating movie contracts and giving press conferences at the Cannes film festival, but handling stuff on the criminal side is a whole other ball game. You need a specialist, Kai. The D.A. means to get very nasty, and what you do makes you a good target, unfortunately. In the morning, I think I should call F. Lee Bailey or—''

''I already have someone to defend me,'' Kai said. ''He'll be here tomorrow.''

''Well, I hope it's someone good. You deserve to come out of this perfectly clean.''

''He's damn good,'' Kai said. ''Maybe the best.''

"Who is it?"

The answer came softly: "My father."

She had never forgotten it—that first moment she'd seen him striding into a court room, taking command, casting his spell over a jury to win the verdict he wanted. Whatever had passed between them, Kai still believed no one could give her a better defense in a court of law.

But if she summoned Randall Wyler, it wasn't only because she needed his knowledge and talent. Kai reached out simply because it was time. Alone, and afraid of what might be done to her in the wake of Mitch Karel's savage act, she called out for help as any fearful child might call for the most reliable pillar of strength she knew—her father.

She had no more fear of him. She had thought often about the last time she'd been with him in Baltimore. As she recalled the earnest appeal he had made on behalf of Vanessa, she felt increasingly unsure it had been right to turn him away. She remembered him saying that he had entered therapy to remake himself. How could she believe in her own work and not believe he deserved a second chance?

A few hours of fitful sleep after returning from the police station was broken easily at sunrise by the sound of the door chime. Evidently, he had caught a plane right away. Wrapped hastily in a robe, Kai was almost at the door when she wished she'd taken a moment to neaten up—still the child, eager to look her best.

Opening the door, she went awkwardly silent with surprise and embarrassment as she stared out at the tall figure in the early morning haze.

"I wasn't going to risk a call this time," Jim Bolton said. "It would have hurt too much if you told me not to come."

It was just another second before she tumbled into his arms. From her father she would get defense and protection. But this man brought something else she needed no less, the balm to her heart that would keep her strong through any ordeal.

"Dear, darling Jim," she sighed, nestling against him after a long kiss. "I've been so damn stupid, keeping you away." In an instant it was clear to her—for he hadn't come now to indulge himself in pleasure. What had brought him was the willingness to share her pain, give her strength and support.

She had never seen the *haku* do that for his *manuwahi*.

In the kitchen, as she began to make coffee, he sat at the table and told her he'd come from New York, where he'd been setting up financing for a new venture. With the three-hour time gap, the story about the murder had made the eleven o'clock news. An hour after he heard it, he was flying west.

"How long can you stay?" she asked. Not a challenge this time, but an expression of her need.

"No limits, Kai. I won't be here one hour less than you want me."

"But your business—"

"I've got perfectly good people to run it. This is where I belong."

How long she had waited to hear it! She sat down beside him and took his hand. "I'll want you every day. I've always wanted you. I've been wrong to ask you to give up anything—"

"No, you weren't unfair. There was no reason for you to tag along with me instead of doing your own work, and I was too caught up in proving something. It really struck home when I thought about Mitch. I don't know exactly what sent him off the deep end, but it's pretty clear he was chasing the wrong dreams."

"There's no comparison, Jim. Mitch has been a troubled man for a very long time."

"Whatever drove him, Kai, his tragedy came from not knowing when to stop—when to take stock and put changing himself ahead of everything else. God help me from making a similar mistake. The first change I'm going to make is having you in my life, close to me, all the time, every day, always."

She heard the sincerity in his pledge, and that mattered far more to her than insisting he fulfill it in any way that limited his goals.

She leaned over to kiss him again, and the heat started to rise through her. When they paused breathlessly, she pulled away and stood up.

"I don't need coffee now," he said.

"Neither do I. I'm just turning it off."

They went to bed, and he had begun to lay a trail of hot kisses across her body when a thought struck Kai that she had to share. "Do you realize that the total sum of days we've spent together add up to just one week?"

He spread himself along the length of her, and she shuddered at the thrill. "Then it certainly is about time," he answered, "that we start getting to know each other."

Her father arrived that afternoon, and she met him in the lobby of the Beverly-Wilshire Hotel, where he had booked a room.

When she entered and spotted Randall Wyler waiting in one of the chairs across from the reception desk, she had a momentary shock. He had aged significantly in the years since she'd last seen him. Now in his early seventies, heavier, his face seamed with the lines of worry and experience, the man who stood to meet her was no longer the sleek matinee idol he had been, merely a very distinguished-looking older gentleman.

They gazed at each other for a long moment before he said, "I'm grateful you called me, Kai. I've never wanted anything so much as another chance."

"I'm just sorry I had to be in trouble before I gave you one."

"Getting daughters out of trouble is one of the things fathers do best." He smiled, his eyes glistening.

They held back from each other one more second, then he spread his arms and Kai went into them. As he held her tightly, she whispered the word that best expressed her forgiveness. "Daddy."

"Well," he said at last, easing her away, "before we get down to cases, I have one more thing to do." He motioned to an adjacent chair where a handsome older woman had been sitting, unnoticed in the heat of emotion. "This is Norma Farnum, Kai. Norma and I . . . are going to be married in a few weeks."

She rose and seized Kai's hand in hers. She was gray-haired but not chic or thin or even especially beautiful. Yet her face, the clasp of her hands, her voice, were all filled with a glowing warmth. "Hello, Kai," Norma said. "I hope you don't mind my intruding on this family reunion."

Kai felt an instant rapport with the woman. "Of course not. I need all the support I can get."

"I wouldn't have come, but your father insisted I join him."

"You bet I did," Wyler said. "I'm going to be here awhile. I couldn't leave you behind that long." He sent Kai a look to say he knew the irony in his words, and he hoped she understood that it was his way of saying he understood all the sins of the past and would never repeat them. "Besides," he added, "I was pretty scared about facing you again, Kai. I needed a little moral support of my own."

"Scared to face me alone—really?" Kai asked, feigning surprise. Then she laughed and turned to Jim, beckoning him to come and join them.

Being all together gave Kai the secure feeling of being enfolded in a family. She'd never had that before, she realized, not even when Mak and Lili had joined her mother to look after her. Things had always seemed so temporary then, and her mother had been so unstable.

From what she could see of her father now—and his intended wife—she understood how much he had truly changed. Norma Farnum, a social worker in Chicago, had met Wyler through the *pro bono* legal work he did these days representing the interests of women and children who were victims of domestic violence. Only when Norma described their meeting did Kai learn that her father had been doing this sort of work. She perceived that it was part of a penance for his own past abuses.

Wyler and Jim also got along well. Of course, in the context of business, they had long known about each other. But the personal chemistry that developed was just what Kai longed to see between her father and the man she loved.

As they all rose after having lunch in the hotel restaurant, Wyler put a hand on Jim's shoulder. "I know this may be an old-fashioned question, son, but since Norma and I have announced our plans it seems only fair to ask: what are your intentions toward my daughter?"

"Randall! Dad!" the two women scolded in unison.

But Jim answered with absolute sincerity. "I mean to marry her, sir, if she'll have me. And," he added drily, "if you'll grant me her hand."

Kai's adoring eyes gave him the answer before he swept

her into a kiss, unmindful of Wyler or Norma or the dozens
of other people who turned to stare.

Later the same day Mitch Karel was apprehended in Seattle, trying to charter a plane to take him out of the country. News reports said detectives from Los Angeles had been
dispatched to bring him back for arraignment.

The district attorney promptly made contact with Kai,
summoning her to appear at his office.

She arrived with her father, and as soon as the D.A. began threatening again to file charges, Randall Wyler stepped
into the discussion.

"You want to prosecute my daughter?" he said challeng-
ingly. "I'd be almost happy for you to try, Mr. Webb, because I'll wipe the floor with you in court." Eyes blazing,
he rose out of the chair that faced the D.A. across his desk.
"You want to question the propriety of what my daughter
does? I'll produce a thousand experts in the field and tes-
timonials from people whose lives have been made better.
And just as she helped them, she wanted to help Mitch
Karel. She failed, and for that you think she should be punished. But she wasn't able to control what happened in his
mind. He was acting on his own sick impulse, out of his
own need. If the ghost of his poor victim could come back
and speak to us, I'm sure the last person she'd blame for
what happened to her is Kai Wyler."

Webb smiled thinly as Wyler kept glaring at him. "That's
a very good speech, Mr. Wyler. Was that a dress rehearsal
for the trial?"

"You bet your ass, son, you bet your ass."

The D.A. pulled a file folder from a corner of his desk
and flipped it open. He scanned the top page inside, then
looked up at Wyler. "I wonder what the jury will say, sir,
if I bring out in court that a former wife of yours once swore
out a complaint against you for being guilty of incest with
the very daughter whose brilliant work in sex therapy you
are now so happy to defend."

Both Kai and her father were struck speechless by the
bold vindictiveness of the prosecutor's tactic. Kai stood and
glanced anxiously at her father as she saw the color flood
his face, and his fingers start twitching as if the itch to
strangle his tormentor was tingling in his hands. If he lost

control—as the D.A. no doubt wanted—it would deepen the shadow that hung over Kai and her work, and probably force her father to disqualify himself. She was about to move to him and pull him back when he began to speak. His voice trembled with the effort of controlling his rage.

"That was a terrible time in my life, counsellor. It happens that the accusation wasn't true—though I'll admit here and now it was close enough to the truth that I am mortally ashamed of the way I behaved. And yet, if you are scum enough to want to use it against me, I would be the last one to discourage you. For I'm not the man today that I was then . . . and I believe my daughter has completely forgiven me." He paused and glanced to her, seeking affirmation. Only after she nodded, he turned back to the district attorney. "All of which is testament to the fact that there are afflictions of the human spirit that can warp our desires . . . and that cry out for the compassionate treatment that people like my daughter provide." He turned from the desk and extended his hand to Kai. "C'mon, sweetheart, let's get out of this cesspool."

It felt wonderful to have her father fighting for her, though Kai worried he might have overplayed his hand. But the chastened D.A. let them walk out of the office with no more than a shouted warning he might call Kai in again, or issue an arrest warrant at any time.

"Like hell he will," Wyler said when they were leaving the police station, punctuating it with such a good-natured chuckle that Kai realized he had purposefully smeared on the theatrics. "Mr. Webb knows every bit as well as I do that he'll have one hell of a hard time making any of those charges stick."

"I guess I feel on shaky ground," Kai said, "because I am partly to blame."

He put his arm around her. "I may have done some ham-acting back there, Kai, but that doesn't mean I thought what I said was baloney. People need what you do." He paused as they stepped out into the California sunshine, and then turned to her. "I missed your graduation, but I guess any old day is just as good a time to say . . . I'm proud of you."

"Any old day," she agreed as tears welled in her eyes.

* * *

No charges were ever filed against Kai. When it became clear that she would no longer be harassed by the D.A.'s office, her father left Los Angeles—but not to return immediately to Chicago. Kai had given him the address she had for Vanessa, and he went first to Florida, intent on rebuilding that bridge, too. A week after he left, he called to report that Vanessa had returned with him and Norma to Chicago. She was indeed trying to kick a drug habit, but with their loving determination—and Norma's particular experience as a social worker in helping other youngsters through the problem—he was optimistic she would succeed.

Five months later when Mitch Karel went on trial, Kai sustained her claim of confidential privilege in discussing her treatment. But when called by the prosecution, she was willing to say that it would be wrong to excuse Mitch Karel from being held to account by accepting his plea of temporary insanity. In her opinion, he was a man who knew right from wrong at all times, even if he had lost perspective and believed his money entitled him to make his own rules.

Judged guilty of "intent to cause physical injury which had led to the victim's death," Mitch was convicted of manslaughter in the first degree and sentenced to prison for twenty years.

While Mitch had been under indictment, all his business interests had languished. Bankers who controlled the debt on borrowed money Mitch had used to keep extending his empire began pressuring for companies to be sold off, and one afternoon Jim was called to a meeting with several financiers who had flown to Los Angeles to ask if he would be interested in adding Allstate Communications to his portfolio.

When he collected Kai at her office that evening and told her about the possibility, she was enthusiastic. "I wouldn't mind having some sympathetic management again," she said cheerfully. In Mitch's absence, her contract had never been renegotiated, and her show remained in limbo.

"Then I hope you won't be too unhappy with the answer I gave them," Jim answered. Kai glanced up at him expectantly as he continued. "I told them I'm not looking for any new deals. In fact, I'd like to dispose of all my own companies." As he saw Kai's look of concern, he added, "Oh, not because they're in trouble. Every one is very sound and profitable. There won't be any trouble finding buyers."

The expression of concern hadn't left her features. It was the ultimate compliance with what she had once asked of him, yet now it seemed not only selfish but unnecessary. They were together, they had found their balance in a relationship where there was mutual respect for their separate careers.

"But if you sell everything," she said, "then . . . what will you do?" Suddenly Kai had a vision of Jim doing nothing but playing golf or sailing a yacht around the world. It wasn't a playboy she'd fallen in love with, it was a man of action and accomplishment.

"Well, one thing is for sure," he said, "I'll have pots of money that I'd like to put to work somehow. You know, one thing that's interested me for a long time is conservation. . . ."

During the months she'd been with Jim, she had seen he was a major contributor to many causes involved with environmental preservation.

"I've sifted through a lot of opportunities lately, and I've found one I like. It requires a huge chunk of cash to take the next step—and it might even mean moving away from L.A.—but it's a major conservation project, and I can't think of anything more worthwhile."

"Moving away . . ." Kai echoed in dismay.

He put his arms around her. "Not without you. I'd only do this if you gave it your okay—if you'd want to be part of it."

Kai thought: could she leave here? Why not? If she wanted to continue her work, she could do it anywhere. If this was important enough to Jim, then she wanted it, too.

"Well, tell me more. What's the project?"

He gave her a smile, slightly mischievous as though pleased that he had hooked her curiosity. "I don't think I'm going to tell you," he said. "Tomorrow I'm going to show you."

It was nearly sunset of the next day by the time they were standing side by side at the summit of the hill, the highest point of land within the thousand-acre property.

Without canceling all her appointments on short notice, Kai had been unable to get away until mid-afternoon, then there had been the five-hour flight. All arranged with great mystery by Jim. He had a chartered Lear jet standing by at Los Angeles to take them whenever they were ready.

Of course, as the plane banked west across the Pacific, Kai had suspected their destination.

Sure enough, they had landed in Honolulu, where a car and driver were waiting. As they were driven out into the countryside, Kai said little, and Jim respected the silence. Filled with memories, many of them unhappy, Kai couldn't quite pin down her emotions about coming back. Jim was obviously aware of her mixed feelings. As they had grown closer, she had talked more about her background, told him some of the circumstances that had led to their first meeting, but not all. She hadn't admitted that her mother had been a call girl when Wyler left her, or that Lokei had virtually sold herself into sexual slavery to a Hawaiian landowner.

At last the car turned off the main road and began a winding ascent until it had reached the top of the hill. At the foot of the long, gentle slope on one side, a beautiful beach rimmed the ocean, and looking in the other directions she could see the cleared empty fields of a sugar and pineapple plantation, fringed by workers' shacks. On a hill that jutted up three or four miles away was a large white house.

"What do you think?" Jim asked finally.

"About what?"

"Buying it"—his hand swept across the view—"everything you can see."

"Everything? But that would cost—"

"A fortune. But I told you I want to put money into conservation. This land is going up for sale, the whole block of a thousand acres. I'd like to see it preserved instead of getting chopped up piecemeal and developed. There's any number of hotel chains that would love to slice pieces off that beach, but it could be kept together if one buyer is ready to pay the price."

She scanned the vast property once more, and at last her gaze settled on the distant house. At the same moment a shaft of the setting sun knifed through a cleft in a low blanket of clouds and focused on the mansion. Magnetized by the vision, Kai moved forward to the edge of an outcropping. That house—suddenly she realized exactly what it was. She might have known sooner, but she had never driven onto the property—and had never seen the mansion from this angle, up high, instead of looking at it from down below.

Jim moved behind her, his arms encircling her waist, a safety line to keep her secure. "Of course," he said, "I wouldn't go through with it if you don't—"

"The seller," Kai broke in, "who is it?"

"A family named Trane. Or perhaps I should say their creditors. Most of what the land sale brings in will go to pay off their debts."

"But they had so much," she said, thinking aloud. "How could they lose it all?"

"Maybe it was greed. They overextended themselves in a number of ventures, and also mismanaged their assets. I gather there was a pair of brothers who inherited a fortune, but one of them died young, and the other was a drunk who gambled and played around and didn't watch the shop before he died, too."

Greed? Mismanagement? Or maybe, thought Kai, they'd finally been forced to reckon with the gods of the volcano.

Jim turned her gently around. "So, how do you feel about it? We'd make it a nature conservancy . . . and live here." He looked across the valley between the two hills. "That house over there is part of the property."

She smiled up at him. "It sounds like paradise," she said. "Except for the house. Don't you think it might be much nicer for our children if we live right on the beach?" She reached out. "Come, I'll show you a beautiful spot." With him, she thought, it would be beautiful, the last of the ugly memories purged forever.

He paused to give her a questioning glance. But in the next moment the light of understanding came into his eyes, and he just nodded and grasped her hand, happy to follow wherever she would lead.